Death of a Past Life

By Robert N. Reincke

SPUNKY BOOKS

Death of a Past Life
By Robert N. Reincke

Published by Spunky Books
West Hollywood, CA

Although all of the stories after 1906 are actual and all the
characters are true, some of the feelings, dialogue, and pre-1906
activities have been re-created based upon interpretations.

LIBRARY OF CONGRESS CATALOGING-IN-
PUBLICATION DATA

Reincke, Robert
Death of a Past Life/ Robert N. Reincke – Third ed.

ISBN 978-0-9794241-0-6
Library of Congress Control Number: 2006929953

Cover: Illustration by Ann L. Fackler
Photos: Leonid Siewert & Nicholas Katschalin
Photo of author: Lorraine Galloway
Design: Michael J. Mackel
Editor (first edition): Stephen Herzog, Ph.D.
Editor (second edition): Toni Kelley

THIRD EDITION
2008

Lovingly to Ann

In Memory of

Nina
(1906-2008)

and

Nicholas
(1903-1963)

Acknowledgements

This book could not have been created without my grandfather Nicholas and his inspirational prologue. And while I miss not having had the opportunity to meet him in person, I know that he stood over my shoulder at some more ethereal level, observing and assisting in the manifestation of these words on computer keyboard. Thank you dear namesake Nicholas, wherever you are.

My grandmother, "Omi," Nina, from whom I heard the majority of the stories throughout my life, was an amazing woman. She passed away several months after reaching the age of 101. Her longevity was equal to her fortitude and steadfast belief in positive outcomes despite seemingly insurmountable difficulties, often in the face of incomprehensible uncertainty. I'm grateful for the endless hours she spent patiently reliving some unconscionable events to help me write this book.

Thanks are also due to my great-uncle Vova. His photo (most likely his last) sits on my credenza, with eyes evoking the passion and sadness that was Russia. It reminds me that the atrocities we have committed against ourselves, each other, and our planet cannot continue. The travesty that was the murder of millions of innocent Russian citizens by its dictators, and the horror of the Second World War, cannot be left forgotten and therefore repeated or revised to be played out by yet another set of misguided world leaders.

The other family members mentioned in this book, and whose presence or essence I also sensed while transcribing their lives and experiences, I feel also participated in a level similar to that of my grandfather and great-uncle above. I thank Vera, Josephine and her mother Josephine, Leonid, Karl, Roman, Sophia, Tatiana, Svetlana, Claudia, Uncle Erich and the others. I adore their strength, creativity, and willingness to work through the oppressions they faced within their lifetimes.

Of course this book could not have been produced without help from the living. I'm grateful to my mother for assisting me during the most difficult of times in my life, when I was first inspired to write. I also thank her for her recollection of some of the later stories told here. I'm indeed fortunate to have as loving a mother as she.

I thank Michael Miller of the North Dakota State University Libraries for publishing the first edition of this book, and Margaret Freeman and Dr. Ray Heer of the American Historical Society of

Germans from Russia for their initial and continued enthusiastic support. I sincerely thank Dr. Stephen Herzog for his historical editing of the first edition, and Alex Herzog, for his initial enthusiasm by forwarding the work on to his son. Thanks also go to Ms. Toni Kelley for editing, Bob John for his kind and timely suggestions, and his brother for assisting in proofing. I thank Kira for giving me a tape of her aunt Swetlana and Claus von Kursell. Finally, I thank my partner Michael J. Mackel, for his design work, and whose love and support is a continual blessing.

CONTENTS

Family Tree Krümmel xiii

Family Tree Siewert..xiv

Prologue xvii

Book I

1. La Belle Époque—St. Petersburg (1911) 3

2. The Walking Stick (1912) 20

3. Endless Journey (1913) 35

4. First Flight and the Caged Canary (1914) 51

5. War and Peace in Tsarskoe Selo (1914)................................ 65

6. The Goat the Bear and the Great War (1915)........................ 81

7. Eve of the End (1916)... 97

8. February Revolution (1917) 114

9. The End—The October Revolution (1917) 130

    Photographs 149

Book II

10. Civil War (1918–1919) 153

11. The Dacha and the Russian Countryside (1919-1921) 168

12. The Crow's Eggs, the Chicken and the Treacherous Journey
    (1921–1924) 185

13. Yaroslavl: Vova Brushes with Death and Nina Explores
    Independence (1924–1927) 197

14. Reunion and Dissolution (1928–1929) 215

15. Leningrad (1929–1932) 233

16. Integration (1932–1933) 249

17. Nicholas (1934-1935) 266

18. The Great Terror & Another Approaches (1937–1939)..... 283

    Photographs 299

Book III

19. The Siege (1941) 305

20. The Escape (1942).. 323

21. The Caucasus (April 1942 to January 1943)..................... 338

22. Fleeing Russia (January to April 1943)............................. 360

23. Berlin (1943) 372

24. The New Onslaught (1943).....................................384

25. Evacuation from the Capital of The Third Reich (1943)....397

26. In the German Countryside (1944–1945).........................403

27. Attack (May 1945)...411

    Photographs 419

Book IV

28. Marburg-an-der-Lahn—Life Amongst the Ghosts of WWII

    (1945–1946) 424

29. Anni (1946–1948)..435

30. Passage Beyond (1949)...447

31. New York (1949) 461

Epilogue

Nina 469

Author's Note..475

Bibliography...477

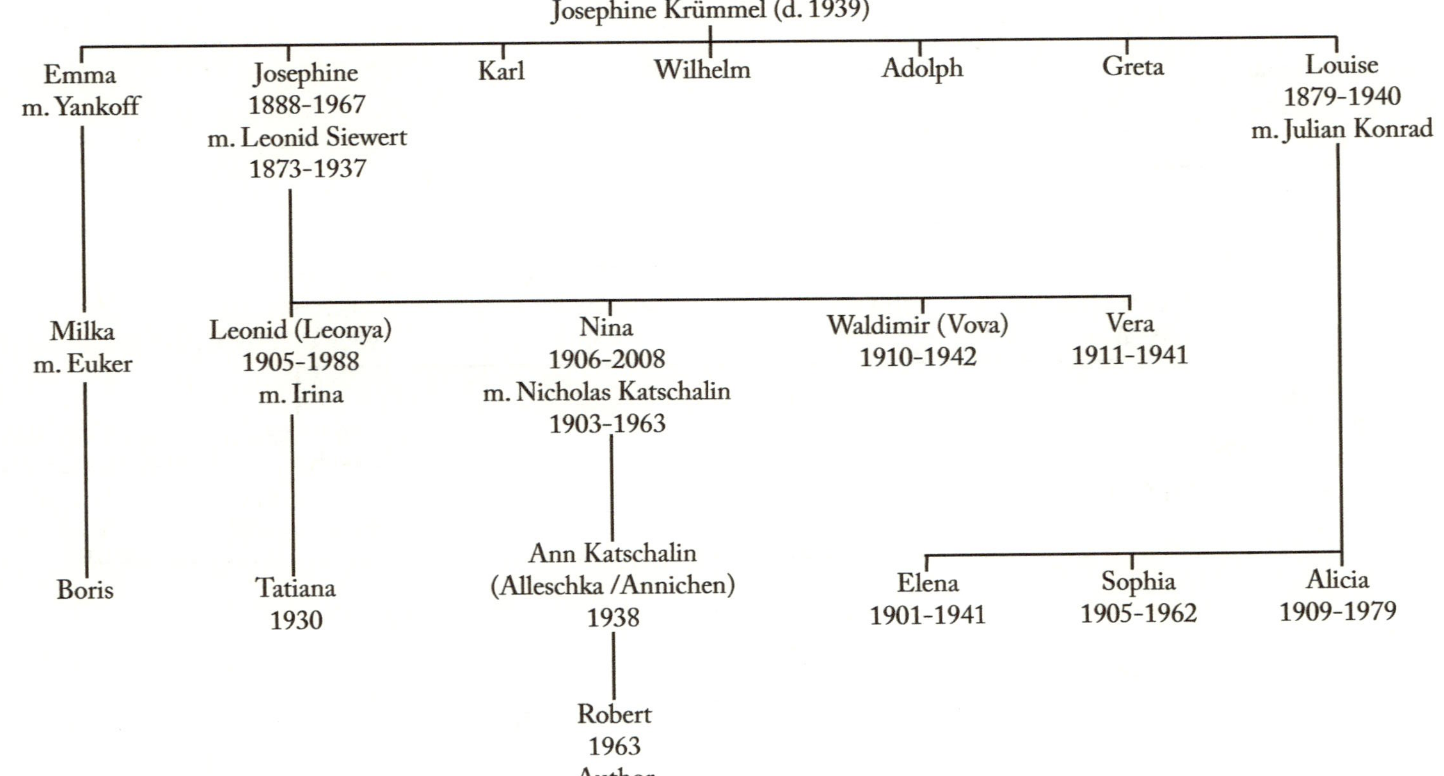

Family Tree Krümmel
Karl Krümmel (d. 1935)
Josephine Krümmel (d. 1939)
Emma
m. Yankoff
Josephine
1888-1967
m. Leonid Siewert
1873-1937
Karl
Wilhelm
Adolph
Greta
Louise
1879-1940
m. Julian Konrad
Milka
m. Euker
Leonid (Leonya)
1905-1988
m. Irina
Nina
1906-2008
m. Nicholas Katschalin
1903-1963
Waldimir (Vova)
1910-1942
Vera
1911-1941
Boris
Tatiana
1930
Ann Katschalin
(Alleschka /Annichen)
1938
Elena
1901-1941
Sophia
1905-1962
Alicia
1909-1979
Robert
1963
Author

Family Tree Siewert

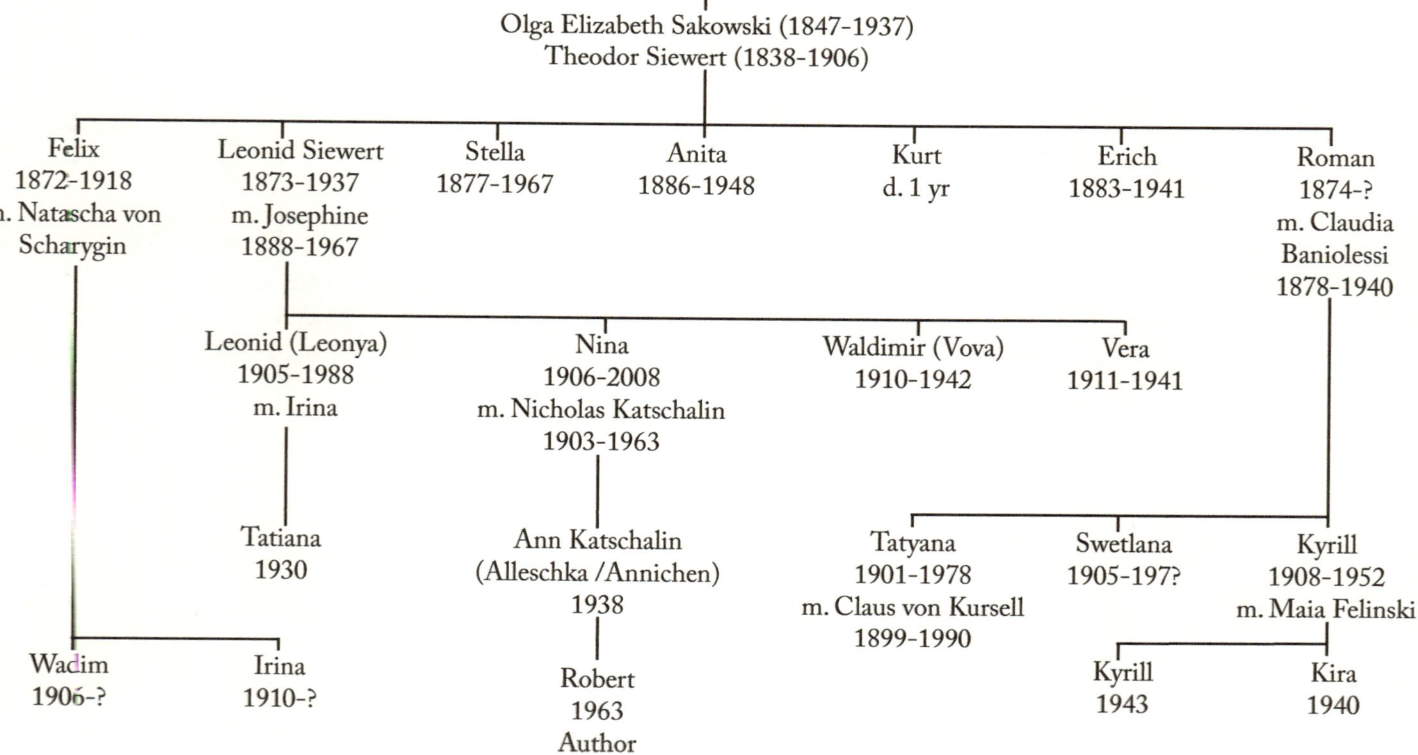

Death of a Past Life

PROLOGUE

Nicholas, an old spirit weary of his life, trudges slowly into the small room where he works and sleeps. An old, once-elaborate, French clock chimes, indicating it's ten at night. The mechanism works well thanks to his clever mind and dexterous hands, but the casing is long gone, destroyed by the Second World War. The exterior is now as simple as Nick's life has become in America, replaced by a wooden structure he's created for practicality.

Nick's heart pains him as he turns on his simple desk lamp and draws the shades. Even though the windows reflect nothing but the moon's glow off the fine layer of snow outside, he wants peace, knowing he is alone in his silence. Nina, his wife, knows not to disturb him, and remains in the kitchen folding laundry. His daughter Ann works on her homework while watching the black and white television in the living room.

The cot in the other corner awaits him for a much-needed rest both from this day and this life. His resistance has ended, although too late. There's a mission he must now follow—he must write the story of his young daughter's tormented early life. Although all are safe from the war and the starvation they've suffered, he feels he must reveal what happened, if only to prevent future generations from making the same tortuous mistakes. Luckily, his friend Serge has promised to translate from their native Russian. Sitting down in silence, he writes five pages, which is all he will ever be able to complete.

From the Life Of Ann K.

The first time Ann suffered a real big fright was when a bomb exploded. She was then 3 1/2 years old. We were at home. Her mumy was out waiting in line before a store to buy food. During this time I had to do all the house-work. It was getting dark outside. Then all of a sudden the sirens were howling; sounding an alarm. We were already quite used to that. For more than one month the battle had been raging not far from the town. We now realized that the noise from guns shooting and shells exploding, which always made the night sky reflect with a red glow, was heard much closer on that particular evening. I took Ann on my lap and soothed her trying to act as if nothing had happened.

"Where is mummy?" asked Ann in a voice filled with fright.

"She will be coming back soon." I comforted her. I took my cigarette case and counted the cigarettes aloud, "One, two, three, four", and made Ann repeat the counting. She then played with the cigarettes placing them in another box. In the meantime, I was very nervous myself wondering what I should do next. Maybe we should go down to the basement, as we were living up on the fifth floor.

"five, six, seven,.." we continued to count, when all of a sudden a terrible crash shook the whole building. The glass-panes in the windows splintered, the hanging lamp gave a bounce in the middle of the room, the kitchen door banged open and the looking glass hung side ways on the wall. Our "Pussy" cat leaped into the room staring at us with frightened eyes.

"Oh, what was that?" exclaimed Anna

badly scared.

"...eight, nine, ten." I continued to count, but I could not get Ann's attention anymore. She trembled and hugging me tightly trying to hide against my breast. I managed somehow to show a calm front. I wanted to teach Ann that she should not be frightened by explosions. I took her on my arm and without hurrying I stepped over to the wall and straightened the looking glass, but my hand shook a little bit.

"It's just a heavy thunderstorm." I said quietly and lit a cigarette. The noise of reports and explosions subsided.

A few minutes later mummy came running back. Everybody was safe and sound. Ann started telling Mummy what fun it had been when our house had been shaken and how poor "Pussy" got frightened.

From this day forward, these occurrences were repeated oftener and oftener and we started to take refuge in the cellar. In the beginning, Ann, upon hearing the howl of the siren, kept her happy mood, took her dolls and carried them to safety in the basement. There was a heap of sand and other children to play with, so Ann was happy. But then came the

times when we had to get down to the basement
several times during one day and several times
at night. This was no longer pleasant for little
Ann. Finally the cold and the dampness of the
cellar made her fall ill with pneumonia. From
that time on, we remained in our apartment
on the fifth floor. We never went down to the
basement again in spite of bombs and explosions.
We left our lives in the hands of our Lord.

When Ann recovered, the air raids
became less frequent, but then the town was
taken under fire by artillery. Any minute we
expected a shell to hit our house. In fact, many
neighboring houses had been hit and severely
damaged. But in a way this did not frighten us
too much anymore; another danger was turning
up. We were to suffer from hunger. Mummy
was out the whole day standing in line at the
food store and, which is worse, returned at
times with empty hands. Three times a day we
cooked a watery soup with just a few teaspoons
of flour in it for the three of us. It was a mere
muddy liquid.

I don't see anything floating in this soup,"
complained Ann tearfully.

"Tomorrow there won't be anything at

all, " said Mummy.

Ann bursted into tears and held tightly on to her plate as if fearing that it would be taken away. Then she gave a deep long sigh, seized her spoon and this first spoonful mingled ing with her own tears was swallowed.

After such meals, I walked up and down trying to find something fit to be eaten; something with which I could stop this awful feeling of hunger with in my body. I took some mustard, put salt on it and ate it slowly. It seemed to help for a few minutes.

Ann came close and asked me, "Daddy, what are you eating?"

"Mustard," I replied simply.

Whereupon she looked at me incredulously. Then she sighed and went away to sit in a corner. She did not play anymore. Hunger abstracted her somehow. I felt a mad pity for her. I even felt ashamed that I had eaten the mustard. I I had found some means of stunning this awful feeling of hunger for a few minutes, while she was feeling it continuously. I decided to eat no more. I took Ann on my arm near the stove and started telling her some wonderful fairy tale about some good uncle bringing us a big box filled with bread, potatoes, and maccaroni. Ann's face showed animation. She even remembered her Teddy-bear and took him on her lap and told him in a soothing voice, "don't cry, little Teddy-bear, soon the good uncle will arrive and give you plenty to eat."

In order to save our lives, we had to eat our dog, two cats, joiner's glue, and the skins of animals intended for leather factories. Many of our neighbors died. The granny, Ann's nurse, died. Also my brother-in-law died. There were no lights and water anymore. We made ourselves a small night-light with vaseline. We had to go very far to get water. In fact, all the way to the river; thus exposing our selves to severe bombing.

Ann was very pale. Her hands were red and swollen. My hands became thin and blue. This was from hunger and cold. The temperature outside fell to 5 or 15 degrees below zero. We had no wood nor other fuel. Already part of our furniture had been used for heating--chairs, tables, shelves and almost all of my books.

When I tore the pages out of those books thrusting them into the stove, Ann enjoyed the sight very much. Paper burns easily and made the room warm. Ann even wanted to help me. Having seen a book on the table, which I had intended to save, Ann seized it and tore it to pieces to fling it into the stove before I noticed her. Indeed, to Ann all this seemed rather normal.

When I tore down a door from our cupboard to serve as fuel, Ann started to break her toys and placed them in front of the stove. When I started to saw the pieces, Ann gathered the sawdust and tried to eat it thinking that they were bread crumbs. We reproved her.

The most trying loss Ann suffered was our "Pussy." She often recalled Pussy sighing and asking, "Why did we eat Pussy? I pity him. He was such a darling."

We had to endure more suffering and trials, but in the end having lost absolutely everything, with just one suitcase and a handbag to carry, ourselves half dead from starvation, we were forced, to evacuate from our town.

By Nicholas Katschalin
June 14, 1955

Book 1

1

LA BELLE ÉPOQUE
ST. PETERSBURG
1911

White steam mixes with bitter cold as the slow, wide-gauge train comfortably carrying her father and mother begins its acceleration out of the busy St. Petersburg station towards Berlin. Josephine takes her gloved hand and holds it tightly around her tall fox collar as her leather shoe hits the crunchy snow still encrusted on the bustling Neva Prospekt outside the station. She breathes a gulp of St. Petersburg's December air—icy cold even for Russian standards—and tastes the residue of burning timber and coal from so many city fireplaces and industrial furnaces. A flock of pigeons scatters. "Odd creatures, these birds, to still be here in this frozen winter," she thinks as she steadies her impractically large, feathered hat.

Nothing less than calamity has reigned beneath the surface of life in St. Petersburg since January, 1905, and what is now known as the Bloody Sunday Revolution. It was then that guards of the Tsar's Winter Palace shot hundreds of workers—workers who marched peacefully, carrying religious icons and respectfully requested reform. The shootings ignited a storm of terrorism and clashes between the classes. The so-coined "terrorist endemic" which followed killed over 4,000 and resulted in workers' demonstrations, naval mutinies, and the horror on the battleship *Potempkin*. "The Black Hundred" death squads massacred Jews in the villages, burned manor homes, and maimed cattle that walked mooing in pain on country roads. And students, professors, and theater workers joined the metal and chemical workers in strikes.

The subsequent six years have become somewhat better, not by their bandaged outward appearances but by true internal changes that are slowly gathering hope and momentum. Prime Minister Stolypin's initial response of hanging perpetrators and implementing policies to create a new, wealthier class of peasants has had some obviously mixed effects. The Tsar's responses of a paltry and unconvincing verbal concession of freedom of "speech, conscience, and association," and a new, puppet parliament named the "Duma," have had equally lackluster approval. Especially given the fact that while in theory the Tsar is now responsible to a legislature, in reality he can and does disband it whenever he so chooses. Nonetheless, the inherent changes are vital to the increasing economy and the potential for Russia to finally develop like its European neighbors.

Something of particular but equally unrecognized importance, during those post-Japanese war-torn days, was the development of a so-called St. Petersburg "Soviet." But this is gone now and of no interest at the moment to Josephine, who momentarily ignores the distrust and misery that still reverberate amongst the workers coming from small villages for their temporary winter stay in this city of her birth. Of importance now is the immediacy of stopping by her husband's law office before the coming darkness of winter's nineteen-hour-long night begins. Her jewels are in his safe there, and she'll need them for the ball tonight. Only she can select the most appropriate.

Her children will be cared for and fed by the time she comes home to the warmth of her large, affluent, central Liteinyi District apartment, without any need for her to lift a finger. Indeed, during the time of the initial turmoil Josephine became pregnant with her second child Nina, who was born on November 28, 1906, of the still-in-use-but-outdated Russian Gregorian Calendar. Of course, the Tsar's family was growing to its current five children at the same time Josephine and Leonid continued to increase theirs to the current four. In fact, wealthy families as well as the middle and lower classes all continue to have large families, just like the Tsar. After all, who has any choice in the matter?

The cold continues to make its presence known as snow accumulates on the v-shaped hollow of her tall fur collar, but soon enough she is in the warmth of her husband's office above the bustling first-floor shops. Her husband's secretary greets her as she proceeds to his private suite. Josephine and her husband speak openly about household matters as Leonid opens the safe for her. She chooses her jewelry and leaves to continue her journey.

If her husband's office and their enormous second-floor apartments were not as near one another and Nevsky Prospekt, she would have hired a sled. "But no matter now," she thinks, as she continues home, the pouch sewn inside her full-length fur coat filled with a diamond encrusted silver hair pin and brooch, a stranded pearl necklace, oversized, ostrich egg-shaped pearl earrings, and her favorite ruby bracelet. Like the Tsarina Alexandra and many of the Tsars since the time of Peter the Great, including Nicholas II himself, Josephine is German-Russian by blood and is proud of her resilience to the calamities brought on by man and nature.

It is not that Josephine is unaware of the strife of the city around her caused in part by the financial strain jeopardizing the country from the shoddy completion of the trans-Siberian railroad. Certainly, she is aware of her just-departed father's desire to profit from the recent invention of the automobile—especially since he currently owns the largest carriage manufacturer in the country. And, in fact, beneath her forced nonchalance, she is only too aware of the city's restlessness juxtaposed against her own social requirements as a St. Petersburg elite. But Josephine doesn't often choose to consider broader societal issues as she goes about her daily life. While noting the familiar faces of her city, she thinks instead of her extended family in Berlin, the Baltic Grand Duchy Provinces and the Crimea, and the likelihood of their attending a ball like the one she anticipates attending tonight. For tonight, she will dress in her elegant satin gown and wear her collected jewelry.

She briskly continues her walk across the windswept, snowy boulevard, which is covered with ruts carved by sleighs, and sliced by the tracks of trolley cars. The street, adorned with butcher shops, tailors, offices, restaurants, banks, businesses, and large department stores, is busily trafficked by clerks, foreign businessmen wearing beaver collars, dignified wing-collared workers, and the bourgeoisie *burzhui* in their pencil striped pants. The unemployed and disenfranchised do not mingle with office workers and the ranks of servants, who in turn do not mingle with the hectic lives of the established elite.

Josephine looks in the walnut-framed mirror of her dressing room as she pulls her cream-colored, smoothly delicate gloves up past her elbows. Her blue-green eyes sparkle as she regrets her choice of necklace remembering now the sapphire that she curiously overlooked in the confines of the safe. Her dark brown hair shines in its arrangement like the mink coat her maidservant hands her. She is ready to disappear from her household and motherly responsibilities and engage in social ones. She wants to waltz tonight and embraces the thought of expressing herself.

Leonid, tall, solidly framed, with a sparkle of Russian charm on his flushed German-Russian face, prepares for the ball in his private room as well, albeit discontentedly. He puts on his decorous emblemmed overcoat that identifies him as a member of the Tsar's civil servants. As one of ten official city notaries and a lawyer, he looks dignified. His beard has been clipped, his mustache waxed, his short blondish brown hair bristles atop his head. He buttons the long row of silver buttons on his topcoat.

Society life disturbs him. He far more appreciates time spent hunting or gambling with his peers. He is troubled by the Tsar's weaknesses, of which he learns many in his distinguished occupation. He is well aware, in his dealings with many differing socioeconomic and intellectually divergent countrymen and resident foreigners, of dissatisfaction with the business and administration of his native Russia. Nevertheless, he is amazed at these rumblings as he has seen some of the more public displays of the protesting bastions of the people and philosophically supportive intellectuals condemned to Siberia and to death. The constant worldly friction and discontent grates on his mind and disturbs the serenity he has managed to muster in his young life.

He knows the later evening's requirements will include discussions on current philosophical thinking among members of his class—which will be trifling, given their emphasis not so much on current issues, but instead on their individual political and social ambitions, goals and values. It isn't so much that he is incapable of taking part in this discourse, but more that he disdains the constant jockeying for position and social one-upmanship that such a gathering inevitably inspires. He'd rather be betting on the races than be at one tonight. Tomorrow, he'll go hunting for bear. And as for the questions he'll undoubtedly be cornered on—some that so much as question the Tsar's competence as autocratic ruler of the vastness of Russia—Leonid thinks it's been this way for decades, why should anything come of it now? Tonight he'll make the best of dining with his brothers, and then fulfill his obligations to his wife and society.

A servant taps on the heavy wooden door of his private room, "The coach is waiting sir." He answers, "Another minute, I'm not quite ready yet." Embarrassed, he wonders how it is that he is somehow behind even his wife in preparing to go anywhere

⇛

Leonid's family is one mostly dominated by their men. Leonid has three brothers: Felix Carl Frederick (the eldest), Roman Jeannot, and Erich Leopold (both younger than Leonid), a fourth—Kurt Herbert Robert—died at twelve months of age. He has two younger, spinster sisters: Stella Marie Adelheid Wilhelmine aged 33, and Anita Alide Olga, aged 25. Father Theodore, God rest his soul, who passed last year, had been a prior governor general of Russian-controlled Latvia, and his mother Olga is the daughter of the capital of Latvia's Lord Mayor and a descendant of the celebrated von Schwarzenberg line (whose ancient title was bequeathed upon her family by the Prussian Emperor Karl V after the Turkish war of the late sixteenth century).

The boys have all been educated in St. Petersburg at the acclaimed gymnasium, the Tenishev School. Leonid and Erich later graduated in law from the Alexander Lyceum, established by the Tsar. Roman graduated in engineering from the May Academy, internationally renowned for its highly intellectual and cosmopolitan character. Erich, like Leonid, is a notary—a position held in high regard and privy to all the details of Russian society. They are two of only ten notaries that exist in the entire capitol. Given that they, together, control a fifth of all possible affairs which circulate the city, they know they hold their own sway, but conscientiously choose to not misuse this power for their own personal interests.

Felix is governor general of Crimea, partially a German-Russian enclave since the time of The Great Catherine. It is also a famous retreat of the imperial family and the wealthiest class. Felix gained this position through his father's influence. Of course Felix won't attend this evening's family celebration. Rarely in Petersburg, and only then on official business, he and his noble-born wife and two children, find the city stiflingly lacking the warmth and conveniences of their Black Sea coastal, provincial enclave.

Roman, the wealthiest of the brothers, holds a position as consultant to the Bank of Belgium in its financing of loans to Russian coal companies. His earlier post-graduate work, for the largest mine in the Urals owned by Belgian Capital, allowed him promotion to his current, enormously financially and socially influential position. Roman's Florentine-born wife Claudia, the hostess tonight, will be present, as will their daughters Swetlana and Tatyana, and their young son Kiril.

The widowed mother, Olga, will appear quiet, and still be uncomfortable with the loss of her lifelong companion and husband, Theodor. Stella and Anita will be certain to sit on either side of her, taking care of her every need. Erich, the youngest and a bachelor, will most likely be dressed in his dapper best.

"Quite enough for an evening dinner," thinks Josephine, as she takes it upon herself to rouse the family together, inspect her children's appearances, and in her customary fashion, asks whether each of them has remembered to bring their handkerchief.

That the family is large, growing, and constantly in motion exacts its responsibilities upon Josephine in ways that are mostly appealing to her. Of German nationality, the Sieverts and Krümmels, Leonid's family and Josephine's family respectively, have not been in Russia for small opportunity, but rather for large ambitions and privileged welcome. For beyond what may seem to be a backward country to some western elites, there is opportunity for great amounts of money to be made. The sluggishness of Russia's ability to catch up with the worldwide industrial revolution has created some opportunities for wealth creation that only existed in the European West decades earlier.

Josephine, Leonid, and the children accompanied by their

governess and nanny, enter the expansive floors of Roman's Kazan district St Petersburg town home. Members of the household's staff immediately appear to remove Leonid's floor-length sable fur coat and Josephine's ermine wrap. There are more servants than there are guests arriving for the baptism, dinner, and evening discourse. The children and their governesses are equally fretted over and then escorted by one of their cousins' governesses to the children's playroom at the end of the children's corridor.

As is customary for Roman's home, a large worked-silver icon hangs illuminated by guttering candles in the "red," or beautiful, corner of the dark wood-walled front alcove hallway. Custom would dictate that Leonid cross himself and kiss the icon, but the family on both sides is loosely Lutheran. Roman is the only member of the family to follow the Russian Orthodox tradition to the extent of raising his children in it. Equally motivating for his social rank and profile, the absence of the icon would simply be unacceptable.

The scents of the chefs' preparations of Russian and French appetizers and main entrees emanate from the kitchen. There will be hors d'oeuvres of fish baked in parsley and stuffed with rice, herring fillets and fresh caviar, steaming Borscht with its attendant pervasive smell of cooked red cabbage, very cold Brut Imperial champagne as developed by the French for the ancient Romanov Tsarist monarchy, chocolate mousse and German pastries.

Nina unselfconsciously plays with her cousins Swetlana and Tatyana—who are approximately her same age—in the enormous playroom while the youngest children are attended to by a bevy of nannies. An elegant woman enters the room. Aunt Claudia, the Florentine-born and educated wife of Uncle Roman, wears a straight, silk dress and an oversized, black pearl necklace. The dress is unusual, inspired by the orientalism displayed in the Ballets Russes performance of Scheherazade last season. Nina's cousin Tatyana tells her in French that the dress is Parisian. The nannies and governesses politely stop their conversation.

Claudia approaches the children and, in a reserved, commanding Italian accent, invites the eldest, Nina and Leonya, Swetlana and Tatyana, to join the adults at the dinner table. The younger children will eat in the children's room attended to by their nannies, and the elder children's governesses will eat in the kitchen with the chefs and other servants.

Nina steps out into the foyer, which is the turning point in the hallway where the rooms of the governess, nannies, chef, first and second maidservants, and butler and her cousins' rooms intersect. She, her brother and cousins, walk beyond the stairway and small elevator leading to her uncle's parlor, chamber, and private dining area, and into the main living room where the parents are assembled.

The room is framed in pooling, thick curtains. The adults' nearly perfectly-poised postures are draped in their gowns of elegant silks and satins, jewels, and formal wear. Candlelight reflects from immaculately polished gold and silverware that adorn the linen covered tables. The delicate porcelain china bears a bevy of assorted international meats and pastries. And an enormous, tiered platter, filled with cheeses and odd fresh fruits from tropical climates, is the crowning centerpiece.

Conversation swirls in French, Russian and German—all languages spoken in wealthy and noble homes: "the Imperial Neva Yacht Club…the Imperial Maryinsky Theater latest…what is art?… no ballerina like Anna Pavlova…intellectuals on Vaselevsky island… Diaghalev in Paris…Stravinsky and the Ballet Russe…finally the West is only now discovering what we…who are these Futuristic poets?…Pushkin will always speak for…"

Dinner having concluded, the children are sent home with their governesses or to their rooms as the parents continue their evening. The men retire to Roman's mahogany-veneered, plush, red velvet-draped gentlemen's lounge. Fine cigars from Yugoslavia are trimmed and lit, and after-dinner cognac is served in lieu of the more traditional vodka. The women congregate in the distinctly eclectic mix of both French Art Nouveau and traditional Italian Renaissance decor, which reflects the tastes of the effervescent and extremely well-traveled Claudia. The room is illuminated by the warmth of a smaller, acacia-leaf motif fireplace, a crystal chandelier, and several solid gold, heavy, Russian candelabra. They'll drink their steaming hot black tea, served from a giant silver samovar, with lemon.

"What do you mean the peasants have no land?" Roman exclaims to his brother Erich. Not waiting for a reply, he continues,

"Statistics indicate that peasants have appropriated a larger number of their communes and, looking at Russia as a whole, own a good percentage of the arable land," he concludes with a slightly reddened face. Indeed, he feels justified in his resolve given the well-known fact that, since the Tsar created the Duma legislature in response to the 1905 revolts, changes have slowly taken place allowing for greater freedoms, travel, and land ownership for the lower classes. The man held most widely responsible for these is Prime Minister Stolypin.

Leonid declines the offer of a thick cigar. As he is the middle child, he is unwilling to be overshadowed by the terse debate he already has had little control in developing. He begins, "Speaking of the Duma, I am happy to acknowledge that their programs of increased industrialization and European style capitalism have helped the People." Clearing his throat, he continues, "They've even considered health and medical benefits. But look at how many tens of thousands of men are needed to work. And look at the substandard conditions they work in, and the utterly low wages they get paid. The continual influx of these countryside recruits has made a mockery out of the municipal authorities' ability to improve housing and sanitation conditions. It has put our great city into an administrative crisis that it has found impossible to reconcile."

Erich, the youngest, is sorry he brought up the questions of the Duma and reform in the first place. Even though his professional position is one of great esteem, he knows he can never make a point with his older brothers. He accepts the cognac offered by his brother's servant while wondering what the women are talking about in the other parlor. Perhaps it would be more comfortable to leave the room and join them? He has always felt more comfortable in the presence of women as the hotheaded discussions of his three brothers have become an annoyance to him. His life is different from theirs in that he has never chosen to marry, and his ambitions have been thwarted given his lack of need to prove anything to his family.

Roman knows his brothers' concerns as they are not only discussed at the highest levels of society, but are also more and more frequently published in the many newspapers that circulate the city. His position connecting him with the largest foreign investors in the world requires he promote Russia as a good investment. Therefore, he maintains a more monarchist and politically correct approach to his more liberal-minded brothers. Unlike his absent elder brother Felix, however, his international travels do allow him to moderate his conservative viewpoints when confronted personally with a need to voice his true inner understandings. Nonetheless, it is important for him that his brothers reflect a strong consensual ideal to his, if for no other purpose than to alleviate him of any potential embarrassment in their relatively small social circle.

He pounds his fist on the table, "Absolute monarchy is a requirement in this land until the day when these feeble legislative attempts at education of the masses, use of significant foreign investment, and full industrialization take root. Hasn't the attempted assassination of this Prime Minister Stolypin, of whom you so proudly speak, five years ago proved to you that the people don't want change?"

Leonid uncharacteristically bites back, "The government is unable to alleviate the antagonism that I see between the manufacturers, who lock out their workers in lieu of profits over worker's welfare, landlords who defend their property rights to the point of dismissing grain production, and the refusal of management to raise wages and improve living conditions." He surprises even himself, unaware that so much of what he's been told or read has made such an impact on him.

Roman exchanges, "Continue a dialogue like that, dear Brother, and you may find yourself in a situation you will not be able to get out of. I say this not so much as a threat to you but as a concern. The Tsar, and I say this to you in confidence, may make a better country squire than the leader of one of the largest land masses and peoples of all civilized societies, as I believe his cousin the Kaiser has said, but always remember that his temperance and patience are unrelentingly short sighted."

"And," Roman continues, "as far as wages are concerned, our workers make a disposable income roughly the same as those in France, and they have 90 holidays a year, and similar working weeks. Even if the actual pay rates are higher there, food and lodging is less expensive here. Please remember these facts when your more liberal intellectual types corner you on a discussion, dear Brother."

Josephine enters the men's parlor, which smells of smoke and a whiff of cognac, not in the least intimidated by the masculine room set with heavy, red leather furniture and dark mahogany inlaid walls.

Having four brothers of her own, she sees no threat in the mindset or camaraderie established by the sanctity of the male bonding that she could not help hearing as she walked down the carpeted hallway leading to this wing. Her presence has made clear that it is time to leave the dinner and go to the ball. The children, who are not invited to the adult festivities, have already taken a sleigh ride home.

☙

Josephine nods her head as she walks through the crowd of well-adorned familiar faces, her left arm loosely fitted through her husband's. Servants walk by with trays of caviar and champagne. The parquet-floored, gold-gilded ballroom is fresh with lavender and rose smells of expensive French perfume. The orchestra plays Tchaikovsky, Schubert, and Rimsky-Korsakov under the illumination of drooping chandeliers and upright candelabra. Beneath the echoing sounds, Josephine's ear picks up the rustle of taffeta and lace next to the satin and silk of the ladies gowns, and the clink of gloved, expensively jeweled hands holding crystal champagne glasses. The mansion ballroom throbs with the intensity of the city's well-to-do's most formal face.

The violins soothe, the marble gleams, the mirrors multiply, the warmth evokes, confidences and asides soar, and then the quickening moments, more opulent than anticipated, pass fluidly as if in a dream for Josephine—just as life passes nearly unrecognizably quickly from day to day. What are moments of illuminated pleasure suddenly become yesterday's events—mere memories in the collective conscience until no one is left to recall them at all.

The evening complete, Leonid and Josephine ride home in a varnished sleigh, their legs covered in a thick bearskin blanket provided by their red-velvet capped driver. The sled makes its way through the crystal clear, frigid St. Petersburg night, whisking by illuminated embassies, schools, theaters, museums, ministries, courthouses, regimental barracks, the domed St. Isaac's Cathedral, and the sparkling Winter Palace—all of which lie between the exclusive residential neighborhoods of Roman and Leonid's families. The brightness of the lights make the frozen Neva River, embanked in pink Finnish granite, radiate with the reflected hues— ochres, crimsons and blues—from the glowing dull red facade of the Hermitage to the pastel stucco of palaces.

Across the river to the northeast are the slums and teaming factories of the Vyborg district and the surrounding proletarian districts of Nevsky, Moscow, Narva-Peterhof, and Vasil'evskii, and the majority of the other twenty-five districts of the city. Workers and entire families squeeze into abysmal quarters called *kamorki*, where rags and sheets replace walls to separate families sharing the same room. Yet tens of thousands of workers, considered fortunate to have factory jobs at all, rent wooden slat beds in cavernous lodging houses. Water and plumbing is far below any European standard and many public sources of water are a stew of infection, creating widespread epidemics, disease, and high infant mortality rates.

2

THE WALKING STICK
1912

Soon to be six-years-old, Nina sits perched next to her mother on the high-backed black leather seat in the first class compartment of the Russian Express, curiosity in her eyes. Her mother's tall ostrich feather seems to float in rhythm to the acceleration of the train now leaving the St. Petersburg Finlyandsky Railway Station far behind. Her father, Leonid sits across from them, with his starched white collar, finely tailored, vested suit and hat, reading the Russkoye Selo newspaper. Brother Leonya, nearing eight, sits in his navy suit and dangling legs next to father.

A first-class compartment containing her two-year old brother Vova, her year-old sister Vera, the younger children's nanny, the elder children's French governess, and the cook, is across the hall from them but of no concern to Nina. Instead, she focuses out the window at the endless columns of birch trees covered in their chalky white bark and imagines them to be white guards standing at attention like those she saw when the four Tsarinas rode in their carriage past the family's St. Petersburg residence. Nina now pictures herself a princess, the guards saluting her, as the sun reflects its rays off the sparkling leaves like so many golden epaulettes.

Already the big capital city is far behind, as the wide-gauge, lulling train first sweeps past what is the often gray and damp, many-canalled Petersburg, and then plunges headstrong into the thick green woods, denser forests, and heavy, piercing and more-prevalent, warm summer sunshine. The train continues its journey up the peninsula as it passes small stations. The railroad has formed the backbone of industrial and agricultural trade amongst the towns of what has been the free peasant, Lutheran, Autonomous Grand Duchy of Finland since the Swedes ceded it to Russia over a hundred years ago.

Nina knows the deepening forests are filled with deer, bear, and wild untamed nature, and the villages with roaming gypsies and superstitious peasants. The names indicated in Cyrillic on wooden boards are unimportant to her except for the last one. The toothless, melancholic peasants, frenetic businessmen and merchants, old wooden-framed substations, and the increasingly prevalent advertising posters she passes create only a general perception to her that is mostly forgotten as soon as her destination is reached. The majority of her memories are mostly marked by excess of tragedy, generosity, and joy.

Nina's mother Josephine sits quietly nearest the patterned, inlaid door that leads to the corridor. Alerted from a near slumber by the sound of the conductor's whistle, she takes notice as the train stops to let passengers on and off in a small hamlet near the Finnish town of Terioki where they will disembark. The majority of Russians live in the country, but, while Josephine enjoys spending time in the fresher air, she doesn't necessarily love the country. It is too rugged for her. It's remote and somehow lonely, regardless of the fact that she will be in the midst of so many of her and Leonid's, visiting family. he sounds of the country more often alarm and haunt her than relax her. The quiet she perceives belies the brutality of nature with its wolves and bear preying on god's smaller creatures. The rustlings of animals agitate her, for she doesn't know which is prey or predator.

She watches, first as service girls and working men depart at an earlier destination, and then as nobility, intellectuals and artists depart closer to Terioki, In recent years it has become known as a gathering spot for artists, poets, and musicians, although it wasn't chosen as such at the time of her father's purchase of the compound of dachas they now visit. Indeed her father, Karl Krümmel, bought the houses and land in a rather shrewd investment strategy.

The original owner first built the large wooden structure now occupied by Josephine's parents. It contains several guest rooms and a large extensive porch circling three-quarters of the house where the family often gathers, and on Sunday is called to dinner at the sound of the cook's gong. Unfortunately for the first owner, his continual inebriation began to wreak havoc on his finances, resulting in his need to sell this first home. Karl was the lucky buyer.

With a strong determination yet impossible to deny, the original owner built another house on his adjoining property. This second home is now occupied by Josephine's married sister Louise, and resembles the first, although smaller. Karl bequeathed it to his first married daughter, who also benefited by a lavish wedding gift of two apartment buildings in St. Petersburg. Josephine does not readily forget this fact, particularly since her sister's husband Yuri is so often unaccounted for.

The Finnish man continued to drink but, bolstered with additional finances and a predisposition toward grand schemes, built yet a third, a fourth, and fifth property. Continuing to lose his ability to manage his life and seeing it deteriorate before his eyes as quickly as his vodka vanished into his throat, he was again forced to sell each dacha in turn to the lurking Karl, until finally Karl, one-by-one, had purchased the entire compound, including the adjoining small swan pond.

The third dacha is now occasionally used by Josephine's sister Emma, who is married to a Bulgarian nobleman and has the ability to summer at any number of dachas spread haphazardly from the south of France to Italy, Bulgaria, and the Crimea. Josephine and her family now occupy the fourth cottage, given that Josephine was the third of her seven surviving siblings to marry. The fifth dacha Karl rents to another city family on vacation. An adopted sister, Mila, recently passed away from cancer in a Paris hospital, younger sister Greta is still unmarried, and brothers Karl Jr., Wilhelm, and Adolph remain unmarried—conveniently so, given that there is only one cottage left; the prior owner now vanished.

Josephine sits back into her heavily cushioned seat. Traveling outside the confines of the city whether to the cottages or abroad seems to make her more reflective. Willful and intelligent as she is, Josephine's mental reminiscing more recently has begun to reflect more soberly on the relations between herself, her husband, and his continually destructive relationship with gambling.

Married to Leonid, eight years her senior, she wonders now if she's made the right choice. There was a time, she remembers, when the society pages would comment on how she and her sisters dressed and gentlemen would joke that of the four sisters—Louise, Josephine, Emma, and Greta—it was impossible to choose the most beautiful. Their father Karl always made every effort to allow his pampered daughters to be seen at public events in the most splendid, utterly tasteful costumes.

As the train continues its journey to their country retreat she cannot avoid seeing the similarities between what she knows of the prior owner's behavior and her own husband's; whether the problem was drinking or gambling, the results were somewhat similar. Finding her thoughts disturbingly intolerant, she realizes that whether Leonid gambled on horses, greyhounds, durachki, or poker at one of his clubs, in the city or the country, it was always the same—he would either be overly joyous or deeply somber.

She can't understand it. He's an accomplished gentleman and a conscientious and caring father. How can he be so insane as to gamble away what everyone knows is a fortune? Just last year even her ears caught the rumors that he had placed their cottage (which in actuality didn't belong to him) on the poker table and lost, only luckily to make it up again the next night before any documents needed to be signed. Josephine ponders his thoughtlessness, glancing at her husband across from her as the train begins its motion again.

Money had never been a problem in the past and certainly nothing worthy of concern. Even her earlier married years allowed her financial freedoms and opportunities and the occasional embarrassingly lavish gift—embarrassing in the sense that she never needed these items as confirmation of who she was. But now that they had four children, expenses had increased with the need for more servants including governesses, nannies for the babies, music lessons, tutoring, private education, and clothing. Money had become more important then ever, and yet they had less and less of it.

She wonders why her marriage crowds into her thoughts today. Leonid has been gambling for many years, that much is true, and odds are that he will do the same at the cottages again. Still yearning for more, she isn't even sure what "more" is, but she knows there is something terribly wrong with her world. Last year was so rainy, perhaps this year will bring more sunshine, she thinks as she conceals her concerns from herself. Yes, more sunshine! That's what she wants, even though it will require extra effort protecting her fashionably pale skin from it.

The decorative wooden clapboard Terioki train station comes into view as the train reaches the family's destination. Less than an hour away from the city, it feels like a completely different world. Josephine lifts her long skirts and holds onto the large brim of her oversized hat as she gently works her way down to the platform. Following her are her son Leonya, then Nina not far behind, the governess, Leonid, and the nanny carrying Vera. They calmly traverse their way through the small station and to awaiting carriages that will taxi them to the compound.

As the carriages make their way through the quaint town, cafes are busy, restaurants serve cosmopolitan foods, artists sell watercolors, and an open market allows the visiting tourists and locals a place to converse. Nina, who is already developing a young, tomboyish nature, although inclined to fidget like her idealized older brother, tries her hardest to mimic her mother's stately reserve. But as the carriage turns the corner, she finds it ever harder to contain herself.

Eagerly, she points toward the sign that reads "Property of Krümmel—No Trespassing," which is situated at the boundary of the property's long windy street. The sign, though ominous and bold, is welcoming to her. She isn't quite sure what trespassing or its consequences mean, only that for her or anyone she knows, it means nothing. The movement of horse and carriage breaks the tranquility of the surrounding quiet. But Nina knows that beyond the clatter and stomp is a cacophony of birds and chirping of crickets. There up ahead she now sees the river she knows is filled with fish and banked with croaking frogs, and then the outline of her grandparent's large cottage appears. It rises divinely and invitingly from the brush, its large wooden porch encircling the front and sides framed by geometric, patterned latticework.

Nina's excitement builds as the second large dacha comes into view; two stories of pretty, carved wooden window frames. Peering into its lacey curtained windows Nina wonders if her three cousins, Elena, Sophia, and Alicia, are in or if they are already playing at the lake or river, or even down by the seashore beyond the boundaries of the property compound. But there it is—the small lake that is home to geese and ducks—then the proprietor's quarters near the stable, and the clay tennis courts where she looks forward eagerly to one day becoming strong enough to play.

She counts one, two, three…and yes, Nina still counts, the fourth cottage, surrounded by birch and aspen with a little path that leads around the back to where Nina has her own door leading to her own room. Located in the front is a long porch enclosed in beveled glass where the immediate family will eat and spend hours looking out at the trees. She can barely contain the enthusiasm now bursting inside her, but knows she must, remembering Mother's fragile patience for energetic childish outbursts.

Farther down the road is the last cottage—last vestige of hope for the destitute and nameless prior owner before even this was too much for him. Although it is the smallest of the five cottages, it contains a coop for chickens and a sty for hogs. Nina can already hear the chickens, and imagines the sloshing and rut of hogs. This year, however, Nina will soon discover that the small yard contains a goat, brought by a renting bourgeoisie family, instead of pigs.

Already fatigued from the trip and uncomfortably dusty from the carriage ride, Josephine immediately enters her room to rest, change her clothes, and apply a damp washcloth to her face. Her parents' servants have already prepared all the prerequisite conveniences, changed the linens, and brought fresh water. She wonders if her brothers will be visiting from Berlin this year and staying at her parents' cottage, preferring the mixed company that her bachelor brothers bring.

&cs;

Dressed today with a large blue silk ribbon perched atop her head and another one at the curve of her tiny back, Nina feels as ridiculous as her cousins now seem to her. She would by far prefer being less encumbered in shorts and shirt like Leonya. Tugging at her floppy bow, she bounds out of her back door and skips toward her Aunt Louise's dacha.

Once at Tante Lulya's she joins her aunt, grandfather, and three coquettish cousins on a carriage ride to the beach. The Gulf of Finland, which far to the East touches St. Petersburg, is a mere few minutes' ride away. Here endless pebbly beaches surround it.

Grandpa, as always, is dressed in his three-piece suit, bowler, and beautiful black walking stick crowned with an ornamental gold handle, used more for a grand appearance and as a statement of his gentility than for any practical necessity. Once arrived, he makes a rather quick disappearance to find a comfortable spot to nap on one of his favorite boulders.

Nina scans the surroundings, seeing long wooden bridges jut out from the beach. Large clumsy stones and random few boulders line the shallow waters for many yards out to sea. Small, wooden bathhouses are found at the end of wooden, plank bridges where swimmers change into bathing clothes. A small ladder leads from the end of the docks to where the sandy bottom finally begins.

Nina can't go in the water. Her fast metabolism, quickly growing little body, constant activity, and finicky eating habits have made her terribly thin. The family doctor instructed her that salt water is bad for thin little girls, and swimming should be avoided for fear of being carried away on the buoyant, powerful sea.

With this in mind, she nonetheless lackadaisically follows her aunt on a long bridge. Tante Lulya is not hard to see in her full, long, pale green dress, hat and sun umbrella, but she is quite a distance away and nearing the bathing house. Alicia, Sophia, and Elena are already changing as Nina continues to walk, now alone, over the long musty-smelling boards that stand high over the water below.

Nina hears the sound of the chilly gulf water splashing against the large rocks jutting through the surface as the water becomes deeper and darker, but also beautifully appealing. She's infatuated with the way in which the small waves mingle on the long shore and in the shallows. As light sparkles on the tips of the waves within waves she finds herself looking too closely now, feeling as if the water wants to grab her like a giant living being luring her with a false sense of tranquility only to reveal cold, frightening, underwater creatures and darkness where no light shines.

Her heart begins to race. The sound of the sea comes from below her shoes and through the wooden planks, from the sides, from in front and behind. Terrified, she quickly turns on her heels and begins to run as fast as her little legs will carry her. Faster, faster, back to the land.

Suddenly, for no apparent reason her feet fail her and she begins to fly, then falls uncontrollably toward the churning, unfamiliar depths. Her mind goes blank as her instincts take charge. She struggles to grasp something solid from the air as she is enveloped by the chilly, airless sea.

As soon as she tries to stand up, the pounding waves knock her down again. Unable to swim, she begins to swallow the salty water until her lungs burst with pain. Struggling with the waves, the water, and her painful lungs, she tries to get hold of something, anything, but can't. She knows she is drowning.

With all her strength she pushes herself up through the increasingly shallow water—waves that have been pushing her down have also pushed her closer to the shore. She's able to stand briefly and yell to her grandfather asleep on a large boulder on the shore.

"Grandfather, grandfather! Help, help!," she gasps between gulps.

Through cloudy eyes she sees him awaken, as if from a dream, and rub his eyes. Nina gasps with lessening breath, "Grandfather... heeellllp me!"

Grandfather Karl jerks awake, rubs his eyes, and runs the short distance of the wooden bridge. Nina, now standing and holding onto a rock watches him look down at his black leather shoes and full suit. Realizing it isn't necessary for him to go into the shallow water, he takes his cane and reaches its gold-knobbed handle out to his favorite granddaughter. "Come Nina, come on, Nina come."

Calmed by his confidence, Nina reaches for the cane and, holding onto its comforting gold knob, walks bravely toward him the remaining distance out of the water. It is not the first time grandfather has saved her in such a way; last year her sandals slipped on the muddy banks of the river running through their property, jettisoning her into the water and in need of her grandfather's cane.

At first she cries uncontrollably, confused on so many levels and wondering why it is that she always falls into the water, thinking that might be why she's her grandfather's favorite; for after all, he saves her life almost every year now. And then she thinks of how crowded the beach was with not only her grandfather and aunt nearby, but also with other strangers. How can it be that she was so alone and at risk of dying when so many were so near?

Josephine's mother, after whom Josephine was named, the matriarch of the family, sits in her large, cushioned rocking chair on her extensive front porch of the main compound dacha. Her daughters Josephine and Louise and eternal bachelor sons Adolph and Wilhelm, who have come from Berlin, surround her. The June weather has been consistently hot and humid creating a heavy, restless fatigue over the northern native family.

"What's the use of bringing any more children into this world," Wilhelm espouses?

"I completely agree," Adolph responds. "There are far too many people on the earth already and I see no need to add to the overpopulation. You know Berlin has grown so much in this decade alone that there is a shortage of housing? The lowest classes move from the country to cities everywhere, including your beloved Petersburg where they remain impoverished and working for ungodly low wages in intolerable conditions."

Josephine listens silently in agreement. She has already decided that four children have pushed her limits and her patience as a mother. How her upper-class, Alsace-born mother could stand fifteen children—seven stillborn, and one adopted—is beyond all reason to her. When a child Josephine marveled at her motivations and dedication, sitting by her bedside so often when mother was ill with the demands of yet another birth. But her mother recovered quite resiliently to still travel back and forth between Berlin and St. Petersburg, always at her husband's side. Out of respect and sheer incredulity for her mother's experience Josephine remains silent.

Wilhelm continues, "World affairs are treacherous and horrendously nationalistic." Everyone knows he enjoys listening to himself talk, and so they make no effort to dissuade him as he goes on. "Still, working conditions and the growing bourgeoisie are far better situated in Germany as a whole than what I understand them to be in Russia." He fiddles with his thumbnails and hammers his final point, "Nonetheless, it's abhorrent to think that we should allow children into this disaster we call civilization."

Adolph adds, "Oh so proud, proud... proud of ourselves for all of our modern day marvels in Germany, in Russia and France... not to mention England. But what accomplishments are these when that mighty ship, the *Titanic*, went down a few months ago? My god, all of those innocent people; how advanced are we...really?"

Josephine remembers the event, knowing exactly where she was in April. She remembers her father later defending technology and blaming it on the errors of the British, explaining, "That's why they are losing their dominance to Germany and Russia." She remembers her horror and those of her peers at the utter dismay at the lack of protection all those people had when they thought they were participating in an event using science, engineering, and comforts unheard of before in the modern world.

"Children," the matriarch responds, "here we sit in this beautiful forested enclave. Why discuss such atrocities? What in heaven's name has caused you all to be so glum? I support whatever decisions you each make in your own lives concerning children, for heaven's sake, but this is neither the place nor the time to discuss them."

Nina walks dejectedly around the side of the house after her devastating afternoon. She knows her mother was quite concerned to the point of being unusually verbose when speaking with Tante Lulya, but now she hears a different story. Josephine is close enough to her to be in earshot, speaking with her brothers and sisters on grandmother's porch. But is that laughter she hears? Nina creeps up closer, not yet seen by the others.

"…all dressed up in her beautiful silk bows and sopping wet like a drowned little creature," Josephine muses in her own semi-dramatic fashion, yet adding a bit of her charismatic humor; her motive to defer to her mother's request to add levity to the prior conversation and relieve her own terror about the situation works well in polished communication. Nina, however, is too young to grasp her mother's complex motives. "How can Mother be so cruel as to make light of my almost dying?" she thinks in her childish state of mind?

Immediately she runs back to the cottage, knowing that the chef will soon ring the dinner gong calling the entire extended family to its customary huge Sunday feast. Nina doesn't feel hungry at all.

3

ENDLESS JOURNEY
1913

Public transportation is utterly stifled during the thousands of strikes of 1913. The city is often at a standstill. Working hours are long in unsafe conditions, yet some progress is slowly being made; hours are cut due to new laws and child labor has been banned. Intellectuals, many from wealthy families themselves, urge apathy among the newly industrialized peasants who come in droves from the country. "Soviets" or small workers' management groups sprout in the largest factories where tens of thousands of workers earn the best wages. The majority of the city's peasants and lower classes work as domestic servants and administrators and are not represented at all.

The comfortable lives of the growing middle class and the eccentric ostentation of the wealthy are more than blatantly obvious to the least educated or socially connected. What's worse is the Tsar—the king and "god-gifted" leader who had been thought to be capable of no moral wrong—is now increasingly seen by the masses as uncaring, disconnected and corrupt. Religious fanaticism amongst the wealthy is rampant. Some claim the coming of Armageddon. The Tsarina herself has taken to seeing a mystic monk, Rasputin, who has been said to have the ability to foresee the future and to have curative powers over her son.

Karl Krümmel's frequent trips to Berlin, now an industrial wealth-producing machine, has allowed him the knowledge and wherewithal to invest in the infant automobile industry in St. Petersburg, by purchasing a fleet of automobiles he's had commissioned and named after himself. Financially fortunate for him is Russia's lethargy in industrial, entrepreneurial, and capitalistic advancement resulting in its continued reliance on his old carriage business. But times are changing, and his carriage business, while providing the financial horsepower for new investments, now takes a backseat to his interest in the automobile. The wealthy won't be stopped by the strikes, and now his most recent Russian triumph will be blessed.

Josephine walks ahead of Nina, suede lining her floor-length dress to protect it from the muddied streets on this dull and drizzling day in late April. The two press their way past pedestrian onlookers toward a round, four-story brick building. Together they enter and walk up the stairs to the rooftop where a small group stands. Here on the roof also are Father, Uncle Erich, and other members of the extended family, journalists, bankers, businessmen, and their wives. Grandfather Karl stands on a platform in his brusque, stately manner and casts a friendly glance at Nina.

A Russian Orthodox priest from the Cathedral of St. Petersburg stands nearby, fully robed from collar to feet in richly colored, gold and silver gilded habit and pointed, richly embroidered headpiece. He swings incense into the chilly early spring air. His thick beard is slightly damp from his concurrent exaltations. Another priest, exquisitely ornamented in a cone-shaped robe with a brilliant headpiece of semi-precious stones, sprinkles holy water in the typical Russian tradition of blessing most material objects.

Karl continues his discourse in a measured, confident tone, "As you all know, St. Petersburg, like so many European cities, will soon have little space to park its modern automobiles. In light of this problem, I have built a solution. The center of this building contains a large mechanical lift, an elevator for horseless carriages. At the bequest of a lady or gentleman, one of several chauffeurs residing at all times of the day and evening in the apartments next door can be summoned to retrieve either one of the fleet of automobiles I have developed or one of their own fine automobiles from any one of these four floors. Once ordered, the chauffeur will simply drive onto the lift, which will then take him and the auto down to the first floor, where he can then drive to the requesting personage. Those city dwellers with their own drivers can lease space in this modern marvel and retrieve their vehicles whenever they wish."

As grandfather lectures on, Nina looks up imagining herself

as a bird taking flight above the city, high above the clouds, and then soaring back down and around, with the city surrounding her. She comes back to her current reality just in time to see the satisfaction in the faces of the adults around her. And standing next to her is kind-hearted uncle Erich.

He takes her hand in his, which in itself is very unusual for Nina as she isn't often touched by any adult member of her family in any way. The simple physical contact and warmth of an adult's nurturing hand is reassuring. Together the two leave the building and walk to one of the automobiles parked outside. Nina is familiar with autos, as she's seen Grandfather Karl ride in many, and Uncle Roman arrive in his large chauffeured vehicle—something called a Rolls Royce Silver Ghost. But she's never ridden in one.

Erich opens the door of the boxy, enclosed vehicle and helps Nina in. As she watches, he goes to the front and turns a metal handle attached to the front grill. "Jjjjjjjrrr," she hears the sound of metal rubbing against metal. Then again, "jjjjjrrrrrr," as a roaring cough emanates from below and in front of her, and the mechanical animal comes to life. Her uncle gets into the front seat and the horseless carriage jars forward frightening horses and displacing bystanders. She'll remember this ride for the rest of her life, and the thrill of the vehicle lurching forward through and beyond the mass of humanity.

Time passes quickly for Nina, punctuated mostly by large family banquets, ceremonies, holidays, and wonderful trips to the dachas. The family, St. Petersburg and Tsarskoe Selo are Nina's foundation and she expects that everyone else in the world lives a similar existence to hers. She doesn't comprehend the life of the workers, the serfs, or the servants, as their history and lifestyles aren't presented in her studies. Albeit filled with neatly dressed people, etiquette, and language studies by French and German governesses, tutors, and her Aunt Stella, her life is simple.

Nonetheless, as the summer again approaches, Nina has begun to grow from incoherence to childlike reason, from complete surrender to the world around her to the beginnings of judgment and discernment. She more readily moves from lack of conscious awareness to the pangs of certain memory. She wakes up to the world like Russia itself, and, like Russia, her awakening is not without its fits and tantrums.

Nina and Leonya have left for the dachas earlier than the rest of the family. Their new young governess and the rest of the servants will be coming tomorrow. Josephine for the time being has remained in St. Petersburg to attend to the illness of Nina's younger sister. And father Leonid has escorted the pair into the first class compartment of the St. Petersburg to Terioki Express train, where he knows they'll be safe. Tonight they'll stay at Tante Lulya's dacha.

It's unusual to be left alone like this, but Nina is confident in her mother's judgment. Besides mother will be coming tomorrow, as Nina has been told there is some issue with one of her two youngest siblings. Being four years older than her brother and five years older than her sister, she is far too concerned with her own life to focus on the details of her younger siblings' lives. For now brother Leonya has been given money to hire a carriage in Terioki that will take them to the cottages, and both sister and brother have waved goodbye to father Leonid.

Nina doesn't mind any of this at all. In fact, she loves it. Her brother is still her idol and she trusts every move he makes. Now that he's almost nine Mother obviously trusts that he will be responsible. Besides, they've made the trip from Petersburg to the cottages every year of their lives so far.

The first class compartment is similar to past experience, and the other passengers are polite and helpful. The train ride is not long as Nina sits quietly on her best behavior, much like a little lady, across from her brother. The signs and villages they pass are infused with subtle and not-so-subtle changes in the lives of those who live there. But these changes go unnoticed by Nina. Where before she imagined the Tsar's White Guards, today she imagines everything being just the same as it always has been.

As the two disembark in Terioki, Leonya feels the weight of the coins between his fingers in his pocket. With a sudden rush of adrenaline and lift of his eyebrow he turns to Nina and says, "Wouldn't you rather get a frozen ice in the village first? Then we can just walk instead of taking a hired carriage," he adds convincingly.

"A frozen ice?" Nina wonders. She weighs the options. But even though Leonya chastises her more often than befriends her, he must be doing no wrong in a bonded plot together. Getting into trouble seems out of the question, he continues to assure her, since, "…who would know if we don't tell them?" Favoring her brother's suggestion and bored with the other option, her answer is an almost immediate "Yes!"

Together they walk out of the station, beyond the carriages and directly in the midst of the thriving village where cafes, restaurants, and retail shops line the main thoroughfare. Farther down near the end of the main district is the apothecary that serves special flavored ice. Nina follows her brother somewhat shyly as he sits up at the counter barstool and orders two frozen ice; a strawberry for him and a blueberry for her. She wishes she could have the same, but nonetheless, he's ordered, and apparently some need for differentiation exists. Nina accepts this, silently rejecting the inequality between herself and her bigger, domineering brother.

The sticky-sweet sugar turns their teeth and lips red and blue when Leonya instructs her, "It's time to go now." As they walk out of town the dirt road becomes narrower, and the forest denser, with only random large farmhouses. Farmers and, relatively well-dressed, visiting tourists in their carts slow down so as not to spread dust on the two youngsters. An occasional automobile drives by with a well-adorned woman's scarf fluttering in the wind. Leonya waves them on, as he proudly skips, walks, and throws twigs and stones into the air, intentionally increasing the distance between himself and his sister.

Nina keeps up her pace the best she can, using two steps

for his every one in a frantic effort to not be left abandoned, and to prove she can be as fast as he. As the distance increases, her cheerful mood starts to turn as sour as her iced stomach is becoming. She tries to not be perturbed by the now seemingly endless journey as she licks her dry blue lips. Her little black shoes and white stockings carry a fine layer of dust that makes her wonder how on earth they'll go unnoticed once they arrive at Tante Lulya's.

"Where is that rotten boy," she thinks to herself as the trees and bushes meld into one another. Everything looks different from the ground compared to riding in the carriage. Landmarks that were always obvious are less so as seen from a different perspective. She's not sure which trees are familiar but feels a compelling certainty in her direction that helps carry her forward even amidst her fear. And then there, up ahead, beyond some obviously maintained hedges, appears the familiar "No Trespassing" sign. Relieved, she knows she's getting closer to home.

Entering the kitchen of her aunt's dacha, she is greeted by the maid. Nina asks to be directed to the young governess of her cousins who she knows will help her clean up. Luckily, Tante Lulya and those three little rascals are nowhere to be found, she realizes as she proceeds to the children's rooms.

Sure enough, she finds the young governess who has become an intimate of the four girls. A couple of years ago they all had quite a surprise when spotting a lost yellow canary in a tree. The governess climbed up, tucked the bird into her large peasant's blouse, and returned with it. No sooner had she done that than a neighbor, claiming to have heard the chirps of her favorite pet, came to retrieve it.

Just as planned, Nina greets the friendly governess, who proceeds to promise to keep her story safe. After a nice lunch of fresh sliced cucumbers and bread, Nina is off again to look for her brother. It isn't long before she realizes the folly in her concern in the first place; for just as soon as she's been cleaned and fed, she is off getting dirty in the endless summer forests.

⁊

Dressed in her requisite costume, her soft and naturally curly, shoulder-length hair pinched by another bow, Nina is disregarded by brother Leonya as she tries to follow him throughout the late afternoon like a baby chicken follows its hen. Nina peruses the forest near the house. She is hunting small mushrooms, which are her favorite, and fried mushrooms thick with butter are best. The smell of the mulching forest in her little nose, and the feel of dirt in her little hands, which she rubs off the newly discovered mushrooms, enlivens her. The late burning sun makes giants out of tree shadows that were barely there only a few hours before. The breeze tickles the bow on her head and flips her fine hair as she considers her inability to be respected by her older brother. She heads back to her cottage looking for Papa with a decision in mind.

Leonid digs the shovel further into the sandy soil, and takes another clump of ochre earth from the garden as he transplants a sickly specimen of shrub rose. The plants border the pathways around the gardens of the house, looking strangely like people with their long stalk-like necks and round blooming heads. The crimson, bluish white, and his favorite deep yellow are faring much better this summer, he realizes, breathing in their fragrance as his shovel scrapes the earth.

Gardening is one of his favorite past-times and he goes about it with the patience and serenity afforded him by having ample free time. Much like the Tsar himself, Leonid enjoys his domestic life and numerous hobbies far greater than any number of more complex political or worldly burdens. He favors the title of "Little Father" that the people endearingly call the Tsar, remembering fondly his own happy childhood.

Leonid was born in the spring of 1873 in Dunaberg, Lithuania, where the family had moved from Libau. Much of his youth was spent in Minsk, where his father's increasing political success required the family to live before moving to the capital city of St. Petersburg. It wasn't until he lived in St Petersburg and began to involve himself in societal functions that he met his wife Josephine, who was born there. Always given every opportunity to carry out whatever interests he had, much of the time he enjoyed the countryside. Now that he's just turned 40, he finds himself involved even more with family matters and, quite frankly, enjoys his children.

On this particular day, he finds himself thinking about little in particular except for an underlying gratitude to his father-in-law. As in the past, Leonid has been provided for. His father-in-law Karl has generously gifted him a large sum of money to cover some of his gambling losses. Leonid has promised himself and Karl to not gamble any more. He feels strongly that he can manage this urge for he knows that it has become irrational. Nonetheless, he goes about his day with a continued nonchalance to outside matters.

Nina is emboldened by her growing self-assuredness as is most evident now with her victory of finding a full basket of mushrooms. Tired of what she considers unwieldy hair, she is now determined to have it cut short like Leonya's. After all, it's summertime, she thinks. Perhaps she can convince father into letting her have a haircut. Why not?

Nina flirts, "Hello father. See I picked some mushrooms. They're very pretty."

"Oh, I see," replies Leonid, smiling at his daughter and wondering curiously at how she finds the dirty basket of mushrooms to be pretty in contrast to his own beautiful blooming roses. But the two share a common bond beyond the apparent state of dirtiness. Nina has always held a special place in Leonid's heart as his first-born daughter, and Nina realizes his love for her.

Together they investigate Leonid's roses, as Nina begins to carry with her a fondness for the flowers that she will maintain for the rest of her life. Not distracted by her initial concerns, nor at all apprehensive of her father, she eventually asks outright, "May I get a haircut so that it's shorter like Leonya's'?"

Leonid thinks for a moment before simply responding, "You'll have to go and ask your mother."

❧

Josephine manages the cottages as she manages the apartment in the city, mostly busying herself with evening wardrobes to choose; an outing on the ferry to plan for tomorrow; coordination with the chef over choices and timing of meals; managing the governesses and nanny with respect to care of the children; and visiting with her family. But at this particular moment she stops and looks out the window catching a glimpse of the breeze flowing through the million shades of green dotting the landscape and hears the punctuating sound of a crow. She notices the cascade of humid light, and admires the crisp whites, creams, and blacks of a clump of birch trees in the distance.

Tranquilly she admires this rare, quiet moment. Feeling inspired, she picks up her velvet-lined basket filled with silk thread and needles and a prepared, ruby red silk canvas, and walks to the glass-enclosed porch. She's recently finished a *petit-point* portrait of a beautiful young woman with a large feathered hat, but hasn't quite made up her mind on her new project.

"Mother" Nina says, now bravely approaching the porch and interrupting Josephine's moment of artistic escape.

"Yes, Nina."

Nina suddenly becomes worried about her request. She is never sure what her mother is thinking. Normally she is not exposed to either her mother's or her father's rationale for decisions. Conversation between the two parents is subdued and anything of any importance is said in one of the parlors behind closed doors, away from the servants, away from the children, and often in hushed tones. Sometimes the less said with mother, the better: "May I please cut my hair short like Leonya's?"

"What an odd little girl," thinks Josephine, placing her silk thread upon her lap, grateful now that she has another daughter who may turn out to be less odd. "Your hair is too thin and fine as it is. But if it is cut it may grow back thicker."

Nina is thrilled, seemingly conquering everything today, including the fear of her mother. There is nothing she can't do, and doesn't care about how she looks to anyone. She just knows how she feels—and she feels great. Best not tempt fate, however.

Josephine's silence momentarily breached, she reminisces upon the conversations of this summer, her recent introduction to current impressionistic art, the complexities of her life with her husband and children, and the actual beauty she's noticed today. An idea starts to form; "Where is that odd photograph Leonid took of the young peasant boy with the tattered dress shirt and hole-filled straw hat; the one with the boy oddly holding a cigarette," she wonders. Inspired, she sets down her thread to search for the photograph. A peasant boy in silk for her new needlepoint, she decides. And she is happy with her decision, for internally she knows the world of beautifully dressed women in large flattering hats is changing as wardrobes and cities change back home and abroad.

☙

A bright burst of light momentarily illuminates the already sunny day. Nina, Leonya, Vova, and Vera blink to clear their eyes from the now familiar flash of Papa's camera apparatus. Nina, her hair cut down to a uniform two inches, holds a large string attached to her wooden monkey on wheels, Leonya holds onto a miniature wooden horse and Vova is posed between the handles of a decorative wooden wheelbarrow that contains his sister Vera. They stand on the rose-bush lined path that leads to Nina's no longer secret back door, now captured for everyone to see.

Leonid is very pleased with his hobby. He'll develop this shot in his darkroom and add it to the ones taken earlier of the ferry ride, the day at the beach, the posed picture of Nina with her cousins on the ladder behind one of the cottages, and Nina sitting in the dog house where his hunting pointer Stopka lives.

Like the Tsar, he feels compelled to record these majestic idle days and his growing family. And like the Tsar, Leonid's preoccupation with this more readily available technology only represents what he chooses to see of his preferred, idealistic world. The pictures develop with his world—some more avant-garde than others—revealing not so much the total picture of the reality of the world around him, but more what he chooses to focus his lens on. The developed two-dimensional form motivates him to create art and record events, however it also allows him to avoid his worries over troubled times and his own personal demons. His photographs are selective pieces of his perception, which mirror only slices of life. Nonetheless, the images will outlive him, framed with their perspective of a dying yet stubborn reality. For who can say whether or not the ideas presented by his photos will ever change?

❧

August has nearly come to its conclusion and so too have the sunny, warm, twenty-two-hour, northern days. Fall will approach as it always does within a couple short months. Its appearance, if not yet felt, can be observed in the first odd leaf that has turned to dull gold or bright yellow in the weakest of the trees. The majestic days—idle, yet fully orchestrated—have coalesced into disappointment for Nina, who realizes that, for some inexplicable reason, they must end. But they'll end for her this year with a new understanding of her own competence in dealing with the difficulties that have befallen her even amidst the pleasure.

For now, the city beckons her back complete with its lessons and stringent codes of conduct. She will soon be attending private school with other little girls just like herself, held away from the masses of other children who do not wear school uniforms nor have books to read at all; most of the working classes in bustling St. Petersburg are still illiterate. Nina doesn't worry about this, and only hopes for next summer, more sensitized to her feelings, which are as resilient as her young flexible mind and body.

The coachman places the last of the bags in the coach and heads back to his room. Nina watches him with her observant curiosity. She looks into the one-room, dirt-and wood-floored apartment while he briefly retrieves his hat, and sees a humble fireplace surrounded by old metal pots and pans. There are two small beds on each side and a table in the middle. She sees his wife and young son sitting quietly in the dimly lit room. It's strange she never really noticed them much before. "How odd to see three people in such a small room," she thinks, registering this memory in her mind where no camera goes and no photo will record. Her governess is calling.

4

FIRST FLIGHT
AND THE CAGED CANARY
1914

Josephine pushes the long crushed-turquoise velvet curtains aside as she enters her dressing chamber to dress for the theater. A large, dark green fern plant breaks the chill of the seemingly endless imposition of winter and, along with the warmth of the room furnace, transforms the evening into far more pleasure than the late spring outside might imply.

She reaches for a silver handled brush noticing her reflection in the mirror. The somber seriousness on her thirty-three-year-old face doesn't belong there, she thinks. She worries about getting older and the constant responsibilities she feels towards her children. She pushes back her unpinned, long, dark brown hair in an effort to look more beautiful to herself, and then sets down the brush and sips some hot tea poured from the steaming samovar her maid has

51

brought in.

The beginning of 1914 has been filled with more balls and gatherings than any season in recent memory. The art scene is burgeoning with Modernism, Impressionism, Symbolism, Cubism, Fauvism, the Bolshoi Ballet, and new opera at the Maryinsky Theater. Josephine is mostly relieved that the huge Easter feast is over. Soon it will be summer and everyone she knows will leave for the Crimea, Finland, France, Germany, and the Baltics.

Nina knows her mother is preparing for her evening's activities and is occasionally allowed to visit her at such times. She enters her mother's room today proudly wearing a gold Easter necklace with eight golden eggs, each received as a gift from Aunt Emma for each Easter of her life, attached by miniscule gold hooks. Her latest egg is cream-colored enamel with a gold and diamond band. Feeling like an adult, she approaches her mother, who sits at her large mirrored dressing table.

"How is my Nina," questions Josephine in the unusual manner of addressing her daughter with a question about her feelings, as she continues with her preparations.

"I am very well mother," says Nina flatly, holding her head high to expose her gilded eggs, but gaining no response.

Josephine opens an elaborately embellished box with navy blue velvet lining and an assortment of jeweled accessories. She takes out a ostrich-feathered fan, with decorative silver clasps and roped silver handle, and sets it aside, looking for something else. Nina, always enamored with birds and their feathers, notices the fan.

Josephine catches her daughter's observation in the reflection of the mirror.

"Would you like the fan, Nina?" asks Josephine.

"Oh yes mother, if I may," responds Nina shyly, still bolstered by her regally necklaced appearance.

"You may have it then."

Nina carefully takes the beautiful object with her tiny fingers and awkwardly flutters it, obscuring her face. Pretending to be a grand dame at a ball, she can only see the large feathers in front of her, and then her mother's jeweled fingers gently grabbing them, folding them, replacing the fan in its box, and closing the lid.

"You must learn to say "thank you" when presented with a gift," Josephine remarks as she continues to place a silver hairpin in her hair. Nina holds back her tears in order to not further offend her mother.

"I'm sorry, dear Mother." She curtsies and bows her head grateful to hide her red, puffy face. She continues, "May I be excused?"

"Good night, Nina," Josephine allows, practicing her belief that showing a child too much love will spoil it.

Nina turns on her heals and quickly walks out of the dressing room and down the hall to her room. The eggs rub against her neck as she bursts into tears, all the while chastising herself for being so inconsiderate.

Josephine continues to adorn her evening costume with bracelets, rings, necklaces, and brooches. German-Russians have recently fallen into disfavor as the German-born Tsarina has been increasingly blamed for her and Rasputin's influence over the Tsar, yet Josephine, herself a Russian with German blood, is going to one of the grandest balls of the season held at the German consulate.

She thinks twice about replacing the sapphire and diamond bracelet upon her wrist. It almost feels too ostentatious. What a shame, she thinks, that the Tsar's three hundredth Anniversary Celebration last year was so bitterly criticized by the press and the people. She considers the evident rudeness not only to the Tsar's family but also to women of her class. For beyond her evening's appearance she is patently aware of the facts that continue to influence her intuitive if not severely analytical thinking.

The city contains too much distress and the children are growing older. It is true that the pollution is such that even little Leonya became ill with fever and coughing. In fact, one in three poor children die shortly after birth as a result of an array of maladies from poor sewage treatment. And the chronic strikes, disturbances, and even occasional shortages are beyond tolerable. As she again looks at her refined and beautiful appearance, Josephine senses that the city itself seems to be wreaking havoc with her nerves. And why is it that the Tsar and his family don't live here and haven't for the past nine years, she wonders to herself now.

Roman works busily at his enameled, oversized desk. His powerful position as a consulting liaison to the Bank of Belgium offers him fluid connections with the international banking community as well as rare and intimate knowledge of the heated international flow of capital. His authority over Russian coal companies seeking financing and investment provides him exceptional knowledge of the intimate workings of the Russian economy. His influence, increasing diplomatic standing and prerequisite sense of political balances, combine to create a delicate framework for his politically correct public statements versus what he knows privately to be true.

He places the heavy-handled, silver earpiece of the telephone on its wooden box-like base, concluding an international call. He's just learned some of the year-end latest figures and indices. The supply of money between Belgium, France and Russia is moving with more and more rapidity and volume, either in spite of or regardless of continued apprehension of German imperialistic motives and Berlin's ever-expanding industrial growth. Britain and France continue their ancient infighting to the exclusion of harmonious financial decisions. And concern about the force used and blood spilled during the latest worker conflict in Siberian gold mines has mostly gone forgotten.

Roman is frustrated by what he sees and knows. Although dressed in ascot, gold-handled walking stick and large diamond pendant, he has never lost his knack for speaking directly with engineers at the factory. It doesn't take a genius, is his thought, to know that there is absolute misery among the normally perseverant workers in the field. They don't feel heard because they are not. Russia nonetheless continues to grow in industrial and financial strength as the Eastern European center of power, despite, by Western standards, its odd and old-fashioned methods.

It will be a typical evening for him. After he concludes his day at his office he will attend a social function or his club, mingle with nobility, or visit with an acquaintance. Perhaps he may visit his mistress, a popular, highly recognized ballerina. Then again, he may attend an early evening meal with his family, to whom he is an attentive and loving father and husband.

There is nothing within his power that he can do to stop the tortuously-slow wheels of progress from creating the conflicts that seem to pervade this land that he loves so dearly. Tonight in particular, this cold and barren January of 1914, he chooses to go home, where, sitting in front of the fire, he converses quite readily with his wife. Claudia will hear all he has to say and add insights of her own. His two daughters will have attended to their evening Orthodox prayers and the nanny will have put his son to bed. Roman will end the day and the week as he has for years.

&

Nina shyly wipes the tears away from her eyes. She isn't really sure why she's crying. She's always liked adventure. But the shock of this announcement, coming from her mother's mouth as Nina sits on the sofa that day in the living room with her two brothers, upsets her.

With no warning from anyone, not even a snip of information from her siblings or governess, Nina hears Josephine abruptly inform her children, "As you all know, your brother Vova has been increasingly ill due to congestion in his lungs from the city air. Because of this we are moving to Tsarskoe Selo."

At seven and one-half years old, she likes her stability and even though she really doesn't like the city as much as the country, she's afraid of actually moving to this new place, this city of the Tsars. But if it will help her brother get better, she can put her own fears aside.

It's not that Josephine has become totally disillusioned with the city of her birth, but after weighing the options of a move to Tsarskoe Selo, where the Tsars family has resided for nine years, and to what some consider a stunning new place, as well as considering the health of her child, the decision has made itself. Besides, it is only a short twenty-minute train ride from St. Petersburg to the opulent town and retreat built by Catherine the Great. It is now the most exclusive residence in all of Russia and the center of the Tsar's innermost circle.

Josephine stands in her dressing parlor and inspects a large wooden box containing a ball gown from what seems to be a bygone era. She remembers when it was such a glamorous dress with its slight bustle in back and its beautifully stitched semi-precious jeweled ribbing. Everything seemed so simple then. She remembers the ball, the ballet, the quartet and theater, and the endless nine-course meal for over one hundred and fifty guests attending her parents' wedding anniversary. She recalls with great pleasure how many fine gentlemen asked to dance with her and her sisters, and how she waltzed to the music—lulled by the quartet of harp, violin, cello, and piano playing Beethoven. They watched the small theater performance of *Cyrano de Bergerac* as she fanned herself while avoiding the unrestrained looks of the debonair, young men. As if it were yesterday, she recalls how proud she was of her parents, and how much sincerity they appeared to have for one another after twenty-five years of marriage.

Josephine collects herself and pushes the dress aside. She'll have the semi-precious stoned ribbing removed and the rest of the dress will go in the crate that won't be moved. It seems as if she has endless things to look through as the servants continue packing.

Leonid keeps his distance from the household's myriad activities. As on any other normal weekday, he continues to see clients and work in his office suite. There a secretary and a live-in maid and her husband (who works as a document carrier) attend to him. Together the man, wife, and their two-year-old son live in one of Leonid's adjoining rooms for fee rent in exchange for their services.

Leonid is unconcerned about the details of the family's move to the smaller city. For the most part, his interest in this move is to a large degree inconsequential, as the new arrangement will leave him staying in the city and renting a suite at the St. Petersburg Hotel. Only on weekends will he take the short train ride to be with his family in their new, extensive second-floor apartment.

This arrangement is not completely impractical as many

people of his stature and among the nobility have spent years living both in houses, palaces, and apartments in Tsarskoe Selo—or attending receptions by the Tsar there—and working or living in the capital St. Petersburg the rest of the time. In fact, the frequent train rides between the two cities may offer him more opportunities for discourse; something Josephine has always been in favor of.

❧

The summertime is here again. Nina awakens to a humid sunny morning, seeing the shadows of the gently fluttering birch leaves cast through the lace curtains of the dacha and onto her bedroom wall. She hears the crow of a rooster in a far off farm urging her to become excited about all the activities that await her. It is another wonderful summertime at the dachas, even though the trip here this year required a transfer through St. Petersburg.

Nina rushes to put on the outfit her governess has left out for her and rolls up her sleeves to hide its lacy cuffs. She ties her ankle-length leather shoes, and pushes down her lace trimmed socks. Little Leonya will have a similar cream-colored, collared, long-sleeve shirt, but will also wear shorts with shiny silver buttons.

She won't have breakfast, knowing that mother and father won't even be up yet, and no one will miss her as she walks outside the external door of her room leading down the side path. Running for the sake of running, breathing in the smells of the fir trees, listening to the morning music of so many birds, and imagining the wild boar and bears that must live beyond the thicket, she runs beyond her cottage, past her Tante Lulya and cousins' cottage, and toward the flattened, dark clay of the tennis courts.

"What is that silly girl doing now," she thinks as she approaches Alicia, who is dressed in her frilly bows and laces and, as usual, is holding her toothbrush and a glass of water, and is furiously brushing her teeth.

"Look Nina," Alicia points towards a tree, her mouth foaming with baking soda. "It's a little yellow bird. I saw it this morning through my window."

Nina squints at the sunlit tree, finding what she recognizes as a lone canary. It must have flown out of the window of some neighbor's cage. She worries it can't survive here, lost and living off leaves.

"I want her. I want to save her," Nina says to her cousin.

"What do you mean you want to save her…she's free after all… you'll never catch that bird," Alicia says condescendingly.

Spurred on even more by her cousin's challenge, Nina will have none of this. Nor will she take the time to explain her reasoning, surmising that in order for the bird to truly be saved from starving or freezing to death, it will need to be captured, caged, and fed by human hands.

She thinks fast. Thank goodness she had snuck around the house, rummaging through the storage shed with her brother a few days ago, and noticed that fancy empty birdcage. She runs quickly to the storage shed where she also finds some seed, some string, and a pair of hedge trimmers. Then just as quickly, she runs back to the tennis court to find Alicia still standing there and the bird happily or nervously chirping in the tree.

"What do you mean I won't catch that bird," she says. "Watch me."

Tying a small piece of string to the cage door so that it stays held open, she then places some seed in front of the cage and a larger portion inside. Aware of the fact that, if she places too much seed in front of the cage, the bird won't be tempted enough to venture inside, she picks up some seed from in front of the cage. "Hide now," Nina shouts to Alicia, as she too races behind a large metal roller used to flatten the court.

"Come down, come down," Nina thinks. "Come back to this pretty little cage. I know you will."

Nina holds her breath as she sees a splash of flying yellow against the green backdrop. The canary darts directly to the ground in front of the cage. As expected, the docile creature begins to eat and then hops over to the door. Exactly as planned, Nina's feathered conquest moves into the cage where it seeks its bonus of food.

Nina's heart races as fast as the bird's. Adrenaline pumping, Nina rushes to the cage and cups her hands over the door.

"Alicia, Alicia, come here and untie the string...come quickly!," she shouts to her cousin, who dashes over, detaches the string, and allows Nina to shut the door.

Momentarily baffled by her good luck and barely holding

onto the pride garnered by her accomplishment, she suddenly becomes conscious of what her mother may think.

Alicia has left her toothbrush and glass alone, and in her most practiced politeness says, "Thank you, Nina, for catching my bird."

"What do you mean, *your* bird?"

"Well, I did hear it and see it first, so it is my bird, Alicia says.

Nina assertively says, "We'll see about that, takes the cage and starts immediately for her private door to her cottage. She knows exactly what she'll do. She'll show Leonya. He'll know what to say to Mother, and in the meantime, she'll hide the entire cage under a blanket and sit with it as long as it takes her to know all will be safe.

Of course it isn't long before the entire compound has heard the story of Nina catching the bird, or before Tante Lulya, as always siding with her dearest, once-sickly, Alicia, has claimed the bird for herself. Nina knows her mother has spoken with her aunt but, until now, nothing has been said to her. Nina still holds her own beliefs even though her conscience sometimes cringes with the knowledge that she has another canary back home in Tsarskoe Selo, received as a Christmas gift.

Dinner is served for the immediate family on the glassed-in front porch of their dacha. Nina proceeds to the table unintimidated, and plops herself down on her chair, her puffy waist bow hanging out from behind like a floppy, feathered tail. A servant girl passes

Russet potatoes to each person and then some funny flat piece of meat that Nina instantly knows she will not like. Some green and orange vegetables are then served, causing Nina to completely lose her appetite, as she begins to feel more trapped at the table than her bird in its cage. As Nina pokes at the food with her silver fork, she looks up and over to Josephine who glares with disappointment at Nina's apparent sluggish distaste for the food.

Josephine with a slight tilt of her otherwise upright head begins, "About your bird, Nina." Nina places the weight of her fork on her mushy carrots and looks up as her mother continues, "I've spoken with your aunt Lulya who claims that your dearest cousin Alicia wishes the bird. I've also learned that you caught it…and how you caught it. Although I don't understand how you've possibly spent your free time learning such interesting tricks, I think it's fair and appropriate that you keep the bird. Therefore, I've told your aunt that it is rightfully yours. You may display it in the house, and you may not make any forthright statements of any pretense of conquest. It's only a caged bird after all, but you've earned the right to call it your own."

Nina, victorious, immediately thanks her mother and father, quickly smiles at her brother sitting to her right, and then straightening her back as she's been taught, digs promptly into her carrots, getting them out of the way before quietly finishing the rest of this hindrance that is her food.

 ☙

It's not infrequently that Nina's summertime excursions are so full of excitement, but today even her father seems to have a newfound respect for her. He's taken her out on one of his small game hunting expeditions and Nina couldn't be more pleased.

It's a small group of finely dressed men in their hunting boots and jackets, the ones with the leather sewn on the side and elbows. Leonid carries a long Scheutzen rifle as he and his daughter trail the other men in the forest path not too far from the compound. Nina tugs on his sleeve and asks him, "Father, when you are about to shoot something can't you please just tell me first?"

Leonid looks down at his daughter and says with a smile, "if we're talking we'll scare the prey. I must ask you to be as quiet as possible."

"Well perhaps you can just signal to me then, Father" Nina insists.

"I'll tell you what I'll do then. When I see the prey, I'll signal you as I lift my gun. You can then plug your ears, as that is what you want to do."

Nina beams in understanding and watches as her father's dog, Stopka, the one that stays in the kitchen with the maid, runs about. No sooner has the discourse ended than a rabbit dashes suddenly down the trail and directly over Nina's feet. She looks at her father, and he holds true to his promise. Quickly she covers her ears as the gunshot reverberates across the field.

5

War and Peace
In Tsarskoe Selo
1914

Leonid approaches the expansive front porch of his parents-in-law's dacha where so many of his brothers and sisters-in-law, and visiting brother Erich now have gathered in their cream-and-white suits and long summer dresses. A breeze blows off the gulf, cutting the sun's heat as the sun itself evaporates into the distant horizon. Leonid maintains a calm, distinguished presence, although his facial expression shows he is obviously disturbed. Taking off his hat, he first greets his family, sits down, and then begins; "I've just returned from the village, where the news has come that the Archduke Francis Ferdinand of Austria (heir to the Austrian-Hungarian throne) has been assassinated in Serbia. I don't have any more details than that, but I assume Germany will respond."

As Leonid speaks the family registers shock and great

concern from all sides: "Assassinations aren't new," invites Wilhelm cuttingly. All know that the predecessor of the current Serbian King was assassinated, as was their own Russian Prime Minister, Stolypin, who was considered responsible for some of the advantages given the serfs during the beginning years of the parliament or Duma. Most pertinent of all was the 1881 assassination of Tsar Alexander, grandfather to current Tsar Nicholas, by handmade grenades thrown at his carriage from Nihilist members of the revolutionary party called the "People's Will."

As the news is absorbed by all present, what was a welcoming and cooling breeze has suddenly become cold enough for the women to replace their fans with shawls. The underlying concern for both sides of the family—in Russia and in Germany—is how this current catastrophe may affect the ease with which they may continue to maintain such strong familial relations.

ॐ

Josephine oversees the packing by the servants of the temporary belongings brought to the cottages. The family is leaving early this summer. The outbreak of war on July 30, 1914, changed the familiar, peaceful vacation into endless discourse about fear of the future. Events in the larger world began to coalesce quickly. First, Austria-Hungary provided an unacceptable ultimatum to Serbia. Second, Russia, Britain, and France came to the "rescue" of Serbia and peaceful Belgium against the alliance that quickly formed between Germany and Austria-Hungary. This response was presumably necessitated by overbearing nationalism and existing foreign treaties among the world's major powers. The threats and responding prideful arrogance of the combined countries' leaders resulted in the "Great War to end all wars."

Josephine will have more brought home than on previous summer trips. Nothing can be certain about next year's visit even though everyone, including her husband, says the war will be over soon. "We only need to throw our hats down and the Germans will run away," she overheard him say. Josephine can't help but wonder whether this is true. It feels odd to be leaving so soon and even stranger to be the last to leave. Mother and father Krümmel have already gone back to St. Petersburg, her brothers left immediately for Berlin, and the coachman has begun the process of boarding up the windows. Her sister and nieces have left early also, and Emma never came.

The compound feels deserted as the carriage pulls away past the "No Trespassing" sign written in German—now the soon-to-be-banned language of an enemy country. Josephine feels a slight chill in the normally warm air. "Maybe fall will come early this year," she thinks, feeling the loneliness of the season's change—a loneliness that is now aggravated by the emptiness of her family's evacuated compound.

❧

The city of St. Petersburg revels ecstatically as the extended family makes its way across town to the apartments of Tante Lulya. The transfer train to Tsarskoe Selo has been delayed. Josephine, Leonid, the children and servants will need to stop by Tante Lulya's until the trains are running again, along with their odd assortment of possessions. Nina clutches her awkward birdcage as the entire entourage makes its way into her aunt's extensive suite.

While the family concludes their vacation, Russia's army (the largest in the world with over one million, four hundred thousand troops) is fortified with an additional three million, one hundred thousand peasants and working-class reserves. Crowds cheer for "Faith, Tsar, and Country" in St. Petersburg as the Tsar proclaims his desire, the same as his assassinated grandfather's: "We will drive the last soldier of the enemy off our land!" Behind closed doors, his advisor, Count Sergei Witte, tells the Tsar a German victory would mean a world that could not even be imagined. He furthers his statements by adding, "Even if we are the victors it will be the end of Tsarism in Russia." As the Tsar replies, repeating the feelings of his condemned grandfather, the Tsarina turns pale, closing her eyes in fear.

As the children play in Nina's cousins' rooms, the conversation of the immediate family is subdued. After servings of tea and lunch, the visitors, determined to make their way to Tsarskoe Selo, begins to gather their assortment of packages. Josephine, having had yet one more disagreement with her sister over the disposition of Nina's canary, has lost all patience with what she considers its triviality. Directly, she instructs Nina, "The family has far too many packages to carry," and adds that Nina's new pet will have to stay for safe keeping at Tante Lulya's. "Everyone is already overburdened," is her final remark to her distraught daughter. Leonid has to stay behind in the city to attend to his work. To buffer her exasperated last remark, Josephine suggests that he will bring Nina's canary home on a future trip to Tsarskoe Selo.

It is unusual for Josephine to compromise with her daughter, but even she feels betrayed by the current state of affairs. And if nothing else, she wishes to not only convey hope to her daughter, but hope to herself for what she knows intuitively to be a horrendous catastrophe.

Right now there is little Nina can do but stare at the sly look of accomplishment on Cousin Alicia's face. She wishes at this moment that Alicia hadn't recovered from a recent bout with a malady of the heart, but then she softens her thoughts, knowing it is not good to wish evil things on people. Instead, she chooses to believe her mother, trusting that Father will bring her canary with him when he comes home.

Josephine inspects the new furniture the family purchased

from an evacuating prince. Odd that not long after their arrival in this new city of Tsarskoe Selo, some of the neighbors are now making exits. She looks at the newly hung, thick curtains, added to protect the rooms of their new second-story apartment against the harshness of the oncoming winter. Although their new city is becoming familiar, it is different than what it had been in more peaceful times. Military horses seem to be taking up lawns that normally were vacant, and the Imperial Gardens and palace courtyards are populated with guards in uniforms.

Josephine now calms herself by reading one of the numerous art journals and newspapers in her parlor. She sits on her cream-and-blue striped silken chair that, like her other exquisite, feminine furniture, differentiates her parlor from her husbands. The main living room, with its large central fireplace, is shared by all, but Josephine finds herself most comfortable here. It is here that she can sort through the choicest of the many publications that had been coming with regularity out of Petersburg and Moscow. It is here that she reads, beyond the current atrocities, about the latest poets blowing in every direction like the leaves off a tree on a windy fall day. She sets aside an article with a photo of Chagall, a relative newcomer on the art scene. It was obviously printed before the movement of so many artists back to Russia or from Russia to Berlin or Paris. Inquisitively, she wonders at what seems to be the coming of a new Russian renaissance in art, now that artists are back after having spent the last decade abroad making Russian art, poetry, theater, music, ballet, opera and painting recognized the world over.

Tsarskoe Selo has met her expectations. Her new home is truly the most advanced city in all of Russia. She hesitates as she touches the book entitled *Tsarskoe Selo* by Benois, published in 1910 that helped motivate their move in the first place. It has taken its rightful place on the tea table, always visible to any who visits. "The greatest water and sewage systems in the world…The first city in all of Europe with a citywide electrical system…," she notices as she flicks through the pages one more time. "The city is already the future of European brilliance…" Stores, shops, palaces, and gardens are close by and picturesque. The Alexander, Bablova, and Catherine's parks encircle the entire city. There is a wonderful lake and river, and the entire region's higher elevation makes a noticeable change in air quality.

It's a relief having Leonya and Nina attending a private school not far away. The youngest two now have a governess, trained at the Academe in the city, as their nanny is no longer required. And then there is the volunteer work available to Josephine, with all the charities and hospitals for every group, from aged women to ill infants.

಄

Leonid works at his desk in his ornate, dark, paneled office suite on the second floor of the building outside of which hangs a sign advertising his name. His desk lamp sheds light through its transparent ruby-red and blue glass shade onto the newly published *Pravda* newspaper that he has enjoyed reading almost since its inception two years earlier. It seems so unfamiliar to see its publication information as *Petrograd, 12 November 1914.*

He reads about the swelling patriotism overtaking the country in support of the war—about the Tsar's pre-eminence as the country's military, political, and religious leader. He reads about the workers kneeling at the sight of the Tsar and Tsarina on the balcony facing Palace Square in… "Petrograd."

Leonid misses St. Petersburg. He doesn't like the sound of the new name of the city originally named after Peter the Great over 200 years ago. He reads further about the ban on the use of the "offensive language" of German, about the humiliating defeats in the Grand Duchy of Poland, about bread rationing and typhoid, and he shudders.

The days are growing short, and it is already quite dark outside. Tomorrow he is planning on going back to his family in Tsarskoe Selo, but today, like most weekdays, he spends in Petrograd living at the newly re-named Petrograd Hotel. He organizes the folders on his desk, putting the most important of these in his safe directly in front of the wooden box containing his wife's jewelry.

He'll leave the rest for his secretary to organize. The live-in maid (wife of his live-in errand man) and her son, will soon clean up. Putting on his fur-collared topcoat over his dark gray suit he walks out into the cool night air wondering if Roman will still be working. Perhaps he'll stop by his brother's office and see if he can shed some light on the situation. Leonid walks out to the always active Nevsky Prospekt, and briskly covers the short distance to his brother's even more grandiose office.

Roman is, in fact, still in his office now that his wife and children spend less time in the city. The chronic disturbances and strikes before the war grated on Claudia's nerves. She felt as if Petersburg was a powder keg ready to explode. The new patriotism did nothing to sway her belief.

"Leonid, sit down," Roman says as he signals his assistant to pour some tea from the silver samovar, then gestures for his brother to sit on the plush, ornate sofa across the room from his overbearing and oversized desk. "What brings you here so late? Aren't you usually early to bed these days?" he asks Leonid.

Leonid conceals his emotions. His brother doesn't have the capacity to understand his character. The thought never crosses his mind, as a man, to discuss with Roman his feelings of loneliness and isolation, his feeling that somehow he doesn't fit in with anyone or anything in the entire world at this moment. Change is happening so quickly. And now he doesn't even recognize the name of his own city.

"I just finished reading Pravda and…"

"Oh that liberal trash," Roman interjects, "Who's 'truth' do they speak of I wonder?" he continues, playing a pun on the meaning of Pravda as "Truth."

"It worries me that…" Leonid tries to finish.

"And worried we all are, Brother. How perceptive of you. Do

you know we've already lost nearly one million men on the Eastern front alone? And beyond all the human suffering and loss, in fact, the true cause of so many ill-equipped soldiers and lack of medical care is the reality that there isn't enough money in all of Russia to support this war. Are you at all aware that one-third of this country's industrial output had been supported by foreign investment? And that money is drying up!" Roman relishes the opportunity to hear himself speak unchecked, in safe company, without fear of political reprisal.

Leonid continues to listen, completely aware of all the statistics his brother is spouting obviously in an attempt to relieve his own tension. This isn't exactly what he'd had in mind, but he continues to be a good sport about it, giving his brother his ear.

Roman continues, "The Tsar's Minister of Finance actually told our industrialists to halt production because he felt that the reduction in foreign trade would decrease demand. He's insane. Our infant new economy is already at great risk. What's worse is the boys going to the front don't even have enough weapons, supplies, appropriate clothing, or even ample supplies of food. And the cities; do you know how many displaced Poles, Jews, Slavs, and Russians, who had been living in our vast country's outer regions, are returning to the already overcrowded cities to get out of the way of the advancing front? It's a disaster waiting to happen, I tell you, Brother. You were wise beyond your own knowledge to move out of Petrograd."

Leonid hears that name again and cringes. He doesn't want to hear it anymore. Perhaps, he realizes now, it was a mistake to visit his brother. Even his own brother is now using that foul word. Feeling the urge to gamble, he knows he can lose himself in a game of cards. But would that solve anything? It doesn't matter; his mind reverts to the same solution as always, and he has no defense against it.

Roman continues, "…and the railroad system. It's been inadequate to supply the needs of the mining companies my bank finances. It's already proven wholly incapable of mass transport of troops. Yes, we are making progress. Slow progress in Austria-Hungary, but…"

Leonid interrupts him as aware of the details as he feels he needs to be. "I appreciate your information, Brother, but there are some duties I must attend to. Until later," Leonid says, as he sets down his tea and leaves his brother's office. It's decided. He'll go to his favorite haunt. He'll lose himself in cards. His body seems to have carried him there already.

⁊

Nina looks with dismay at her vocabulary list of French nouns as she sits at her little desk in her room. Not very happy to be studying French, she is nonetheless relieved to be free from German. For the time being Aunt Anita will not be giving her German lessons. The language is no longer allowed, let alone considered a positive attribute. Anyone speaking it is viewed with great suspicion, no matter his or her level in society, and Aunt Anita is now a widow and still living far away in Petersburg; her husband, Uncle Herbert, the prior editor of the largest German-language newspaper in all of Petrograd, was recently found dead in his office.

Leonid has recently returned from Petrograd. One of his first duties will be to speak with his daughter regarding the disposition of her bird. He sees this as a relief compared to the insanity of his outside world. And for the moment he isn't particularly interested in speaking with his wife. Nina, having been summoned by one of the servants, is quick to see her father, certain that he will have good news for her.

Leonid unbuttons the lower button of his white vest, just below his dangling gold watch, and sits down on the large sofa in his personal parlor, at eye level with Nina, who now stands next to him. He clears his throat after their initial greetings and confesses, "Nina, your aunt does not want to return the bird." Watching the sadness in his daughter's face he continues, "She feels it is Alicia's since she saw it first. We do not want to have any disagreement with our relatives. I'm sure you understand." The feeling of loss he witnesses is almost too much for him to bear. For unknown to anyone other than himself, he has recently lost quite a lot, including some of his wife's most cherished jewelry. To make matters worse, what he gained the following day is a two-year-old racehorse named "Lightning," which he is planning on keeping in Tsarskoe Selo. Subverting his own better judgment and to alleviate his guilt, he adds, "Perhaps you'll have another canary of your very own for your birthday."

Nina at first hates Tante Lulya. Whenever an issue or argument arises between herself and her cousins, her cousin's are always right. Of course, if a challenge is with anyone else outside the family, Nina gets to be right. But this is wrong. How could her father agree to such a crazy thing? Leaving her bird with her aunt in the first place was devastating enough. Hadn't she been told that she caught it and what's fair is fair? Nothing seems to make sense, but she knows better than to express anger at either of her parents. Hurt and betrayed by the man, of all men, in whom she's put her trust for as long as she can remember, she will still consider his proposed gift.

Just then, Josephine walks into her husband's parlor. "Your governess is here to take you to the park where you'll practice your French, Nina. Your father and I have important matters to discuss." Nina understands and leaves promptly as Josephine shuts the door behind her.

"Leonid," Josephine proceeds, still standing as he withdraws further into the corner of his couch. Her cool tone courses through him and he is not sure what to make of it. He's never heard this tone of voice before.

"My father and mother, as you know, still German citizens, have been detained. They are being sent away to some small village in Siberia in an effort, as they say, to protect the Russian people from possible German infiltrators." The sound of her own words causes her to stiffly take a seat, breaking down her well-practiced emotional detachment.

Leonid is shocked. "Why wasn't I informed? When, 'Fina?'" he asks pityingly, using his affectionate term for his wife. Josephine sits at the edge of a facing chair. She places her hands upon her knees and keeps her feet crossed at the ankle, as she leans forward and continues; "Yesterday, Friday, we tried to contact you at your office, but you weren't there; and the hotel said that they had left a message for you. Roman telephoned that he saw you on Thursday night but you left abruptly, that you looked pale."

Leonid retorts with an excuse of having stayed with his mother and sisters.

Josephine continues, un-deflected."Here it is Saturday morning…I don't know…Why didn't they move back to Berlin? Why does he insist on his residence here? He could have just left the businesses here, managed by…Oh, Leonid, I'm afraid!" Josephine is not used to admitting this, but it has indeed been fear she has been feeling. It's been fear for a long time. It is only now that she puts it into words. It is the compilation of years of accumulated stress caused by unexpected, unheeded, disruptive national crises evident to her in every aspect of the old Petersburg. "Don't worry Fina," Leonid uses his affectionate term again. "I will see that what appears to be a grave mistake is immediately corrected." His personal worries and self-absorption have vanished; he is here, outside himself, and will do whatever it takes to utilize his credentials to see to the assistance of his parents-in-law. He wishes he had taken precautions earlier, been more aware. But he finally feels justified in having moved Josephine and his children to this smaller city outside the complexities of

Petrograd.

⁋

Nina breathes in the crisp cool air. She knew deep down inside she would never get her bird back when they left it with her aunt. But confirmation of what she instinctively knew to be true stings almost worse. Nonetheless, there is little privacy for personal sadness and no one to condone such behavior.

The park is beautiful even in winter. The now bare birch trees look elegant still, with their black-spotted white bark distinguishing them from the fallen crusty white snow. The colonnaded palace and neoclassic temples and pavilions are also part of the park. Nina continues to repeat the phrases her governess dictates as an armed guard on horseback briskly trots past them.

Her new Russian-born French language tutor walks beside her, fur muff in hand. The French governess had returned to France at the outbreak of the war along with the French chef the family had used for years. Now she studies French from a Russian and can detect the slight difference in the phrasing of the already familiar Latin-inspired words.

A last, lone brown leaf falls off the branch of a barren tree. The ground below is hard. Winter has come with full force this year. But it is her mother's principle that, like the Tsar and his family, the children must get two hours a day of fresh air no matter what the temperature. Nina wants to tell her tutor of her horrible day, but the tutor will not speak or respond to her in her native Russian, or even her almost equally competent German. Together they must muster French.

"Huit anee," her tutor instructs, the age Nina will be in two weeks. Nina remembers the embarrassment she felt after her mother reprimanded her last year for proudly using her German skills and telling her German grandfather that she was "neun." "Sieben, not neun, Nina," Josephine reprimanded. "Haven't you been learning anything about German with your aunt?" Grandfather merely laughed after he realized he wasn't mistaken in the rapid aging of his granddaughter.

Now she will be eight. How fast she is becoming a big girl, she thinks, not comprehending that her birthday will not be celebrated as it has been in the past. Grandfather is now in Siberia, Germany is the enemy, and her older age has found her in a smaller, more isolated world.

Nina responds, "Huit anee," not liking her foreign language lesson any more than she likes the fact that she has lost her bird. But she knows how to do what's expected of her. And as for the bird, there is no need for sorrow, she rationalizes. For, as the villagers say, "What is done is done…what is, *is*…and what has fallen off the wagon is already gone."

6

THE GOAT THE BEAR
AND THE GREAT WAR
1915

It's strange for Josephine to be visiting the cottages again this year. The train ride from Tsarskoe Selo is longer, involving a transfer after the initial twenty-mile ride to Petrograd. And it's odd for her to ride through a city that previously had been her home. Nostalgia and a flood of memories coincide with an uncomfortable feeling that all of the difficult and unpleasant changes have occurred without her input, participation, or involvement.

It seems to be even clearer to her the city has been transformed from one that—though rife with strife, overcrowding, and poor sanitary standards for many—had a semblance of growth and progress. Now queues for bread and lack of consumer goods has created a look of hopelessness on the faces of so very many—not only city residents, but displaced evacuees, returned and injured soldiers, and transient, unemployed peasants. Even the palaces overflow with a motley assortment of the city's new homeless. "How conditions have deteriorated in one year's time," she thinks to herself in horror.

Even she has grown disillusioned with the increasingly explosive Petrograd and knows in her bones that, this time, the ugliness is not going away. She recalls the looks she sometimes received from the growing disenfranchised, and the more boisterous disaffected, as she took her customary walks through the boulevards before the war's enthusiasm. Now queues for bread, extending for blocks, make her heart heavy because she knows these workers; she's seen them working in her father's factories since she was a little girl.

At some level she is aware how difficult it is for these people to make a decent wage. After all, her father is a self-made man. He diligently worked first in the coal business, then in carriages, and more recently in the new automotive industry. She recalls now the story of the very early days of her parents' marriage; they lived above the coal processing factory that her father owned before he purchased his carriage manufacturing business. She knows how he came to St. Petersburg as a young man from Berlin, against the wishes of his family, to do what so many men, rich, poor or aristocratic alike, had done for centuries: transform Russia into a modern, cosmopolitan country.

The compound seems empty without her father and mother. Emma is in Bulgaria, and Josephine's brothers, living in Berlin, are completely unable to travel to their new enemy-country's territories.

Only sister Louise will be there this year, and the fifth cottage is rented again to a bourgeoisie family.

The decision to come here was itself strained, but in the end Leonid won out in his insistence that life should continue as close to normal as possible. After all, "We are not or ever will be a defeated land," was his argument. This was closely followed by "So, too, must we follow our Tsar's proclamation." Josephine's motives are less patriotic, fueled more by a need to inspect the property's condition for her parents, with whom she has maintained written communication. It is they who also suggested the trip. Not to be undervalued is her equal concern that her four young children should be out of the increasingly military, claustrophobic atmosphere of Tsarskoe Selo. It will be good for her to watch them playing in the freedom that their beloved natural countryside provides.

❧

This midsummer's warm and breezy morning, Nina has found herself on the way to Tante Lulya's chicken coop with a pail full of kernels. Tante Lulya's dacha contains a large coop adjacent to the back kitchen similar to the one Nina's family has at their own dacha. And today she's been given the task of feeding the chickens while Tante Lulya, her cousins, and their governess are away in the village; even the cook and young maid are away purchasing supplies.

Nina volunteered. After all, she loves animals as much as her father does. He also feeds their chickens and ducks at times, as well as the wild geese and occasional swans in the contained lake of their compound. Earlier this summer she even brought home a cat from a neighboring farm. At first, of course, mother Josephine had been surprised to see the cat. But, fortunately for Nina, she surprisingly agreed to let her keep it as long as it stayed in the kitchen when inside. Cats being what they are, it has taken ownership of the entire dacha and compound.

This year the compound seems to be full of animals. The fifth cottage is rented by a family whose young son keeps his pet goat in its adjoining stables. Nina's seen the goat, and has been told to keep her distance. And she knows why. Two years ago the same family had a different goat. One day she watched as the very young boy walked alone around the front of his rented dacha. Then she saw the goat mercilessly charge, knocking the child down. It was only after their maid came running out of the house that the goat was contained and the boy rescued. Still, this seemed unusual to Nina, for her own experience with animals had always been pleasant.

Overall, Nina's pleased to be at the dachas again, even though she's still slightly miffed at her cousin Alicia. As it so happens, she's found out the canary she caught last summer and lost, has escaped again. Apparently, Alicia left the cage door open when the maid was cleaning and airing out her room. And, as before, the bird simply took the chance to fly away, out the open window. Nina knows that it can't survive alone in the big city without anyone to feed it. She's sorry that she played a role in its dislocation, but her feelings are lifted by her rather sinister joy that Alicia, too, has lost the bird.

In addition to this, she feels forlorn about not having the rest of the family around. Grandmother and Grandfather's absence is strongly felt. Uncle Erich won't be visiting this year. This won't even be a year with the rare visit from Uncle Roman and her cousins on their way to their own dachas. Aunt Emma is in Bulgaria with her husband, now a military officer, and their new daughter Milka. And Nina knows her uncles on her mother's side of the family, Wilhelm and Karl, are occupied in Berlin.

Nina makes her way across the tennis courts nearest her aunt's dacha. Unexpectedly, there is the strange, squat goat, standing uncontained. It appears to be quite harmless. Wondering if he might like some of the kernels she's bringing the chickens, she puts down her metal bucket, fills her hands with corn, and shouts to the goat. "Here goat, here goat…come and get some breakfast…would you like some breakfast?"

The coarse haired, long-nosed beast just stands and watches with a charismatic unpredictability. Then, instead of approaching, he begins to back up. Nina isn't quite sure what this means but knows it's highly unusual for him to back up if he's interested in food. Suddenly he charges and brutally knocks her over; obviously choosing hostility over acceptance of chicken feed. Nina pushes herself to her feet, shouting for someone, anyone, to come to her aid. No one seems to be around.

But just as Nina is upright, she sees the goat start to back up again. This isn't a game she's interested in playing any longer. Thinking first, and then becoming quite certain that he's backing up to hit her again, she feels angry instead of frightened. She thinks to herself, "I'm *not* stupid, and I'm *not* going to stand around here anymore just to get butted." Adamantly she makes a quick dash for the house. The goat immediately follows. Nina thinks, "He's not stupid *either*!" as she quickens her pace, running around and around Tante Lulya's empty cottage. She continues to scream, but still no one comes. The goat starts to shorten the distance between them. Her legs are tiring. "What do I do now?" she thinks, frantic to escape. And then she again serenely reverts to bravery. She speaks under her breath, "We'll just have to see if it *kills* me," as she stops and leans her back against the storage shed wall.

Indeed her fate seems to no longer be in her control, as the goat stops and looks at her, his large eyes with their rectangular pupils peering from both sides of his head. Slowly and deliberately, he once again backs up. And then, with a slight shirk of his thick neck, he moves in to butt her in the stomach. Nina remembers what she learned from the talk that resulted after the little boy's experience two years ago—something about holding the goat's horns. Quickly, she grabs them with her two hands just as the ferocity of his momentum carries him toward her. She feels his strength as she now stands grasping both horns in her firm little fists. The beast has frozen just before striking; she's got him!

"Now what?" she thinks to herself. Alone in a place usually filled with brothers, sisters, cousins, and visitors, she realizes she must continue to fend for herself. And then she thinks about her dacha. It's only about a quarter mile away. Someone must be there and at least she could run in the door. If he behaves while I hold him like this, she surmises, then perhaps he will walk with me to my house. It's the only choice. And so, with the assurance of a risk-taking gambler, she starts taking steps backward and sideways the entire distance to her house.

The goat somewhat amiably complies. Moments seem like hours as this odd couple gradually crosses the space between dachas. When she spots the five small wooden steps that lead up to her front porch, she calls out again. But there is still no one to respond to her pleas. Slowly, the two make it the rest of the distance to the front porch.

"Mother! Mother!" She screams again, "I have hold of a goat. Help me. Let me in the house." No response. Mother must be in the back somewhere, maybe in the bedrooms, and probably the cook and maid have gone with Tante Lulya's servants to the village as well. Leonya might have joined them, but who knows? It doesn't matter now, as she wonders what her next move should be. Perhaps she can walk up the stairs and get through the door. She hesitates to guess whether the door is unlocked. Surely it must be. It normally is. Nina begins to move up the first wooden step.

The goat continues to be led as she now walks up the second, third, fourth, and fifth step. Now the concern is how to let go of one of the horns to open the door. Nina considers this for a while, knowing the pain involved if the door is locked after all. She can't very well stand there, she knows. So, she devises a plan. She knows she's small and skinny, and if she opens the door only a little bit, perhaps she can jump in and slam it shut, before the goat follows. Everything will have to happen very quickly. But she's ready. First, she'll let go, and then try the tin doorknob, and, if it's open, she'll jump in.

Gathering her strength, she lets go of one horn. Instantly she grabs the doorknob. It's open! Quickly now, she turns and skids through the gap, slamming the door behind her. She's safe and inside the house, looking at the goat through the door.

"You nasty goat!" she shouts through the door. "I was going to feed you, and you just wanted to ram me. What's the matter with you anyway, you mean goat, you!"

The goat, either growing bored with the lecture or sensing the approach of more people, slowly takes its leave. Josephine, exhausted from tending to her ill daughter Vera, has been taking a nap in a back bedroom. She opens the door leading to Nina and the enclosed front porch. Her look is stern rather than concerned. "What might you be doing, Ninatschka?" is her immediate question. Nina begins to rapidly explain, but is interrupted by her mother's comments; "I have neither the patience nor the endurance for your antics this day or any other, Nina. It must be clearly understood that you are to behave like a lady. Shouting as you did is not condoned regardless of what mischief you've created for yourself. Am I understood?"

Nina nods her head more in embarrassment than self-pity, then waits while her mother exits the porch. In the distance she can see the carriages coming back with all the other people. At least no one will know, she thinks to herself, not even that brother of mine who would love to pick on me. Nonetheless, she'd rather not interact with him at all right now. What a shame she's still too jarred to go out to the garden and maybe pick some mushrooms. That always makes her feel better. In haste to recover her composure, she enters the house and cleans up instead. Just like her mother might want her to, she thinks.

❧

Nina spends the next several weeks at the cottage fully engaged in playing with her cat, tending to the chickens, hunting mushrooms, and sometimes playing wit her her cousins or, on a lucky day, her elder brother. Her father has taken a photo of her sitting alone, wearing a dress, in the doghouse. Somehow it seemed fun, even though obviously less becoming according to her mother. She holds these visions in her memory now that, once again, the day has come to leave.

Overall it's been a perplexing summer, but one that Nina truly appreciates even at her age. Unfortunately, several days ago she's had to find a new home for her cat, which wasn't invited to return with them to Tsarskoe Selo. But she doesn't argue with this decision, and the cat's new home with yet another farmer is familiar to the cat. Nina knows it loves the freedom of the wide-open countryside rich with mice and birds.

Leonid and Josephine don't make a point of implementing any drastic conditions on their evacuation of the compound. On several occasions in the past, they've visited the cottages in the winter and leave open the possibility of doing the same again. It's been a relief to them, as always, to enjoy the comforts of winter repose. The children are entertained as well; the groundskeeper normally making traditional ice slides in the yard similar to those found throughout old Petersburg and the countryside for centuries; large wooden structures covered in ice and used by the Imperial Family since the time of the Great Catherine.

The proprietor and servants have packed the coach. And as the family leaves, Nina looks one more time at the dachas disappearing in the distance, the manicured forest, and the winding dirt road. The only difference in the scenery this year is that the sign saying "Property of Krümmel…" has been removed, the proprietor having suggested that the property might be better protected by not advertising it as owned by Germans.

ආ

And so it goes over the weeks of fall for the family, much as it had before the war. As with the Tsar's family and many of the upper class, there are family events, social functions, dinners, baptisms, ceremonies, marriages, and the like. And so they continue, relatively unobstructed by the worsening conditions of the less fortunate around them.

The news of war dead is reported and compared to familiar war dead in neighboring countries. Tragedies are reported, but absorbed as matters of fact, or as mechanical breakdowns, rather than as the misery suffered by human spirit. Denial makes events appear nearly normal to the elite group conscience. And since they are living in the midst of the deterioration, the complexity and scale of the change goes relatively unnoticed.

In the war's first year alone, four million Russian peasant and working class soldiers were killed, wounded, captured, or missing. This number has more than doubled in the second year. The Duma has issued a list of "what we have learned" to the Tsar. It states that "Russia is short of machine guns, artillery and ammunition—items with which the enemy is plentifully supplied; that every enemy soldier has a rifle, whereas 'hundreds of thousands of our men are without weapons, and have to wait until they can pick up the rifles dropped by their fallen comrades'; that 'Neither bravery, nor talent, nor competence, nor military worth influence appointments, and that the able are rarely given important commands'." A military commander tells the Duma that "Germans plow up the battlefield with shell bursts, devastating trenches and bury the defenders of the Russian people in the process…They use up metal, we use up human life."

❧

Leonid is quite happy to be combining two of his favorite hobbies, his photography and his big game hunting. Very much like his fellow hunting comrades, he is completely determined to have an enjoyable time in the Russian forests. Today, in fact, he plans on fulfilling his elaborate plan to photograph a bear.

It has been no easy task to trudge through the thick snow in this outlying forest, many kilometers away from Tsarskoe Selo, in order to find her. But there ahead in a cave they know lies a bear in hibernation. As usual, the hunting party is composed of wealthy hunters and an odd assortment of peasant farmers who are trained in leading precisely this kind of excursion. Trained to not only find bears, but also rouse them to their feet, in order for the city hunters to have the best chance at shooting the animals.

Leonid has taken the time to set his camera up on a large tripod, and covers himself with the black cloth that will protect the camera's aperture from too much light. The peasants stand in a semi-circle holding a number of metal pots, pans, sticks, and other noise-making instruments. One holds a large stick and another begins to scout around the outskirts of the cave. Two of Leonid's gentlemen hunters stand nearby, dressed in their hunting jackets and plumed hats, ready to shoot the creature that is more than likely to be extremely angry.

Leonid signals that he's ready to get the shot as one of the peasants, who appears slightly drunk on vodka, ostentatiously enters the cave. The men position their rifles, and the other peasants move knowledgeably to prearranged positions. For although most are familiar with the particularities of this type of hunting, no one ever really knows the exact reaction or direction the bear will take once instigated.

As planned, the man in the cave shouts, backing up to a position where he can easily run. The clatter begins, echoing from all sides. A horrible ear-piercing howl emanates from the cave along with the man who entered it, now falling over himself as he stumbles into the knee deep, drifted snow. The bear bounds outside, immediately takes a stand and projects a howling guttural roar.

The gentlemen hunters fearfully lose control of their weapons, one dropping his gun, as both turn around in alarm, bolting in both directions. Leonid is too amazed to either move or snap the photo, and feeling falsely safe behind his canopy, does nothing. A shot is fired by a peasant, but to no avail, as the bear, in several short but powerful strides, bounds nearer Leonid. Leonid, at the last possible moment, ducks. In an instant the tripod, camera, and black canopy are ripped from above him as the bear crushes the wooden structure.

Leonid crouches on the ground as another shot rings out finally wounding the bear. The bear hesitates briefly and then runs, crippled, into the forest with the peasants following. Leonid regains his composure, brushes the snow off himself, and steps over the decimated ruins of his camera, following with gun in hand. Another shot, a second, and finally a third is heard as the bear tumbles to the ground, killed by the three remaining men. Leonid, who fired the first successful round, and most severely threatened, will win the prize. The servants will carry the animal's carcass to the cabin where they'll skin, gut, and butcher it, and do what they will with the meat.

❧

Nina and her father are beginning to share a relationship that has grown quite special for them both. Having just turned nine, Nina supposes that now she's old enough to share some of his confidences. Leonid realizes that, being away from home most the time, he misses his young family. And it is no secret to either of them that they share a common fascination with the animal kingdom.

Together they sit on the sofa in the large living room, warmed by the fireplace, a bear rug directly in front of them. Leonid has just told his daughter the harrowing details of the hunting story. While Nina loves animals, she also isn't that distant from reality to know that they are slaughtered for food and hunted for sport. Nonetheless, the bear story upsets her, if not only by the bear's death, but for the risk that she knows her father took. Male Russians, she hears, are proud of their gamesmanship, and she knows all too well talk of peasants and gentlemen alike participating in even scandalous drunken behavior. Russian roulette, duels, and chivalry are far from dead in this modern world.

"But Father," Nina says, "don't you think that hunting bear like that is dangerous?"

"Well yes, it is, Nina…that is very true," responds Leonid, thinking quickly of how he can explain his interest to his young daughter; his mind trained in the legal profession to manage debatable topics as rapidly as a young child can spew out unprejudiced observation.

"Don't you think…" Nina begins.

"Let me explain to you," Leonid softly interjects, already prepared for the question. "Do you remember last summer when you were attacked by the goat?"

"I shall always remember that," Nina responds. "I was very afraid and then…had a moment to think, and was able to quickly take care of the situation."

"Exactly, my dear. Except this time, we made a game out of it."

"How can fighting the bear be a game?" Nina wonders.

Leonid tries to rationalize, using the first thing that comes to mind.

"Picture the goat as Germany," Leonid calmly explains. "Right now, as you know, we're at war with Germany. A war is fought like a game is played. Strategy, risk, fear, temptation, reward are all considered. In your case, if the goat were Germany, at first you were afraid when he attacked you. Then after a moment when you could still catch your breath, you out-maneuvered her. You took her by the horns and although you had to trudge a great distance, you came to safety and, in the long run, weren't much more afraid of her than you were in the past. In fact, now you know what to watch for."

Leonid's handsome face begins to flush as he becomes fascinated with his own analogy. Continuing, he says, "Now, think of the bear as great Russia. You know the bear is the ancient symbol for Russia anyhow. Russia has been hibernating. Some think that she's been sleeping for quite some time. She needed to be woken up to protect herself and to interact with the world more efficiently. Do you understand what I'm trying to tell you, Nina?"

Nina does understand that what Father is talking about is a game, and what adults often do even to the point of war can be considered a game. What she doesn't understand is, if the bear is Russia, why in the end did the bear die, and why would great Russia want to kill Father? And what of the broken camera which records great Russia? Obviously, she notices, her father is quite pleased with himself. And the observation that he is pleased makes her feel satisfied. She'll choose not to argue the point even though she knows she's quite capable of doing so.

7

Eve of the End
1916

Nina walks through the living room the toward an elegantly set dining room table. The bearskin rug lies in front of a fireplace that burns less brightly than usual because of the scarcity of wood. She particularly doesn't like the stuffed bear head now facing the couch. She sees the entire spectacle as a bad omen. But she doesn't dwell on the deceased animal for long, happy that it is Christmastime and that her cousins Swetlana and Tatiana are visiting, along with Uncle Roman, Aunt Claudia, and young cousin Kiril.

Josephine has prepared for this Christmas-week dinner party for the last several days. It's been difficult making the atmosphere festive given the morose conditions caused by the war. There are fewer servants now that much of the available domestic help has been recruited to either fight or work in the factories. Prices for staple food items, which Josephine had heretofore never considered, have been raised well over three times as much, wood and eggs four times, and butter and soap five times. There are reports that some peasants and working poor are found starved to death or frozen inside their dwellings, and the middle-class (or *Burzhui)* are having difficulty keeping their home temperatures above freezing. Superfluous luxury items are more than plentiful as few of the formerly bourgeoisie can afford them at all. And anything *can* be had in Petrograd, for the right price, with exquisite boutiques brimming with mostly untouchable, old-fashioned, luxury products.

Nonetheless, the aristocratic and wealthy social whirl continues unabated. Dinner menus have changed to accommodate more patriotic Russian courses, even if the French did invent them. Some families invite officers and soldiers to dine with them, since military rations are so severe.

Josephine's sister Louise did not make the train journey from Petrograd because the train is so unreliable, even for those fortunate enough to still be able to travel. There is hardly enough fuel for the army, let alone any for civilian travel. And although Leonid still commutes between Petrograd and Tsarskoe Selo, Josephine rarely attends the numerous social functions that she is invited to. Her German brothers in Berlin and her sister Emma in Bulgaria are a war away, and her husband's mother and sisters are well ensconced in Petrograd, with brother Felix locked into difficult matters in the Crimea. Josephine is grateful that at least Roman and Claudia and their children have interrupted their busy social schedule to drive to

Tsarskoe Selo this year.

Even Nina notices the differences at the table this Christmas. Most of the rich, heavy sauces that are difficult on her finicky palate are missing; the new, Russian cook is far less skilled than his French predecessor. For this she is grateful. How often she has had to wait at the table after everyone else has left to finish her food. And how much she hated the liver and onions, or the broccoli in cream sauce, or the Beef Burgundy. At least tonight she won't need to hide the remains behind the dish cabinet when no one is looking.

Something else is missing this Christmas. Even though Nina did receive gifts, she didn't receive the usual gold coin that her German grandfather had given her every Christmas since she can recall. Those coins of years past are all far away now in Father's safe in his office in Petrograd, reminders of her "bright and shining future," as Grandfather often said—locked away in a dark safe in a city far away.

Nina and her female cousins, ranging in age from Nina's ten to Tatiana's fifteen, are allowed to join the entire family at the formal dining room table again this year. All having been raised with many servants, they remain quiet and unassuming as they sit gracefully attired and eating unselfconsciously, exhibiting proper table manners. Nina sits through her dinner quietly and, as usual, trying her utmost to not pick at her food.

After dinner has ended and the adults have had their evening tea, Leonid and Roman excuse themselves, retiring to Leonid's gentlemen's sitting room. Seated now on the heavy, red leather-upholstered club chairs and surrounded by bookshelves adorned with Russian, French, and German classics, the two converse more freely.

"So tell me, Brother, what are the latest shocking revelations from this Rasputin that everyone is either so crazy or incensed about?" Roman asks openly, without his customary defensive, all-knowing, posturing.

Leonid is prepared to again discuss the loss in investment by foreign countries or the crashing halt of Russian capitalistic expansion. He's prepared to discuss the effects of the frightening scarcity of everything from fuel to food; prepared to offer his comments about workers losing all the benefits they had so painstakingly gained before the war, or the devastation to the recent reversal of improved working conditions that were finally taking affect. He is neither prepared nor does he desire to answer this question.

Knowingly, he responds, "Rasputin the *starets*, the 'holy man?'" His tone is readably cautious. For even beyond Leonid's full awareness of near universal disappointment with their autocratic ruler's management of the war, finances, and food production, he's not willing to criticize the Tsar on how he conducts his personal domestic life. After all, Leonid idolizes the Imperial Family to the point of mimicking its behavior in a most bourgeois way; Leonid hunts bear like the Tsar, and is inspired by photography; his family practices the same frequent outdoor activities even in the harshest weather, and even little Nina has been exposed to tennis, much like the Tsarinas. Leonid and Josephine had at one time discussed having five children who would be, as a whole, slightly younger than the Imperial Family's. Beyond this, they have made the sacrifice of moving from the capital city, the city where Leonid works, to the enclave of Tsarskoe Selo, where the Tsar's family has lived as virtual recluses from society and politics for the prior eleven years.

Leonid continues, "Well, Brother, I know Rasputin's power over the imperial family is considered outrageous, especially in Petrograd. And I know that both the Duma and the intellectuals consider his behavior and conduct appalling. But I…you know, Brother, Nicholas is first a family man, and then his father's son. Some of his lack of *enthusiasm* in having so many great matters decided by…he doesn't have the, shall I say, broadness of mind… I understand, to concern himself intimately with some of these concerns…you know since he's been away at the front…"

"You haven't answered my question," Roman insists, bored with his brother's fidgeting. "You know I am probably the most politically visible Russian citizen of our entire extended families, and have stood my ground supporting the Tsar. But this obscene holy relic of a man seems to have absolute power over the thinking and decisions of the Tsarina to such a degree that he even suggests appointments of government ministers. I'll be specific: NO LESS THAN FIVE interior ministers, Three WAR ministers in only TEN MONTHS, all at the urgings of that MONK! Alexandra is obsessed. Therefore, who do you think is making decisions on behalf of all of Russia? Who, in fact, acts as our new Tsar and Emperor— Autocrat of all the Russias, Sovereign of the Circassian Princes,

Prince of Estonia, Grand Duke of Finland and Lithuania, Lord of Turkestan and the Armenian Regions, Lord and Master of All Northern Countries, etcetera, etcetera—during the Tsar's absence?"

Leonid is infuriated, yet his brother has made a clear and distinct point; one he cannot deny. A year and a half older than Roman, and not wanting to appear weak, Leonid chooses to egg him on. "Do you truly think that the advice of Rasputin is being taken to heart, with all of his doomsday predictions? The doomsayers have been claiming the end of the world since before the Revolution of '05. Run to the hills they say…bah! We never needed to run to the hills then, and we won't have to now…" He sits back confidently in his chair but wonders silently at the possibilities. But what is he to do, as Roman volleys further debate. After all, he is neither a military man nor a politician, and he is far from being a social agitator; where could he and his family possibly go if things really did get worse?

Roman persists in his argument, "True, Brother, but our biggest enemy right now is a psychological one. The people, the Duma, and even the imperial family have grown listless. There's a loss of morale amongst the troops and an impending sense of doom even in the highest ranks and, in my understanding, in the Tsar himself. Nothing can be accomplished while this attitude prevails, and it will only lead to less, never more."

Leonid agrees. There is little he can say to such a startling truth. It occurs to Leonid that perhaps his brother doesn't see things in such a different light after all.

Claudia sits perched near the end table in Josephine's sitting parlor, radiant in the latest, simple Parisian fashion; something by a relative newcomer named Coco Channel. Her jeweled hand holds the dainty silver handle of a glass of black tea. Removed from the conversation of their husbands and with the children looked after by their governesses, the two women speak with animation.

"I am thoroughly impressed by the movement into 'Suprematism' led by Melevich and some of the other returnees… what a coup to have had Kandinsky back from Munich at the outbreak and then, of course, Chagall and Bogoslavsky from their long stays in Paris…the Ballet Russe has entered its fourth season touring the West, you know…I am overwhelmed and utterly amazed at Stravinsky's composition for 'The Fire Bird'…" Claudia interjects an opinion between these courteous, knowledgeable contributions by Josephine. "…The Ballet Russe will never set foot in Russia during this war. It hasn't been in Russia since its inception."

Josephine maintains an attachment to the arts, feeling her Russian patriotism re-emerging as the warmth of the room and strength of the hot tea both sedate and invigorate her. She forms a silent, prideful opinion of her own, "Claudia has actually spent *too* much time abroad, from Paris to London to Moscow and elsewhere, whereas *I* have spent much of my time *in* Russia and the Grand Duchy of Finland where I have been exposed to the arts and theater of which we speak."

Confidently Josephine adds aloud, "Even though I completely dislike this new, bizarre Cubist Futurism, I did find the two exhibitions *Tramway V* and *The Last Futurist Painting Exhibition* held in Petrograd, to be well attended, and if nothing else…thought-provoking." And then, beginning to lose her desire to maintain what she suddenly considers a charade of appearances, she looks directly at her sister-in-law seated next to her on the small settee, and says, "And now what about the war, Claudia?"

Claudia puts her hand on her sister-in-law's arm honestly coming to terms with the reality of the times. She says, "I want your opinion on something that even Roman does not know." An intimate connection between the two women has always existed on a level of sophistication that was inherently understood. Both women— passionate, well informed, educated, and fiercely independent—have been struggling far too often with issues that they speak far too little about. Josephine will be happy to listen.

Claudia continues, "You know that even beyond the war, the city has changed dramatically in these last several years. Oh yes, there is still a myriad of activities; social events, balls, theater, opera, ballet. And this war will be over sometime. But our city has lost its old charm for me. It's lost more than its colorful past, what with all this turmoil. It seems to have lost its *raison d'etre*. Do you know what I mean?"

Josephine nods, "Yes, my dear. Tragically, I do. It's like an inspiration that, if not acted upon, is lost. Life often feels so disjointed, so superfluous. What once was such a clear sense of our country's common, cohesive understanding, or spirit, seems to have left us. Nothing could have been more evident of this than the poor reception of the Tsar's 300th anniversary tour. We seem to have lost more than our compassion. It feels to me as if we have indeed lost our common thread, which is the soul of Russia."

"Yes," Claudia agrees. "I don't feel at home in Petrograd anymore. And once spring comes I will be taking my children and moving to the Baltics. As you know, we have an estate in Estonia near the coast where we will…" she looks away as she hesitates, then continues, "I don't know if I shall return even when the war is over. You know, things don't look good for Russia either way."

Josephine looks admiringly at her sister-in-law, relieved that she is not alone in her sense of loss. She sets down her glass of tea. There isn't much more to be said. A large part of her wishes she could leave as well.

☙

Josephine takes a moment to relax alone in her parlor this sluggish, hot, late summer's afternoon; she often finds her time alone to be indispensable. Her maid interrupts her silence by first knocking, then bringing in the afternoon mail on a silver tray. The bedroom maid has taken on many responsibilities since the household servants have been even further reduced. The men who worked as coachman, butler, handyman, and one chef, have all been sent off to the war. Amongst the women, their laundress and two maids have found higher-paying jobs—and are more needed—in a factory.

But the responsibilities associated with raising an eleven-and-a-half-year-old Leonya, nine-and-a-half-year-old Nina, six-year-old Vova, and five-year-old Vera, have only increased for Josephine. Recently she's begun to feel distracted. And, where before she might have taken her servants for granted, she is now greatly relieved to still have her favorite, faithful maid, a governess, a new chef, and a part-time laundress.

She takes the letters, noticing one from her sister Emma and one from her mother in Siberia. It's a sad reminder that she receives the letter today, August 11, 1916, the day after her youngest daughter Vera's fifth birthday; the daughter who was born at the summer cottages.Under normal circumstances the entire family would be spending this wretchedly hot and humid day, with her parents included, at the dachas.

Now the cottages no longer belong to her family at all. For earlier in the year she learned that the entire compound had been taken over by a fiasco devised by the former property manager. The property manager had not paid the taxes with the money he had been sent by Josephine's father. And after the properties had, unknown to the family, been repossessed, he then purchased them on the open market at a huge discount. In general, Finnish citizens had long resented being controlled by Russia. Now that the war has been going so poorly, its people have become restless in their opposition to Russians and Germans; some siding with Germany and others Russia, but all for a free and independent Finland. No one knows what this means to the legal case Leonid has initiated, but at least he has sympathetic ears in the courts of Petrograd.

It's been some time since she's received a letter from her parents at all. The military's commandeering of the Siberian Railroad (exacerbated by chronic breakdowns) has made mail delivery a slow and uncertain process. The cheap materials and slave labor used by the Tsar's father, Alexander, to build the railroad, have come back to haunt Russia. And the telegrams that her husband's office has received from her parents usually deal with legal tactics that are being employed to reclaim the lost properties and assistance to Leonid in his efforts to ensure their early return from imposed exile.

Josephine, her exhausted thoughts now perturbed, wants to know what only a handwritten letter can tell. Using her gold letter opener, she first slices the envelope, revealing crude brown paper and pencil in place of linen stationery and pen. She notices the date—June 16, 1916, two months ago—as she begins to read:

Daughter,

We are as comfortable as possible for political exiles living in a small village far removed from life in Petrograd. It is calm here compared to recent difficulties caused by the war in other places. We have freedom of movement outside the small house, which we rent. We pay for food prepared by a rather colorful and superstitious peasant family, who also do our laundry and some household cleaning. We have what we most urgently need, and actually more food than what is rumored to be available there.

While touched by the letter more deeply than its matter-of-fact words might convey, Josephine is also angered. She wonders at how the politicians with whom her father still has connections can be so weak as to continue to allow such an atrocity to happen. Her anger is somewhat mollified by the embarrassment and shame of her parents' sending her such a simple thing as flour. But shortages are a real problem. And while Tsarskoe Selo doesn't have the extreme bread rationing that Petrograd and Moscow are experiencing, with their need to feed tens of thousands of factory workers, prices have quadrupled. Josephine has verified this herself on a recent trip to the market to examine her cook's claims of higher pricing.

Though still alone, her composure and fortitude now regained, Josephine sits upright in her chair as she opens the second letter, from her sister Emma. "Yes Emma," she hears herself thinking, as she reads Emma's disappointment over the latest fashion declaration; A Russian-inspired burst of colors, the turquoise, the lapis lazuli, the orange and cerise, the Rose Vif, the Nuits d'Orient, all in vogue recently for fabrics, cushions, and general décor of the *civilized* world, are now declared *passé*. "Doesn't she know there is a war going on," she whispers in exasperation, forgetting that just a moment before she also hadn't focused much on inconvenient reality.

Shuddering, she observes for the first time the contrast between the two late-in-arriving letters. She looks out the window at the tree-lined boulevard. An occasional, well-dressed woman enters the jewelry store situated on the first floor below her apartment, and a disheveled soldier and uniformed military officer walk down the street. Can all this be *normal* now? Have they all grown so accustomed to life in these times so filled with horrors, so layered below the surface of seeming complacency, that they can't really see below the surface at all?

She stands up and goes to her closet, as she needs to choose a hat fit for the luncheon she will be having with her friends. Again she stops, and thinks to herself, "Is it really over?" Everyone knows there will be some sort of revolt. And the term "revolution" is not in the least new or unheard of. The papers are full of these predictions, contradicted by published opinions that state such things as "No revolution can occur, simply because revolutions require a surprise tactic…and we are all well beyond surprises." Some say the army is on the brink of mutiny. She must convince Leonid it is time to discuss their options. "What a waste are these huge, cumbersome, feathered creations," she says to herself, as she sets hatbox after hatbox aside.

❧

Leonid locks the metal door of his Petrograd office vault, where he keeps the neatly organized stack of manila envelopes containing the case notes for his father-in-law's stolen properties. Beside the documents, Josephine's jewelry box sits missing a couple of pieces of its most lavish contents, which causes him panic, then he realizes his luck as his wife hasn't been to any recent functions in the city, and so hasn't needed to stop by to choose her jewelry.

In an effort to ease his conscience, he conjectures that card playing with the newly-elected Duma members pays off in ways that losses don't make obvious. While he looks at his reflection in the oval mirror, the thought adds a boyish sparkle to his eyes as he straightens his bow tie. He pulls a silver-handled flat brush through his short-cropped blondish hair, and applies some wax to his long curly mustache. Feeling buoyantly self-confident, he puts on his feltlapelled, black overcoat and walks out onto the Nevsky Prospekt, toward his temporary home at the Petrograd Hotel.

He walks into the quickly-darkening, brisk fall day and onto the bustling main artery of his beloved city. But now, despite his good mood, he cannot help but notice, as if suddenly awakened to the presence of an oncoming winter storm, the poorly clothed pedestrians, some still in summer clothing. Mingling with them are refugees from the lost territories and Poland, and injured or deserting, soldiers; all crowding out from the cellars, overflowing hotels, private houses, and vast palaces, onto the street. He's read about wooden sheds serving as houses, hastily erected in the factory districts outlying the city, and he's heard of the trains of wounded pouring into the Warsaw Station at all hours of the day and night.

He continues to walk past bread queues endlessly snaking around whole city blocks, even in this district, knowing many won't be able to eat without coupons or ration cards. As he approaches his hotel he sees cafes and restaurants bursting, as usual, with well-to-do patrons.

❧

Roman removes his hat, sable-collared, black, dress overcoat, and cream kid leather gloves as he takes a seat in the private club, relieved that his family is living in Estonia. He mostly dines out, as he is doing tonight, He tugs at his shirtsleeve, revealing his gold and ruby cuff links, as the servant carrying his coat, hat, and gloves walks away. He nods to a few of the select crowd of princes, counts, barons, and aristocratic elite, some adorned in epaulettes and military costume, now worn at the most exclusive men's clubs, even at ten in the evening. He knows that his intimate knowledge of the mining concerns of the country—always critical, yet now even more so—affords him confidences that few enjoy.

Roman's mind is filled with information as he makes his presence known. Amongst countless facts, he is aware that there are over eight million Russian soldiers dead, the hospitals are crowded, food shortages are becoming epidemic, and many once-patriotic solders, taken from the working and peasant classes, march in the cold with a hopelessness, void of emotion, knowing it is to their death. Tired and dying officers have been known to order their troops to shoot at fellow soldiers in their dull, colorless trenches, in order to force them onto the battlefield—sometimes with no weapons or artillery of their own. The Tsar, relieving his brother, the Grand Duke Mikhail, has left Tsarskoe Selo, and now foolishly performs as Commander-in-Chief; and the country is now left, as everyone here knows, to be run by the Empress, the distrusted German-born Alexandra, who, until recently had entrusted so many important decisions to Rasputin.

However, Rasputin has been murdered. Prince Yusupov stabbed and shot him before shoving the body into a hole in the ice. Yusupov is now considered a hero and too popular to be tried. Alexandra is left to visit the Tsarskoe Selo Alexandra Palace Gardens, where Rasputin is buried. She writes her husband daily. The Tsar writes back, asking about simple domestic matters, his daughter's recent bout with a cold, and inquiries about the well-being of his dog.

With this knowledge Roman knows his government has become isolated and universally distrusted. He needs to keep his focus tonight. Purely Tsarist, purely Russian, and ever hopeful for solutions, he walks directly to a group of high-ranking inner-circle members and, without hesitation, makes his presence known.

"God save the Tsar. Gentlemen…"

8

FEBRUARY REVOLUTION
1917

Josephine walks down Nevsky Prospekt, in Petrograd, in her full-length red fox overcoat, mink hat and muff. The ornate street lamps glow with a feeble light that is barely perceptible through the falling snow and darkening day. She quickens her step, avoiding eye contact with the disheveled passersby.

Josephine notices the difference in so many new faces, strangers wearing calico shirts and tall boots, some without proper coats. These newcomers are still so countrified, a different breed from some of the skilled, politically aware, peasants who have worked in the city's industries many winters past. These thousands—so many thousands—work in factories, like the Putilov Metalworks, to support the country's massive armament build-up. They are new Russian workers who are badly trained, badly paid, and inefficient compared to their European counterparts. They perform the treacherous and repetitive work now done more and more by machines elsewhere with increasingly long hours, and mounting industrial accidents. In return they are treated to brutal, repressive reprimands and unheeded complaints.

Her trips to the countryside in the past have made her familiar with these people, so different from herself in so many ways. She remembers their simple contentedness—or was it simply acceptance? These memories contrast greatly with the overwrought expressions she sees now. She feels sympathy for them; their simple life disrupted by the atrocities of war and the government's decisions to force them into dehumanizing labor.

She comes to Petrograd infrequently now and does not visit her in-laws often. She'd rather think that her brothers are doing well in Berlin; she knows her parents are managing well, given their situation in Siberia, and regards their resiliency with incredulity and respect.

Josephine never brings the children anymore. There have been rumors of food hoarding by all but the wealthiest classes now that even potatoes have increased in price. She worries that if even the wealthy are resorting to unsavory practices, what other dangers might lurk here?

The air feels heavy with the weight of so many dead. And so many more are dying from disease, cold, hunger, and wounds from the war. Over 170,000 reservists—made up of the injured, the shell-shocked, and the poorest of the Cossacks—are in Petrograd. The best men are at the front. Hopelessness is palpable; casting such a sinister pall over this city of her birth she cannot recognize it. If it weren't for Leonid's insistence on staying in the city to work, she would have left Russia for good. After all, her mother-in-law has noble old Germanic ties in the Baltics, Emma has welcoming royal relations in Bulgaria, and if needed, there is extended family and high-level connections in Germany.

But, Leonid's logic does make sense. He supports the family by his law practice, and Law doesn't easily move from country to country or region to region. The language of law that Leonid knows is the language peculiar to this capitol city at the least, and to Russia at its broadest.

The wind lashes her face, making it difficult to breathe, This January, 1917, is the coldest on record. She passes a flickering street lamp, makes a turn down the short side street, which leads to the railroad station, and notices that the top lantern is crooked, looking like a broken neck. Her heart beats faster. Her entire being wants to get out of Petrograd as soon as possible.

Originally she planned on attending a dinner thrown in honor of her mother-in-law's seventieth namesake anniversary, and then returning to Tsarskoe Selo on Monday. But, as she went to the safe in her husband's office to get a selection of jewelry, she began to feel afraid. She'd heard rumors of wealthy friends being stopped and robbed. And so, she decided instead to leave at once, to not go to the safe, and not attend the celebration. Leonid will have to do without her. Besides Claudia is out of town, and she often enjoys her company amidst the crowd of Leonid's extensive family, friends, and well-wishers.

Between the terrible snows, the offices and factories closed due to the incessant strikes, and the constant fuel shortages, there is no good reason for her to stay. She certainly doesn't want to risk being trapped in the city, wondering when the rail connection will go down again. And the train *is* running now. Having made up her mind, she walks quickly, to take the next train to Tsarskoe Selo.

❧

It is late morning on February 23, 1917, International Women's Day. Snow has cut the main railway lines and strikes are cutting the remainder. Leonid is working in his large, wood-paneled office suite, his secretary in the small room next door, and his errand man, maid, and their young child are in the apartment adjoining. The weeks of sub-zero temperatures have unpredictably transformed to relative warmth and the heavy layers of snow are now covered in a glow of unusual sunshine.

He can't help but hear it. A large crowd marches below in the sunlit, snowy Nevsky Boulevard. It is made up of women workers, authorized in their rally for equal rights, joined now by some of the remaining men, who complain of lack of coal and bread. Leonid walks to the window, pushing aside the thick, embroidered, blue curtain to view the demonstration. He is startled to see hundreds of people below. He shouts to his secretary to join him. "What amazing freedoms we have in Russia to allow this sort of demonstration," he says. "I remember the day when this was not tolerated, and it wasn't that long…," his comments are interrupted by marchers' shouts reverberating up the decorative facade of the brick building, "Down with Hunger!!…Down with high prices!!…Bread for Workers!!… End the WAR!!"

Meanwhile, not too far away, women protestors pelt windows of small engineering shops with snowballs shouting, "Stop your work"…"Join us…" They are encouraging additional, willing men onto the street. Armed guards and policemen, themselves hungry and forlorn, watch as the protesters go by. They do nothing. The crowd intensifies.

Leonid continues to watch as a Cossack sneers at a group being led by an elderly woman, "Who are you following? You are being led by an old crone!" The woman retorts, "Not an old crone, but a sister and wife of soldiers at the front." The Cossack lowers his rifle as another woman yells, "Cossacks, you are our brothers, you can't shoot us." Beyond his vision a large bakery is sacked as the crowd senses the irresolute nature of the authorities.

It's a quiet and peaceful day in Tsarskoe Selo, In fact, it's almost too quiet. Nina, proud of her independence, has been allowed the opportunity to take her walk alone today in the Catherine Park. The snow has created large drifts, but this doesn't matter. After all, Russia's princes and princesses, Tsars and Tsarinas, have always had the strength and constitution to withstand, in fact conquer, even the most severe weather. Besides, Nina misses the outdoors. Being stuck inside all day is stifling, and the fresh air is welcome.

"Funny, even the animals are silent today," Nina thinks as she skips down the well-trodden road. Continuing her walk, she peeks around the door frame of the stables nearest the back of her family's apartment building, which adjoins the large park. There she sees her father's beautiful racehorse—the two-year old he brought home one day from Petrograd. Nina admires the horse, so beautiful with its dark black mane and silky, brown hair. She admires the horse's obvious strength, while having no desire to ride it. Her older brother has ridden before, but that's one thing she doesn't care to imitate.

Happily, she continues to skip down the sunny boulevard toward the most beautiful palace of all—the one where the Tsarina is, right this very moment, taking care of her ill daughters. Even Nina's heard that they all have terrible colds.

Alexandra, in her palace, hears of the demonstrations in Petrograd. She writes her husband that these events are nothing other than youngsters running about…that if the weather were colder they would have stayed home.

Leonid remains in the city over the weekend, unable to leave. The protesting that started with several hundred women on Thursday increased to over 200,000 men and women on Friday, and turned to bloodshed on Saturday. Nonetheless, a well-attended party at the palace of Princess Radziwill was held Sunday night, not to be delayed, while nine people were shot down on Nevsky by a cavalry squadron. Police officers disguised themselves in army greatcoats and fled the city. Protestors released those who had earlier been taken by police snatch squads. The Duma received a command from the Tsar to dissolve. But, this time it did not heed the directive. Instead it defied his directive, and its deputies rename the legislative body created after the Bloody Sunday Revolution of 1905. They call themselves the 'Provisional Committee."

Leonid holds back his emotions as he pens a letter to his wife:

> *Monday, February 27, 1917…The entire city has shut down. Not a single working place is functioning. The rail lines have been cut. Streetcars are burned. The streets have been swarming with hundreds of thousands every day for the past three days. Like all true Russians, my heart is breaking in fear of what is becoming of my Russia.*

What sounds like mass hysteria emanates from the streets outside. Leonid stops writing, now terrified. Can he do anything? Where is the army? Where is the military? Even the reserves have now joined the march, abandoning their posts and their oath to the

Tsar. He leaves the unfinished letter on the credenza in the guest room of his brother Erich's apartment. There is no need to finish it today. There is no mail. He needs to get to his office…to his papers, his responsibilities…to the safe.

Dressing quickly, he instructs the butler to tell his brother that he has gone to the office. As he walks out into the chill, sunny day, haze from the still-smoldering court buildings and prisons obstructs the sunlight. Banners now wave…"Down with the Tsar!" Shouts have changed to, "We will stop only when the generals hang from the gallows!" The guards who shot nine people on Sunday have now shot their captain. Rifles are seized from battalion stores, with no response from officers. Many officers, frightened of their troops or contemptuous of the government, make themselves absent and report in sick. A disorderly mass of men spreads from the barracks, carrying ragged banners. The oldest regiment in Russia bayonets its colonel. Locked doors of the ammunition storerooms at the engineering battalion barracks are pillaged. The gates of the main arsenal are battered, the depot commander killed. A soldier yells, "We're going forward into the unknown…" Teenagers run shouting out of side streets while firing their guns at pigeons roosting on streetcar wires.

Leonid weaves his way toward his office, around marching masses and past pillaged apartments of the bourgeoisie. An armored car rumbles by with a red pennant flying from it. Suddenly Leonid hears bullets ricochet off the building nearest him. Trembling, he jumps inside a doorway. A young boy on the other side of the street hides behind a lamppost. The firing continues. Shouts and screams reverberate in his ears as hats and cloaks are left on the street. He stands frozen in place. The shooting dies down slightly. "Don't move," he tells himself. But, in fact, he's too petrified to move.

He looks across the street and notices the boy. In a split second the boy pokes his head out from behind the post. Leonid's scream, "NOOOOO...," is lost in the roar of a bullet. The boy crumples to the ground in an unnatural heap, his skull opened and bleeding. Leonid, his back against the wall, slides down the side of the doorway where he has taken cover. He stays there, slumped and shivering.

The Tsar is cabled a warning at 8 p.m. that only a handful of his troops remain loyal. A state of siege is proclaimed and posted on the railings. The night breeze picks up, floating the detritus of the day; papers, bloody bits of clothing, ashes and proclamations.

❧

"Would you like some more tea?" Josephine offers a high-ranking general and two of his commanding officers, who have just completed the dinner she's provided them in a fashion not unusual for wealthy families these war-torn days.

"No, thank you," answers the general, in an almost pained tone, uncharacteristic of his otherwise imposing, authoritative manner. Instead he bows his head and stares vacantly at his plate, appearing to Josephine to be a man who has lost all hope. Nina, her brothers and sister, sit silently around the table knowing that something has gone terribly wrong.

Josephine will not be daunted, and continues to make polite conversation. The general's entire being remains expressionless and disoriented. "General, please stay here tonight, get some rest and be on your way in the morning," Josephine offers with a sense of civic duty and wartime hospitality, as well as a motherly instinct to protect her family from what she clearly understands to be an impending danger. The Tsar, God help him, has been en route to get back to Tsarskoe Selo but is constantly delayed.

"Madame, do not be overly alarmed for your children," the General pulls himself momentarily together as he rises to leave. "This city is not of key industrial importance. The factories and ammunition depots are mostly in Moscow and Petrograd. I believe all is lost, dear woman, but the nature of this so-called workers' revolution is such that the lives of the civilian population in general have so far remained intact." With these words, he wearily stands up, bids his goodbye, and leaves with his aides.

It is evening, and the streets outside are completely quiet. Nina feels so frightened she can hear her heart beat. She lies awake on her bed, listening as the wind howls outside, and hears the abrupt crack of what could either be ice on tree limbs or a far-off shot. The temperature is well below zero. "What if a bullet tears through my window," she thinks, remembering the general's comments about ammunition. She shuffles across her dark room, having been told firmly to not turn the lights on. She takes one of her large, overstuffed goose-down pillows from her bed and places it against the window, straightening the corners of the linen pillow case to block the frost encrusted glass from any stray bullet shots, then walks back to her bed.

Morning comes and the sun shines through the corners of the linen pillowcase across the room from Nina's bed. She has fallen asleep for some time. As she looks out the window, she rubs her eyes. No, the glass isn't broken, and her room looks and feels safe. The night was silent. She takes the pillow down and timidly looks out. The frozen trees are covered with a light dusting of snow. Icicles hang from the gutters, reflecting the sunshine. It all seems so normal.

❦

Leonid looks through a stack of aging documents placed on his desk by his secretary, not sure of what to make of them. His notary business has changed radically in the last three months. New laws have been created but very little information has been disseminated about what they mean or how they are to be enforced. Traditions remain, and for now most day-to-day activities appear to progress as normal.

After abdicating his throne on March 3, 1917, to his brother—who in turn abandons the ancient form of imperial monarchy—former Tsar Nicholas now lives as a prisoner at his Tsarskoe Selo Palace a short distance from Leonid's apartment. Josephine and his children continue to live their lives as normally as possible. The children's schooling has been disrupted, but private tutors still educate. The general whom Josephine entertained for dinner was found assassinated.

The government has changed most of all. Now there is something called a Provisional Government that is made of up old-school diplomats and politicians who have lost their ability to govern effectually, and are almost equally disdained by the workers and the bourgeoisie. A Soviet, or committee, of Workers' and Soldiers' Deputies made up of a Bolshevik minority faction headquarters itself in the wing opposite the formal Provincial Government in the Tauride Palace. Most of the known "rabble rousers" belong to this faction, which advocates an end to the war, land redistribution to the peasants, and an eight-hour day, in addition to demands for food.

Leonid reads the papers profusely and keeps himself abreast of current changes, but for the most part continues his life as he did before the abdication of the Tsar, which has marked the end of over three hundred years of Romanov power, and centuries longer of absolute monarchy. Leonid's thoughts are torn on the subject of the war. Although truly Russian in heart and spirit, his identification with his own distant German heritage enables him to want an end to it just as much as he wants his in-laws to be released from Siberia. To that degree he can sympathize with the liberal, protesting socialist mobs.

On the other hand, he disdains the mutineers and protestors that seem to have the run of the city. Trucks patrolled the streets, carrying men with rifles and bayonets, in those weeks shortly after the rebellion. Rumors circulated of aristocrats abandoning their mansions with nothing but a case full of jewels, and still others thrown out of their own dining rooms while their servants were forced to feed soldiers and sailors, pouring glasses full of expensive wines. The otherworldliness of this was beyond anything in his comprehension.

In the factories, Soviets now represent the workers, and sometimes manage the factories themselves. A man named Lenin has been returned as a "gift" from the Germans on April 3rd. Leonid has heard him spewing slogans that drive the deepest aspirations of the most radical elements and the new worker leaders, mostly the skilled metalworkers of the Vyborg district. Leonid found himself scoffing out loud at this Lenin's claims of "Peace, Bread and Land" that supposedly replaces the widely disdained "War, Hunger and Landlords" of the current regime.

It is true that some of his acquaintances and many of the aristocracy have been directly affected. But Leonid has found himself to be quite stalwart in his continued mocking of the change. Perhaps he's been lucky so far, for his disdain is directed both at the Provisional Government's inability to manage the worsening situation with the war and the new Soviet's sophomoric pleas for worker power.

Effective command of troops at the war front is disappearing. Entire regiments now merely dissolve as thousands of deserters stream away from the front, killing any officer who tries to stop them. Civilians, crazed with fear, flee when they see soldiers. Railroad car axles are so overloaded with the weight of deserters that they catch fire. Taking advantage of so much disarray, the minority faction of the Soviets (the Bolsheviks) lay claim to the need for them to take effective action.

Leonid is more intrigued with the events around him than he would care to admit. It's odd to him that this ancient country is now seeking direction by reading other countries' constitutions for ideas. But so much is now, in reality, different, while, at the same time, so many are artificially trying to maintain the *status quo*. He's glad that his mother and sisters have gone to live with distant relatives in the Baltics, even if that means he has less family nearby. These days he sleeps at Erich's house or in his office. Erich had even married briefly during the initial uprising, an unusual thing, given his years of staunch bachelorhood. But his wife soon left him for another man.

Leonid has taken the opportunity to meet his brother Roman for dinner at a posh restaurant near the Winter Palace. He tidies up his appearance and leaves his office, walking down the boulevard as he would have at any other time. He hopes he can put some of this chaos to rest with this evening's discussion. He enters the restaurant and sits down at the table where his brother is already enjoying hors d'oeuvres and champagne.

"So, my brother, you look well, given all of the anarchy around us," Leonid says, now seated across a white tablecloth from Roman. They are in the private dining room of the fully-operational restaurant.

"I am well, Brother," Roman responds. "It seems as if the new Provisional Government as well as the Soviet Executive Committee are still interested in obtaining any possible funds they can from foreign enterprises; and, since I represent those banks that still could be of use, I think they are keeping their hands off." He leans a bit closer to his brother and admits to him, "I don't think their hands will be off for long. The situation is precarious at best. It will not last; it is as stable as the Romanov Dynasty was."

Leonid, feeling a meeting-of-minds with his brother that he's never felt before, adds, "There is nothing more hypocritical than a government—Provisional, that is—telling a committee—Soviet, that is—that it is interested in peace: only later to be exposed by the papers publishing the Foreign Affairs minister's letter to our allies confirming Russia's dedication to a victorious military conclusion."

Roman, feeling like a cohort in a family game, responds, "Yes, Leonid, that has only given clout to the workers, who are having their say—and it has only just begun." They both know very well what the unfortunate reality is; that the workers are justified in their belief that the Provisional Government is a pawn of the capitalists, that it has no real ability to cause change, nor does it have a true dedication to anyone other than the landowners and bourgeoisie.

Leonid nods in agreement, adding his own comment, "And add to this the impossibility of inflation that is running near 1000%, even when workers received a pay increase of 30%, and the situation is grave beyond comprehension."

Roman asks, "Do you know that they're now issuing bank notes on uncut sheets of paper? The printing presses can't keep up with the demand, so people are being asked to guillotine their money themselves."

Dinner has been grim for Leonid, even though both he and his brother have taken pleasure in the challenge and dynamic of the situation. He laughs briefly as he shares Erich's idea for Leonid to change his law practice to a law office "…for the people." And then he fully feels this late spring's damp chill in his body, as he hears Roman's completely sincere remark, "I've kept gold in lieu of paper money for some time now. I hide it in the chandeliers. No one looks up. Remember that. Take caution."

9

THE END
THE OCTOBER REVOLUTION
1917

Today, July 3rd, 1917, Leonid watches as a large and well-organized protest of the Bolsheviks against the so-called "bourgeois-landlord Provisional Government and their imperialist war" makes its way through the quarter. He again hears shouting in the streets below his office window, where he stands just above the large wooden sign that indicates his name, *L.F. Sievert, Notary Offices*, and the row of mostly closed first-floor shops. The reverberation from the chanting protestors is hauntingly familiar. Banners wave in red, "Resign Capitalist Ministers," "Power to the Soviet Executive Committee!" So many strange looking faces wearing red stars pinned on their caps.

"What a diverse, intriguing group," Leonid thinks to himself as he watches confidently, with contradictory feelings of empathy and contempt; "How amazing and sad to know none of these people has even the slightest idea of where the 'People's Revolution' is leading. It's as if they are walking into an unknown destiny, taking the rest of us along with them. He speaks aloud to himself in exasperation, "These large, mostly illiterate masses can't go on running a huge country like Russia, can they?"

Suddenly, gunfire rips through the air. Beyond his line of sight, an assembly of old-guard regiments, loyal to the government, fires on the demonstrators and counter-demonstrators haphazardly. Leonid hurriedly shuts his curtain and, now more agitated than frightened, retreats to his inner-office.

As the weeks immediately following the botched July Revolution go by, The Central Executive Committee of the Soviets denounces demonstrators as "counter-revolutionaries," creating confusion amongst the workers, who later issue a statement that "We trust the Soviet, but not those whom the Soviets trust." Rumors circulate that Lenin is an agent of Berlin, and has accepted payments from the Germans to his Bolshevik cause. Trotsky is arrested, and then he later escapes. Kerensky, Russia's new prime minister (who had the horrendous task of arresting the Tsar and his family), reinstitutes the death penalty from his imperial suite in the Winter Place.

The worsening economic crisis is called Capitalist sabotage. The "bony hand of Hunger" continues and is used as a weapon by the Bolsheviks to persuade the masses that the old bourgeoisie wants to strangle the Revolution. Every large factory contains a workers' committee that is sponsored by the Bolshevik minority;

oddly enough the majority of businesses are not large, but as is usually the case, the largest are the most visible. And as was typical in the Russia of old, Jews are targeted as being the perpetrators of workers' suffering; the old-school and new Bolshevik religions are in agreement on one horrendously evil similarity; pogroms against Jews continue unabated.

$$\wp$$

A creeping despondency begins to capture Leonid. He spends time in Tsarskoe Selo when he can, yet still returns to Petrograd where, he feels, he must continue working as best he can in order to stifle his growing grief-fed malaise. He takes to painting porcelain plates when home in Tsarskoe Selo and journaling in Petrograd. He spends most of his time at his office, although he has plenty of opportunity to carry on his social life as before; but then again, he never really preferred that life. He still gambles with old acquaintances, and some new ones who have achieved political power (the only reason he is in the same rooms as they are). He sees a few old-school comrades who are still left unmolested by the new regime.

At other times he spends evenings with his brother Erich, as he is doing this dreary, late April evening. Brother Roman has become something of a liability. Arrests are common; Tsar Nicholas lives secluded in his Catherine Palace as a prisoner; now Roman has become active not only in the Provisional Government, but also aids in orchestrating a counter-revolution amongst certain hidden factions of the decimated White Guard.

Taking quill in hand, Leonid journals at his credenza in Erich's house:

The government now takes on a precarious name. The villagers who now rule this city—Russia's most venerable—call it the Revolutionary Government of the Proletariat. The poor peasantry are incited, sometimes by intellectuals from wealthy families (even Lenin comes from a wealthy family), to ever sharper class hostility and support of Bolshevik control in the Socialist Executive Committee. Of course the Bolsheviks are becoming more empowered because they represent the largest factory workers' groups and support an immediate end to the war. They've even created an order to give arms to the workers so that they can organize a Red Guard.

He continues to journal, sticking with the evidence so that his mind can comprehend the otherworldly new facts of life: A new cabinet is appointed, the fourth provisional government since the revolution. Everyone talks and talks. Barges are filled with the treasures from the Hermitage. His pen shakes as he writes this, knowing that Russia's national heritage is being shipped away in the night. He continues writing, barely believing his own words:

He sets his pen down. It is clear to him things are not getting better. If he's to continue to make the best out of this situation perhaps there's some hope in the efforts made toward a resolution of all this governmental chaos. But is Roman right to want to bring back the monarchy in Russia? His mind quickly calculates the pros and cons. He's used to this. His work in legal affairs is fraught with gray areas of analysis. Luckily he's not a Russian aristocrat, yet he staunchly sides with the upper classes. He'll figure out a solution, and in the meantime he'll walk a delicate balance between the daily conflicting interests that he's presented with.

Roman has taken extreme precaution in his dealings with the counter-revolutionaries and has somehow protected himself, up to a point, from being arrested. On August 28th, his invincibility is no more. Kerensky launches a Rightist coup, led by the new Supreme

Commander-In-Chief, General Kornilov, with the aim of crushing the Soviets. The coup is a miserable failure due to resistance from the railway and telegraph workers. The coup's forces are captured within striking distance of the capital, frightening working people, and raising arms for an extreme solution to yet unheeded needs.

Roman packs his things, dresses in his servant's working clothes and leaves, heading for the south.

❦

Leonid raps on Josephine's parlor door, and then enters. It has always been her custom to spend time alone before the evening meal is served. Even though they have been reduced to one servant, Josephine still does not know how to cook nor does she participate in the setting of dinner. He finds his wife dressed for dinner, as usual, though her costume is a slightly toned-down version of the new shorter dress lengths and loose, less cumbersome blouses.

"Fina," Leonid says, admiring the stately figure of his beautiful, thirty-six-year- old wife, "I have some information that will please you."

Josephine turns from where she has been standing in her parlor, sorting through her children's old school books. These now must be destroyed for their over-emphasis on inaccuracies that are counter to the revolution of the people. She feels a longing pity for the elegant man he once was. The man who stands in front of her is a man who is obviously disheveled by current events, events which have eaten at his understanding of who he is and where he belongs. With increasing arrests of once-substantial citizens of old St. Petersburg, the threat to his life has indeed strengthened his character and his old belief system, but simultaneously forced him to redefine his concept of himself in a system that no longer defines it for him.

"Yes, Leonid," she acknowledges him.

"I've worked quite diligently on the return of your parents' confiscated Finnish property. The window of opportunity with a feistier Provisional Government and their dissatisfaction with the atrocious independent behavior of the Grand Duchy of Finland, has allowed a resolution to the suit against the thief who stole the property. Monies have been awarded your father's estate in full repatriation of the properties lost."

Josephine sets down the books, relieved that, at last, one unresolved family problem has resulted in a positive outcome. She says nothing, looking instead at her husband as if this were the only expected and possible outcome. She nods her head slightly knowing he has more to say.

Leonid continues, "Furthermore, I've been in contact with your parents via telegram. They wish for you to have the returned monies to do with as you bid. They believe the settlement will be more beneficial to you than to them."

For this Josephine is again grateful, but shows not the slightest reaction. Talk of money had always been something inappropriate for her in the first place. However, she has no hesitation in responding. "I would prefer the money be given in gold once the property issues are settled. We all know that paper is a mere trifle."

Leonid responds with a nod. But there's so much more he wants to tell her of his struggles with emotions for what is becoming of him, of his country, of his feelings of loss, of his need for nurture, and a longing for life to return to what he used to take for granted. He clears his throat, feeling an urge to weep. But, in fact, he cannot.

The maid, Masha, knocks on the door of the parlor. "Comrade Sir and Madame," she says, mixing current titles with old familiar ones, "dinner has been served." Together they walk through the doorway and down the hallway leading to the dining area where the children will have been summoned to join them.

&

It is mid-October, and the chill in the air bites through layers of clothing, as is usual for the early and fierce, oncoming Russian winter. The wind sweeps off the already barren and browned trees. A few branches hold the remnants of what had been oak leaves turned red, brown and then fallen to the ground, where they are left.

Nina takes a walk today, holding on to the hand of her five-year-old sister Vera. The only governess is overburdened with additional household duties, and Nina has insisted on her walks, with her mother's approval. Not too long ago, when the Tsar and his family hadn't been moved away from Tsarskoe Selo to be "safe," they would often take walks around the guarded enclosure of the Alexander Gardens. Now they are gone.

Father's racehorse, stabled briefly after the Revolution in the yard behind the apartment, is now long gone—confiscated by the Peoples' army. In its place are many more horses, nuzzling hungrily beneath the snow for morsels of food. Nina and her sister continue past the stable, but don't go very far before they come across one of many palaces. Nina looks through the beveled-glass window of one of the large, once opulent, mansions. The yard looks unkempt, with summer-dried branches, now dead, poking up from the dirty, low layer of snow. She thinks she can see some light inside but then realizes it must be a reflection from the street lamp. he days are so short. She pretends a family is at home beside the warmth of a fireplace. But no one will be home ever again.

Vera has become a very sensitive and quiet five-year-old. Polite and unusually responsible, she follows Nina without much hesitation. But today Nina feels her sister's hand slipping and tugging, as if Vera is nudging her to go home. It is true that it's awfully chilly outside, and perhaps her sister is a bit more sensitive. Nina continues to go the distance that she had set out to walk. But there is something odd today about the feel of the usually quiet, aristocratic neighborhood. Many of the neighbors no longer live in their homes. And some of the palaces now exhibit garish red banners with names of this or that Committee headquarters. Perhaps it would be okay to turn around and go home.

"Come on, Vera," Nina easily coaxes her little sister to turn around. "Let's see the horses in the garden." Of course, there are horses in other gardens as well, and Nina finds it strange that the military has seen it necessary to keep horses there. She feels a need to coax Vera past the horses, remebering her own bout with the goat. Nearing their home, Nina stops to allow her sister to look at the horses as she promised.

Vera stands listlessly while Nina's gloved hand brushes across the temporary wooden picket fence encircling the yard. It's rough and jagged. Nina sees how thin and restless the horses are. "They're eating the wood," she thinks, "…they must be hungrier than I thought." She notices her sister standing awkwardly below a horse. By instinct or assessed risk, she moves to push her sister back. It's too late. The horse suddenly bites Vera on the head, knocking her over.

Nina rushes to pick up her sister, thinking what a little fool she is to have ventured so close to the horse in the first place. "What a silly little girl," she thinks, as she takes her wailing sister's hand and rushes her back to the house. She knows Mother will not be pleased.

In Petrograd, Leonid has a heightened sense of panic that conflicts with his stubborn insistence on maintaining the conditions of his prior life; his palms sweat as he signs customary documents.

Likewise, while the city maintains its sumptuous feasts and opulent social events, the newspapers shout of conspiracies on both sides of the political pendulum. The Provisional Government and powers-that-are assume a major rebellion or coup is unlikely. Their rationale, odd as it may seem, continues to be that, since a revolution relies on surprise, no one would be surprised, and therefore it is unlikely to occur.

Conditions in the outlying Russian countryside, while not as well documented as in Petrograd or Moscow, are similarly tragic. Landowners and shopkeepers are beaten to death by clubbing with such frequency that the newspaper *Russkiye Vedomosti* apologizes to its readers since it can run only a fraction of the stories about mutinies and pogroms, which flood its newsroom each day. But as life goes on, events multiply in ways, which only the future will attempt to decipher with any semblance of accuracy.

Made up of the experience of individuals, information is accumulated in the consciousness of each person that will later be recorded as a history of the collective whole. And while the extended-family members perform their own appointed tasks, the greater society around them changes based upon the words and actions of a surprising few. Most are simply left lethargically uninvolved.

It is Monday, October 24, 1917. Tolstoy's play *The Death of Ivan the Terrible* shows at the Alexandrinsky Theater; The Restaurant de Paris turns away diners without reservations; cinemas, bars, and nightclubs are full; Karsavina dances ballet at the Maryinsky Theater. Meanwhile, two hundred female soldiers are sent to guard the winter palace.

At 6:00 p.m., Lenin paces the floor of his secret, dingy apartment and writes a note, "We must, at all costs, this very evening, this very night, arrest the ministers." With a wig and a handkerchief wrapped around his face, feigning a toothache, he catches a tram part way to the Smolny Institute, now being used as Bolshevik headquarters, and then walks the rest of the way on foot. As he arrives, he announces, "The time has come for an armed rising."

Nina, one month shy of her eleventh birthday, continues her studies and attends to some of her increased household responsibilities, joining the cook for a walk to the market. Vera and the youngest, Vova, now seven and six and dressed in picturesque childhood clothing, play with their wooden toys before their afternoon lessons. They have been completely sheltered from the reality occurring about them. Leonya, two days after his thirteenth birthday, marvels at the new camera his father generously gifted him, and now studies old photos, fascinated with the scenery.

Wednesday, October 25th, 1917; small groups of Bolsheviks move out of their barracks and take control of the Neva River bridges, the main telegraph office, the post offices, the railroad stations, the Central Bank, and the power stations, with no resistance. Kerensky, prime minister of the Provisional Government, borrows an American embassy official's Renault and chauffeur under pretence of going to the front so he can get troops to protect the city and government. The limousine drives straight through Bolshevik cordons. Pedestrians recognize their besmirched leader as he occasionally rises and salutes them. The driver asks for directions for the easiest way out of the city...forever.

Everyone ignores Lenin's published declaration, and the Bolshevik Committee, meeting for hours, finds many of its participants dozing off in boredom. Trams run, factories work, and business is conducted. At 2:35 p.m. Trotsky makes a much-exaggerated claim to the Soviet session that "The government has ceased to exist as a result of a movement of such enormous masses for which there is no parallel in history." Meanwhile two cyclists arrive at the Winter Palace (where the ministers of the Provisional Government are still waiting for Karensky to return with troops) with a message from the Bolshevik Committee. They give an ultimatum that the Bolsheviks will open fire if the palace does not surrender by 7:10 p.m.

Bolsheviks begin to wander the palace corridors without resistance. A couple of American journalists are escorted around, their coats taken by servants. At 11 p.m. live rounds are fired from the six-inch guns of the Peter and Paul Fortress. Most fall into the river. One hit is recorded. It chips a cornice.

The war at the front continues unabated, albeit compromised by mutinies; men die in droves. Leonid walks to his office from his brother's home. Everyone else continues in his or her normal fashion. Distractions are rarely noticed.

Josephine maintains her decorum and discipline, and continues to mingle with like-minded, powerful women, attending a volunteer luncheon where they discuss and implement activities to help the elderly and the widowed. Roman has left Petrograd and settles in a grand hotel in the Crimea, where he hides his gold in a chandelier and conspires with old-guard generals on the counter-revolution. Grandfather Karl's manufacturing businesses churn out axles and carriages still used by the modern army, his properties accumulate rent while his automotive business stagnates without his leadership; his French and German wife is engrossed in managing their lives with the other wealthy political exiles in the now-frozen Siberian hinterlands.

Early in the morning on October 26, 1917, in Petrograd, a cadet rushes into the room where ministers are napping on divans. "What are the orders of the government," he asks, continuing with the assumption, "…to fight to the last man?" Wearily, a minister replies, "It's not necessary!" A second declares, "it's useless." A third chimes in, "no bloodshed!" A little man with a wide-brimmed artist's hat rushes into the room. An armed mob follows. The man pushes back his red hair and raises his voice amidst the clattering of the crowd. "I inform you, all you members of the Provisional Government, that you are arrested. I am Antonov-Ovseenko." The ministers obey and march out of the room.

Josephine's brothers in Berlin, wealthy bachelors, enjoy non-military, domestic duties. Leonid's brother Erich downplays his role as a notary, dressing in simple clothes while attending to his business on a much reduced scale. Their elderly mother, Olga, and sisters, Anita and Stella, live in their customary fashion in Latvia. And Leonid's brother Felix, once Governor General, is now missing and rumored to have been assassinated.

Josephine walks through her elegant home, alone, late at night. The children and Masha, the remaining servant, are fast asleep. The outside chill is no longer as prevalent as it has been, making the house feel a bit warmer than on past sleepless nights. She thinks the warmth is deceiving, questioning how there can be such a shortage of wood when forests surround them. She walks to, and opens, the china cabinet filled with fine crystal and silver. She takes the set of twelve silver salt bowls that have her initials on them, a wedding gift from a wealthy family friend, and their accompanying silver spoons, and wraps them in fine linen napkins. She's startled at her own behavior and isn't quite sure where to place the balls of silver; then she decides—a hatbox, she'll place them in a hatbox.

Next she studies the large, silver, serving bowl, wondering what to do with it. Then there are the gold-plated utensils; she is mentally inventorying more and more items. She walks into Leonid's room. There are gold, eagle-wings-crested pendants from his gymnasium, and pearl cufflinks and silver collar clips. Perhaps they'd be safer in a sock? And much like a squirrel, she spends the evening burrowing and hiding.

Morning arrives and Leonid reads a flyer delivered to his office with the proclamation: "The Provisional Government is overthrown. State power has passed into the hands of the organ of the Petrograd Soviet of Workers' and Soldiers' Deputies…the cause for which the people fought—an immediate proposal for a democratic peace, abolition of landlord property rights, workers' control over production, the creation of a Soviet government—this cause is assured...Long Live the Revolution of workers, soldiers and peasants!" He sets the proclamation down on his desk and holds his hands to his face for what feels like hours. Finally, he leaves to walk through the familiar streets to his brother's apartment. Somehow he now feels himself to be a foreigner in his own city. "Damn the Bolsheviks!" he mutters under his breath.

❦

Municipal cleaning gangs leave the puddled mud and slush on the streets of the city. Damp winds blow off the Gulf of Finland. The mud splashes on Leonid's black leather shoes as he hurriedly walks to his offices, his mind preoccupied with the conversation he has had with his brother. Under threat of arrest, Erich, dressed in worker's clothing, his original staff dismissed, pretended to be a simple administrator at his own office. Leonid visualizes the wretched conditions of prisons as he continues down the increasingly filthy boulevard. The wind hisses as if echoing the plethora of new ghosts emanating from Russia's past privileged classes. He holds his fur collar tightly to his neck. He does not look up or around. So many old familiar faces are either gone or hidden.

His earlier conversations with his wife come to mind. "We have the option to leave, Leonid. We can go to the Baltics or Finland and there are ways into Bulgaria or even Germany, you know," she suggested not too long ago. "Fina, I have responsibilities in

Petrograd," he remembers telling her. "I am committed to my work in Mother Russia. It's all we can do in these times to continue our life as best as we can until the government has established itself more solidly." His own words, his denial of reality, his pride, now haunt him. But he still does not regret them. Not now...not ever, he continues to convince himself.

As he approaches his building he notices his large wooden office sign hanging unmolested. What once was a busy retail environment below it, however, now feels forebodingly empty. Undeterred, he resolutely hastens his step toward his office. "Why should I hide from these people," he thinks to himself. "I have done nothing wrong, and have nothing to hide."

He enters through the creaking, front door and goes directly up the carpeted marble staircase leading to the second floor. The cold air enters with him as he brushes off his coat. Upstairs he'll find his employees tending to his offices, he's sure. The wife will have cleaned and organized, and the husband will have secured the day's papers and mail. Their little son will be there also, as he hasn't attended school since the beginning of the Revolution. Surely there will be a fire lit.

As he turns the corner of the staircase facing the double wooden doors emblazoned with a bronze plaque containing his name, he notices something unusual. Both doors are wide open, and he hears the voices of men inside. He hesitates momentarily, gathers his strength, and confidently enters.

The family (husband, wife and their son) and his secretary are seated on couches in the parlor. Two men wearing worker's clothing and jackets emblazoned with red stars on the pockets, stand on either side. His employees glance at him with weary, empathetic eyes, as if to say, "we have not betrayed you, Father."

"Comrade Leonid," a third man, with a battered jacket and red emblem on his hat, asks.

"I am he," responds Leonid. "And in what service may I assist you?"

"You are the owner of this establishment?"

"No, I do not own this building or these rooms. I rent them from a landlord and pay my workers, whom you see sitting here, who have worked for me for the past ten years."

"This building, these premises and everything contained here are now the property of the People."

"That makes no difference to me," responds Leonid. "I am grateful to the People for use of their premises."

The men exchange glances, confused yet stern.

"What do you have to declare," the obvious leader spits at him.

Leonid is dismayed by the tone and its implications. His legs feel weak. But he's played cards long enough to know that he must maintain his poker face, even though he has been dealt a bad hand.

"As this is not my property, and all of the documents contained herein have always belonged to the People, whom I represent, I have nothing…to declare," he responds, regaining his composure.

"You will leave this office, and it will be best for you if you leave the city. These workers who you have been exploiting have indicated that you have family in Tsarskoe Selo. We recommend that you return to them. There is nothing for you here any longer."

"I will gladly divest this room of my toiletries and such items that aren't of any use to the people, and…"

"IT IS NO LONGER YOU who decides what is or what is not important to the People!" a previously silent, skinny, disheveled Bolshevik screams. "We are aware of a safe that you will open for us. We have already told you that the entire contents of these offices belong to the People. You no longer have any authority to represent them unless the Council, by whom you will be summoned, allows."

Leonid holds himself strong, glances at his former employees with a respectful nod of his head, then turns and walks to his safe. He turns the knob using every bit of his strength to keep his hand from shaking. In it is his wife's jewelry box containing all of his children's remaining gold coins, Nina's Easter egg necklace, and many of Josephine's jewels. Some of the contents, however, had been gambled away. Leonid wasn't sure how he would have brought himself to disclosing this to his wife. This will no longer be of concern.

As he walks down the stairs he stops briefly, his breathing choked by his rising anger. Everything he's worked so hard for all these years is now lost. "We'll see about this," he thinks to himself. "We'll see about this."

Josephine and Leonid circa 1900

Grandmother Josephine

Leonya and baby Nina (1908)

Nina and Leonya

Nina in the doghouse at the dacha

Leonid

Vera, Vova, Leonya, and Nina at the dacha

Book 2

10

CIVIL WAR
1918–1919

Leonid taps on Josephine's door, and enters the chilly, dimly-lit room. The bitter winter light from the parted window curtains is turning to twilight. His wife stands looking out the window to the busy street below, the heavy over-curtains drawn by her hand, the sheer under-curtains protecting her from the outside world. He finds Josephine, on her 37th birthday, to be as stately as always even though she's dressed in a simple jacket over her subtle, refined dress. Josephine, aware of her husband's entrance, does not turn, but continues to look out the window. Still looking out, she remarks how strange the times seem to her; that this, her birthday, isn't like any she remembers. True that the small family is alone and with little food, but also strange is how the recording of time itself has changed. For this year, the Council of People's Commissars added

Russia to the list of those countries that count their years by the Gregorian Calendar (used by some since the sixteenth century), doing away with the Julian Calendar created by Caesar. Russia, in a day, went from January 31 to February 14th; Josephine remarks on the difference in temperature this cold March 7th, 1918, previously February 21st.

Today she seems more melancholic than her usual controlled placidity. The servants are all long gone as it is now considered unacceptable work to bow to petty demands of the bourgeoisie and former aristocracy. Josephine knows nothing of cooking, having never had to physically prepare a meal, although she's supervised the formation of the menu. It helps that rations for the former elite are so severe that the simple allowances of bread and cheese don't require cooking. Nina, having learned (from Masha, the former maid) to boil potatoes and cabbage and to fry chicken, fish, and meat, has been of great help to the family.

In the five months and some days since the Bolshevik Revolution—or what is now called "Red October"—events have spiraled away from any semblance of what their initial thrust had been. "Free elections with universal suffrage in Russia's new parliament," went the endless promises. The old Provisional Government had advertised "free elections" since the February Social Democratic Revolution. Indeed, in November, three weeks after Red October, lines of peasants, workers, women voters, bourgeoisie, old fallen aristocrats, Bolsheviks, Mensheviks, Democratic Revolutionaries, Social Revolutionaries, trade union representatives, Factory Socialist

Committee members and every citizen possible, waited to cast their meaningless ballots—meaningless because the Bolsheviks had no intention of honoring the results.

When the ballots were tallied, the Bolsheviks, in fact, won only 24% of the vote and the Social Revolutionaries had 40%. The first and only Constituent Assembly was held in the Tauride Palace on January 5, 1918. In only a few hours, armed Red Sailors broke it up and Russian democracy officially died.

What happened after that affected the lives of everyone in every city, village, and town. Most radical, was the ensuing civil war, fought in outlying areas of the vast Russian countryside, pitting Bolsheviks against Cadets, Mensheviks, Socialist Revolutionaries, landowners who lost their estates, factory owners who had their property nationalized, devout members of the Russian Orthodox Church who objected to the new government's atheism, and imperialists who wanted to restore the Tsar. Some defined the events in the countryside as a free-for-all as the differing sides were not always well-defined. By February, however, the old-guard Whites held no major area in Russia.

In addition to this, 1918 had become a year of wholesale massive arrests, outright assassinations, and imprisonment for entire categories of people. Many of Josephine and Leonid's friends and acquaintances have been personally attacked; some have fled the country, others have been assassinated, and yet still others have lost everything and live now in one room of their former palatial residences. In one fell swoop, Josephine's sister Louise, lost ownership of the two apartment buildings in Petrograd gifted to her as a wedding gift by their father Karl. Luckily, she's been able to maintain her personal apartment where she is allowed rooms for her, her husband, and children. The Central Committee Headquarters had obviously taken into consideration the fact that her husband, Yuri, had served so many years as a rather non-disciplinarian civil officer, easily transferring his allegiance to the communists. Louise wisely obligated herself to her new role as property manager of the two apartment buildings.

Leonid speaks affectionately, admiring Josephine's grace in spite of her internal grief, "Fina, I know you are deeply concerned and well-immersed in the state of our affairs." The level with which the two speak to one another is on more socially equal terms than it has ever been. And both are fully aware that Josephine's uncelebrated birthday was immediately followed by news of the signing of the Treaty of Brest-Litovsk, which ended the war with Germany. Leonid continues, "I know you have been completely absorbed by the disposition of German political prisoners such as your parents."

Josephine turns and looks at her husband with little expression. It's been a miracle that their home hasn't been disturbed. During the days of the initial chaos that followed the Revolution, the landlord, before his arrest, made a point of telling local Committee hoodlums, that the family who lived in the apartments was German—even though Josephine and Leonid and all of their children were born in Russia. The Bolsheviks, who now officially call themselves Communists, have stood ground on wanting an end to the war with

Germany, and therefore Josephine and Leonid, being of ancient German heritage, were ironically protected during the worst of the hostilities immediately following the Revolution.

It's been years since Josephine has seen eye-to-eye with Leonid. She hasn't been so foolish as to let his gambling go unnoticed. After all, his risk-taking behavior has affected the entire family. And though he's often moderated his temperament to dissuade any questioning of his behavior, this in itself has made her more aware of what he might be hiding. Despite all the risks he has taken since the world changed, he continues to insist on staying in Russia. This she has difficulty in reconciling. Estonia, the entire Baltic region, and Finland have either claimed their independence or become independent; fortunately, many of their relatives, Claudia, Leonid's mother, Olga, and sisters, Stella and Anita, are now living in non-communist countries. Friends abandon everything to get to the newly coined "Russian Berlin." Yet how can she argue with his reasoning? That he will be unemployable as a lawyer elsewhere and ill-equipped for any other occupation is true.

"What do my parents have to do with our situation anymore, Leonid?" She phrases her reply slowly and deliberately, holding back the anger rising not only at what she feels to be his continual poor choices, but also at her embarrassment; for the past several months they have survived by using currency from the confiscated Finnish properties that had been returned to her father and gifted to her, along with their other savings at 1/10th their original value.

"Josephine, what I'm about to tell you, you don't know," Leonid starts. "Shortly after the Revolution, I was summoned to the Central Committee here. I didn't want to tell you. There wasn't anything I could do. And I needn't worry you excessively. The outcome was out of our control."

Josephine looks at him, the severe look on her face relaxing, and gestures for him to sit down on one of the soft chairs near her. She waits and sits down herself. Leonid's face saddens, as he clears his throat to hold back his emotions.

"I was told I was to be tried as an exploiter of the People, as a pawn of the demagogic government, as a tyrant of the classes of Russian workers. There was little I could say to such groundless and vague accusations. I weighed my words cautiously, and then deliberately asked for the basis of their complaint."

Josephine places her hands upon her lap and listens intently. She's heard much from her husband in the past, but this she feels to be the truth.

Leonid continues, "One of the larger men, with a grizzled beard and a filthy cap, simply shouted, 'Landlords such as yourself should be punished. You're lucky you are even still standing here'. At this I knew an answer, 'But I am not a landlord. My family—a wife and four children—own no property, and never have. We rent our premises as do all working families.'"

"Don't believe him, he's an exploiter of workers, I've read this case," another shouted. " I responded, "But I'm not. I have paid the administrators fairly who have worked for me and have never had a complaint from them or any other individual who has assisted me in any capacity. My files are open for your discretion, you have them yourselves already."

Josephine sits back in incredulity, recognizing her husband's ability to talk his way out of anything while simultaneously feeling betrayed once again at what was happening just under her own feet. "That you're still here, Leonid, is testimony to your skill with these men. But can it not be any clearer that we are not wanted any longer?" Josephine is immediately moving to the next step without any comforting compromise at her husband's victory.

"I'll tell you, 'Fina. I've been speaking with some of these workers' committees and various lower-level judicial officials. They're not so horribly frightening once you understand them."

Josephine surmises he's also played cards with them and perhaps purposely lost. It is true that he doesn't wear his past life on his lapels any longer, although the dignity etched on his 44-year-old face is hard to camouflage. Nonetheless, she's sure he's been able to work his way into knowledge that others may be too frightened to seek.

"Through the connections that I've been able to make in the local Soviet here, I've learned of your mother and father's situation. In fact, Dear, I've spoken with the officials responsible for the transfer of your parents' case. The administration is still intact. How can even the Bolsheviks, I mean Communists, change so many offices overnight? And I've taken it upon myself to call on old acquaintances, before many of them lose their jobs or move in the shuffle of moving the capitol out of Petrograd to Moscow, which you know, my dear, was also announced on your birthday."

Josephine is noticeably surprised by her husband's information. She's learned to become cautious with so much news in every direction. She nonetheless feels touched by her husband's perseverance. She sits upright with her legs crossed at the ankles and leans forward, looking directly in Leonid's eyes.

"What I've learnt is nothing less than remarkable, 'Fina. Here are the facts. Your father, as a wealthy dual citizen, German and Russian, has clout in Berlin. The signing of the treaty was forced upon the Communists based upon their own promises to end the war. The Germans have taken White Russia, as well as made declarations of independence for Lithuania, Latvia, Estonia, the Ukraine, and Poland. Your father's holdings in Petrograd are therefore not only the holdings of a wealthy German entrepreneur, but of a German citizen. All of these properties are to be repaid in gold, as demanded by the highest Berlin authorities. And, 'Fina, your parents are free to leave Siberia, and are to be provided access into Berlin!"

Josephine feels the first true joy she's felt in what seems an age, propelling her to clap her hands together and release a laughing, long sigh. It's too much to believe. Though relieved, she still remains guarded.

Leonid smiles broadly at his wife, his own reaction uninhibited. He feels as if he's just won at the races. "We'll go to Petrograd together 'Fina, when it's time. The treaty has only just been ratified. The process of obtaining a fair exchange will need to occur first."

At this last statement Josephine takes comfort. She cracks a smile at her husband, something she hasn't done for a long time, and relaxes, remembering the many festive occasions that unified them at times, which she acknowledges on secret levels were deliciously exhilarating. Together the two sit and talk nostalgically, missing their supper, well into the late hours of the evening.

❧

It's been a long and trying year that has brought Josephine to this intolerable late spring of 1919. Her clothes resemble her newfound situation. She wears a loose fitting dress and blouse with a jacket. Her maid, Masha, the last to have left, still visits under pretense of being a family friend. Josephine pays her whatever she can. She's in the children's room now, complaining to Nina, "I used to get gifts of diamonds from your mother, and now what have I?" Nina will always remember, as part of her own forming opinion, how terrible Russia has become.

If it weren't for this help, Josephine would be lost. She has no idea how to care for the children on her own. The opportunity had arisen, once her parents were allowed to leave Siberia, for her mother to stay. In fact the senior Josephine insisted, wanting to leave her husband's side for the first time in their fifty-year marriage. Josephine had to advise against it. It was imperative, she felt, that her mother leave for Berlin along with the holdings her father was

161

so fortunate to take. Everyone knew that *that* opportunity wouldn't last for long.

For a moment there had been some hope, as the United States fought on Russian soil with the Whites, and as the war with Finland took twists and turns. But then, of course, the bloodshed of the imperial family that felt like a death knell to Josephine's own, the smashing of the peasant revolts, and the assassinations of the Grand Prince's nephews, made clear things would not change. Josephine has since become resigned to her condition.

It's peculiar to her, not only to have to clean, but to have her daughter Nina as a cook and helper, fulfilling the duties and responsibilities that the servants fulfilled just a short time ago. Josephine has modified the extent to which she informs her daughter of proper, elegant etiquette. Of what practical use can this be now? She's had to reconcile her new reality with what she had been taught as a child and young adult. Her daughters will not have the luxury of managing servants, of their assistance in washing and folding the laundry, purchasing or preparing the meals, maintaining the household, washing the dishes, or even disposing of the trash.

Josephine places her hat, now faded, smaller and floppy, compared to the stiff, feathered, broad brims of her past life, on her neatly combed hair. Paper money has become useless and the rations used for butter and sugar have long been used up. Nina and she will have to see if they can barter some household items with the farmers at the market for more food.

The breeze, normally so precious to this region, has picked

up. Partially decayed leaves from last fall are now revealed under the melted snow and are blowing all over the un-swept streets and sidewalks. In these post-Great Wars, post-Revolution, Civil War years, Tsarskoe Selo, the once-beautiful retreat of Catherine the Great, has quickly deteriorated to a dirty village. None of the palaces have been painted and even the glass on the street lamps is dirty. The only new color is the red seen everywhere from posters to pamphlets to uniforms.

Josephine's concerns are no longer of color schemes, or modern art, poetry, or literature. She instead worries about sustaining the family, obtaining suitable clothing, wood, and food; all utterly demoralizing and bleak thoughts that never had a place to rule her day before. She disdains the propaganda that the new regime spews heedlessly in its attempts to create a worldwide Revolution. The new Russia is catapulting her and her family into a condition far worse than simple mediocrity. She abhors the anxiety of continuous subsistence-level needs her family faces to feed and clean themselves, no reasonable toiletries to be found, and the ceaseless errands required to merely function.

Josephine looks matter-of-factly at the wilted produce available to her for the price of her mother-of-pearl hair comb, the one she received as a sixteenth birthday gift from her father, which is reduced to barter. She sees the daughter of another formerly-wealthy family selling hats at a nearby stall. They are old hats, reconditioned to look modern—reconditioned to reflect the style of the newly-emerging workers of the new era. Josephine simply glances at the girl, looks down at her daughter, and coolly says, "Nina, come on now, we must move quickly." Nina politely obliges.

It's odd for Nina to be with her mother shopping for groceries. She knows her mother isn't familiar with the process of cooking or the accurate choosing amongst the dregs of vegetables, potatoes, or an occasional piece of raw horsemeat, rarely available. The marketplace, a place she had visited once or twice in the past, has changed as well: Communists are everywhere. Nina notices a boy, only slightly older than herself, passing by, with ripped clothing and dragging a gun almost larger than he is behind him. Even though she is still a young girl, she thinks to herself in ways that never concerned her before. "*This* is the new Soviet army," she comments to herself judgmentally. She watches as her mother reaches for the potatoes that a peasant woman hands her in exchange for what used to be a personal item. The woman makes a rude comment to her mother, "We'll see what this common thing brings us."

"Come along, Nina. Let's go home." Josephine says quietly, as soon as the difficult transaction has concluded.

Together they pass the raggedy soldiers guarding what once was the Imperial Family's Tsarskoe Selo summer palace, then their prison, and now a reminder of the dead past. Nina looks away, like her mother, no longer making eye contact with anyone. She recalls watching the princesses in their carriage. She thinks how pretty and kind they all seemed and she wonders why they were taken away as enemies of the state. A poster glued to one of the outlining wooden walls exposes itself below the remnants of more recent ones. It has a red background and a depiction of Lenin and the words "Peace, Land and Bread," a remnant from the early days just after the world changed, before the civil war raged on, and when the Bolsheviks politicized their need for power. She wonders to herself what that all meant. It seems as if none of it was true.

They pass through the garden and past the stable. Although the racehorse is gone, at least Father still has his dog Stopka ("stay"). Nina wonders briefly about the state of the precious animals she so adored. For, in this precarious new age, obviously domesticated cats and dogs are seen scrounging on the streets, trying as best as they can to fend for themselves, until other larger predators have their way with them, and then the frozen winter finishes off those still left.

⅍

Leonid quickens his pace as he walks through the radically changed and empty sidewalks of his Tsarskoe Selo home. He curls his fingers as they hang by his side, as if holding onto the reins of a horse, as he distances himself from the old, once picturesque, mansion where he's met with the local Communist Central Deputies, not aware that his eldest daughter and wife have just passed this intersection on their way home from shopping for potatoes. Still the lawyer that he was, he's discouraged by the meekness with which he's had to present himself in front of this regime that now fills his mind with hatred. The conversation just finished replays itself in his thoughts, "…you will be able to work, Comrade Leonid…and your family and you will take up residence in a village outside of Yaroslavl."

There was little he could say other than to thank the committee, he assures himself. While still seething with anger, he covers the distance to his apartment. His hand no longer releases his fist. "…of course since you are not, nor cannot, become a member of the Communist Party of Workers…" Of this fact he's glad. Tens of thousands of military officers once true to the abdicated and murdered Tsar, joined the half million Soviet troops under Commissar Trotsky, who destroyed the last vestiges of the White Army. He would never, even if it killed him, join the Communist murderers.

Yes, he has picked up some work—minor administrative cases here and there. His past employ was not only prestigious but *required* in Petersburg and Petrograd, and not easily dismissed, he realized. Though laws had been added, Communists only did so to snuff out previously-growing liberties, weighing down the books with reams of additional doctrines. How can he be considered anything but indispensable? This fact has been well proven by his own brother Erich's continued work, though done in worker's clothing while performing the same functions as before.

But now, he is to be banished. Why this hypocrisy, this harassment, this continual admonishment? Who amongst the many elite he's known could be so despised as to bring me in his wake? And then to send me as a judge to the mid-section of greater Russia, to a distant village where I am to rule over civil infractions, domestic disputes, errant crop theft!

Their final statement, "…you will only be able to take the minimum…your apartment here is allocated to the People…you will leave…all behind…" was the worst. Leonid unclenches his fist and jaw as he enters the door leading to the stairway of his apartment. "At least I'll be paid," he reconciles with himself, as he prepares to approach his wife and family.

11

THE DACHA
AND
THE RUSSIAN COUNTRYSIDE
1919–1921

Josephine locks the heavy, inlaid door of her apartment with the thick skeleton key she'll drop off with the new Worker's manager. Strewn about the now-locked and uninhabited rooms are wedding and baptism gifts, Josephine's gilded mirrors, elegant dressing gowns and robes; Leonid's uniforms, awards, and honors; and the children's wooden toys, little navy outfits, dollhouses, and dolls. Left behind are paintings and sculptures, Czechoslovakian and Baccarat crystal, Bristol glass, Tiffany lamps, vases, urns, serving bowls, and other items that Josephine hasn't had the capacity to sell, barter for, or give away. Even Josephine's sister Louise did not have the need for, nor the capacity or audacity to obtain and transport Josephine's most precious objects.

Below and around the array of quickly-sorted-through

and abandoned items are "meuble de style" Art Nouveau furniture, a fourteen-person dining room table and chairs, parlor sofas—Leonid's in fine leather and Josephine's in silk—mahogany armoires and wardrobes, carved wood paneling and ceilings, Italian marble sconces, and Bokhara rugs. Long gone are Josephine's most exquisite diamonds, rubies, sapphires and pearls, Nina's Easter-egg necklace, and the children's golden coins, along with the childhood dreams that went with them; someone else is trading them for potatoes and corn.

Together they walk to the train station with only what they and Leonid's brother Erich can help them carry: a photo album of better days, Josephine's silk embroidered pictures, engraved silver and gold spoons, and other small jewels and precious metals. It's an undignified exit from what had been such a welcome entrance to this centuries-old retreat of the Tsars. The Tsars are gone, and now so are their subjects. The train ride out of their former home is weighted with the knowledge that none of them will ever venture back.

Silently, uneventfully, they exit the train to transfer in Petrograd, the city of the children's birth that they haven't seen since before Red October, before the Social Democratic Revolution, and before the darkness of war. But this trip to the countryside is very different from the days of vacations in Finland. Their travels today will instead take twelve hours, and they've had to bring their own food. They carry bread, pickled fish, a pasty-salty substance, some goat's milk, a chunk of cheese, and some potatoes for their eventual supper. Fortunately, they've arrived in Petrograd un-harassed by the new Communist administrators that have replaced the vacationers, merchants, and former Tsarist administrators that used to make the trip between these two, now politically reprehensible, cities.

Josephine notices Petrograd is less active than when they lived here, while Leonid, all too weary, knows why. The priests, landowners, judges, civil servants, bankers, factory owners, officers, stockbrokers, shopkeepers, grain merchants, oilmen, mine owners, and speculators from former days have all been targets. One by one they've been taken into custody and asked repetitive questions by rote: to what class do you belong? What is your origin? What is your education or profession? Ironically, the tawdrier the answer, the less likely one is to be sentenced to a hard-labor camp or worse. But with no representation to aid the convicted, even former waiters, barkeeps, and ticket takers, with the misfortune of having worked at formerly posh or famous hotels, restaurants, and theaters, have been incarcerated.

The foreigners that made up such a large part of the city are also gone. Nina's little friend, a young British boy, a member of long-time family friends of her parents, and who had been considered eligible for her to marry, is gone; the entire family of five children left for England shortly after the February revolt.

The banks, chemical and metal factories, as well as Grandfather Karl's coach business, are all now owned by the state. As such, and given the end of the war, eighty percent of the factory workers have left for the countryside or other industrial areas. Administrators and tradesmen, even tailors and clerks are gone—either because they've no work, they've been arrested, or their jobs have moved to the new capitol, Moscow, the final insult to the glory of the Great Peter who, it is now said, built this city with forced labor and poorly treated workers. Leonid's old friends have been identified and destroyed with the crassness that one discards of annoying insects.

There will be no time, as in festive journeys of the past, to visit Tante Lulya or any of the now-abandoned posh eateries, tourist kiosks, fine cigar stores, trinket merchants, or toy stores. The family takes their place on the dirty, over-loaded train that will make its way on the route so many take to Moscow. Taking many of the seats are those sick with dysentery, typhus, typhoid, and cholera all of whch are beginning to hit the city with epidemic force. And with the sick are the hungry and "bezprizorniye," or homeless—entire families fleeing the city to scavenge the countryside for work and food.

Josephine sits in the third-class wooden seat near the aisle, dressed in a floppy hat and large, loose-fitting overcoat that protects her hidden precious jewelry and small possessions—objects so similar to those of the Tsarina, whose gold, silver, diamonds, and sapphires at first shielded her from the onslaught of bullets that eventually killed her. Vera sits next to Josephine. Father Leonid sits behind with brother Vova. Nina sits on the aisle with brother Leonya next to her, both in front of Josephine and Vera. Erich sits awkwardly, further in the back amidst the large suitcases, unaccustomed to such movement of people and possessions.

Leonya sits by the window looking out at the altered scenery passing by his window. The countryside is in ruins. At one time the

White Army threatened the former Bolsheviks within 20 miles of the city of Petrograd. Today, signs of the fighting still exist in burnt-out houses and shops. Stragglers board and fill up the rest of the train in their failed attempts at finding a better life. They are once-prosperous Kulaks and farmers, now a bedraggled spectacle making their way by train to somewhere… anywhere. Inflation has led to a barter economy here, where orphans deal in muggers' gangs.

Josephine watches in horror, too weary and overwhelmed to control what can possibly happen on this trip to a village far, far away. She thinks back to the governesses she had, so many that she let go. The one, having been highly referred, who needed to take so many naps for her headaches, only to be found out to be suffering from hangovers. The other she caught putting opium in Nina's milk to make her go to sleep. She no longer worries about such things; her senses overcome by the sight of little children now roaming the countryside for food and shelter.

Halfway to Moscow, the train makes a stop in Yaroslavl, the ancient capitol of pre-Romanov Russia. This will be their exit before they take cabs to the Volga River, where they will need to transfer to a barge for the journey up-river, and eventually to horse and buggy to the remote village, the name of which neither Leonid nor Josephine will ever speak. Leonid leads the family out of the train.

Checkpoints are set up along the way to confiscate assorted plunder, gold rings, watches, cameras and ornaments, from smugglers who have pillaged abandoned countryside manors, city mansions, palaces, apartments, and museums. Josephine has prepared by hiding what she has in her floppy hat and filling up the children's coats and socks with the silver and heirlooms they could manage to carry. Even though it's nearly summertime, Nina wears her felt coat with velvet collars and lapels over a simple dress; eccentric attire that formerly-wealthy and orphaned children can get away with. They pass the checkpoints unmolested in their hired cabs.

The barge they now board has some passenger sections, but is mostly used to transfer goods, machinery, and supplies for the army, up and down the banks of the Volga River. It's uncomfortable and the family is weary, but the children are well behaved, knowing the harshness they will receive from their overwrought mother if they so much as peep.

A chilly breeze drafts through the windows as the boat saunters up the river another hour and a half beyond the historic city of Yaroslavl. Josephine feels the same chill of damp water that she disliked at the cottages. Nina feels no sense of comfort from her mother or from this experience. She sits forlorn on the rolling, long benches. Finally, they disembark at the village nearest the countryside dwellings they still must reach to have shelter.

The humble, hay-filled, peasant wagons make their way outside the village and on into the country. Nina sits with Erich on the planks that are used as seats, the two of them surrounded by suitcases. Her younger brother Vova sits across from her with Leonid. Her older brother, younger sister, and mother follow in a second cart. The children sit quietly, all wondering in their own way, what has become of them and what will happen next. The drivers seem friendly enough, in a customary, peasant sort of way.

As the cart makes its way slowly, Nina notices several, and then counts—twenty, maybe even thirty former retreats that remind her of the dachas in Finland. Although they are a bit rundown and either empty or newly inhabited, they are mostly one-story houses with a few somewhat larger. And many of them include stables and pens for animals. Entire fields nearby are full of wheat and corn, and everyone seems to have a vegetable garden.

Nina's cart now makes its way into a yard surrounded by an untended fence. The yard is thick and lush and full of green pine, birch, maple, oak, walnut, and even some hearty apple trees. Wildflowers mix with tall grasses. And there, up ahead, is a large, pretty dacha, enveloped in a porch with many windows on all sides and a perched rooftop. Beyond it are an old barn where horses were once stabled, a pen for pigs, and an empty chicken coop.

Josephine notices its roof is encircled with carved wooden latticework, its exterior is milky brown, and its eaves and sashes are slightly bowed. Some windows are open. But it is of good size, obviously once stately and well-managed by owners now long gone. It seems as if the house has settled into the resignation of its lost past inhabitants. It's also clear to her that, with all of its windows, it was built primarily for summer use.

Leonid speaks with the driver as Nina sits patiently watching her mother, feeling immense empathy and sadness for what her mother, a lady of cosmopolitan society, might do here. Josephine's buggy halts and she immediately exits. Erich sits with his niece for a moment, waiting in exhaustion for what might be behind the closed doors.

Josephine's skin, hair, and clothing is covered in dust and caked with the unbearable feeling of sticky sweat. Her mouth tastes of the soil and river of Yaroslavl. After the torment she's suffered, she feels no apprehension in staunchly being the first to enter the house. She pushes on one of the large, carved, double wooden doors. It opens with a creak as she tries to keep her reactions to herself. Quickly-fading light filters in through the smudged windows onto the dusty and deserted entrance hall, which in turn opens to the living and dining rooms; fortunate for them that the days are so long. She can still make out the large hallway making its way to the left to what appears to be a master bedroom and a kitchen.

Josephine looks to the right, into the large central living room, empty now except for a randomly-placed, upholstered couch, a couple of scattered wooden chairs, and one small table that do not appear to have anything to do with the decor of the house. She immediately suspects that the old furniture was either stolen or possessed and then replaced, either by request or demand. Another larger table, minus chairs, rests in the dining room beyond. The walls are stained except for square or oval shapes where paintings, portraits, or icons once hung.

Unaided, she continues past the dining room and into the kitchen. Cracked pottery bowls and some old dishes line the open cabinets and shelves. Counters and cabinets are greasy with the handprints and remains of what must have been a village of people taking the cooking utensils, lamps, pots, oils, and soaps from the old owners, who obviously abandoned the estate in a hurry. Josephine picks up a tin spoon and sets it back down on the counter. Sadness, anger, and frustration mixed with some relief that they have such a large home, tremble through her. She forces it all down, as she looks for a kerosene lamp or candles to illuminate the almost faded day.

She continues examining the kitchen, looking into the pantry, and then around the other door leading back to the front hallway. She hears the tired, yet enthralled, voices of her children exploring the other side of the house where another hallway leads to two other bedrooms. Musty brown wallpapered walls and a long red runner lead back toward the master bedroom. She enters. Along one wall is a large bed, perhaps original, as it was probably too large to easily dismantle. And against the far wall is a large brick fireplace formed like an oven, square in shape, like a box with a chimney.

Josephine fully realizes that even though what she had known life to be had been slipping away by degrees, the familiarity of her Tsarskoe Selo home and furnishings brought with it a sense of comfort as well as a certain denial. And even that is gone now. It is here and now that she comes to the conclusion that she'll have to adapt to a completely new life…and suddenly she just doesn't care.

Hearing the voices of her children, husband, and brother-in-law heading her direction, she walks back to the door and shuts it. She takes her hat off, and then pulls her large gold pins out, as her long, dark hair cascades down her back. She sets the pins down on the wobbly dressing table, walks over to the bed, and lies down.

Roman places the slightly soiled fabric footrest underneath the chandelier in the ornately furbished hotel suite. He is in the Caucasus region near the Black Sea where, in the days of the Tsar, wealthy patrons would spend their summer holidays. Today is a damp and ugly April 20th of the new 1920's, perfect for the ghosts of the past to live, but not suitable for comfortable human habitation. Roman steps up, reaching above the dusty, dangling crystals and takes the weighty pieces of gold he's hidden there. He's been assisting General Anton Denikin of the White Guards. The position has led him here, to one of the last outposts of the lost battles of what is loosely regarded as the Civil War. And now it appears as if all will be lost in this region as well. A British ship will be taking him and other fortunate aristocrats, wealthy civilians, and officers who still have their lives, out of Russia forever.

It's been difficult these past months and years for him—years in which events have continued to be unexpectedly bad. And although he has stayed away from the height of activity, Roman has kept his finger on the pulse of change. He knows that the Tsar and his entire family had been taken to Ekaterinburg and shot two years ago, and how some of those loyal to the hateful new regime have made the victims' former home into a tourist destination of sorts; how the Cossacks have been defeated, their institutions destroyed; how Orthodox churches are left in heaps, their treasures stolen or destroyed and desecrated. All of this makes him ashamed of humanity.

He's unaware that his wife and children, after living in Estonia during the Revolution, moved to Finland and then on to Berlin; but he is aware of Estonian independence and knows that Claudia has access to their bank accounts abroad. It has been best he not try to contact his brothers, sisters, or mother; he knows not to threaten whatever security they may have developed for themselves in the rubble of their old, yet cherished, dead society.

Roman was apprised of the defeat in the Crimea where his brother Felix, the prior governor general, had been assassinated, and where the Bolsheviks (now the Soviet Army) pushed the White Army directly into this same Black Sea, where they were trapped and left waiting for the absent British Navy to save them; it was said you could see their bodies, thrown into the sea with rocks tied to their ankles, waving in the water like so much seaweed. Roman hopes to avoid such a death.

He takes his gold coins, places them in his attaché case, and dresses in what remains of his crumpled dark suit, felt hat, gloves, and his fine cane. He, others like him, and the last remaining White Army officials, wait on this creaking wooden dock dressed in their old formal clothes. Listless, quiet, mourning so much loss, Roman imagines it must have been like this shortly after the French Revolution. The British ship can be seen in the distance. They stand. They wait. Soon they'll board and leave their native home, their estates, what remains of their families and friends, and most, if not all, of their belongings…forever.

It had been a cold and sparse winter, and 1921, has entered with unseasonable snows throughout most of spring. As their new home is a summer dacha, it isn't equipped with appropriate furnaces or fireplaces in all the rooms. So in order to stay warm the family closes the door leading to the living room, dining room, and two bedrooms. This leaves only the master bedroom, kitchen, and front entrance hall as living space. The kitchen's oven has a fire burning all day, and the whole family sleeps in Josephine's bedroom. The bedroom fireplace is also used to heat this room, and later at night when it cools down, Leonya takes his mattress and places it on top to sleep. Vera often sleeps with Josephine, and Nina and Vova bring in their own little single beds, setting them up around the circumference of the room. Father Leonid is rarely ever home.

Many of the farmers hoard their own food, secretly not giving all that is requisitioned by the authorities. By good fortune, wheat and domesticated animals are so well grown and stocked here, everyone has a reasonable sufficiency. Meanwhile, widespread famines plague the outlying Volga regions, and epidemics have wiped out hundreds a day back in Petrograd. Leonid, Josephine, and the entire family, have learned that they must plant more of their own food and raise cows.

Still groggy in the early hours of this July morning haze, 14 ½-year-old Nina brushes her hand through her wavy hair, pulls the sheets over her iron-framed single bed, and makes her way through the living room, furnished with an eclectic assortment of furniture, through the kitchen, and out the back door. There will be plenty to do today. She's normally the first up, but today, as she passes by the garden, she can see the thin body of her father sitting in the dirt of the plot nearest the house.

Leonid loves working in the garden, and has obviously taken an early start this morning, surprising his young daughter. There are a multitude of flowers—geraniums, summer lilies, and rose bushes in blue, red, pink, and yellow—and even wild poppies mixed in with those reinvigorated plants that musht have been originally planted by the previous owner. Leonid turns the soil with his old spade, refreshing the ground, tearing out the new, quickly growing weeds and vines with a passion. His thoughts are on the roses he used to plant in Finland for beauty's sake only, and about the vegetables he'll plant here of necessity for food.

His oversized jacket pockets are filled with seeds for tomatoes and cucumbers, and roots for carrots, cabbage, potatoes, beets, and rutabaga, which he's bought and bartered for. Vegetables are available again now that Lenin's highly-publicized New Economic Policies are in effect. The Communists have allowed peasants to sell on the open market that which they don't need to supply the government. Forced requisitioning for the time being has proved unsuccessful for the country's food needs. Unaccounted for in the evolving administration of a new Communist order is this paradox: it takes motivation to grow crops, but anyone showing ambition is officially looked down upon. Why produce anything when you cannot benefit from your efforts, and you risk being denounced for your success.

Everyone still has his or her own plots. The peasants seem to know better: they don't necessarily dislike the Communists, they don't like them either. Peasants complain that life was always bad in the country and things never really change; the only change is just a different set of statues in the city, so the saying goes.

Leonid has made a circle of friends he plays cards with in the village when he's in town and not working in outlying municipalities. Cards have become less risky because, even though many here live off the land, no one has much money and everyone else knows it. One disturbing fact that he's learned from the local gentry, of sorts, is of the demise of the former landlord whose dacha he now resides in. Sometimes when he works in the garden, he feels his presence. "Poor man," Leonid thinks, "who had to run into the woods to hide after the Revolution, only to be hunted down like a fox—and later found shot to death." Leonid brushes the thought out of his mind.

Just as he does, he places his spade, looks up, and notices his beautiful, young daughter Nina walking through the garden to feed her beloved animals. He feels pride at seeing such a fresh sight, and smiles at her. "How is my Ninatschka," he shouts at her as he watches her heading barefoot for the barn.

He regrets that soon he'll have to pack his bag and leave again. His job has been taking him to ever more remote villages to rule on civil cases, domestic matters, divorce, petty thievery, and sometimes even non-political homicide. The political issues are always left to a communist judge not trained in civil law nor educated in any formal courtroom proceedings. He pities the people that are called before angry power mongers. He does what he can to be fair and to compensate for the huge delays and inefficiencies of what can hardly be called a legal system. However, his training and experience can only do a little to aid rural areas where local laws are haphazardly made to serve the few and punish the many.

He resides in small hovels and huts with peasants who make their homes in these God-forsaken, distant, forested villages which resonate with the howling of wolves in the middle of the night. He's seen the bones of the stray cow or lamb that has been eaten lying in the middle of a dirt road. When away, he misses his family. It's frightening to be alone in these far reaches of humanity. But soon the cart will be coming to pick him up and escort him away. He relishes the thought that it's no longer winter and he won't have to make the hours-long journey by sled.

Nina keeps herself busy on all days. She helps her father with the garden and tends to it when he's away. Mostly she takes care of the animals, feeding and milking the cows and goat, and letting them roam in the pastures. She takes pleasure from tending to and feeding the chickens, ducks, roosters and rabbits. Cooking is less fun, but she approaches it with an earnest desire to make her contribution. She's learned how to peel and boil potatoes, fry chicken, duck, and fish, how to make cucumber salad in summer and hearty soups in winter.

No one else helps with these duties much—neither Father nor brothers nor younger sister Vera. Mother has learned how to cook, but when it comes time to clean, she has told Nina, to her surprise, "Why bother, just leave it." And the family has hired a local woman for a small wage to do the necessary laundry.

Vova is growing to be a bit of a good-tempered, handsome rascal. Leonya is quieter now, and spends a lot of his time in solitude, either sketching or entertaining himself in ways that neither Nina nor anyone else is informed of. Vera is turning out to be quite a little lady, a duplicate image of her mother, with a natural predisposition to a regal bearing.

Nina smiles at her father shyly. She's grown quite fond of him, even though the two rarely speak. This she doesn't question. For, even in the middle of the countryside, her parents still act toward the family and one another as they always have: gentrified, civil, and with an old air of blooded nobility. On the other hand, Nina knows her father and mother don't agree on much, even though their disagreements are veiled by silence and glances rather than any verbal attacks. Overall, nothing seems out of the ordinary even though everything is unusual compared to what it was. For Nina it's easy to adapt, so she takes on her new responsibilities without any judgment or predisposition. She knows her mother has little facility for this lifestyle, so that means Nina has to help.

Josephine, also having awakened early, looks out onto the sunny, green forest encircling the house. Doing as much as she's amenable to, she begins to prepare for her only pleasure, her morning walk. The bed and bedroom have never become comfortable for her. Having spent most of her life in her own private quarters, she finds it inconceivably difficult to now be sleeping with her husband and entire family in one room during winter. Even though she's physically here this summer morning, her mind is elsewhere. She not only misses her morning tea, but also cannot seem to adjust to the lack of letters that would have arrived in the city from friends and family informing her of social responsibilities.

Although letters are infrequent, those that haven't been tampered with tell her that her father has invested the monies he received from the properties and businesses he had owned in Berlin. His one-third payback was large compared to the one-tenth exchange rate she and her husband were awarded. He now owns property and apartment buildings near the Brandenburg Gate in the center of Berlin. These are properties he bought relatively cheaply with Russian gold in the current hyper-inflated Germany.

Nina finishes with the cows and heads back to the garden to see if she can't help father with the planting. But he's gone now, the plot barely begun. She'll look for the seeds and roots and do it herself. Digging in the garden brings her the same peace of mind that feeding the animals does. And she can play in the dirt in her summer dress all she wants, knowing mother will have nothing to say about being properly elegant and ladylike when their lives now depend on her very willingness to get dirty.

12

THE CROW'S EGGS, THE CHICKEN AND THE TREACHEROUS JOURNEY 1921–1924

Vova wakes up early this morning and flips the page of the calendar he's received as an eleventh birthday present to July 21, 1921. He likes the repeating numbers, similar to June 10, 1910, when he was born. It's summertime, his favorite time of year, and he's got plenty to do. Though he barely remembers the trips to Finland and hasn't been to school since just after the Revolution, summer always means time for a lot of activities, and today he can't wait to start.

Many days he plays in the forest with the other boys, although he often gets into fights with them. He's beginning to read more now that father secretly brings home banned books by old authors. The writings instill in him a love for his people, more so than the Communist rhetoric can possibly set his mind against them. And even though he doesn't see eye to eye with a lot of the Kulaks he plays with, he respects them as Russians.

Last fall he and his brother spent a few days with father cutting hay in a farmer's field, which they later used for the cows and goats. And in winter he's begun to cut wood for the family. He likes being helpful this way. It makes him feel strong and grown up. But today, he's got another item on his agenda. Nina had mentioned that she thought she heard noises up in the fir tree outside her bedroom. This is significant because about a month ago he devised a plan to replace the crow's eggs in a nest up there with chicken eggs.

On a couple of occasions he's already climbed up to check on them, but they hadn't hatched. But today will be different. Brushing his thick blond hair back with his hands and throwing on his big calico shirt and a pair of father's old pants, he rushes out of his room. First, he'll tell his older sister Nina. Long gone are the days when he had to fear her pushing him away just for being underfoot, but he's grown to respect her nonetheless. The tree is under her bedroom, and he'd rather not shock her by just climbing up the tree.

Nina wakes up to a busy day. First she'll feed the baby lambs, affectionately called Bulka and Arabka, which are kept in a box beside her bed. Normally, she suckles them with a makeshift baby's bottle and some goat's milk. She took this task over after noticing that their true mother hadn't nurtured or fed them. Now they think that *she's* their mother. But, in the last few days, they've gotten to the point where they follow her around the house and yard and seem to be eating solid food.

"Tap…tap," Nina hears a knock on her door. "It's Vova," her brother says politely. She walks to her door and opens it a crack, knowing what he's up to.

"Nina, I'm going to climb the tree and check on my chickens."

"Okay," Nina says, "wait until I feed my lambs and I'll go out with you." It isn't long before Nina throws on her dress and runs out the door, barefoot as usual. Vova, already quite sure of himself, makes his way slowly up the first branch of the tall tree. The crows' nests aren't very close to the ground, but the tree has many solid branches. He makes his way up the second rung, and to the third. Nina waits below, curious and entertained. She wasn't quite sure about the idea in the first place, but now that they've hatched she's fascinated.

It seems as if her little brother's making good progress as the large, dry pine needles rain down on her. Vova precariously shimmies across the final thick branch, ignoring the risk of the situation. He's almost there and, with a slight pull up the branch above him, he looks inside the nest to see what his ears have already informed him to be true. There, sitting in the center of the nest, are three baby chickens. One by one he places them in his large calico shirt pockets, and then lowers himself to each descending branch of the precarious, spindly tree.

Going down is much more difficult than going up, especially since he doesn't want to crush the birds. Nina yells from below, "Do you have them?"

"Yes, Nina," he says, as he grasps the branch nearest the

ground and hops down, joyous at defeating and confusing nature all at the same time.

☙

It's been brisk and rainy most days of this September, 1921. But today the sun has made a re-appearance all morning and well into the afternoon. The mud has caked and dried enough for Nina to spend time in the yard covering the earth in the garden with hay to protect some of father's plants for the winter. She likes it because it gives her more opportunity to be outside with the animals.

The chickens Vova caught are old enough to be fed by Nina on bits of crumbled-up egg. They follow her about the yard as much as her lambs do. They, too, have decided to consider her their mother. The heavy rains have made what was a small pond in back of the house grow into a larger body of water, and Nina's chickens freely wander near it. In her growing isolation, Nina speaks to them as she would to a person, enjoying them more than she does most people. She has felt as if she doesn't truly fit in anywhere for so long now, and she's beginning think she never will. But that no longer even matters as she's proud of who she is.

She's almost finished pushing the straw next to the house to both cover the garden and insulate the house, when something nagging makes itself known: there are only two chickens instead of three.

Making a clicking sound with her tongue, she quickly starts searching the back yard and the chicken coup. The other three hens have a difficult time keeping up with her so she locks them up. And then, as she rushes back toward the far end of the garden, she sees something floating in the shallow edge of the pond. Her heart beating like heavy rain, she runs as fast as she can, with memories of her own conflict with the blasted water surfacing. With the skill of a lifeguard at the public beach in Finland she grabs the water-bloated, limp chicken. It's lifeless, but this does not dissuade her. She won't waste time shedding tears.

Nina holds the bird by its feet while spinning around, hoping the water will fly from its lungs. She rubs its chest and warms it under its wings. Then, remembering what she's heard of villagers saving drowning victims, she runs to the house. She tears through the linen closet, grabs a sheet, and runs outside. She places the bird in it, and swings it round and round—round and round, again and again and again. The bird still appears to be lifeless, so she sits on the ground with it, continuing to warm the body.

Josephine, having become aware of Nina's behavior, exits the back porch and walks toward her dirty and wet youngster. Her glare is enough for Nina to understand she must explain herself. To this Josephine's response is curt and blunt, "The chicken is dead. Now leave it alone." Nina obeys, sets it down nearest the coop, brushes it off, and goes back in to shuffle hay.

A strange thing occurs as she walks one last time to the shed. A solitary chicken clucks as it wanders, trying to find its siblings.

Terribly relieved, Nina will not hold her tongue for a second in telling everyone how she saved the chicken.

❧

It is late summer, 1922. Communist Russia is now called the Union of Soviet Socialist Republics, a fact that Nina could care less about. She pauses at her work in the garden to look up past the endless trees, bristling in the cooling breeze, radiating yellow, red, ocher, and brown. It's a simple day. There is no need to dwell on anything in particular.

A young, lanky, peasant farmer, who looks old beyond his years, comes up behind and startles her. She looks up and sees his once-round, still jolly, partially toothless face. He chuckles in a jovial manner; still chipper from the resonating effects of the vodka he drank last night and this morning.

"What's that you're picking," he asks good-naturedly.

"It's a tomato," Nina responds, hands dirty and basket nearly full. "Haven't you ever eaten a tomato before?"

"No, but are they like apples?" He responds curiously.

Nina picks a ripe one and says calmly, as she brushes it off with her strong hands, "Remember it's a vegetable and not a fruit. Normally you cut it up and eat it with some salt and oil." She hands it to him. He studies it briefly and then takes a big, messy bite.

"Oh that's horrible. Uck, it makes my gut churn," he says

in his heavily accented slang, while handing the wet sample back to her. Nina laughs, grabs the half eaten vegetable, and places it in her basket. She'll save it. She knows what its like to go to bed still hungry.

The man bumbles back to the road he ventured off of. Nina chuckles to herself confidently. She feels good about herself. After all, she's grown quite beautiful with her curly, jet-black hair, and thin, shapely body. Boys haven't been a reality even though she'll be sixteen this year. There's certainly no one suitable that she's ever met in the village. "They're all uneducated farmers and peasants who couldn't hold a conversation with me or my parents," she's rationalized. Plus, she's reasoned it's hard to be selfish with her time because she has had so many responsibilities.

Everyone in the area must hoard large portions of their food in order not to have to give away too much of their hard work from private plots of wheat, corn, little vegetable gardens, and livestock. No one trusts that, even with the New Economic Order, things will always stay this way. But some food is still requisitioned, so later she'll help Leonya and Vova bring the milk from their cow to the village Party office. One especially good part of this, though, is that, after the officials have skimmed the milk, Nina and her brothers will be able to drink the remaining cream. With this in mind, she goes back to finish picking the thick, ripe, red tomatoes.

1923 has been a very good year for the family, all things considered. There is plenty of food put away for the approaching winter, and, for Nina, plenty of animals. As mid-day turns slowly to late afternoon, Nina makes one more trip back to the barn to check on the cows and calf, the lambs, the baby goat, and the many chickens and ducks, worrying if everyone isn't full and happy. It's sad to her that another calf she's been raising will have to be slaughtered again this year, and, like the last, hung to freeze in the storage shed; bits of it hacked off all winter for food.

She puts on her coat, the one that she got when she was ten. It's now so small on her sixteen-year-old body it fits like a jacket, the velvet lapels worn down where she's let her favorite dairy cow lick her. Inside the barn, she talks to the animals while tidying up the hay in the goat's pen and feeding the chickens. She then leaves to inspect the cows and calf, which she let out earlier to roam freely in the yard to eat the tall, fall grasses.

She shuts the gate and calmly goes to look in the yard, knowing she must have been too preoccupied to notice where she left them last. Looking from front to back, the search bears no fruit. A rather ill-tended gate separates the fenced in larger yard from the adjoining immense forests. Nina approaches, and finds it open as well. Growing more alarmed, she now thinks that perhaps one of her brothers, who should be taking better care of the fence in the first place, must have haphazardly left it this way. Nina has no doubt; the cow *must* be in the forest. Shutting the gate and immersing herself under the thick canopy of green leaves and trees, Nina thinks about her father's frequent stories of bears and wolves.

Normally, she enjoys the forest for the mushroom-picking excursions she's taken on humid summer days. But summer has mostly faded and fall is on the horizon, the animals already stocking their food for winter. The forest is rich in life. Though the leaves are beginning to slowly change colors, the trees feel very much alive, and the mulch from felled branches and vegetation smells good. The hoots, taps, trill, rush, snap, and crack of small animals surrounds her.

A trail distinguishes itself, probably carved from the movement of larger creatures. She quickens her pace, her heart beating more rapidly, keeping pace with her rising anxiety. The fact presents itself that she's come quite a distance, well beyond familiar territory. The forest is dark with overcrowded vegetation. She can't imagine her cow having come this far, and has no idea as to where it could have wandered. The possibility of being lost punctures her consciousness. Sounds that earlier didn't concern her take on a more ominous tone. The rustle in the leaves and snap of a rotten branch begin to signal a more sinister presence than that of a squirrel, chipmunk, or skunk.

The path she's been following merges into less trodden areas or nothing at all. To the right, a narrow passage may or may not exist. On her left, the semblance of a trail seems to bend, maybe circling, maybe ending in the den of a large animal. Tired and not wanting to take any more chances, she chooses the more direct, yet less distinct, path on the right. She anxiously tears through the shrubbery.

Unfortunately, the trail narrows from both sides and above. Nina is forced to come to a crawl. Once majestic trees and airy canopies have shrunk to ugly bushes and strangling vines. She imagines a wolf crying in the distance as night begins to fall. The sound of a squirrel moving across a branch becomes the threat of a wild boar or hungry bear. Exasperated, Nina stops moving as tears slide down her cheeks, knowing that finding her own way back is nearly impossible.

A comforting sound breaks her tears. A rooster crows off in the distance. That can only mean one thing, that there must be a house or village nearby! Optimistically, strength regained, Nina pushes her way forward through the bramble, toward the sound. And there up ahead, exposed to the dwindling sunlight, is an open field. In the middle of the field is a small herd of cows and a young boy. Tears mix with cries for joy as Nina runs to the boy.

"I've lost my cow," she says embarrassed.

"Is it that one over there?" he asks, not quite sure what else to say to the crying young woman. Nina looks in the direction he points, relieved that, indeed, it is. She walks toward her cow while wiping away her tears with her dirty hands. There's no doubt in her mind about not going back into the woods, so Nina asks the boy how to get to the nearest road. She'll take her chances on a road, knowing someone might come along—maybe even her father, or brothers. But in either case, once on the road, she *will* find her way back.

❧

Leonid pushes open the door of his home and trudges heavily into the kitchen where his family sits eating their evening potatoes, cabbage, and bits of beef. His beard is caked with frost and his boots are wet with ice as they clunk against the hard wood floor, surprising and alerting the family to his return on this bitter February day of 1924.

His face shows exhaustion. His hair is disheveled and he is pale. Nina stands up, walks over to him and helps him take off his snow-encrusted felt overcoat. Josephine sits quizzically aware that her husband's occupation requires more of him than he's capable of dealing with. Leonid sits down, puts his elbows on the stocky wood table in an uncustomary position, and cradles his face in his hands. He then sits back in his chair and uncharacteristically begins to recall his adventures to the entire family. "I'm afraid that I have been wrongly accused and arrested for the past week and a half." Everyone at the table remains respectfully alert and completely silent. Josephine continues her gaze in her upright posture directly across the table from her husband, expressionless.

Leonid continues, "While in a small village three hours by carriage from here, the local party officials arrested me, under false charges, that I had accepted a bribe. They took me to the cellar of a large house used as a communal court, where I lived in the basement jail for two days." "I later stood," he continues undaunted but revealing his anger, "in front of a Communist judge for such cases.

He was so full of hate for my person and what I have stood for all of my life that he literally foamed at the mouth! I had no defense but myself, and stood my ground."

Everyone remains silent though visibly disturbed. Vera begins to cry, and is immediately reprimanded by her mother. As the little girl stifles her tears, Leonid continues, "I demanded that he name my accusers and rightfully denied any wrongdoing." With this statement he regains his former familiar confidence, standing up and positioning himself at the table in a stance he often reserved for the courtroom. Nina and her siblings have never seen him like this before, but admire him all the more now. He continues, "Of course none were to be found." He leans forward, "And they released me." Point proven.

At this, Nina stands up, takes a ceramic bowl, and walks to the stove to refill it. He stops her. Holding back his emotions again, he clears his throat, and pronounces in a loud and clear voice, "I've spoken with my superiors regarding this matter and have been instructed that I have been reassigned to Yaroslavl. We will all be moving no later than this coming spring." The rest of the winter will be difficult without any more money, Leonid knows, but he's shared more with his family than he has ever done in the past. Josephine stands up from the table and walks into the bedroom. Nina refills the bowl, while everyone else remains silent and still. The children know it isn't their place to exhibit anxiety or displeasure with their father.

13

YAROSLAVL: VOVA BRUSHES WITH
DEATH AND NINA
EXPLORES INDEPENDENCE
1924–1927

The animals were eaten or sold, giving Nina little time to appropriately absorb their loss. And father's dog Stopka is gone—the dog he had for so many years since before the War. When Nina asked him what had become of Stopka, he replied, "Oh, I sold him to make sausage." Nina didn't know if he was joking, but assumed he must have been.

Lenin is dead since this January, 1924, his body lies supine in an open glass casket in the former Petrograd where people, it is reported, line up for hours to view it. Nina's birth city, once St. Petersburg, then Petrograd, has now been renamed Leningrad in his honor. Nina knows too well the story of how Peter the Great almost sacrificed his own life to save a worker from drowning, and wonders what acts of bravery the intellectual revolutionary Lenin ever did to deserve such an honor. Unbeknownst to her, the city's renaming is more of a political move than an honor. The new rising power, lead by Stalin, has nothing but fear, disdain, and prejudice against the founders who claimed they were fighting for workers' rights. Trotsky, Lenin's accomplice, is proof of this by his having been ousted by the new powers-that-be.

The mugginess of the heat today is unbearably like the moist summers in the marshy old St. Petersburg. It seems as if this ancient city, founded by Yaroslavl the Wise nine hundred years ago, is muddled in the weight of heavy, unmoving air. Medieval churches appear on most every corner; their relics pillaged, and their ancient carved doors either shuttered or reopened to their current use as public buildings. But, this city has had its historical and cultural moments. For Yaroslavl is the traditional birthplace of Russian theater and was the ancient second capital to the new Soviet capital city of Moscow.

Nina walks briskly with her bread rations in hand. She passes a market where items are being sold by peasants and the newly-made poor. She notices a stand with some worn and chipped crockery pots and bowls, probably from what once was a wealthy family reduced to nothing. The table is covered with what looks like an old flag with an emblem of a bear and silver axe on it.

She approaches the young woman, who also appears to be about seventeen, who tends the table. Nina has no extra money but likes the bear image. It's strong and powerful, and shows the bear as conqueror, not as conquered. It seems redeeming for the poor hunted creature that is such a beautiful, powerful animal. The woman looks at Nina. They share something in common; an intelligent, sensitive glance. They smile at each other.

"Hello, what's this tablecloth with the bear, Comrade," Nina asks.

"Hello, Comrade, responds the woman. It's the old flag of Yaroslavl." The girl notices Nina's mannerisms, studied politeness, and shy, coquettish glance, and feels confident in sharing. "Yaroslavl was the name of the first Tsar," she continues. "Legend has it that he slew a magical and tyrannical bear near the center of the city, and then civilized its people. We use this as a tablecloth now. No one would buy such a decadent reminder of our now-modified city history. But I like it, don't you?"

Nina nods briefly in approval and then reaches for one of the large bowls, as she casually looks around her, hoping that no one has noticed their illicit conversation. Father's arrest has added to her sensitivity. Replacing the bowl, knowing that such a purchase is beyond her means, she starts to walk away. The girl calls out to her, "I haven't seen you here before. Are you new to the city?"

Nina responds with a quick "Yes," feeling untrusting and embarrassed at not being able to buy the needed bowls.

"Perhaps, I'll see you again, sometime, Comrade," the girl continues. Nina simply turns, nods her head, and goes on with her appointed tasks along the sidewalk of empty storefronts and ragtag people.

Nina enjoys the city life bustling with the activities of so many people. And, even though most of those she meets behave quite differently from her, the combination of her urban upbringing and more-recently adopted countrified experience disposes itself quite well in fitting in here. Nonetheless, she'll quicken her pace, conscientious of meeting her expectations to prepare the evening's meal.

In a short walk, she arrives at the entrance of the old, and once beautiful, three-story apartment building that Leonid secured during the last few weeks before the family left the countryside. The apartment building is packed with many families where it had once only contained a few. A constant influx of migrating families has escaped famine and decreased farming in the countryside to find work in Yaroslavl and other big cities. Living space is divided per head, no longer determined by one's financial means and free choice.

Nina passes young boys playing on the front sidewalk in their worn and frayed smocks and caps. Clasping the bundle containing bread, salt, and butter, she walks up the twisting three flights of stairs to the top floor. Turning the corner of the darkened hallway, she enters the main door and cluttered entrance hall of a once-large, single-family apartment. Just beyond, a family inhabits the living room, their belongings filling every crevice. To the right is the kitchen, which is communal. Nina must pass through it before pausing to slide open a door into what had been the dining room. This is the entrance to where they now live.

It's twilight and nearly dinnertime. The entire family is home already, waiting for Nina. Vova sits on a mattress which lies on the floor. Vera sits studying on makeshift wood panels spread over chairs. Josephine sits nearest the window, reading a book. This one room has become an entire apartment for Nina's six-person family. Most discomforting of all is the room beyond their dining-room apartment which is occupied by a man, his wife, and son. This family's only exit is through the dining room.

Nina places the bundle on the table and walks around her brother and sister, who have begun to adapt to being constantly under each other's feet for the past four months. At least both Vova and Vera are back in school during the day, and Leonya, already nineteen, has found a job working as an assistant photographer.

Josephine looks up. The light from the window accentuates her wrinkles. She's aged in this tiny room, in her impoverished condition. The light does not do her justice. That conditions have deteriorated from bad to worse is a fact that she comprehends every moment of every day. Never in her worst nightmare could she have imagined her life would come to this, and she has little patience in understanding the justification of the menace that constantly threatens their lives. Her only constant thought is that this reality, like her past reality, will not last, and if it means taking on the responsibility to do something about it, she's resigned to that destiny. No one but her need know how much and how constantly she suffers. And if silence is her chosen means of survival for the time being, then silent she will be. For this existence—this new, imposed existence—is not due the respect of even her feigned acceptance.

Josephine realizes that living and existing in a room with none of her former possessions is survivable; and beneath her polished, elegant exterior is the sharpness and dexterity of a darting hummingbird. She says nothing, closes her book, and walks to the dresser to take out some of the old plates brought over from the country house; they are odd and un-matching remnants from various periods of their ever-changing life. She cleans off the table, repeating to herself that this is only temporary.

Nina's heart aches, not for herself, but for the perseverance of her mother. She wants to do everything she can to help her, to protect her, but there isn't anything she can do. This knowledge pains her. She also says nothing and begins the process of making the family's dinner. It's still early, and the other families living in the subdivided apartment aren't using the kitchen yet. First, there will be soup made out of a hearty vegetable base, as Josephine's distaste for fish has eliminated the practicality of a more traditional fish soup. Then she'll make *cutletki* out of hamburger, breadcrumbs, onions, and potatoes. All in all, everyone will be adequately fed, although there is never enough for extra.

Everyone spends as much time out of the apartment as possible, especially now that it's summertime. Luckily, the neighboring family moved out of the parlor adjoining the dining room late last summer, allowing the family to expand. It is also fortunate that Uncle Yuri, Tante Lulya's husband, insisted on shipping some extra furniture to Yaroslavl, furniture they had taken from Grandfather Karl and Grandmother Josephine's abandoned home. Now a large, old-fashioned couch, where Nina sleeps, sits in one room, and a large bed for Josephine and Leonid is in another. A full dining room set separates the twin bed where Vova sleeps and the mattress on the floor for Leonya. Vera still sleeps on her mattress on top of wooden doors. The first room contains an old, formal, upright piano left by some prior tenant and a large armoire also shipped from Leningrad by Uncle Yuri.

Vova has made a makeshift cage for some Carrier pigeons. The sounds of their constant rustle and coo softly descends from the attic. It's an odd arrangement, he knows, but additional wire needs to be attached somewhere to expand the cage. From another collector, as a favor, he has just received four more perky. dusty-gray birds, making a total of thirteen. First, he'll expand the cage, and then he'll begin training them. The birds have all flown back so far. It helps that the apartment building is in a heavily-treed, slightly elevated area, and some distance from the center of the city.

He's considered using the rooftop as a staging ground for their flight. But, last winter, when he climbed there, he lost his footing on some black ice and slid to the gutter. If it weren't for quickly punching his heels through the partially frozen ice in the gutters, and using his pocketknife to hack his way back up, he would be dead by now. Even though it is summertime, he has no intention of climbing up there again.

Vova reaches around outside the small attic's window, feeling for something to attach the strand of wire to. There's an old rusty metal pipe he can feel, just outside his view. As he bends the wire around it, the entire pipe breaks off and falls to the ground. So, too, does the electric wire supported by the pipe. It lands with a jumping spark.

Vova looks down wondering what to do. It occurs to him that he shouldn't touch it. Something about electricity, he's learned, is dangerous. "Well," he thinks, "I might as well just start to clean up here and see if I can't find someone to handle this wire." But then the thought occurs to him that when the children taking summer courses come home, one of them might touch it. He sees them everyday, and some of them he knows from the school he and his sister Vera attend most of the rest of the year.

Nina has a small garden to maintain, in the back of the apartments, that the family has been awarded. She's spent most of the morning stringing tin to a line to keep the crows away, and now works her way around to the front of the building.

Vova's walked down to street level, not thinking very clearly about what methods to utilize to move the wire. Outweighing this more practical concern is his fear that if someone else touches the wire, not only might they get terribly hurt or die, he might end up in the gulag for murder. At fifteen this doesn't seem right to him. "Perhaps, since it hasn't moved in a while, the energy isn't in it any longer," he rationalizes. So he reaches down and grabs the electric snake with his right hand.

Nina turns the corner just in time to watch her brother fly up in the air—up, and then down. Her brother, too shocked to scream, continues to fly, attached to the long chord. Nina knows she can't touch him or the wire, and frantically wonders what to do. "An axe," she thinks, "I'll get an axe. The wooden handle will protect me from the electricity." Turning, she runs to the back storage shed. Just as she begins to turn the corner, she sees Vova shoot to the ground, suddenly released from the wire. He lands hard, with a sloppy bounce, as Nina rushes over to him. Shocked and embarrassed, he ignores her, picks himself up, and wobbles away like a drunken sailor. Nina stands motionless for a while and then rushes into the apartment to Josephine. Vova enters shortly thereafter, shaken and sullen. Josephine contacts the authorities. Everyone watches as they turn off the power and take the wire away.

The days are growing shorter by the week. Mother and Father's impatience with their situation has grown to a semblance of beaten-down acceptance. 1925 has been a mediocre year, at best, in a world otherwise bourgeoning with new styles, new attitudes, and new post-war value systems that no longer include Trotsky and some of the original revolutionary leaders. TASS, the new official Soviet News Agency, works relentlessly at exposing how good everything is. Josephine's beloved Russian art is alive and well, exhibiting its Extreme Rationalism concepts of super workers. Leonya's photography is gaining a broader acceptance, and he's had his first exhibit of photographs of young, upstart musicians. Father Leonid is home much of the time, and Nina has surmised that somehow he's lost his job. Vera spends her time playing with pretty, little girlfriends as delicate and quiet as she. And, for some time, financial concerns have made life difficult. But then, a miracle happened, and money was awarded from the stolen Finnish properties all these years later; money they so badly need to keep the family afloat another year.

Nina and her parents walk together this still, light, summer evening. The cooling breeze feels good against Nina's short hair. Together they make an uncustomary threesome as they escape the confines of their apartment to visit an old lady friend of Josephine's.

So much of social activity in days past had been for multiple purposes—purposes now worn through to obviousness like the material on Nina's dress; the material purchased by Josephine with the last of Nina's initialed childhood silverware. For now that Nina is 18, her parents find it important to socially introduce her as best they can in the *old* ways. To a large degree, Nina is happy with this. Because her parents want what had been and still is, in their minds, the elitist best for her, she hasn't felt any pressure to meet any of the inappropriate boys around town.

The sidewalks are often busy, as is usual for any large city here, regardless of the continuing persecution of the formerly bourgeoisie and wealthy classes. Many are arrested or long gone, having immigrated to friendlier countries still recovering from the Great War. And though dressed in simple jackets with old-style lapels and tailoring (remnants from friends and their own recycled wardrobes) Nina's parents still retain the innate elegance natural to their beings. Nina's proud of this, and, although raised for half of her life outside the confines of the stricter, more regal society of her birth, duplicates her mother's mannerisms as much as she possibly can.

The apartment building they've now reached is a beautiful old building, the entranceway framed by an elaborate façade. Broken wrought iron lanterns hang on both sides, but the building maintains the majesty of a forgotten era. They walk through the front door and up one flight of stairs, the lower level apartments always having been the most prestigious given the lesser number of stairs to climb. Josephine knocks and is greeted by an elderly woman wearing a lace collar and pleated ankle-length dress. She welcomes the threesome gracefully, then escorts them through the front entrance hall into a back room that was once the master bedroom.

The woman explains that the entire floor had belonged to her and her husband, now deceased, who was a ranking officer of the Tsar's army. She says this with the confidence that comes with her age. She is neither awkward nor afraid, having survived the purges that decimated her social level of friends and acquaintances. Her son, too, had been murdered in the last war.

Nina takes in the room as the woman ushers her mother, father, and her, to sit down. Old clocks, beautiful inlaid tables, chairs covered with fine wool textiles, an old French crystal chandelier, Asian china, and an ornate silver candelabrum adorn the room. Every corner is full of opulent objects. All open spaces contain the most precious of what had been a household of delicate and priceless heirlooms.

Nina makes herself comfortable in a manner similar to her mother's straight-backed posture, on the soft fabric of the mahogany-framed loveseat. The old woman pours tea from a shining silver samovar. Nina is neither completely familiar nor unfamiliar with the setting surrounding her. She knows of the life the old woman lived prior to the revolution. But something odd and uncomfortable of a past now dead and buried haunts her. It triggers her imagination of the life lost to her. Perhaps it's the bizarre nature of so many beautiful things now placed carefully, yet inharmoniously, in this cramped setting, that makes it so strange.

Nina looks through the beveled glass of an old cabinet, sees the fine china and delicate crystal propped there, and realizes the value in them beyond that of price or possession. It's the value of a life that she was once born to; the value of membership in a society that no longer values loyalty to the ideas that created these objects—that no longer cherishes the craftsmanship inherent in the delicate, tangible effects reflected in the cuts of the fine, handcrafted crystal.

The open conversation of her parents discussing the horrid state of culture, politics, and communist economics, only confirms the restlessness she feels. She is overwhelmed with the conversation and the position that her parents have placed her in. The other adults unrelentingly continue reliving the life that was stolen from them and glorifying what is gone. Nina answers when questioned, as she has been taught to, remembering her etiquette and posture, while simultaneously enjoying the smooth feeling of a silver spoon against her palette, as she licks off the sugar she's allowed herself to stir into her hot black tea.

Just as Nina's comfort level begins to improve with a revitalized, ingrained privilege and familiarity and acceptance of her new adult status, the conversation comes to an end. Josephine and Leonid, aware of the elderly woman's depleting energy level, have considerately toned down their conversation, signaling that it's time to leave. The two hours have been a magical transition for Nina, although an imperfect one. This afternoon has been her rite of passage to this new, strange old world.

❧

At sixteen, in the year 1926, Vova is mostly self-educated from the old, popular Russian books his parents have been able to procure. He's read Tolstoy, Pushkin, and Dostoevsky. But of course, Vova has also obligingly been exposed to the perfunctory Lenin and to the German philosophers that inspired him, Marx and Engels. Vova has a great sense of himself, and looks at obstacles in his young life as challenges. His good experiences with all he remembers of his time in the country, and the brief memories of the big, old capitol,

209

have given him a self-confidence that easily mixes with his adoption of his father's warm nature, as well as his naive, earthy idealism and tendency to be headstrong. Taking risks and making decisions are inherent to his nature.

The city is filled with rivers and tributaries. It surges, most of all, with the strength of the Volga. The Volga feeds the city, has been a main source for its development, and surrounds it with a nourishing source of ebb and flow. Products, people, and ideas move from the capitol of Moscow, from Siberia, Asia Minor, the Caucasus, Leningrad, and greater Russia, hundreds of miles away.

Vova and his young comrades aren't intimidated by the loud, burly loggers who work on the long barges of felled logs bound together and floating down the river. Instead, he and his friends taunt the loggers and use the floating forests as jumping platforms for their antics. Splashing each other, they jump into the powerful, thick water, freely clad only in swimming trunks.

Vova disobeys the annoyed raftsmen's shouts from a particularly large floating island of logs. He runs past the edge and lands with a cannonball splash into the surging river. Underwater, he opens his eyes and sees light penetrating through the edges of the bound logs. He hears the muffled thunder of the heavy tree trunks bashing against one another, and feels the push of the current.

Glancing to his right from his underwater viewpoint, he sees only wood interspersed with bluish-green and yellow light. Looking to his left, he sees a ceiling of more felled trees, with no exit. Quickly he swims, turning his agile body around and around endless corridors of logs that move in all directions.

He contains his anxiety, familiar with this aquatic world, having swum since he was a little boy. His lungs are strong and can hold a large amount of oxygen. His heart beats with his awareness of the tomb of weighty, wooden behemoths surrounding him. Sleekly, he moves toward a bubble of air also trapped below the surface. He stops his thrashing and breathes.

Not deceived by the momentary comfort of the air bubble, Vova knows he must move forward. If he waits too long the thrashing movement of the logs will break his air pocket anyway. Weighing the options, he contemplates whether to swim horizontally with the logs or vertically against them. Swimming the wrong direction, he knows, will most certainly trap him longer than he might be able to go without breathing. Of course, either direction may lead to nothing but more logs and certain drowning.

How can he be sure which way to go? There isn't adequate information. So he just makes a decision much as his father might in a game of cards. He relies on gut instinct, hoping his feelings will lead him to salvation.

The current rushes against him as his body undulates with the rolling log forest above. He thrusts forward, yet again and again. An angular wall of sunshine penetrates the surface of a clearing up ahead. Vova arcs through with one last, powerful stroke, to the surface, where he pushes his mouth to the sky and gulps his redeemer—oxygen. After a few renewing, life-giving gasps, he hears the shouts of his friends on the shore and the comforting bargemen.

He is the center of attention, as he beams a confident smile, and swims to the shore.

೪

Nina walks alone down the boardwalk which follows the shore of the large, turbulent, Volga River. This is where the city's life force is centered. This is where young adults like her mingle in this second-to-last year of the 1920s, cooling themselves in the breeze and entertaining each other with their antics. She sees girls dressed as prettily as possible, flirting with young working boys, and thinks to herself how silly the boys are that she's met so far. True, Yaroslavl has offered more intelligent boys from good families than the country did. But, they're still far inferior to the boys she knows she should date. Besides, she really has little interest, and is mostly irritated by the boyish behavior she's seen exhibited by her brothers throughout her young life.

There's so much more to life that she wants to explore; so much more she wants to know before she bends to a life of mending socks and making babies. Mother and Father have been at silent odds with one another since before she hit puberty. This is all she knows of family relations between man and wife. Father has added to their discourse with his unceasing anger against the current regime, which is only soothed by his new hobby of painting flowers on ceramic plates. Mother is unrelenting, despite moments of acceptance, in imposing her perfectionism on a world and life that are anything but.

Laughter emanates from giddy and drunken young men and women in the restaurants Nina passes. But she doesn't go in. Drinking is impossibly unladylike to her, and only leads to debauched behavior unfit for a woman identifying with the manners appropriate to another generation and time. Plus, she just doesn't like it. It makes her nose red.

Nina pauses to sit on a concrete ledge in a well-lit area away from most of the activity, to consider her own future and that of her immediate family. Leonya works as a professional photographer and has found a girlfriend that Nina thinks is married. Vova, always active, defying death, and loved because of it, is well taken care of, well-adjusted, and happy here. Vera, five and a half years younger, has girlfriends of her own that are just as quiet and sensitive as she. Nina has little in common with her and hardly ever notices her, except for the one occasion when Vera became loudly upset with her inability to understand her homework.

Nina feels the hem of her only lightweight, summer dress. It's frayed and worn, mended so many times that it can't be sewn again without shortening it to the point of indecency. Her thoughts wander to the propaganda she's seen encouraging young women to join the work force. Everywhere there are cries of "It is the 'Cultural Revolution,' after all!" The Communist Party's Five-Year Plan of 1928 is claiming to encourage the People to work harder, to invigorate the country's drive for industrialization and to increase agricultural production. "More wheat, more coal, more electricity!" is plastered on posters and billboards everywhere.

It strikes her at this moment to ask herself, "Why not me? Why not go back to school and get the education I've missed since the Revolution took it away? Why not go back to old St. Petersburg/ new Leningrad? Perhaps there is a life for me there." She has quietly made a decision.

Most family members are old enough to support themselves without her, she realizes. The independence that she's denied herself all of her life is surfacing with a sudden rush of adrenalin, making Nina smile. Her own refusal to accept repeated displacement and stunting poverty, so evident in her mother's subdued anxiety, propels her up from her concrete bench. Self-determination affirms itself in her as it has never expressed itself before. She's set her mind to it. Now that the choice has been made, the hardest part is over. There will be no looking back.

14

REUNION
AND
DISSOLUTION
1928–1929

Nina carries the one small bag she's packed with her brush, toothbrush, pins, a couple of old family pictures, two used books, mother's perfume bottle as a gift to Tante Lulya, and her one other dress, through the sidewalks of Yaroslavl toward the train station. Buried in her blouse is the gold watch she received from her father on her eighteenth birthday; the watch that caused such a stir with her mother, who knew it must have come from a gambling victory.

Josephine walks at her daughter's side, seeing her off as she so often did her parents. Though it is inconvenient, she understands Nina's ambition for a better life as well as the need for her daughter to work and earn an income. Josephine has done what she can to help. Conveniently, her sister Louise (Tante Lulya) has been concerned that she must take in a boarder before they attract the attention of the authorities for having too much space. Leningrad lost half its population after the Revolution through arrests, assassinations, emigration to the countryside, and the communist move of the capitol to Moscow. In spite of available space, the enforcement of the new regime's police orders and doctrines that set strict limits on the amount of space each individual or family may inhabit is relentless and unforgiving.

Nina will be able to live with her aunt, uncle, and cousins while she tries to get into dental hygienist school. At least the school will be paid for, and Nina will have both a roof over her head and food rations. Uncle Yuri is never home much, which suits her fine. There will only be women around her most of the time, and she can visit Uncle Erich.

Nina knows the Leningrad of 1928 won't be the Petrograd/ St. Petersburg that she left years ago, and she has tempered her expectations accordingly. At the same time, she doesn't feel nostalgic about the life she is leaving. Coming back to visit Yaroslavl won't be practical until she's finished her schooling and found work. In the eyes of the current regime, she's young and she has family to live with, and the administration is hungry for new workers. Stalin has declared that the children of those persecuted are not to be persecuted for their parents' frailties. Together, Josephine and Nina enter the train station they haven't been to since they arrived from the country. It's an unpleasant reminder that adds little to the nostalgic memories that such a departure represented prior to the Revolution. Nina,

21, and her mother, 47, sit on the wooden pew-like bench, silent in their own thoughts which are similar in an odd way—concern with moving to another destination where life can possibly be better. Soldiers of the Red Guard, farmers, a few families, workers, and the dwindling number of artists and intellectual revolutionaries shuffle by with papers in hand, scrutinized by the ominous yet simple-looking officials with red stars on their hats and stripes on their jacket shoulders. Josephine breaks the silence, as only she can, to instruct Nina on what to say or not to say to Tante Lulya about the family's personal affairs.

The conductor hails the northbound passengers on board. Nina stands, picking up her suitcase. Turning to her mother, she says "Good bye. I'll write when I'm settled in the apartment," then adds, "Please tell Vera to take good care of my cat, Moorka."

Josephine has no more words of instruction and, in her mournful silence, only worries whether her daughter *can* create a life. Sadly, she turns and walks away.

Vova brushes his short blond hair, puts on his smock shirt and cap, and pulls up his tall, brown boots, which look like those worn by the peasant party members that he has befriended. No one will mind his leaving the apartment and going to the stables again. The military men there are nice guys, very friendly, and have formed an older-brother camaraderie with him. He hopes they'll let him and his friends take their horses bareback riding to water at the river again, as they have all summer so far.

Sure enough, they are there as usual; his teen-age friends, idle-but-better-dressed civilian men, and military men and their horses. All are present at the aging brick compound of what once was a mansion with adjoining stables. And, as usual, the men are happy to just sit around or play cards instead of watering or exercising their mounts. The exchange will be a win-win situation, and lots of fun for Vova and the other two boys.

Vova is first, as he climbs bareback onto a horse and charges out of the barracks to the jeers of befriended soldiers. Exhilarated and completely unrestrained, he holds his legs firmly against the sides of the horse. The muscled beast gallops faster, stretching his head and neck long and low. Vova grips his legs and his arms tighter around its strong midsection and thick, heaving neck. He feels the animal's sweat, its contact with the earth below; he hears its powerful breathing as if he has become one with it. Wind rushes by, blowing the horse's mane over and around Vova's ears. Sight is blurred and sounds are muffled by the overpowering rhythm of the horse's breath and hooves as it pushes the dirt trail behind. Vova is lost in the exhilaration of movement.

The path he's on comes to a sharp curve and Vova reluctantly reins in the horse to slow its momentum. Keeping his slower pace steady, he allows the world and his friends to catch up with his time-stealing, euphoric moment. Sitting up, Vova turns to look back around the bending path to see if he can spot them. He can't see anyone, but knows they must be coming soon. As he turns his torso forward again, his eyes widen as he spots a stone tunnel archway coming directly at him. Instantly, he ducks into the damp darkness of the overpass, barely avoiding striking his head against the unforgiving stone. Looking back has turned out to be a near-fatal decision.

The river lies just ahead, he knows, as he makes the final distance unhindered by the near calamity. "What an exciting ride," he thinks. He dismounts and then lies against a comfortable grassy knoll, refreshed, invigorated, and proudly waiting for his friends to arrive. The horse drinks the murky dark water in heavy gulps. Meanwhile, just down the river, families of once moderately successful farmers who had earlier in the year protested the shortage of food are being rounded up and sent to prison camps in Northern Siberia. The surging river muffles their shouts.

❧

Nina enters the familiar egg-shell white stone edifice of the apartment building that once was owned by Tante Lulya and Uncle Yuri. Memories rush back of the many occasions she came here, where the children were monitored by a fleet of governesses and servants. Foremost, however, she is reminded of the canary confiscated by her cousin Alicia. The betrayal of that act still makes her feel disagreeable. She wonders how long the bird survived out in the open air of the big city with no one to feed it. Then she reminds herself it doesn't matter. No one will ever know.

After walking up the flight of stairs, she rings the apartment bell and is greeted by her graying aunt. The two exchange cordial greetings, and Nina walks into the transformed apartment, somewhat surprised by its new appearance. Much of the heavy, old-fashioned furniture is intact, with the addition of some of her grandparents' pieces, but the placement of individual pieces has been shifted dramatically. The living room, while still containing the massive grand piano, is now Cousin Elena's (Helen's) and her two children's apartment; Helen's husband works outside of the city and is rarely home. Sophia has moved out and is living down the hall with her new husband. One bedroom is vacant as if waiting to be occupied by some unknown individual. Aunt Lulya maintains her large suite, seldom visited by Uncle Yuri, who spends as much time away from home as he did in the old times. "Some things are ever unchanged," thinks Nina. She will share his old, red-leathered parlor with Cousin Alicia.

It's strange to be back here in the apartments from her past. While the dilapidated external features—the streets, bridges, infrastructure, and buildings—of the past remain, the internal functionings have become completely different; and Nina has no desire to dwell on either. Soon she'll have a meeting with the commission on her application to dental hygienist school and a visit with her bachelor uncle Erich.

The settling-in process is not difficult. The one suitcase doesn't take long to unpack, and Nina heeds her mother's instructions on not presenting any details of their affairs to hide her impoverished shame. Everything is just fine as the night passes for her with the unencumbered ease it always has.

●

Nina walks down the familiar Nevsky Prospekt toward the address she's written on the scrap of paper in her hand. She's borrowed a tight-fitting hat from Alicia, which now serves the duel purpose of holding back her bob-cut, black hair as well as the frown formed on her forehead by the confusion she feels from the meeting with the commissioner. The streets are busy yet less well-maintained and with no storefront shops open for business as in the past. Banners in bold red announce the new teachings of Stalin's Five Year Plan of 1928, Some call "the People" to more action. She doesn't concern herself with this for the moment, nor with the knowledge that spies against oppressors of "the People" position themselves in the throbbing masses squeezing their motley way through the maze of sidewalks and boulevards of this former Tsarist capital.

Nina finds her uncle's apartment, unfamiliar with its location since she often saw him at family gatherings or her parents' old, spacious residence. Like other formerly successful professionals, he now resides in only one room of what had formerly been his own entire grand suite. Seeing him brings back the wonderful memories of her childhood, even all these eleven years later. As the youngest of her father's three brothers, he's reassuringly older, but he's also comfortably approachable. He was always unpretentious and kindly to her then, and nothing in that regard has changed.

Erich settles his forty-five-year-old, thin frame into his narrow sofa and leans forward, pouring his niece some hot, strong, black tea from his remaining samovar while offering some biscuits. Nina takes one because she is hungry, but refrains from appearing too greedy as it is obvious that he, too, lives on meager rations, and is probably entitled to less than families with children or other non-administrative workers. She melts into a soothing, oversized, leather ottoman that is and was obviously his favorite chair. The strength of his old-school voice comforts her as the warm tea sooths her.

Erich decides to treat his niece as an adult and include her in family information, while Nina continues her polite awe of his presence. "Did you know that your Uncle Roman escaped on a British vessel after involvement with General Denisov during the Civil War?" Erich begins. Nina shakes her head, "No."

"Well, he apparently then managed his way to Berlin, where he met up with your Aunt Claudia and your cousins, Kiril, Tatyana, and Swetlana," he continues. "Your Aunt Claudia wanted to get as far away from the Russian frontier as she could, so she abandoned her properties in Estonia just after the Revolution. Your cousins, Tatiana and Swetlana, continued their haphazard education in Berlin, and Kiril is still attending university there." Erich sits back knowing the information is new, but delighted to be able to share now that he is reunited with family. Nina silently takes it all in, pre-occupied with the novelty of it all.

"Tatiana married a German aristocrat, who now leases his family's residence in Estonia to your Uncle Roman, who visits Berlin often, but lives in Estonia. Information is sketchy for me, of course, but my understanding is that your uncle is now involved with the largest German bank, the Mendelssohn Bank, and its development of oil shale in Estonia. Apparently, the government there is in such urgent need of funds that it has offered free land for this development to anyone who wants to take it, and since so much land had been expropriated, your uncle has once again taken on large financial obligations."

The conversation, well above Nina's understanding, is nonetheless fascinating to her. Subtle meanings of inclusion, respect, and awareness of her intellect are perceived by her as clear, direct compliments.

Erich continues his dialogue, watching his niece's reactions and studying her mannerisms. "As you know, Uncle Felix is no longer with us, but Aunt Natascha and your cousins Vadim and Irina have moved here to Leningrad. And my mother, your grandmother Olga, is living well in "Russian" Berlin with your aunts, Stella and Anita."

At this point he stops, and clasps his hands together in his lap. The tribulations that he has weathered show on his face as he recalls the past. Nina sees his gentle nature has been shaken by his own personal misfortune, and it angers her. More passionately now, he continues, "I miss them the most, but what was I to do? I still have work here in Leningrad. They can't get rid of me, and I play a good worker. I've always lived my life a bit out of the mainstream anyhow, you know."

Having survived the emotional and material chaos that her elders have suffered, Nina feels personally immune. Captivated by her uncle's openness more than by the nature of her family's disposition, she, nonetheless, is unfamiliar with such open emotional passion. Ambitious to prove herself, yet remain in the shadows in order to avoid the treacheries of this new regime, she feels conflicted. How can she adjust to living her life unmolested by fear or hatred, while at the same time terribly hurt by the regime's punishment of her family—forcing her once-close inner family to disperse all over the known world?

Erich, having finished his introduction, sits back, rubs his genteel hand across his shaven chin, and laughs, "So Nina, they rejected your application because of your father's position during the Tsar's reign, and because you didn't come from peasant or working-class stock? I'm not completely surprised, you know." Nina doesn't know how to respond, as she hasn't directly been asked to.

Erich recognizing this, changes his posture to that studied, lawyerly grace he's so often used. "So, Nina," he says with genuine sincerity, "tell me quite honestly what you intend to do now."

Nina, finding her tongue, has no difficulty in using it. Questioning back, she says, "Uncle, but what *should* I do?" Frustration at the affairs of her family now easily reflected in her own internal struggle, she continues, "I've left Mother and Father to come here and study to get work. Now I've been denied. What other work is there for me besides licking envelopes?" she asks coyly, surprising even her. The gleam in his eye tells her that she should continue. Unhesitatingly, she adds, "And they rejected me because they've always been after poor Father not being from a peasant or worker's family. He never was an exploiter of the People. He only saved himself by telling them that he's never owned property." After so carefully watching her comments to anyone while away from her mother and father, Nina has let down her guard with her uncle. She feels exhausted after finally expressing herself openly.

Erich conveniently fills in the gap by saying, "You know, Nina, the regime has dictated, albeit foolishly, that it intends to surpass the industries of Germany, France, England and the United States. Russia is larger than all of them and, shall I say, much less economically developed. We're far behind where we were in the 1890's. The country is devoting resources to construction, but even if we don't actually build, resources are needed to plan, design, and draw. I think the most practical and flexible, most-needed occupation here, or anywhere else for that matter, for you to pursue would be drafting. You should learn how to become a draftsman."

Nina silently takes in her clever uncle's forthrightness and the new information. Her logical mind does not take long to grasp the difference between passion and common sense. Quickly it reflects on the disposition of her entire family. On both sides, they had always worked, choosing occupations in business and government that were necessary to the functioning of the society. These choices had proved unfortunate with the coming of the new regime. Dentistry had seemed a good choice because it was practical. After all, Nina thought, everyone has teeth. But now that door is slammed shut.

Instinctively, Nina sets her glass teacup on the wooden table and sits upright near the edge of the chair in a posture that comes naturally to her. With a clear, alert expression, she looks quizzically up at her uncle. He responds to her glance with a simple, confident smile.

Nina's reaction precludes emotionality. She realizes the information could not be more sincere or well delivered or from a more knowledgeable or educated man. "Thank you, Uncle," she says simply, continuing, "I'll inquire to see if the results on the exams I took in Yaroslavl can be transferred to technical drafting school." Starting on this new direction isn't considered an imposition. How many new directions has she already taken?

The conversation concludes as vibrantly as it was initiated. Nina has found a fatherly elder male, and one who seems to express the sensibility most needed now that her father is so far away. Erich is delighted to have a niece he can speak with like the daughter he's never had.

Josephine wastes no time in gathering the last of her things, placing them in the large old suitcase she will have Vova carry for her. Vera has made the appropriate good-byes to her friends and Vova, Vera, and Josephine are dressed as fashionably as they are able. Josephine grabs the photo album complete with pictures of more romantic and comfortable times. Her face remains stern as she lays the cumbersome album on top of the odd assortment of possessions already packed. Anger prevails over simple nostalgia for the years passing, dreamlike, through her mind—memories from before the Revolution 'til now, the fall of 1928.

Emigration was banned two years ago, so Josephine makes a concerted effort to pack as if she were only leaving for an extended stay. Secretly, she and the family all know the unspoken truth. Letters from her mother, father, brothers in Berlin, and sister, Emma, in Bulgaria, have arrived with increasing urgency, telling of Josephine the elder's stomach cancer. Authorities have not bothered to black-out the exaggerated references to her mother's weakened state, hospitalization, and impending death. Even the mediocre, local *apparatchik* wasn't surprised when the paperwork from the highest Berlin authorities arrived, clearing entry into the city to attend to the last needs of daughter Josephine's supposedly dying mother.

But even the lethargic Yaroslavl Central Committee couldn't be dictated to fully by an outside authority, no matter how much Russia intended to lull the Germans into adopting the idealistic "Worldwide Revolution." Indeed, one caveat has made itself clear. The current authorities will only allow half the family to leave to attend to the medical issues in Berlin, thereby creating a "motivation" for Josephine's return.

The decision was not terribly difficult for Josephine to make. Nina is settled in drafting school in Leningrad, and Leonya has gained recognition as a successful photographer. Josephine recognizes that her marriage has been failing for years. She's never forgiven Leonid's weakness for gambling, his continued badgering by the party apparatus, and what, she feels, is his incompetence in allowing the family to live in such poverty in this remote, miserable city.

With the definitive judgment that has been smoldering in Josephine's psyche for years, she informs the authorities and arranges the departure, even reserving tickets for her "return," and attends to the necessary paperwork for her youngest two teen-age children and herself. Nina, Leonya, and Leonid will be left behind. She's fully aware that this will most likely be final.

The risk of confiscations—if not outright thievery—will be a constant threat on the journey. Nonetheless, she's spent weeks sewing and bartering for smart outfits, feeling she must, by all means, present herself and her children in the best light to her awaiting Berlin family—if not for their sake, then for her own. She will not let them be considered a family of urchins.

For, although certain details of her father's wealth in Berlin have either been omitted or deleted by the Russian authorities or by his own conservatism, the stationary and ink used, and the occasional photo enclosed, speaks volumes to Josephine. It is quite clear to her that her father has significant business interest or ownership in apartment buildings and automobiles. While few autos are ever seen in Russia, she's aware that the industry has grown far beyond what her father dabbled with in Russia before the war.

She grasps the stack of letters with their blackened lines and envelopes ripped open and taped shut again before she ever received them. They'll be useful to tell the tale of her departure if the other documents she carries are questioned at the border.

Looking in the mirror, Josephine's face flushes with anger as she thinks of the completeness of the Bolsheviks' invasion into her private life and the lives of her friends. And then the anger fades as she recognizes the blush as oddly attractive on her still-beautiful, high cheek-boned, green-eyed features. And with a look of complacency she has neither seen on her face nor felt in years, she turns from the mirror, leaves the communal bathroom, and returns to her apartment rooms for the last time. "It's time we leave now," she calls to her two youngest. She flashes a glance at her husband, and then, for the children's sake, she kisses him on both cheeks in the customary formal French fashion. "Good bye," she says as she shakes her eldest son's hand, instructing him that she will write and expects him to do the same.

Leonid and Leonya stand frozen in place—neither able to express the deep loss of their abandonment in this two-room Yaroslavl apartment. As Josephine leaves the room with Vova and Vera, Leonid struggles within himself as he wipes away the tears cascading from his eyes.

Josephine marches forward through the swelling population of Yaroslavl. Wealthy farmers, Kulaks, are just beginning to be ripped from their own farms, which will be re-dedicated as communal farms. Their lost lives permeate the forlorn city with human suffering. The trip takes longer than expected, but soon the trio arrives in Leningrad.

Josephine leaves her younger children at a restaurant while she carries a small trunk, filled with items for Nina, through the streets of her once-beloved city. Arriving at her sister Louise's, she finds Nina, who instead of crying, feels a heaviness in her heart hard for her to put into words.

Josephine opens the trunk and hands over a blouse that she hadn't been able to complete. Josephine briefly declares that she had intended it for herself, but since she wasn't able to wear it, perhaps it would be best for Nina. Nina notices that only the buttons are missing and tells her mother that she will finish it for her. Tante Lulya, always privy to any conversation, declares, "I do everything for my children; and here you are, Nina, doing for your mother." Nina says nothing and quickly sews the buttons before Josephine leaves the apartment, and Russia, forever.

Leonid rides the worn, wooden seat of an old railway car in a direction he's never traveled before. Leonya, his last remaining relation in Yaroslavl, escorted him to the station. His salty friends and card-playing buddies were obviously absent from any good-byes.

This departure came as abruptly as it was involuntary. For a long time now they all have silently denied the inevitable—unwarranted arrests are not only commonplace, but also likely.

The other passengers, like him, sit silently on the train as it makes its way northeast into farther reaches of rural, summer countryside. Most were once farmers; others bear a bedraggled resemblance to former-middle-class bourgeoisie, now pried from the crevices of existence they had heretofore found for themselves. Many are middle-aged, but some are young, the spark in their eyes that allowed them to rise to the top of their communities has been destroyed. Those same eyes are hollow, pierced with ridicule, shame and befuddlement.

Yet others, like Leonid—fortunate in days past to have accumulated a pen of sheep, a sty of pigs, a gaggle of geese, a house of hens, a herd of cows, or a responsible or authoritative job—are now condemned for these same things. For in every town are administrators of the new doctrines; Communist spies who have grown in numbers that only the chief administrator, Stalin, can manage. And unless artificial quotas for inhumane arrests are maintained, the spies, too, are sent to concentration camps, hard labor, or death. Industry must have laborers and what cheaper labor is there than political prisoners of the State? The Soviet economy cannot support itself without free slave labor plucked from concentration camps. Serfdom, or the "second serfdom," has been fully reinstated in the Russia of 1929.

Article 58; Item 6, of the criminal code, defines so many minor offenses as "treason" that even the failure to report complaints of treasonous acts made by family or neighbors against the USSR or its leadership will subject a struggling, sincere, soviet worker to be condemned. If a starving farm worker steals a piece of bread, the accusation will read, "When all the people are working hard to construct socialism, stealing bread (which is the property of the people), therefore, is treason." Still other farm administrators are used as scapegoats for the empty bins of grain that are exported with fabricated quantities written on the manifests, while war widows and starving, orphaned children are assassinated for stealing a cob of corn.

Leonid sits, not knowing his destination or his fate. He simply rides through fields and countryside, noticing row upon row of wild orange poppies. Strange, idiosyncratic thoughts cross his mind, like his love of simple flowers, of the porcelain plates he just completed painting. Silently, his body vibrates with the roll of the engine. He is beyond tears, beyond caring, his soul reaching out to the endless fields. It's almost as if the poppies speak to him… "Leonid…Leonid…," as the train, also uncaring, churns its metal wheels onward.

15

LENINGRAD
1929–1932

The August mugginess wearies the two guards who stand on either side of the large factory's metal-framed doors. If it weren't for the heat, the two men would appear more intimidating to Nina, but as it is, they just seem like everybody else in this last year of the 1920's—bedraggled and lethargic.

Nina wears her nicest dress, wishing desperately that her mother had the foresight to send her at least some new material from Berlin. Last winter she was surprised to find a nice woolen suit, but this does little good now. The sign above the door reads, "Baltic Manufacturing and Engineering," and the second lobby door that her escort takes her through, reads, "Specialty Operations." If it weren't for her drafting college professor's special interest in her, she would never have found herself here, looking for a job in the drafting department of a submarine manufacturer.

The last door swings open to a large busy room filled with draftsmen and women. Nina grasps her documents tightly and looks down to avoid eye contact with any number of men and women who pop their heads up at various intervals from their large, tilted, drafting tables. Nina waits for the escort to return, doing as she's instructed by standing alone against the wall. To her relief, a tall lanky man is briskly coming toward her, and has the courtesy to shake her hand. After a moment's introduction, Nina hands over her identification and newly-printed diploma. The man, Serge, the department assistant manager, reads through the oversized diploma, dated July 29, 1929, and the endless lines of listed course accomplishments. He mumbles them aloud as he feigns interest, while occasionally glancing up at Nina; "Let's see here…Geometric Drafting, Technical Drawing, Trigonometry…"

Nina feels like blushing, noticing that he's taking less interest in the coursework, than he is in her. She smiles ever so politely, in a practiced manner taught her by her brother Leonya during private photo shoots.

Leonya felt abandoned by both his family and ex-lover in Yaroslavl. The combination of this and his rising fame and importance in professional photography has motivated him to move back to Leningrad; recently he was commissioned to photograph a famous, young violinist here.

He currently rents a room in an apartment on the opposite side of the city from Nina. Fortunately, he was able to move into an empty room of the apartment rented by their Aunt Natascha's sister, Tatiana, the wife of assassinated Uncle Felix. This distant, non-blood relative has a pretty blonde daughter named Irina. The apartment houses Irina and Tatiana, Tatiana's other sister and their father, who lives in his own room since divorcing the mother. Tatiana has already eyed Leonya as a good prospect for her daughter, whom Leonya, in turn, has found immediately attractive.

Since before moving back to town, he's occasionally used Nina as a photo model. Even though Nina is pretty and daring enough to pose nude (one recent shot has her lying on her stomach wrapped in a sable boa), she knows she's still a simple girl who lacks the refined sophistication her mother was always trying to teach her. Besides, all the years of hard work of animal care and gardening have thickened her wrists more than she'd like.

"…Technical Physics and Materials, Technology and Structure of New Materials," the assistant manager finally concludes with a gleam in his eye as he looks at Nina.

Again Nina is asked to wait as she watches Serge first rap on, then enter a tall glass and wood door. As it closes behind him, she questions her hearing when she overhears him say, "Fyodor, I think you have a job for this young female comrade."

Nina continues to stand nonchalantly as she assesses the room, its people, the propaganda warnings, disciplinary codes pertaining to management, and other paraphernalia plastered on all of the walls. Nina isn't overwhelmed by the climate of robust business, having been raised in the presence of so many family members and friends of the family who truly were significant in their individual accomplishments in business, law, and politics. In addition to this, office politics and group dynamics, which she intuits are an important part of this office, seem inconsequential to her after a life of having to fend for herself against her unruly brothers.

In a relatively short period of time she sees the manager's door open and faintly hears a senior man's voice say, "All are pretty girls in my drafting department…under the age of 24." Nina realizes she must have just made it, as she will be 23 at the end of the year. Serge turns to shut the door again and approaches Nina, who continues to stand innocently by the bulletin board. Walking directly to her with a renewed sense of seriousness, if only for appearances, he announces that she will have to complete some paperwork and, upon authorization from the local committee of workers, can be hired.

"Thank you, Comrade Manager," Nina says, as she reaches to shake his hand.

"We work here from 9 a.m. to 5 p.m.," six days per week," he explains as he walks her towards a hinged slanted desk by the side of the wall. He then takes out a piece of carbon paper and a pre-printed form. Still using a professional manner, he asks her to sit down, fill out the form, and leave it on the desk before she leaves. Nina thanks him and sits down.

The form appears simple enough: *First name*__________, Nina fills out her customary Russian first and father's first names, *Nina Leonidivna*; *Last name*________, Nina writes her Germanic surname; *Nationality*__________, at this point she stops. While true, both she and her mother were born in Russia and in Leningrad (old St. Petersburg), her father was born in Minsk to German Baltic aristocracy who served the former Tsar. Her mother's family is from Germany as well. "I'll just put 'Russian,'" Nina thinks. "It will make me fit in better since the only constant I can trust is that arrests are made for random reasons. I won't give anyone a reason to question me."

With a mark of the pen, she inserts "Russian" on the indicated line, and then continues filling out the rest of the application. Setting the form to the side of the desk, she brushes her dress smooth, stands, and walks around the corner to the attending guard, who escorts her out of the building.

❧

Nina and her coworkers make their way back to the office this cold, weary New Year's Day, 1930. Nina will have to wear the same dress she's worn yesterday, but this isn't much of a stretch from alternating between the two dresses she owns anyway. Public transportation is idle, as usual, after one o'clock in the morning. The Soviet government doesn't officially recognize this day as a holiday, even though most people still do. Revelers weave their way home on foot amidst strong flurries of cold, blowing snow. Later, this morning, Wednesday, January 1, factories and offices will be full of bleary-eyed workers. Nina has sometimes found coworkers so sick and tired from previous night's celebrations that the only reprieve they can get is to sleep on the toilet.

When the Neva isn't frozen over, the bridges are also lifted in the early morning hours. Last Fall Nina found this out on a similar occasion. Having been invited to a party at the apartment of one of her coworkers, Nina and most of the others found themselves staying past the time when transportation was shut down. Everyone had to walk home. As they walked through the foggy mist typical of Leningrad, Nina thought she saw a beautiful blue star in the sky. "Look at that incredible blue star," she said quite loudly to her escorts. With little tact, one of the boys simply said, "that's not a blue star; it's the light of the raised bridge." Nina quipped back, pouting humorously, "Now you've even taken my blue star away."

Nina is in a great mood as she chuckles with her friends and trudges through the thick air of icy side streets. She's become quite popular amongst her Baltic Engineering and Manufacturing co-workers even though, during work hours, she makes a habit of staying silent and avoiding conversation with any of her adjoining work mates.

The evenings are a different story though, and Nina has really enjoyed dating. Men like her, she thinks, because of her simple, natural personality. Most of the younger men that she calls boys and has chosen to date, are engineers, and most of these are German. Dating German men gives her the added benefit of going to the specialty shops that only foreigners are allowed to frequent, even if she hasn't much money to spend there.

Her cousins used to tease her about the fact that she dated so often, yet never kissed a boy. But laugh she let them. Between her aunt's almost militant nosiness and her cousins' constant inquiries, she's found it best to move out. It was her aunt's incessant snooping and eavesdropping that ultimately drove her out; her shallow, trifling cousins simply added impetus to her decision. Alicia, never her favorite, eventually followed Nina and attended drafting school, only to quit the job that Nina found for her at the Baltic plant after a few months' time. Helen works in a candy store and is married to a Polish engineer, with whom she has two little daughters, Elena and Tatyana. Sophia, closest to Nina's age, has married and is already divorced.

Alicia is not married, believing that her marriage chances have been damaged by an omen. Apparently Uncle Yuri had three fine bottles of champagne purchased, one for each of his daughters to open on their wedding days. After the Revolution, when furniture was beings shuffled around, Alicia's bottle broke. Alicia still feels this has hindered her success with men.

Nina has no intention to marry and, instead, enjoys going out with groups of friends to the movies, the theater, parties, and shops. Her physique is slim, with strong, lanky muscles in her shoulders, arms and legs, from the tennis she plays competitively. Shortly after starting work at the Baltic Manufacturing Company, she began using their tennis courts. Eventually she joined their workers' tennis team, and then moved up to a city team. Tennis, gymnastics, ice-skating in winter, and calisthenics, is strongly supported as good for healthy workers in today's "Cultural Revolution." Nina has adapted to this particular dictate with great enthusiasm, given her familiarity with tennis from her summertimes at the dachas in Finland, and the fortuitousness of her highly-developed upper body strength; an attribute from her teenage years working at the farm in the countryside.

Leonya is now married to his former apartment-mate Irina, and the two share a room. Irina's mother, Tatiana, takes the dining room. Her father takes a second bedroom. And the sister of the mother, who works as a doctor, takes a fourth room. Nina has the living room, which is directly connected to the open dining area where the mother sleeps.

The small party continues their walk in the early-morning freeze. No one seems to mind the white blur caused by the now-swirling snow. New Year's Eve was festive and joyful, regardless of the fact that it was also ghostly.

One of Nina's female coworkers had invited the whole gang to an opulent mansion formerly owned by wealthy Russians. The girl's parents were then the servants, and have, for all these years, continued to live in the small room adjoining the kitchen. The rest of the house has remained eerily like it was; its beautiful silk furniture and bedspreads unused, its oversized porcelain vases and urns adorning the many vestibules on large Romanesque pedestals. Polished marble staircases lead to unused, fully furnished parlors, and ancient, painted portraits of ancestors glower down upon empty rooms.

Nina assumes the prior owners are in Siberia—if alive at all—but chooses not to dwell on this subject. The current Polish saying, "Shisko yedno quatrens paszuski," (or, "It makes no difference, its quarter to six."), is a fashionable metaphor for how these comrades in their early twenties like to think about everything—including Stalin. Their conscious minds do not distinguish the difference between their present lust for life and the torment of the past's glory now left abandoned. Living with these contradictions has been a fact of life for Nina since the time she moved into the dacha of the assassinated country gentleman nearly twelve years ago.

Last night everyone used the soft beds and silk couches without question. Nina found the bed she slept on to be very comfortable although old-fashioned. As morning arrived, the parents of their hostess coworker set out cheese and bread and made strong, hot tea, which most enjoyed who weren't feeling too ill from the vodka of the night before.

The trolleys are beginning to run again. Nina gets on one with her friends in order to get to work on time, thinking nothing of the questions she might be asked when she returns to her brother's tonight. The truth is that she's done nothing wrong and doesn't care what anybody thinks anyhow.

☙

Nina puts on her nicely ironed and washed second dress,

continuing her habit of trading off the two dresses on a daily basis. The rest of the household is still sleeping as she brushes off her brown, bedraggled-looking overcoat. As she does, she notices that the material has frazzled a bit more than she had noticed earlier. It's been taken apart and re-sewn backwards and forwards so many times now that it will be hard to fix. It's hard to find a coat, and even harder to get a ration coupon to buy one in the first place. Most irritating is that Nina's mother actually appears to believe the letters Nina writes to her in Berlin, telling of how wonderful everything is in Leningrad. Obviously, neither her cousins nor her brother seem to be writing the same impressions. Her brother received a brand new, very expensive Leica camera this Christmas, while Helen was gifted a silver brush, and Alicia a set of china. All Nina got was a pair of socks. "This coat will have to do," she thinks, as she avoids any contact with Irina's mother and walks out the door.

Her continued practice of not coming home until very late and leaving very early has created some annoying questions from Irina's mother. The inquiries she felt she left behind with her aunt and cousins have now resurfaced in the sometimes sarcastic comments of this elderly woman, who, Nina feels, has little right in making any presumptions at all. Nina often tells her so. Besides, dating, social activities, working six days a week, and tennis-playing keep her very busy. Last summer she participated with her best girlfriend, Sasha, as a city-of-Leningrad, tennis-team member in the Moscow national tournament of 1931. Unfortunately, her only racket broke a string and she and Sasha were left to go home with tales of shopping in the marvelous Moscow stores that are only open to foreigners, executive committee members, and famous athletes.

The early October air blows across Nina's face as she passes the now-familiar but more imposingly rigid guards who are posted on either side of the tightly secured factory. Entering the large room where all draftsmen sit, Nina takes off her coat and hangs it on the communal coat rack.

Unfortunately, work *has* begun to trouble Nina, as has fear of reprisal from the letters she continues to write to her father in Siberia and to her mother in Berlin. Recently, the manager of the design team was arrested, and, as usual, no one knows why. Everyone has heard about the arrest of an entire group of department heads from another factory—for listening to and laughing at a joke about Stalin.

Nina knows that a good job, like this one, isn't easy to find. Former teachers from pre-Revolutionary days are scrubbing floors because their right to work has been taken away. Women who had once been secretaries, if still alive, have no jobs at all. Others work long and laboriously at factories regardless of their prior occupations or training. The thousands that flock to Leningrad from the countryside to avoid collectivism immediately take up the worst of the jobs. And these thousands create the illusion that the millions that die or disappear are not gone at all.

As Nina walks to her desk, she feels someone grab her arm from behind. It is her girlfriend. The girl's eyes are puffy and Nina notices that she's been crying.

"Nina, I need to talk with you," whispers her friend.

Nina replies, "I can't right now but we can meet at lunch. Will that be alright?"

"Sure," responds the girl as she walks away.

Nina sits down behind her drafting desk and picks up her pencils. An emotion deep within her threatens to surface. It's impossible to deny. Her work involves drawing the interior of an inside hatch of a U-Boat. Knowing that the sensitive nature of her work, drafting drawings from engineers, some of whom have also disappeared, exposes her to sensitive and confidential information, makes her uncomfortable and anxious. How can she consider herself safe?

As Nina translates sketches into finely detailed measurements, she thinks about her father, now in his third year in Siberia. The constant thought of her poor father's incarceration disturbs her enough to set down the pencil. Looking up, her eyes meet a tired and haggard, red-headed draftsman sitting nearby. He too was arrested. Annoyed at her own distraction, she lifts her mechanical pencil again and forces herself to continue.

At lunch Nina searches for the crying girl as promised, wondering what she has to say. The two sit together in the large, gray cafeteria. Through muffled sobs, the girl asks, "You know that red-headed man who works in the engineering department?"

"Yes, I do," replies Nina in-between bites of boiled potatoes and small chunks of beef.

"Well, he likes me and wants to go out with me," the girl

continues, trying not to cry harder. Nina wonders why she's crying at all.

"I'm not interested in him," the girl says, trying to eat so as to avoid being noticed, but doing a poor job at it. "But when I said no, he said he was from the GPU." The girl places a fork full of potatoes in her mouth to stifle a fearful cry. Nina looks up and away, purposely not making eye contact with her.

"If I continue to say no, he told me in no uncertain terms that he would report me and have me arrested," she continues. With this last statement the girl stops feigning eating. "I don't know what I'm going to do, Nina," she says pleadingly.

Nina can see other workers sitting around small tables and hears their gregarious voices and some chortled laughter. The seeming normality of this setting hasn't fooled her. "It is true that some of these people, at this very moment, are spies," Nina thinks. Not showing any sign of empathy or emotion, she replies quietly and matter-of-factly, "It's very simple. You'll have to leave your job here immediately and go to work somewhere else."

The girl's face reflects incredulity mixed with rising anger. "What do you mean leave my job? What am I to do? Where am I to go? I can't just…," she says in rapid succession, before realizing that what Nina says is true.

"I'll tell you what," Nina interrupts with a growing intolerant harshness. "If he talks to you today, tell him that you'll be going to the movies with me tonight. You'll then have an excuse. Tomorrow you can quit your job." The girl looks at Nina with understanding, although the understanding makes her no happier, as the two stand up to deliver their trays to the kitchen.

❧

Uncle Erich laughs, as he sits back in his chair listening to the anger presenting itself as confidence in his niece's tone. Nina continues to explain her recent questioning by the GPU (the hated Commissariat of Internal Affairs). Erich listens to her situation, rationale, and final triumph. Pouring some hot tea to warm the atmosphere of the clammy cold spring of 1932, he repeats his niece's statements: "So, you told them that you dated German engineers for no other reason than the fact that you're young, *attractive*, and single, and what's a girl supposed to do?"

Nina knows that he's added the attractive part, and confesses to herself that that did help the interview. She sits back again and laughs with him at the ridiculousness of it all, as she explains the details of their questioning and her confident, fully honest, response. Germans, after Poles and before Italians, have come under the scrutiny of Stalin's henchmen. While once they were sought after for their engineering skills they are now sought after for slave labor. The new approach pains Nina, who makes a conscious decision to take it all in stride. The earlier decision to declare her nationality as Russian proves to be a life preserver. In addition to this, she continues to be impeccably above reproach in all of her work-related activities.

"You are still writing your father and your mother, Nina, are you not?" Erich interjects with a line of questioning now familiar to Nina.

"Yes, but you don't think…," Nina begins. "Do you, Uncle?" she questions knowingly.

Erich continues to coolly analyze Nina's response, phrasing his questions in a way to help her make decisions on her own. He, too, has had to make decisions recently in order to alleviate suspicions. Any idiosyncrasy can be construed as a liability.

"My concern is that the combination of letters to other countries added to the sensitive nature of your work, can be rather, shall I say, concerning, Nina," Erich replies.

Nina understands the information, realizing sadly though appreciatively that she is being given the same advice she gave her coworker. Nonetheless, she trusts it and ponders broaching the subject with her manager. Erich agrees to let her think about it for a day, but urges her to act quickly.

Together the two enjoy a simple meal before Nina takes the streetcar back to her apartment. The following day, during the early part of her lunch break, she inauspiciously visits her manager's office.

"Comrade Manager," Nina begins, "…as you may or may not know, I have a father in Siberia and mother living in Berlin, with whom I correspond regularly." The manager responds with only a look, his tired eyes revealing his personal association and understanding of Nina's particular background. Forthrightly, Nina continues, "Do you believe that there may be any risk associated with working for such a company as this and communicating with my immediate family abroad?" The manager looks down at his hands, his silence telling Nina all she needs to know.

"Comrade Manager, I would like to be fired from my work here," Nina forces the point resolutely.

The manager, with little hesitation, responds, "That would be impossible, as your records show you've done nothing to warrant such action. There are many who want a position in this factory, so many that I cannot count." He waits a moment, and then stifles Nina's rising interjection by saying, "But if you wish to resign, there is nothing I can do to stop you."

Nina isn't taken off guard. She's assumed this to be a possibility and pauses to compose herself for her final remark; "Comrade Manager, I must resign."

"In that case, I will be happy to write you a very good letter of recommendation, Comrade Nina."

Nina thanks him and walks back to her desk, where she continues finishing her most urgent assignments before collecting her referral, her mechanical pencils, and walking once again into the streets of Leningrad and the unknown.

16

INTEGRATION
1932–1933

"You're not home very often, Sister," Leonya says to Nina this early summer morning of 1932, as he passes by her as she irons her dress in the dining room. The question bothers Nina, since now her brother, at home infrequently as well, seems to take an interest in her activities. Tatiana, Leonya's mother-in-law, prepares his lunch and smiles knowingly.

Nina replies to both of them, partially in jest and partially out of aggravation, "I'll be at home when I'm married."

"Fair enough," replies her older sibling, even though he continues to pry. "So who is this Nikolai?"

It is true that Nick has taken precedence over all the other men she's been dating. Biting her tongue to keep from telling them it was none of their business, Nina answers, "He's the chief engineer of the M. Gorki Factory."

"And…," her brother chides her, "…you've been out with him more than any other fellow, so I've heard."

Nina cringes at his remark, knowing the mother-in-law has been keeping tabs on her. "Well, if you must know, he's three and a half years older than I am, originally from Twer-Burashevo, in mid-central Russia, and a brilliant engineer whose currently working on his Master's Degree in Mechanical Engineering." Nina conveniently leaves out the fact that what's attractive to her is that his grandfather was a former serf of a wealthy Russian landlord, and who, because of his brilliance in botany and creation of unique specimens of fruit trees spliced together (apple and pear, for instance), was freed before the emancipation of the serfs. His father, Michael Michailovitsch, was educated in Leningrad, and eventually became a professor in the Caucasus. Nicholai followed in his footsteps, and although a rather rebellious and obstinate boy, graduated from the University of Pensa shortly after the Revolution.

"Well I'm sure there's much more to this story," Leonya teases, knowing that his sister's ethical standards are well above modern norms, and that she knows better than to tell him much anyhow. He continues finishing his thick oatmeal, and begins to walk toward his room to collect his photography equipment. As he leaves, he turns and says jokingly, "So, no more Germans?"

Nina responds fully humorously, saying, "There *are* no more German's left to date," as they both laugh. For, indeed, the German engineers are not only not safe to date but all of them have been arrested at both Nina's old job, and her new job at a paper manufacturing equipment supplier.

"Well, whoever he is, I'm sure you've done a good job looking after yourself," Leonya adds cleverly. The comment irks Nina, although she isn't sure why. Her brother knows full well that Nina uses her looks and practiced, charming naiveté to manipulate situations to suit her needs. In truth, Nina knows that Nick's background can only be beneficial to her. There is nothing in his past, from serf upbringing and intellectual botanist parentage, to mechanical engineering prowess, when foreigners with these needed skills have been disposed of, that can be construed in any way as negative by the current authorities. He's also not a Communist, and that makes him available in the first place.

Nina continues ironing her dress and seriously considers how to refrain from discussing anything of importance with Tatiana in the future.

❧

The snow crunches beneath Nina's feet as she walks down Neva Boulevard, remembering the time when there were so many horses pulling sleighs. The streets are as crowded as in the past, but are filled with despair as well. There were even some automobiles then. Now the few autos to be found are limousines owned by influential party members.

Arrests aren't published anywhere, but, if one wanted to research the matter, one could look in the phone book and see names of all registered Leningraders with a telephone; normally these are more capable, more important people, and they are disappearing with accelerating rapidity. The Communist party under Stalin has become all-powerful. There is no avoiding it, and it concerns itself with every action, every public comment, and every thought that might appear on the face of anyone thinking too deeply. German farmers from the time of Catherine and peasants who showed "vigor" in the New Economic Policy of 1920-1928 have now been destroyed en masse in the Five Year Plan of 1928-1933. The farming community where Nina and her family dwelt has been decimated, unbeknownst to Nina. Over five million people have starved to death as the result of famine in the countryside. Entire families are sent to the gulags and hard labor camps that, by this year of 1932, have over two million starving or exhausted inhabitants. The special settlements extend all the way to Archangelsk and some of the coldest places on earth, where half-clad people freeze to death while using hammers and chisels in slave labor, hacking stone destined for tunnels, bridges, and buildings. The few surviving dogs and cats slink by with fear in their eyes in some villages. In still others, cannibalism is practiced after all the animals have been eaten.

Meanwhile, over 75% of all peasants have been forced onto slow, idle, unproductive collective farms. In order to avoid persecution for being a wealthy farmer with livestock or be interned in the collective settlements, some peasants slaughtered their animals, decimating entire populations of pigs, cows, and chickens. Other farmers left machinery to rot on abandoned farms along with what remained of their grain and livestock before being arrested. Meanwhile, Party activists and Stalin's henchmen search for hidden food. To this end they stop at nothing, including beating up swollen, starving peasants in order to find secret grain stashes that don't exist.

In the cities, filmmakers, artists, newspapermen, poets and writers are carted away and shot. Abandoned children from the countryside beg for bread, while manned carts collect the corpses of the dying in Kiev. Food is held in reserve for the *new* party officials since many of the original Bolsheviks and revolutionaries have been executed, along with the idealism that built the Revolution in the first place. Precious metals are mined for export, along with what little grain there is, in order to prove the country's falsely reported abundance to the rest of the world as well as to fund the straggling worldwide communist revolution. Meanwhile, the propaganda machine churns out articles, like the one written by Stalin in *Pravda*, declaring, "The Five Year Plan is dizzying with success!" It is clear to all that the only true success is Stalin's entrenchment of power by force and terror, and establishment of the monolithic communist bureaucracy that only he can manage, and that has been necessitated to control the feeding, housing, and directing of Russia's millions of inhabitants.

But what can a person do? Work, eat, sleep, visit family, and live, minding one's business as much as possible in the big, restless city. Nina holds her coat closer to her body as the fierce, cold wind blows off the Neva River and against her reddening face. Her pace quickens as she walks across Leningrad's icy and often dirty streets.

Walking down the cold side streets of the Neva, Nina notices a pawnshop filled with belongings that no one can buy. Money has been scarce for her even though she's been employed. Her last job shop shut its doors, and now she works for another paper manufacturing company. In the Leningrad of 1932 jobs aren't always consistent, Nina's realized, regardless of the claims of the government to the contrary.

The biting cold is abnormally unbearable for her, but her eyes are directed, as if by some strange force, to a bedroom suite just beyond the window. She walks in and recognizes the light ash wood carved with images of plants and fruit. It's her mother's headboard, armoire, and dressing table that, for all those years back in her childhood, were part of her mother's private bedroom. And now, here, years later, it sits for sale in a pawnshop not far from her original home. Never wanting so much as to *walk* on the street where she used to live as a child; her thoughts have been to let the past stay buried in the past. Now old memories haunt her as she hurries out of the shop and back into the frigid, bustling street.

Leonid has returned suddenly to Leningrad, where he had pleaded to be sent in an effort to locate his children, after being released by his captors from his three-year sentence. Unable to workably fit into the apartment with Nina, Leonya, Irinka, and Irinka's mother, father, and aunt, he has had to find a tiny, one-room apartment with just enough room for a bed, a hotplate for making soup, an old and deteriorating wooden dresser, and a hook for his now shabby clothing. He lives alone, often sulking and miffed at his fate, wondering how things could have resulted in one brother's assassination, while another has survived in Berlin with their 90-year-old mother and their sisters. His own wife and two youngest children also abandoned him, choosing to flee to Berlin, and now his remaining children don't seem to pay any attention to him.

The three years in Siberia have not broken his resistance against the terror of the regime. However, his absence from the growth in the regime's power has blinded him to the realities of the present day. The fact that he has survived so far has only increased his belief that he is immune to being assassinated. He continues to hold onto his old ideals as one of the few surviving, stalwart advocates of change and dissatisfaction. He sits at the simple wooden table perched below his sixth-floor, round window, finishing a letter to his wife, when he hears a knock on his door.

Nina enters, barely affected by the many flights of stairs she's climbed to get there, and sits on the stool nearest him. She can't help but feel uncomfortable in his presence. Even her own father has become a liability to her and her brother. Two times now he's been arrested, and two times now, by some incredible fortune as well as his own skill at talking his way out of things, he's been released.

But she knows that being released means nothing to future freedom. She remembers all too clearly the scrutiny she received on a daily basis when she worked at the U-Boat factory, and how, on some mornings, coworkers would not return to work from the previous day. Everyone knows of the large black limousines that come to people's front doors in the middle of the night, taking away the residents, who are never to be heard from again.

The two sit for a moment, discussing Nina's day's activities and Leonid's health. Nina notices the letter and asks who it's for. Leonid answers that he's writing to her mother and pushes it over for her to read. She takes the letter, dated Sunday, December 25, 1932, and reads: "There are now not even potatoes…it is difficult in this so-called Five Year Plan to buy food…"

Abruptly, she sets it aside, and, surprising herself with her own anger, says "Father, how can you write such letters to Mother!? Don't you know by now that they open and read them? I always write that there is plenty of food to go around, to show what good workers we are. Don't you see? You're impossible with this letter!"

Leonid says nothing, at first. Indeed it *is* harsh language coming from his daughter, who in the past was never allowed to speak with him on any issue that he did not initiate. Nina realizes this also, but doesn't seem to be able to control herself, nor does she wish to. To her it is critical that she convince her father. After all, she thinks, only family can truly tell family the truth. In this emphatic manner she continues, "Can't you remember your job in Siberia, sitting around the fire making sure it wouldn't go out? Do you want to do that for another three years or longer?"

Leonid looks at his daughter with saddened eyes, much older looking than his sixty-two years would prove him to be. With great effort, his wrinkled face creases in the roots of a smile, as he jokes,

"Oh it wasn't so bad. The hardest part was not falling asleep."

The joke falls on deaf ears, as Nina sits unmoved, with an icy-cold manner that she has often seen her mother use, but never used herself until now. Then she softens her expression as she realizes how sad and old he seems. She won't say much more, for there isn't any use at the moment. And she won't visit much longer or come again any time soon. It is all she can do to guard her safety—and to keep her heart from breaking at the sight of him.

❧

Nick studies Nina's response through the dim light of the theater, as she takes the photograph he hands her. "You haven't been to my apartment, so I wanted to show you a picture of me there, being the good bachelor," he says. "See I'm mending my sock," he points out flirtatiously.

Nina finds the picture interesting and sentimental in a way that reminds her of her father. The fact that he's an amateur photographer is also appealing to her, as she immediately compares his photos to those of her brother. The glimpse of his small studio apartment shows his walls hung with modern art sketches and a handsome clock. The desk next to him is covered with mechanical devices, slide rules, mechanical pencils, interesting sculptures, and another clock. And indeed, he sits with thick, black hair not greased back as it normally is, with high Russian cheekbones and sculpted good looks, working diligently on a sock.

"Please keep the picture, Nina. I want you to be reminded of me at home alone when we're not together," Nick continues.

Nina accepts it, and with little fanfare suggests that perhaps, soon, he can meet her brother Leonya and see some really good photos. Already in love, he disregards the comparison. He feels confident in her response, thinking that meeting her brother is a step in the right direction. Noting how the light reflects off the dark curls peeking from under her hat, her freckled face, and dark brown eyes, he turns toward the stage where the symphony is playing Rimsky-Korsakoff.

As he watches the orchestra, he thinks about Nina—her natural nature and her seriousness. He likes the way she talks to him in a direct yet still feminine fashion. He's a man's man, an intellectual and a prankster, and he knows she enjoys his cunning sense of humor. This pleases him.

Nina takes in the music, remembering that Rimsky-Korsakoff was distantly related to the family. This evokes both pride and fear in her, for she knows that this sort of information is considered anti-government. Sitting next to Nick makes her feel safe. Something about him seems untouchable and secure, and she likes this.

Nina sits on the wooden kitchen chair, reading a letter she's received from her mother. The annoying conflict she usually feels when she reads these letters resurfaces. And although she convinces herself that her life in Leningrad is good, she knows with certainty that her mother, younger sister, and brother living in Berlin must be wealthy beyond her current capacity to imagine for herself here. While her mother has never written of being financially well-off, it is evident, not only in the stationary she uses, but in the gifts she's seen her brother and cousins receive from Josephine in the past.

It's been several months since Nina's last received a letter, partially because Nina has reduced the number of letters she's written herself. The letters she has written continue to lack any real definition of daily events, for Nina feels this is of little use. Still, it is exciting to have some semblance of events from the outside world. And even where some few sentences are censored or blacked out, Nina gleans a great deal from the mixed French, German, and Russian that her mother carefully uses.

Nina tears open the envelope, and begins to read; "Dear Nina, I trust that both you and your brother are doing well…" Nina realizes that there is no mention of her father. Most of the first paragraph seems to be concerned with instructions on proper ways to eat, exercise, and look after her brother. Mother, as usual in these letters, comments on practical matters of how Nina should care for herself, always reminding her to take walks. This in itself is an aggravation because living in the city is always about walking, even to public transportation. Nina does as much as she's willing to in this regard. Looking after her brother, and father for that matter, has included inevitably loaning them money from the small parcel of savings that Nina makes a point of stashing away each payday.

Nina reads on. Her mother normally writes political news only in ways that are agreeable to the censors, but Nina can see that the next statement has no need to be expressed in that regard. A man named Hitler has taken power as chancellor, which appears to be of some concern to her mother because of her dislike of intense nationalism. Even though Nina chooses to be indifferent in external or public conversations about politics, she is highly opinionated in private, in the age-old Russian heritage of being so. And having survived so far to this age of twenty-six, she's unwittingly seen the radical chaotic results of what extreme political movements can cause.

Nina reads on, more alarmed by what follows: her sister Vera's mental health seems to be mysteriously deteriorating…but there are no details. "What can this mean?" Nina wonders, perplexed, as she continues to see if she can't find out more. Vova, states Josephine, has never recovered from leaving his beloved Russia; "What can he possibly be thinking?" Nina asks herself as she rereads this odd statement with eyebrows raised in shock. "Certainly, the many immigrants in Berlin can help clear his mind of any misconceptions about life in Russia during this year of 1933," Nina thinks. For even Nina knows of the famine in the countryside, if only because the papers have finally declared that it's ended before ever acknowledging that it existed.

Nina finishes reading, and then shrugs off the information,

knowing there is no way for her to be any clearer on the details than she already is. Hastily, she tears up the letter and places the pieces in the trash along with the other refuse. There certainly isn't any need to have letters from Berlin sitting around the house.

ℭ

The tennis ball bounces off the cement court, damp from an early October rain the night before. Nina stretches to her right in order to return it. Sasha does not miss a beat as she drives the ball back. Nina instantly eyes its direction and velocity and prepares herself once again. As the ball spins toward her, she attempts to clear her mind of any thought except of returning it, but for a moment cannot. She strikes it with a hard snap of her racket, and it flies out of bounds. Sasha walks over, picks it up, and serves again. Nina is distracted today, and her tennis suffers because of it. Turning to swing, she misses the ball completely. Sasha has won. Nina walks over to the net, shakes her hand, and the two separate to continue on with their Sunday.

Nina walks up the spiral of three flights of stairs leading to the apartment that she's become so accustomed to sharing with her brother. As she turns the last half-flight of stairs she notices a man standing by the apartment door. Immediately she fears trouble, but continues to walk undeterred. There's something else that flashes through her mind, something more familiar. With little choice, she looks up directly at the well-dressed man. There she sees the broad shoulders, gleaming eyes, and bright, white shining teeth of her younger brother, Vova.

"Nina!" Vova exclaims as he leans next to the doorframe, his fine leather luggage beside him. Nina stops in shock, staring at her brother. His blonde hair is slicked back, and he's wearing a finely-tailored suit, neatly pressed pants, and polished, black leather shoes, the quality of which she hasn't seen since she was a child. Instantly she calculates how much he's changed physically in the five years since 1928, when she saw him last.

"You seem so short," Vova says with a gleam of satisfaction in his eyes.

Nina responds with little warmth, "Why have you come here?"

"Well, don't I even get a 'Hello'?" Vova asks, smiling.

Nina, turning red, looks around to make sure no one is watching. "Vova, come in with me," she says as she quickly unlocks the door and lets him in. "You shouldn't have come here," she continues.

"Your letters said all was well here, and what is not well I want to fix. I've been called to help save my mother Russia," Vova replies simplistically as he sets his large case down in the kitchen.

"Vova, don't you know I write what I have to in order to not be arrested? Don't you know what sort of government we have here?" Nina splutters in exasperation.

"Ah, same old sister...some things never change," Vova

responds. "Well if you're worried about me, don't be. I won't be a nuisance. I've arranged for an apartment that will be left vacant by a couple of German ladies soon. It will all work out," he says, smiling broadly at his frustrated sister. Nina sets down her things and offers to make him some food and tea. Vova looks around the small apartment, realizing many people share it.

"When will Brother be home?" he asks, as he watches Nina prepare the food.

"I never know for sure. He has a couple of jobs other than his photography work," Nina answers, warming up to the young brother that everyone so adored. And then she ponders her old theory that he's so adored because he has, so often in the past, put himself in situations requiring he sidestep danger, or death itself. He relished being the daring, courageous death-defying one.

Nina continues frying dried mushrooms in a pan, remembering the times when she used to pick fresh mushrooms from the forests surrounding her grandfather's cottages, and how the cook would then fry them in butter. She loved them then and finds them delicious now. Leonya has returned, and Irina volunteered to fetch Leonid, who does not have a telephone. Nicholas will be joining the family soon, but not until after dinner as he is completing one of his exams.

At first, the conversation is peppered with shock at the return of Vova. Nina and Leonya and then old Leonid explain what has gone on with their lives. As the evening wears on, and Nick joins in, the men share some vodka and continue their conversations. Vova continues, discussing his life in Berlin—of the city and of the wealth that he was privy to but did not feel a part of it. He tells story after story, none of which had been communicated in any of the letters from Josephine.

Vova speaks wearily of opportunities that should otherwise elicit more enthusiasm, and discloses that he always felt melancholy about Russia and his having to leave so hastily. Although Grandfather Karl had amassed a huge fortune in real estate from his early dealings in the upstart auto industry, Vova admits he never completely enjoyed the life presented to him in Berlin. Because his schooling was so far behind the others in his social class, and because he was disillusioned with the social one-up-manship that the colleges in Berlin represented, he chose trade school instead, and is now a certified electrician. He hopes he can use this knowledge to help rebuild Russia.

Vova's garrulousness continues as the evening wears on, and he explains how deeply he disliked the required, two-years' military service in the German army. He expresses concern over some of the new restrictions imposed by Chancellor Hitler, and the lack of balance with President von Hindenburg, now nearly ninety. Most of all, the southern, Munich-led politicizing in Berlin made Vova desperately miss the heart and soul of the always-struggling, Russian people.

Though not a heavy drinker himself, the four measured fingers of vodka that Nick serves him has its effect, and Vova discloses how everyone in the family tried to talk him out of returning; he then admits he hastened his return by abandoning his last year of compulsory service in the Nazi Army.

As the evening concludes, he also speaks of their sister Vera's schizophrenia, which was a recent diagnosis and not published in the medical records of the family doctor, who is also a family friend. Her talents as an artist seemed to blossom along with her beauty in her late teens, but shortly after she began charity work with poor village farmers she began to have episodes. Then, as time went on, her mind became oddly more mischievous. Finally, Vova discloses how she now screams and throws tantrums at the most bizarre times. Their mother, Josephine, has become a social recluse, both for fear of her daughter acting out, as well as in response to numerous occasions of embarrassment in front of others.

17

NICHOLAS

Nick enters his one-room apartment and places the keys to his newly acquired larger, two-room apartment on his desk. He smiles to himself as he realizes how he got away with breaking the rules. Sitting down at his desk to sketch an outline of the new floor layout, he recalls again how he told the authorities that he was married. Of course, public debate over the institution of marriage was at its height before simplification in 1926.

At times all unmarried partners were considered the same as married couples in the eyes of the authorities. Divorce now takes place in a matter of minutes, allowing some rural peasants as many as three or four marriages by the time they are twenty. Other country farmers in their semi-lucrative twenties married husky wives during the summer season for labor and then divorced them at season's end.

Russia claims to be a country of no illegitimate children, only because children are considered the responsibility of the father, whether there is a legal marriage or not. Fathers sometimes had many children from different wives, regardless of their ability to afford them. Other times women knowingly became "summer brides" to wealthy kulaks, before kulaks (successful farmers) became ostracized, in order to get money for themselves and their offspring.

Nonetheless, the rules are still the same in the Leningrad of 1934, where housing is parceled out per person, accordingly. And while the hated, old "bourgeois" tradition of marriage still exists on paper, never truly abolished by those Communists who think it an abomination, it also helped Nick obtain a larger apartment before ever asking Nina to consider marrying him. After all, Nick continues to think, this *might* happen, maybe even soon. He's already met all of Nina's family, and everyone seems to like him as far as he can tell.

The phone on his desk rings. Nick answers and laughs at the far-fetched antics one of his oldest and best friends calls to share with him. It's the same friend he's known since their boyhood, and one of the fellows he used to play the game "Cuckoo" with. The game went something like this: Nick or one of his friends would have been chosen to take a gamble or ploy. Whoever that was would then remove four out of the five cartridges from the cylinder of a revolver. He would then spin the cylinder, snap it back in place, put it to his head, and, when the others called, "Cuckoo!" pull the trigger. The game came from Russian officers who would stage a game in a dark room, where one officer would stand on a chair or table and, when the others yelled "Cuckoo," would pull the trigger as a temptation of fate. There was one chance out of five that the hammer would set off a live cartridge. Nick finally quit the dare after a bullet ricocheted past his ear, nearly killing him on the spot.

When Nick finally gets the opportunity, he confides his newest "deal" to his old friend. After their conversation ends, Nick sets the heavy black receiver on the cradle, sits back in his metal-framed chair, puts his feet on his desk, and leans back. Always having been a thinker and strategist, Nick contemplates his future. Married life will be different, he thinks, but not that much…his old buddies will still be invited over, he's sure. After all, he supposes, Nina's used to having men around. Besides, he's been a good bachelor all of these years and, now that he's thirty-one, he's had lots of experience hosting friends and making *zakuski* (small, dark bread sandwiches served with sardines, caviar, smoked fish, pickled herring, or ham) along with a modest serving of vodka to wash it down. On that point, he thinks again, remembering only having seen Nina drink vodka once, and then eating all the fat off the ham to fill herself up.

Continuing his sketching, Nick ponders the schematic thoroughly as usual. The apartment is a large rectangle in which the corner contains a separate room that can be entered via two narrow doors on each of the adjoining walls. The main entrance is through the kitchen area that contains a small stove and kitchen sink. It is here that Nick considers bringing in a small tub for bathing and perhaps a separate washbasin for cleaning vegetables and dishes. The bathroom is just outside the door and is shared by one other, rather overweight couple who live in the apartment next door.

As he sketches, he remembers the Russian saying, "Dreams, Dreams, where are your sweetness." Thinking it odd to remember this now, he continues to contrive various arrangements. As a bachelor for all these years, he thinks that it would be ideal to take the smaller room as a study/office/workshop and napping area that he can call his own. His bride could then take full charge of the remaining three-quarters of the house, leaving him in peace when he needs it. Above all, he knows that Nina, still harboring old values, wouldn't consider living with him without first being married and, for that matter, has yet to even see his current apartment.

Nick sketches his room, complete with bookshelves, a small couch that can also serve as a bed, his desk, and chairs. It doesn't take him long to project the entire layout and begin thinking about how he can use the tool shop, at the factory he works at, in the evenings to make some of the furniture he's drafting on paper. He works well into the night, forgetting about his homework. He rationalizes that he can sleep on the job tomorrow, as he drowsily begins to fall asleep at his desk. For without dreams, both awake and asleep, how can he make reality work?

∽

It's been a busy day for Nina so far, and it's far from over, she realizes, as she mixes the onions, bread, and hamburger together from the combined rations of all the family members, in order to make her specialty staple food, *kutleki*. Vova has come over for dinner once again, as he has not learned to prepare food for himself, having had a cook the prior five years in Berlin. Leonya will be home soon, as well, but by that time Nina might be well on her way to her cousin's apartment, where, she's promised her aunt, she'll visit with her depressed and forlorn cousin Sophia.

Memories resurface of cooking for her entire family during her teenage years, first in the country and then in Yaroslavl. "Cooking for a growing family of men is not the reason I moved back to Leningrad,' she thinks, as she places the meat patties in the frying pan.

"So I got to work on my first day…My first day, Nina," Vova animatedly interrupts his sister's thoughts from his seat next to the kitchen table. Nina looks up briefly, and then continues peeling potatoes. "…and I'm standing next to the chief electrician who I was supposed to assist until I learn how things are done there," Vova continues, barely restrain his eagerness.

Nina hears the word *was*, and is ready to give Vova a piece of her mind if he's done something wrong at work already. Vova knows this and plays with her. He waits the requisite amount of time before she interrupts her work, and then continues; "Just then the fuse box he's working on…explodes."

Nina stops completely and looks at him. Vova continues, "Oh, there wasn't much of a fire, but the smoke and soot went everywhere; on his face, all over his hair, on his and my clothing…the works."

Knowing that he has a captive audience, Vova demands, "Guess what happened then."

Nina, already compromised in her work, sets down the utensils. "What happened, Vova," she says, "Are you okay?"

"I'll tell you," Vova lingers, then starts, "He asks for a cigarette…," Nina stands and waits. Vova slowly continues, "…and he lights it…" Watching his sister's face, he finally concludes with eyes wide and hands in the air, "…and then he falls dead to the ground!"

"Dead!?" Nina exclaims, morbidly humored by his story.

Vova looks directly at her and repeats, "Dead!"

The smell of meat burning in the pan brings Nina back to her cooking; she quickly gets up to add some water. Vova sits satisfied on the chair while Nina realizes how little anything has changed. Vova is still the same boy that left all those years ago. Finishing the meal she says to him, "You know, Vova, you have to save some of the money that you'll be making from your work." Vova looks at her wondering how she's come up with this. "After all, you never can tell if you'll have to go to the hospital and not work, or what you'll need, so always, always make sure to save." Vova continues to listen, having been lectured by his sister from time immemorial. He does his best to change the subject, with no apparent success, as Nina brings him his plate and begins to eat her dinner.

The meal has concluded for Nina. She's eaten her portion and left her brothers to their own diversions. The cable cars are full, as usual, and provide the extra warmth to take the remaining wet chill out of the spring air. Nina transfers across town toward Tetragoza Terraca where her cousins live, her thoughts now focused more on Nicholas than on what to expect from Sophia. Her primary concern for their future is whether he has any bad habits.

The first time Nina ever confronted her father she found him sitting alone in his room looking pale as a ghost. Knowingly, she asked if he had gambled and lost, and to this he answered honestly that he had. Remembering the scene now as if it were yesterday, she asked, "Can't you stop," and he answered, "No." It's true that Nick doesn't have the same background as hers, but hardly anybody left still does. And those who do would be just as much a liability as a gambling husband, she believes. How interesting that what is or is not desirable in a person has changed so with the times, she concludes, as she walks up the flights of stairs to her cousin's familiar apartment.

Entering her aunt's house, she finds her cousin lying immobile on the sofa, staring into the dry, coal-heated air. Nina knows that Sophia has been spending months on end traveling to far reaches of the country, to various hard labor and concentration camps, everywhere short of Siberia, to find her exiled Polish husband, and bring him a pair of warm boots. Ethnic Germans, Poles, Italians, and Jews have recently been the most targeted "criminals." Beyond all of Sophia's traveling, she's accomplished nothing. Nina wonders whether Sophia is sick from exhaustion.

"Sophia, how can you let this happen to you," Nina says critically, as she takes her coat and old fur hat off and walks over to her cousin. Then, in an attempt to recover from the harshness of her words, she tells Sophia of the time she found Sophia's mother lying exhausted on the sofa. Tante Lulya had returned from the May Day Parade, throwing her hand to her forehead and declaring dramatically that she had marched herself to exhaustion, and then sank ever so gracefully onto the sofa cushions.

Barely audible, her cousin responds in a cool unwavering tone, "I've been told I have to leave the city, Nina."

"But why," Nina hears herself asking, knowing full well that there really isn't any reason that can be rationalized by any measure of the imagination.

"Because my husband has been sent away–my dear, dear Anton, who I spent three months trying to find and bring a new pair of boots to, is gone."

"Yes, Sophia, but what has that to do with you," Nina says coolly, remembering how much older her husband Anton is.

"That's what *I* said, Nina," Sophia cries, not lifting her head far from the pillow. "I told them I had done nothing wrong."

"And so you didn't," Nina says, as she sits on the couch next to Sophia's legs.

"Their answer to that was, 'If you *did* do something wrong, you would be arrested; since you haven't done anything wrong, we're sending you out of the city'."

Nina looks at her cousin's swollen, wet, puffy face, not knowing what to say. "Where are you being sent," she finally asks.

Sophia answers, "To the desert, or it may as well be. It's

dry over there. There are no trees and the grass grows long...it's Tashkent!"

Nina looks into her cousin's pleading eyes and says, "Leningrad is a big city, Sophia. If we ever had any sort of catastrophe, we'd all be in trouble. You'll at least be safe there."

⇟

For this wedding there will be no gifts, no special gown, no large family gathering. Everything in the small civil office is either beige or gray, with some splashes of red signifying the Party's strength. The bored clerk shouts out "Comrades... come this way." Nick and Nina walk together to the clerk's paper-covered, metal desk, and then join a small group of other couples who are waiting to be wed as well.

A wall-eyed, stooped, little man shouts out instructions, "Sign here...Your nationality, citizenship, dates of birth...just follow the questions...each of you." Nina and Nick take turns and sign the document. Nina writes her nationality as Russian, as usual. Once they've finished the official grabs the document and signs his name the only way he knows how, with an "X."

"Thank you, Comrade," Nick says with a smile and then turns to his wife and kisses her. Nina shrugs back slightly, feeling self-conscious in public. The two follow the others out into the street to begin their life together. One of the first concerns for Nick is that the apartment Nina will now call home lacks furniture. He *has* been successful, however, at building some shelves for the main living and kitchen areas, and some of the men in the tool shop made nicely-stylized, art deco chairs with a matching table. Besides these, he has his cot, desk, desk chair, little lamp with fringes on it, and his own bookshelves. Luckily, both have arranged to take time off from work to move Nina in, and then celebrate their union with a vacation to the Crimea.

Vova has agreed to help him bring Nina's couch, which was brought from Yaroslavl and opens to another, larger, bed. Nina also has a large mirror given her by Uncle Yuri, which was one of the excess furniture Tante Lulya and Uncle Yuri were able to retrieve from Grandfather Karl and Grandmother Josephine after they left for Berlin. She also has a sewing machine and a large trunk her mother left her.

After moving Nina's belongings, the two attend a nice dinner at a local restaurant that, like many, requires the diners to bring their own utensils. Nina doesn't criticize the food, enjoying not having to cook. But, because she is new at it, romance doesn't come easily, and she looks forward to the time when all the newness will wear off.

The flight to the Crimea is Nina's first, but she refrains from acting unladylike by showing any excess of enthusiasm. Being a couple is almost embarrassing to her, but she's confident she'll be able to adapt with time.

The quaint hotel they stay in is a three-storied, wood and stone building decorated with rustic latticework on its exterior. It has inviting porches leading out to a view of the sea beyond. The interior touches include Russian lace and embroidered tablecloths in the otherwise modestly furnished guest rooms. The bed is soft and luxurious for Soviet standards, with clean but frail linen. Both Nick and Nina are very pleased to be in this former retreat of the wealthy, one of several Black Sea towns they will visit. Nina has already let Nick know that this is the area where her uncle Felix, well-liked by the local population, once governed before he was assassinated. Unfortunately, she's added, since his assassination, her cousins Irina and Wadim, and their noble-born mother, her aunt, moved to Leningrad, where Wadim became the only person in the family to join the Communist party.

The alarm clock wakes both Nick and Nina to join the organized hike they will be taking today to a high meadow near the top of a steep hill. The area is quite mountainous to the west toward the Black Sea. Unbeknownst to Nina, that was where her other uncle, Roman, made his last daring escape from the invading Bolsheviks at the end of the Civil War. This morning, however, both get ready for their hike, as unfamiliar with the region's history and former opulence as the rest of their young-adult, Soviet peers.

Nick wears his white pants and open-collared shirt. A straw hat covers his dark hair, and beige, woven sandals brace his feet against the rocky soil. Nina wears a pale yellow, light cotton dress she's sewn for the occasion and cream-colored sandals. The two have joined a large group that makes its way up the mountain. A group of eight women follow the leader, and the men trail behind, Nick at the head of this group.

Women speak and laugh with one another. Nina breathes in the scent of flowering fruit trees and wildflowers, thinking she's in paradise. Apple trees line the lower path.

The sun has become quite hot, but a few, long, white clouds occasionally filter its intensity. The sound of loose rocks crunching and shifting beneath sandaled feet is all they hear. The group makes a turn higher up the path. Large hawks fly above and strange tiny creatures dart quickly here and there on prehistoric legs.

The banter continues, the trail narrows and winds around the increasingly steep hill, and what had been just a slope off to the left of the path has turned into a craggy cliff. The mood is gay and jovial despite the long hike made by these athletic, thin-framed hikers.

Nina comfortably walks near the back of the group of women, many of whom have lifted their skirts straight up over their heads to protect themselves from the sunlight. The men are a distance behind, with Nick still barely visible in the front. Nina decides to join in and unashamedly lifts her skirt up over the back of her head as well.

Suddenly she hears dirt shifting and a thud down the side of the hill. Worrying that it's Nick, she turns quickly, only to see a smile on his face. She smiles back at him as she watches him take a large stone and throw it in her direction and down the hill. The path becomes much narrower as Nina contemplates the sound of the rock falling all that distance.

As they continue to rise, Nina notices that a white cloud seems to be hovering just above them, almost within reach. "What a dream, to touch a cloud," she thinks to herself; "Then I could always remember how I touched the sky once in my life." She turns around to see the five men gaining speed and wonders if Nick or the others can see what she sees, or thinks what she thinks. And then there's just one more uphill climb before the path begins to settle into the meadow. Nina reaches on her tiptoes, extends her arm as high as she can, and touches the cloud.

Having done so, ecstatic in her own accomplishment, she quickly looks around to see if anyone else has noticed her or the cloud, too. No one looks, no one feels the cloud, and no one notices. "Stupid people," she mumbles disappointed and alone in this awareness. She moves forward amidst the banter of the mobile, young group.

A couple of days later, Nina still mentions nothing of her experience with the cloud to her husband. The two sit next to each other on another rare and thrilling journey. The roaring of the turboprop engines seems to create turmoil in the air around her as the small airplane lifts Nina and Nick off the ground and upward into the heavens and beyond where Nina's cloud floated. Nina watches in awe as the air field, airport workers, then buildings and even mountains become smaller and smaller below them. If she focuses and squints her eyes she can almost see the Black Sea. Nina is infatuated with it all; how lucky those little people must be to live on this beautiful mountainside this August, 1934.

❧

It's six o'clock in the morning, and Nina is up and dressed. Rumor has it that there are some armoires that will be available today. Nina wants to be amongst the first in line, if she isn't the chances of her getting one will be small at best. She walks over to the small, wooden table in the larger room where she usually sleeps, and splashes some water from the ceramic basin on her face. Quickly, she finishes cleaning up with a face cloth, dresses, and leaves. Nick won't be up for another hour or two, and hopefully she will have purchased the wardrobe by then.

Dashing out of the door she makes it to the shop in time to be the sixth person in line. The line continues to grow with housewives until it snakes around the block. Hours pass as Nina contemplates her lost day of work, and then the doors finally open. Nina feels the push of the crowd behind her, but this doesn't bother her in the least. She's here for one purpose and intends to be successful. Only six wardrobes were manufactured, shipped, and available for sale, and Nina, the sixth person in line, gets the last one. The wardrobe is heavy and large, but Nina is able to arrange for picking it up after work. Nick should be home early tonight, so all will go well. She feels so lucky, as she rushes to her job.

Returning home after finishing the day at work, she notices a letter from her mother. The postmark, as usual, is a couple of months behind, as it is now October, 1935, and the date stamped in Berlin indicates August. Nick isn't home yet, and Nina hasn't time to read it, as she must pick up the wardrobe, even if it means getting one of her brothers to help her. She sets it down on the kitchen table and rushes back out the door to collect Vova or Leonya.

Josephine wrote the letter shortly after her 96-year-old father, known to Nina as Grandfather Karl, passed away. Josephine has inherited his businesses, even though her mother is still alive. Sister Emma has more money than she knows what to do with and wasn't interested in taking over any responsibilities of the extensive estate. Her two brothers are likewise preoccupied. And sister Louise (Nina's Tante Lulya) is in Russia, where it is impossible to transfer possession of such a large estate. Josephine now must manage twelve apartment complexes and sixty-six auto garages, all located on three major intersections that form a triangle of city blocks within walking distance of the Brandenburg Gate, which is the center of Berlin,.

Yet even with this new wealth, Josephine has become increasingly forlorn. Her letter to her daughter mentions the fact that she has moved to the western part of the city, a good distance from some of the other immigrants and Berlin socialites that she, in earlier days, had befriended. Her younger son's move back to Leningrad has caused her nothing but distress. And her distress is only compounded by her daughter Vera's schizophrenia, which has worsened. Shortly before their move, Vera attempted to jump off the balcony on one occasion, and on a separate, started kicking at Josephine in the middle of the street.

The new apartment is smaller than the last, with only two bedrooms to accommodate Josephine and her daughter. The furniture that Josephine acquired since living in Berlin is upholstered in silk, and a large display cabinet sits in the middle of the main living area to show off Josephine's collected objects of art, crystal, and family heirlooms from her mother.

The political situation has likewise become alarming to Josephine, who prefers to have less idealistic men in office. Since the death of von Hindenburg in March of 1934, Adolph Hitler has assumed control of both the chancellorship and the presidency of the country. Josephine's brother Karl has exclaimed that it is the end of the country as they know it. This has, in and of itself, grieved Josephine, who feels she has no place left to run should conditions ever become as ideologically extreme as they had in Russia. The Nazi Party has taken complete control and censors the press, creates new laws without the approval of Parliament, and arrests any and all citizens who oppose Nazi policy. The Jewish synagogue located near Josephine's old apartment has been burned to the ground.

Josephine's letter to her daughter reveals none of these concerns, for she knows that there are censors in both countries. Nina will not notice the brevity of the letter. Her remarks are narrow, at best, as they describe how Vera has given up her charity work with farmers in the village and plays the piano more often to settle nerves; her favorite piece is Beethoven's *Moonlight Sonata*. She closes with a wish for the best for Nina and her brothers, and adds the change of address.

Nicholas returns home exhausted after a full day of work and a full evening of classes. He walks past his wife sleeping on her couch, not noticing the new wardrobe that stands in the area where they eat. In order not to wake her, he quietly steps into his own room and shuts the door before turning on his small lamp to do some reading that is required for his class tomorrow. Likewise, he'll forego eating tonight since the noise in the kitchen might bother her. He knows how early Nina has been waking and how busy she is. So, as his stomach growls, he works late into the morning.

18

THE GREAT TERROR
1937–1938
&
ANOTHER APPROACHES
1939

The October days are short and dark. The air is damp and cold, yet the heartiest of the brown, dry leaves still cling to the branches of the nearly barren trees. An icy circle wraps around the waning moon as Leonid walks with his daughter, Nina, three months pregnant, through the dark, ghostly streets toward the familiar, Leningrad train station.

Leonid grabs for his collar with his empty hand, feeling for the fur that he hasn't worn for decades. His thoughts have grown cloudy, unlike the clean lines of shadows cast by the illuminating moon. In his left hand he carries a bag with all his worldly possessions, a silver brush, old documents declaring achievements from a bygone era, a worn suit jacket, pants and a pair of new boots.

Nina holds onto his arm, feeling a foreboding sense of loss.

She's more emotional than usual, but attributes this to her pregnancy. Then again, she knows it's not. The Communists have despised Father for years, but current persecutions of 1937, by all outward appearances, have been the most extensive in memory. Arrests are so utterly commonplace, and the threat of being persecuted so great, that there are no longer any smiling or–to Nina's way of thinking–intelligent-looking faces on any of the pedestrians she passes by. The tens of thousands murdered cannot be hidden from the grim, anxious survivors of this new Russia.

Leonid has been lucky. His last summons to the authorities has resulted in his being told he must leave Leningrad at once and never return. Leningrad, the old city of the Tsars, continues to be under more scrutiny than many other great cities. It is Stalin's intent to smash any semblance of the city's former society and philosophy, to erase any vestige of hope, color, or energy that remains. And the old bourgeoisie are no longer the only scapegoats. Every man and woman are.

In order to comply with the recent dictate, Leonid's chosen to move back to Yaroslavl to be near his old cronies from days past. Nina strongly dislikes his decision, remembering well how her father was under continual surveillance there, until he was finally arrested and sent to three years in Siberia. She doesn't see why anything should be different now. And besides, there isn't anyone of any worth for him there either, only fellow sick gamblers. But the decision is not in her hands, and she has little influence in molding her father's mind, even though she has tried.

"Perhaps I can speak of times past," Nina thinks, trying to make conversation with her depressed, resigned father. "Remember, Father, the chicken coup that you built at the Finnish dachas that summer? And the pond nearby, where the ducks would swim?"

"Yes, I do," Leonid responds wearily, yet newly animated by old memories that come to mind more quickly than the tortured recent ones. "And I remember how you saved the scrawny chicken who laid those oversized eggs," Leonid says proudly in response.

"Oh yes," Nina responds, happy that he mentioned her favorite subject— animals. "That's right. I came out and saw that she had drowned in the lake," Nina notices her father's interest as the two continue across the damp cobblestones towards the station. "So I used the bed sheet, the way I had heard people in the old days had saved drowned children. Remember, Father, how I almost drowned at the dachas twice?"

Leonid doesn't respond verbally, but Nina thinks she sees the recognition of her question on his deeply wrinkled, yet maturely handsome features. "I placed her on the sheet, and then swung the sheet until the water came out of her mouth," Nina continues with the story. As she does so, she stifles her own desire to ask her father questions that have no answer—questions like, "How long will you stay with your friends?" or "Will you gamble?" or "How will I ever see you again?"

Nina wasn't with her father when he was last arrested, and did not see his reaction or feel his fear. Still, this current expulsion seems more sinister to her than any before. The weight of the verdict rested heavily on her father's shoulders when he visited several days ago to gift Nina four, delicate, porcelain plates. He had painted these with images of beautiful red, yellow, pink, and violet roses. She's since placed them along the tall, wooden shelf that runs below the ceiling of the kitchen area in her apartment.

Nina watches as her father continues to walk beside her, his best suit on below his worn coat with the pin of his graduating law class proudly visible on the lapel. Beneath the glow of the irregularly-placed street lamps, she sees his eyes glazing with tears. "I took my hands and warmed her under her wings until Mother came out and told me...," Nina tries to copy her mother's voice, to her father's rather amused response "...you are to leave that dead chicken alone!" The station, visible up ahead, gradually comes into focus through the darkness. The illumination of functioning streetlamps makes clear that her father's face has the same white and pasty pallor that Nina remembers of the general who ate supper with the family during the Revolution, the night before he died. "But she wasn't dead, I saved her," Nina concludes mumbling now beneath her breath as the damp and drizzling breeze picks up. And then she realizes she is speaking only to herself.

The Leningrad station is busy even at this late and dreary hour, filled with the fellow dispossessed; drunken sailors, Communist officials, wary passengers, spies. The ticket purchased, Nina waits while her father steps onto the idle train and momentarily disappears behind its sideboard. She follows alongside, watching as he moves down the aisle looking for a seat.

She places a hand on her stomach and feels a momentary weakness in her legs. In no uncertain terms she knows she will not see her father again. Now, with clear eyes, she sees his face seemingly larger than life, looking directly at her through the beveled glass window. She lifts her hand to blow a kiss to him as a tear runs down his cheek.

Leonid feels the train's pulse as it advances through the countryside. He's leaving his Petersburg for the last time. Gone are the familiar facades, the echo of the voices on cobble-stoned streets, the dreary, pigeon-stained statues, the smell of vendor's carts selling chestnuts during Christmastimes of old. There are no poppies in the fields to greet him this time. Nothing calls his name to bring him hope. For, this time, there is no such thing.

❦

Vova sits at the small table at his sister's home, where he often visits. Nick pours vodka into a glass to calm his brother-in-law's nerves, as Vova begins to tell them of his trip to Yaroslavl to attend Leonid's trial. Both Nick and pregnant Nina are extremely fatigued, having been awoken once again, at two a.m., by neighbors' tortured screams and protesting pleadings which pierce the walls of their apartment. Yet neither spoke of it this morning, for there was no need.

The hours between eleven o'clock in the evening and three

o'clock in the dark morning are generally when arrests take place. Individuals, couples–nay, entire families–go, often without any argument. What use is there to scream for mercy when there is no explanation, trial, or representation? Some even leave a suitcase by the door in preparation for the inevitable.

Tens of thousands disappear from Leningrad each month. And the arrests are not confined to Leningrad. Stalin's insane, paranoid purges of the countryside where Nina and her family once lived are not recorded anywhere and only known to the inhabitants of their former country home–and of villages like them. The census of 1937 will report a decline in population and the officials responsible for the count will be shot. The majority of the original Bolsheviks have been shot in 1937, as well as army leaders, Poles, Italians, Jews, and Germans. Arrests at Nick and Nina's work do not go unnoticed, but most people have become numb to them; former co-workers leave after work one night and never return the following morning. Nonetheless, posters adorn factory and engineering shop walls reading, "Life Has Become Better," and "Life Has Become More Joyful."

Vova is at a loss for words for the true meaning of what he's witnessed. His motives to evade Hitler's Germany and return to help save his mother Russia have not helped him save his own father. He is left helplessly stunned in a no-man's-land between two demented dictators. The scene at the trial was like a surreal picture show of actors performing the recently deceased Stanislovski's theatrics. Vova, at first, can only describe it as "spooky." Nick and Nina want to know more.

"There was a judge, a middle-aged, surly-looking man with a greasy cap. And there was Father, looking pale but courageous…but most of all sad," Vova tries to explain. "There wasn't any way for Father to win; he knew this, so he said very little."

Nick pours more vodka for his brother-in-law. Nina remains silent. "Then I was asked questions," Vova says, speaking to the glass. "I was there, and being there, I was asked questions. It was scary and I began to worry, but recalled, as you've told me, Nina, the children of those persecuted are not to be blamed."

Nina does not ask about the judgment for she already knows. And while not officially publicized, an arrest anytime after July of 1937 is the same as a death sentence. The Russian Politburo and NKVD–replacement for the Cheka and GPU–have signed Order #447, which mandates that all prison camps in the Soviet Union be emptied–emptied of their six to eight million inhabitants.

Vova finally spits out the information, "He's been condemned!" Looking pleadingly at his sister, he seems to be asking her if there is any justice. In truth, he knows there isn't. They sit together in silence, feeling a deep, aching sadness.

℃

Josephine looks at the picture postcard received from her son Leonya in Leningrad. Leonya smiles, his wife Irinka next to him, and their three-year-old daughter, Tatiana, looks joyous in-between. They are well yet simply dressed, for Josephine's tastes; her son wears a sweater jacket with a white collared shirt underneath, her daughter-in-law a loose bow and a permanent wave in her short, bobbed hair, her granddaughter a ruffled collar and short, naturally-curly, blonde hair. The black and white background is a birch-filled forest with a stream running in front of it. It is obviously a backdrop. Nonetheless, the card, dated November, 1937, exudes simplistic words describing what appears to be a delightful vacation to the Crimea. Leonya obviously went to great lengths to prepare the postcard with the picture, and, by all appearances, his family is happy and well-fed.

And indeed, it has been a happy marriage. Irinka's mother had known from the beginning that Leonya was a good catch, successful, bright, and motivated. Irinka immediately had eyes for her new roommate, who moved in shortly after his father's arrest in Yaroslavl. For that matter, Leonya, suffering from so much loss, yet happy to be back and working in the city of his birth, found Irinka—blonde, confident, vivacious, even if a little narcissistic—perfect.

Josephine sets the postcard aside, to be placed later in the family photo album. It leaves her feeling empty. At home, Vera, her youngest daughter, continues to deteriorate from schizophrenia, and conducts activities that embarrass her. Recently, Vera attempted another suicide. Josephine knew she could no longer keep her daughter safe, and, with much regret, committed her to the hospital in Berlin. Much debate has been circulating of late regarding drastic measures to treat the mentally disabled. Josephine doesn't trust the care she's committed her daughter to, but needed to make the decision for her own safety and sanity. The outcome of the hospitalization has been that Vera has had her uterus removed against her will, as Nazi medical practitioners have forced through a law that those suffering mental illness must be sterilized to guard against bringing sickly German children into the world. To make matters worse, she is no longer allowed to leave the institution.

Josephine feels a tragic sense of loss and powerlessness. Her youngest daughter is now confined and sterilized; her youngest son left to return to Leningrad; her estranged husband, eldest daughter, eldest son and sister also live in Leningrad; her other sister, Emma, is still married to a Bulgarian Prince with Nazi ties; her father is dead, and her own two brothers are in a state of abhorrence and contempt for the current regime.

Beyond this, she is aware the direction events are taking in Berlin. The burning of the Reichstag in 1934, and the subsequent blaming of it on the Communists, was even then improbable. Further blame is directed at Jews, an act of scapegoating that is as premeditated now as it was after the assassination of Alexander II in Russia. The resulting declassification of Jews as "non-Aryan," the taking away of their rights of speech, use of the press, professional practices and businesses are steps that she has seen performed on her own class by the Bolsheviks and Communists. She is again witness to sheer and utter insanity.

True, some wealthy and former aristocratic Russian Berliners have, to greater or lesser degree, endorsed the Nazi "Revolution" as a means to safeguard against or even defeat the Communists. But the Nazi Party has been supported predominantly by old WWI war veterans, the middle class, and farmers. Josephine had voted with her Social Democrat, bachelor brothers in 1933 against Hitler; this was before he declared the Enabling Act, making it possible for him to pass laws without consulting the Reichstag and effectively becoming a dictator.

Though some have disagreed with her opinions her family stands in high regard among prestigious members of Berlin society. Josephine doesn't care. As events accumulate—the forced sterilization of her daughter, arrests of Jewish friends, the Nazi Party, declaring itself the only true voice of the people, and the active speeches and parlor talk affirming these speeches for aggression—it becomes nearly impossible to control her passion against them; yet she knows she must.

Already she is surely watched by the party that she despises, given her son's desertion. But she maintains a detached, resolute, indifferent attitude that she's carried from her early adulthood. She's always held herself apart, erectly detached from those elements around her that she neither agrees with nor wishes to condone. Old Russia was teaming with contrast and she maintained her citified uniqueness along with the duty she owed to her class.

Now age is a consideration. Josephine is approaching sixty, but works against her increasing aches and pains via the ballet, winter ice-skating, and year-long gymnastics to keep her body fit and her mind alert. She's briefly considered the thought of leaving and fleeing yet another burgeoning despotic regime. But where would she go? Josephine knows very few people outside of Russia or Germany. And to leave all that her parents had built? No, she rationalizes. She must stay even though she knows staying means life probably will get worse before getting better. The Reich cannot last forever, despite Hitler's claims.

She won't reply to the postcard. While she doesn't know the technicalities of the Soviet Union's Paragraph 58, Item 6 of the Russian code ("Foreign correspondence by letter is a violation and can be considered espionage by the receiver"), she does know that the world has become increasingly dangerous with every passing month. Writing to family in Leningrad can only add to their danger. Besides, at this point she cannot bear to lie to her children by hiding behind false messages, when she struggles so fervently with her opposition to truly being heard. Life is fraught with horrors enough that she need not impose any more of it on what's left of her family.

❦

Nina sits alone on a wooden chaise on the porch of a dacha overlooking the deep Russian forest. Nick will come on the weekend to visit and take pictures, but otherwise must stay and work and watch Kotya, the cat, while Nina takes her much needed month-long vacation. In a bassinet in the main room sleeps their 16-month-old daughter, Alla Nickolaevna. Alla was born last year on April 15,

293

1938. She's a quiet, blonde-haired, green-eyed baby–a pretty contrast to Nick's jet-black hair and light blue eyes, and Nina's dark brown hair and brown eyes.

The birth was uneventful for Nina. At home alone, while Nick was at work, she began feeling the contractions she knew were labor pains. Without phoning her husband, Nina then walked the distance to the hospital. After all, birthing babies had always been a woman's job in the times she remembers as a child, when she and her father were never allowed near her mother. Once Nina arrived at the hospital, an attending midwife came to the room shared with another woman having heavy contractions and screaming in pain. A doctor was available, but midwives and attendant nurses cared for both women for the most part. Children are needed for the young Soviet Union, and everyone is highly trained in this very important official business. No anesthesia is used so the mother can be "fully present."

The nurses worked diligently on delivering the baby boy as its mother screamed in the bed next to Nina. When the little boy was delivered, beautiful and big, he died a stillborn. The nurses and midwives continued to talk amongst themselves at how hard they tried, how beautiful the boy would have been, and what a shame for the mother to have lost the child. Nina was much more lucky and pleased with her newborn, seven-pound, baby girl.

Eventually Nick, after being informed of the birth of his daughter, came to the hospital after work. He, too, was happy to have a girl, and fell in love with her at first sight, dreaming of teaching her math and science when she got older.

Nina remained in the hospital the customary ten days after the birth of Allechka. Wisely, she exercised and walked around in the hospital room so as to not be too weak from all the bed rest when the time came to attend to her new baby and continue with the endless tasks and inconveniences of sustenance and cleaning for her small family.

A cooling breeze flows past weary Nina, rustling the leaves of the birch trees. These trees still stand indifferent to the storm of philosophical conflict that has replaced those who used to vacation here. Nina has thus far weathered the storm. As in her childhood, she melts to the familiar comforts of the balmy, humid air, smells of sap and mulch, and sounds of birds and crickets chirping.

All has not been easy though. Even getting the bassinet for Alla (whom she and Nick call "Allechka") was trying. Again, Nina heard of the availability of these impossible-to-find items, and woke up early once again to be the first in line. Late in her pregnancy at the time, she luckily obtained one, and then had to lug it onto the streetcar on her way to work. Fortunately, she was able to convince a guard at the airplane engineering company (where she most recently worked) to keep it for her until the end of her shift.

Nina hasn't worked since Allechka was born. She can't return to work when most of her day is spent carrying her young daughter from line to line with ration cards to pick up food and necessities . The month-long vacation has become a necessity not only for Nina but, according to Nick, for Allechka. It was upon his suggestion and arrangements that Allechka has been brought to the fresh air of the countryside while still in the fragile first months of life.

Nina did not disagree. While the apartment is relatively large, it has become smaller with Allechka. At times, when Nick or Nina entertain guests or family, all that separates the sleeping baby from their guests is a blanket draped from a piece of string hung from the ceiling. At other times she rests angelically at the foot of the table while the adults eat and drink.

The breeze has picked up with its increasing chilly dampness, alerting Nina from her rest. Nina opens her eyes, then covers them against the hazy sunshine, and looks up to see the formation of gray clouds off in the distance. As is often the case, a sudden downpour can occur in these parts. But there's no need to rush in the house yet.

Two days ago on August 23, 1939, Nick heard on his radio of the signing of the non-aggression pact between Hitler's Germany and Stalinist Russia. To great fanfare the report declared another victory for Soviet foreign relations. Nick could only wonder why a non-aggression pact would be necessary unless there was a great potential for aggression in the first place.

What he could never surmise nor would ever be told was that secret protocols had been added assigning the countries of Finland, Estonia, Latvia, and Bessarabia to the Soviet Union, and Poland was to be partitioned between the two countries. Within days, Poland will be invaded and its Jews exported to concentration camps shortly thereafter. Within a couple of weeks after this, the Soviet Union will also invade Poland, and, several weeks after the Russo-Finnish War will start by invading Finland with half a million Soviet men. Nina has heard nothing of this non-aggression pact yet, as she has no phone or radio and doesn't speak much with the villagers or with the maid who visits twice a week to help with laundry and cleaning.

The cool, humid breeze prevails as it filters through Nina's light, summer, cotton dress. The clouds in the distance are foreboding, almost black, as the fringes creep toward her and dim the light even more. Nina gets up off her chair and walks into the main room where little Allechka lies recently awake. They look at one another with the knowing comfort and serenity that innately affects child and mother.

Nina's thoughts are disturbed, perhaps by the approaching storm after such a pretty morning and early afternoon. Or, perhaps, by the weariness that has finally made itself known now that she can relax away from her exhausting schedule in the city. Nonetheless, her mind is drawn to the last correspondence she received from her mother nearly a year ago. It was only one sentence, but one sentence was all it needed to be.

Letters have been silenced for the most part. In 1938, at the end of what will be known as the Great Terror, over 600,000 people were arrested or sentenced to death in Leningrad and perhaps greater than 14 million others, the exact numbers never revealed, in the rest of the country. The law enforcing the crime of espionage through letters received from foreign countries has been taken seriously. Fortunate for Nina, she hasn't received any.

At this very moment, Nina is also unaware that her Grandmother Josephine, her mother's mother, has just died. Nina's mother is beyond grief, suddenly made aware that her nearly 90-year-old mother, the stalwart of the family who was born at the epicenter of the forging of the Industrial Revolution, has been the most constant and vital thing in her life. And this woman is no more.

Nina walks to the kitchen where she lights the gas burner to heat up some food for her baby. The first vestiges of rain begin to pelt the old wood and tin roof.

"'You have brought your baby into the world only to die.' What a horribly mean thing to write," Nina recalls, as she stirs the porridge into the pot and the rain strikes loudly against the window.

Nina in Leningrad, late 1920's

299

Vova, Josephine, and Vera in Berlin, early 1930's

Nick as a student and darning a sock in his apartment

Nina on honeymoon

Nick's study

Vova in Leningrad

Nina, Irina and Leonya

Book 3

19

THE SIEGE

"Koko, Koko," little Allechka coquettishly calls her father, in her best effort to mimic her mother's nickname for him, which is "Kilja." "Dinner's ready," Allechka continues undeterred by his customary avoidance of her pleas as she knocks on the closed private door to his room.

"Da, da, yes, yes," she hears, as Nick answers from inside his study while busy repairing his radio. Kotya the cat looks warily at his little tormentor from his perch on one of the shelves Nick has built against the kitchen wall. It wasn't long ago that Allechka decided to pull on his tail, taking the shelf with him, and received a nice scar above her eye from the cat's panicked desire to free himself from the playful, little girl.

If Nina were home Allechka's rambunctious behavior would

be stifled. But as is often the case, she's out with a handful of coupons collecting what can be purchased at the markets. An elderly neighbor, nicknamed "Granny," sometimes watches Allechka when Nick is at work. Allechka doesn't really care for her, missing the affections of her mother, and often acts out in ways that makes the woman prefer to keep away. This weekend Papa is home, which is a treat for both Allechka and Nina.

In the corner of the kitchen is a large pile of wooden toys, dolls and stuffed animals that Allechka's accumulated in her short life of three-and-a-third years. A sled stands upright against the wall which Nick built at Nina's request to help her transfer Allechka and bags she carries from the market in the wintertime. Since it's summer, 1941, the sled has gone without use, but stands dust free in the nicely cleaned corner. Nina's sewing table stands at the other side of the room, covered with pots and pans Allechka plays with in her pretence of making breakfast and dinner.

Allechka continues to knock on her father's door, holding a pan filled with toy wooden eggs. Nick finally relents and opens it, blocking her entrance. Just beyond reach on his desk is his toolbox, a work of art that he made, composed of three levels containing wooden rectangles, squares, and circles perfectly formed to house each of his many tools. Nick pats his daughter on the head and says, "I'll be out in a minute." Allechka watches as the door shuts knowing that he won't actually come out. But she knows what to do. If this door doesn't work, there's always the other. And if she tries really hard to be cute, then he'll let her in. Running around to the other side of the room, she again knocks and repeats, "Koko, Koko, dinner's ready."

Nina trades her coupons for tomatoes, carrots, beets and potatoes at the Workers' market near the city center. It's often a grueling chore to stop at so many lines, using so many coupons to get so few goods for so much effort. Today is no different. Even though Nick has suggested she stock up on extra food, she's fatigued with spending so much time, day after day, in the same tedious lines. Plus, she misses her work. Drafting gave her a sense of accomplishment. "Why doesn't Nick go out and do this himself?" she muses. The war between Germany and the western powers, that Nick is so concerned with, is ridiculous to Nina. After all, everyone knows there's a non-aggression pact between Russia and Germany. She decides against burdening herself by buying extra food. With full arms and hands, nonetheless, she heads to the familiar streetcar that will take her across the Neva River and home—home to Vasily Ochev, where the middle class and workers once lived during the time of the Tsar.

There is an unusual briskness among the passersby this balmy June day; it reflects that certain fear that comes when war is in the air. And it is apparent once again. Germany invaded Poland two years ago. Soon after, on September 16, 1939, Russia invaded Poland. Britain and France ignored this fact when they only declared war on Germany. Stalin's army brutally murdered over 10,000 Polish officers; some were taken out to sea on a barge which was then sunk, while others were buried in mass graves at Katyn, their watches and rings removed but badges of rank and medals-of-honor left on the bodies. Intellectuals and priests were the next to be murdered, adding 15,000 to the mass graves already filled with 9,000 corpses of Russian intellectuals and victims of the Great Russian Terror. By the end of November that same year, Nick heard of the war with Finland on his radio. Of course, only rumors reported the size of the invasion (over one million troops) which lasted 105 days before Russia annexed 16,000 square miles of Finnish territory.

Nina cannot deny that the rumors of these atrocities, as echoed by her husband and conversations of other city people, are true. Nonetheless, she chooses to ignore their implications. Pushing her way onto the always-crowded streetcar, she sits down. A young man climbs on board carrying an assortment of rubber paraphernalia and a gas mask, and sits next to her. Nina is drawn out of her complacency by curiosity as the streetcar jerks forward. With her customary directness, Nina asks, "What are you carrying?"

The man responds, "This is military equipment."

"But what for?" Nina responds bluntly. "We have a non-aggression pact with Germany and the Finnish War is over," she goes on to explain to him and herself.

The man looks at her and quietly and simply responds, "There's going to be another war."

Nina jests in order to rationalize what she's just heard, "You're lying." The streetcar continues its jerky, stop-and-go movement. Perhaps the man is correct; she can't help but wonder, as he continues to sit soberly and unflinchingly next to her. Perhaps he and the military know something that the people don't. She continues looking out the window at the many people always crowding the busy side streets. Everything seems so normal; babushkas (older Russian women) walk, their arms filled with children or the day's rations. Soldiers idly sit at cafes. Undercover agents appear out of doorways—everyone recognizes them these days. Farmers drive horse-drawn carts on the road, and one or two official, Communist vehicles drive by. Suddenly Nina can't wait to be home.

The following day it comes like a streak of lightening in a dry summer forest. Waves of news reverberate through offices, apartments, streetcars, markets, and city blocks. Great crowds gather at loudspeakers placed throughout the city, and as quickly disperse. The Nazi army has invaded Russia. It has swiftly torn through outlying villages, burning and disintegrating them in its wake. Stores quickly sell out of food, leaving only the poorest quality dry stock, and then that disappears.

Everyone learns of the Nazi invasion of Russian-occupied Poland, if not by official news, then by talk on the streets by those closest to the battles. One day, go the rumors, Russian officers and soldiers alike went home to their beds. The next day, the swift cruelty of the rapid, German, automatic weapon made the Russian single-fire obsolete. Everyone was either killed or surrendered. The streets of Leningrad hum with the statement, "They just fire and everyone falls down."

Realizing his earlier premonitions to be true, Nick is inconsolable. Arguments surface about who was responsible for not buying any extra food when they could. Nick writes in a journal, which he begins to keep in a small black book, "…arguing with a woman is like scooping water with a sieve."

❧

Life in the fall of 1941 is suddenly dependent upon rebuilding the war machine and sending supplies to Moscow. Stalin has ordered all plants and factories to begin the process. There are evacuations, but not many and not enough. Soon it becomes nearly impossible to evacuate.

Nick's radio is on day and night with more and more disconnected information in German, Polish, and Finnish. He repeatedly hears the name of Hitler and the sounds of troops at battle. The pulse of the Nazi war machine is in full force. It's strange, after so many years of hearing nothing other than false propaganda of the outside world, the outside world has catapulted itself directly into Russia, and the life Nick and Nina have managed to create together.

Man is fighting against man and the entire Russian civilian world–families, children, husbands, wives, and partners—are directly, immediately and uncontrollably affected. Nina wonders at the nature of Man, thinking the world would be a much better place if women were allowed to make the decisions. After all, goes her reasoning, women give birth and raise children. Women would not want to provoke war when the children they love so dearly are brutalized and murdered by it. Yes, she believes the world would be a better place if only women ran it.

By September 8th, 1941, the Nazi army encircles the entire city of Leningrad. Shells explode not only in the outskirts of town, but directly on apartments, buildings, shops, and offices in the city. Trains that had previously been able to leave, flooded with evacuees, stand idle and unable to use their bombed out tracks. The city has become an island unto itself surrounded by hostile, murderous forces.

Soon the life that had been meager yet fulfilling in its own right begins to reach a breaking point. In the beginning of what everyone calls "the siege," city officials offer small but moderately fulfilling bread coupons. Quickly fewer and fewer are offered. Food rations decrease rapidly as long days recede into the darkness of the harsh Leningrad winter. Women stand in lines for bread. These are not the usual, but long, snaking lines of increasingly undernourished people wrapping around city blocks. The need in the eyes of those in line is far different from anything Nina remembers seeing before. Food to merely sustain the hungry masses was not taken for granted when it was hard to obtain in the past, but now it has become a priceless commodity.

As the elderly, ill, disabled, and children begin to fill the morgues, Nick contemplates the potential mortality of his family. He seeks some undefined answer to alleviate his intellectual mind, and becomes increasingly concerned that his family will suffer the misery he sees around him. Searching for hope, he looks to the spiritual world of his Greek Orthodox childhood, and remembers the strange mysticism of persecuted, now-extinct, wandering gypsies. Desperate, he wonders if it is not already too late.

His job at a printing-press firm ended abruptly when his and all other non-military engineering shops were closed. There will be no more income, and only those who work for the military arms industries continue to have work and food at employee cafeterias. This change in the dynamics of Nick's power has alienated him from the world in which he had, until now, made his mark. Russian men are recruited to military duty, no matter their age, and sent to the front where, rumor has it, only one in thirty-seven are given a gun. The others are slaughtered like cattle. Immediately, tens of thousands are massacred while civilians are still arrested for any sign of anti-revolutionary treason. People arrested for political crimes are immediately exterminated.

Amid the bursting artillery, Nick considers the consequences if he were to be recruited to the front line. What would become of Nina and Allechka? Nina cannot care for Allechka and stand in the bread lines. The old nanny is ill from starvation. Eventually, he is summoned to the military office to be recruited. As suggested by a comrade, he brings an egg with him. When the authorities take a sample of his urine he places the egg white into the piss pot. The results indicate that he has a kidney problem, and he is issued a reprieve. The notice indicates that he is deathly ill, but Nick doesn't look deathly ill. It is clear he will now have to go into hiding; the reprieve has become his sentence. As able-bodied men disappear from the streets, he will be under suspicion. And everyone knows that being under suspicion is only one step closer to death for treason. Although he knows intellectually and intuitively that his family will not be able to fend for themselves alone, he is now condemned to continue with his latest ruse. To do so, he begins to eat tea leaves under the common belief that they, too, will skew medical tests to indicate a weakened heart.

☙

As the weeks that began so horrifically decline into the abyss of oncoming winter, conditions continue to deteriorate. Factories on the outskirts of the city that contained much needed bread, sugar, and salt are hit and windows shake that haven't already been cracked by mortar bursts. Still, in spite of mortar fire and bombs, the philharmonic performs and Stravinsky works alone on his next piece of music. The libraries function but the graveyards, already full, do not.

For a time, the immediate neighbor's stock of food is, to a degree, helpful. Nick suggests Nina barter some of her precious possessions, a Siberian, handmade comforter and pillows, and a little press used to dry ink made with beautiful glass handles, that was gifted to her by her mother. The food they receive in exchange is difficult to swallow—oatmeal tops made from oats used to thresh out corn. But it is better than the dried pigskin that Nick has been able to obtain from friends who used to work at a defunct leather factory.

At first, whenever the sirens sounded, the family walked the five flights of stairs down into the damp and musty cellar. Upon returning, fires could be seen burning in the city. Allechka remained placated throughout this activity for the first few weeks. But, as endless nights of interrupted sleep on empty stomachs multiplied, it became a torture for her. After the baby suffered a bout with pneumonia in early October, Nick refused to allow the abuse to continue. Nina agreed. They no longer take refuge in the shelter, but instead give over their lives to whatever fate has to offer.

Nina still takes her place in endless, looping breadlines, sometimes coming home empty-handed. Nick remains at home during the day, doing what he can to sustain his family. Since electricity has been shut off, he's made lanterns using petroleum jelly. At night he's gathered the components necessary to make a little stove that adds needed heat to the apartment. Also at night, Nick and other men rummage in burnt-out buildings to obtain fuel, which has become impossible to buy. Most begin to burn their furniture. Nick's bookcases are the first to go.

Conditions have deteriorated even further from their already-morbid beginnings. By October 31, Nick writes in a tiny script in his small, black, cardboard-bound journal, "Can't sleep anymore, I'm so hungry." On November 13th he writes, "Bread rations are decreased to 150 grams per person." Nina brings home only chunks of bread for all three people. Three days later the rations are decreased to 125 grams.

Nick sees the reflection of his own suffering compounded in the face of his once vivacious daughter. No longer capable of playing, she only asks piteously where the food is. Nick tries to sooth her, at first by telling her fairy tales of a rich uncle coming to visit with macaroni, or of pretend lands that are overflowing with pies and milk. By November 29th, he notes, she asks him to stop telling her stories. By November 30th, he writes, "We cannot overcome our weakness from starvation."

On November 27th explosions hit so close that the windows crack, Nina's mirror hangs sideways, the lamp swings on Nick's desk, and the door to the kitchen flies open. During the worst of this Nick instructs his daughter on how to count cigarettes to ease both their nerves. Nick uses one of the boxes of cigarettes that he had hidden at the outbreak of the war, realizing they might one day become worth more than gold. Nina rushes back from the bread lines. By the time she returns, Allechka only remarks how Kosichka (Kotya) the cat, himself skinny with hunger, jumped from his perch when the building shook.

December is ruthless. As nighttime has lengthened, eating away the daylight, the temperature has dropped below zero. When not blanketed in soot and fire, the sky is invisible from blizzard conditions. The winter, which came on like the Nazis, is in full stride. The lack of food is constantly on their minds and the pain of starvation ceaseless. With extreme cold comes frozen municipal water without workers to repair the lines. Nina risks her life by dodging gunfire with other women to bring buckets of water from holes dug in the frozen Neva. The bread lines take most of her time as she must arrive early in the morning to reduce the risk of being near the middle or end of the line if the store runs out of food. Communication with Nina's starving relatives is shut off as the telephone lines fail, and all public transportation is at a standstill. Nina thinks it is because the switchboard operators are either dead or dying.

The lack of food is so intolerable that Nick has suggested glue in water as something to eat. After his daughter catches him eating a teaspoon of mustard, he reproves himself mercilessly for his defiant act of eating anything at all. He wonders how he could stoop to such a level as to scavenge for food. He can no longer pace the floor wondering what else to do. Pacing is too tiring as he's lost one-third his original weight. Allechka's pleas for food go unanswered. Her questions as to where Granny has gone are met with silence as well. Nick can't tell her that her nanny is dead, buried when the ground was still soft enough to dig mass graves.

Nina's frustration is so great that it feels as if her very soul aches. Any energy she has left is gnawed away by constant frustration. Nothing can justify the situation in her mind. She cannot explain how the country's former capital and second-largest city can be left to die. Every conceivable option seems to lead to decline. There are simply no options left. The only sensations left are worry, torment, and fear of whether some tiny morsel of bread will be at the end of the next line of freezing, hopeless people.

In response, she uncharacteristically begins to lash out at her husband for not having stocked up on food, while he responds in equal anger that she should have heeded his warnings, and then they stand at a stalemate. The neighbors, who have stocked food, appear to her as greedy. And while she would gladly give her own life, as she gives her rations to her daughter, her responses to not only her daughter but also her husband have shifted. No longer does she have even one iota of the carefree adolescence she was able to maintain for so long. Unbeknownst to her, her sharp, critical remarks have taken on a tone and demeanor that Nick cannot bear. When Allechka complained about the watery soup they had Nina had snapped that tomorrow there might be no soup at all, which caused Allechka to break out inconsolably in tears.

By December 19th the hunger Nick and Nina feel is so overwhelming and their bodies so weary that each wonders how they are still alive. Nick takes one of his night journeys, breaking the curfew and risking his life for his family. He goes equipped with a knife to hunt whatever starving animal he can find. In an abandoned building, burnt by a prior ammunition burst, he hears the moans of a starved creature. Operating out of his own animal mind, he follows the sound. Whimpering, cold, in a corner is a suffering dog. His owners, probably dead, most likely once inhabited the burnt-out building. At the right moment, Nick stabs the dog with his knife. When he returns, he instructs Nina to put Allechka in his study. Nina, familiar with slaughtering animals from her life in the country, helps to clean the meat. Without reservation, she then cooks it.

Brother Vova arrives unexpectedly at the apartment this late evening, the day Christmas had been celebrated before the Revolution made it illegal. He leans against the door, ghostly white, his eyes hollow and bloodshot, and his skin gray and chalklike. Nina sees that it's hard for him to stand and notices the stains on the front of his fine camel-hair coat—stains she assumes are from falling because of weakness. She takes his coat and walks him to a chair in the kitchen.

After greeting his brother-in-law and sister, Vova takes two wilted and frozen leaves of cabbage out of his coat. Nina asks what they are. Vova explains how that morning, feeling exasperated at his condition, he tried to seek a solution. Nearest the front are the outskirts of what had been farm villages. Vova, excused from military service because of his former experience in Berlin, felt he could go there unmolested. He thought he could take the risk and barter for some food with anyone he might find there. The farmers' houses were destroyed and the military had nothing to give. What he found instead were these two pieces of wilted frozen cabbage leaves. Nina takes them and throws them away, knowing that they are frozen with contamination. Instead she offers him some of the sinewy dog meat. Vova jokes, "Now I can say that I ate dog," after first refusing his sister's offer.

After the meal, Nick, Nina and Vova speak briefly. Their exhales form wisps in the chill of the apartment. Vova tells Nick and Nina that he has invited Tante Natashka (assassinated Uncle Felix's wife), her daughter, their cousin Irina, and Irina's one-year-old daughter Natascha to live with him. His one-room apartment is small, but the women were freezing to death in their apartment. Living tightly is the best way to conserve heat and survive. Cousin Wadim, Irina's brother, is the only member of the extended family to have become a Communist. While most starve, the Communist special stores still exist, allocating food in ample proportions as if the war didn't exist. Just prior to the war Wadim warned Irina—only Irina—to stock up on food, so she did. Out of fear that there isn't enough to feed her mother and daughter, she offers none to Vova, who doesn't request any either. Vova shares with his sister that it's hard watching them eat. Nina becomes enraged. She knows her brother has always had a soft heart, yet never learned how to care for himself.

Conversation between Nina and her Leningrad, extended family has ceased. Brother Leonya has been recruited and serves in a subordinate position stocking supplies, as having family in Germany excluded him, luckily, from sensitive or front-line positions. His wife Irinka and daughter Tatiana live alone, well supplied with food from before the war, when they were wealthy by anyone's standard. Uncle Erich had been taken care of by a woman friend. The last communication Nina had with him, however, he was very ill from starvation; Nina is unaware that he too, like many elderly, has already died. Tante Lulya died of a heart attack shortly before the siege. Cousins Elena and Alicia are near death. Sophia is out of the city, fulfilling Nina's earlier prophecy.

The conversation does not last long and silence quickly ensues, as there are no words to express their grief at the final decimation of the long-suffering family. Vova tells his sister it is time for him to leave. Nick pleads with him to stay, saying that there is more chance for survival if they all stay together. Vova wants to hear none of it. He doesn't want to be a burden or dim their potential chance to get out of the city if at all possible, for there is talk that families would be the first to go should there be a way to leave Leningrad. He insists on leaving for his own apartment near the Nicholai Station across town. Nina pleads with him as she watches him stumble while trying to get up, and again as he stands. But he leaves anyway. Nina watches from the window as her little brother, her favorite, leaves a trail with his breath on the darkened, Leningrad boulevard …walking…slowly…away.

The temperature outside this January 23rd, 1942, has fallen to twenty-five degrees below zero. Nick notices his thin, blue hands as he tears the frame off Nina's mirror to throw into the fire. The bookshelves are already long gone, as are the chairs and table. Several days ago Nick made a note in his journal that, "Allechka picks up sawdust thinking it is breadcrumbs." Nina reproves her, telling her, "Don't eat that." Allechka complied. He, on the other hand, no longer has the capacity to reprove her for anything. Though greatly distressed when he saw his daughter throw one of his dearest books into the fire, he said nothing. After all, she's seen him burn many books and knows no difference.

Kotya the cat is so starved that he is only an idle skeleton with fur. Nick is out of ideas for hunting food. The city is void of animals, including vermin, and in some instances smells of cannibalism. He makes the decision to shut Allechka in his room while he sacrifices his daughter's beloved cat. That evening, Allechka says nothing about how they have a small amount of meat with their rations of bread. Later, in the dark, Nick lies awake haunted by her comments, which he also notes in his journal: "Why did we eat Puss…I pity him…He was such a darling."

The next day, convoys of trucks bring military supplies out of the city and some food into it, predicating the increase in bread rations to 250 grams. Nick makes a note of the increased rations and slaughtered cat in his journal.

February 5th, Nina's forehead beads with feverish sweat and she suffers a bloody diarrhea common to those who starve. Hunger has weakened her otherwise sturdy countenance to the point where her organs have swollen. Microorganisms that are normally healthy for digestion have begun to consume her stomach. Her last resources of energy are now utilized to fight off the terrible, demobilizing illness she came down with four days ago. Nina lies dreaming of death and thinking of her lost family. Resonations of the hundreds of thousands of dead and dying in the city of her birth are close to her. Indeed half of the population—over a million people—are already dead or near death. Thoughts are random and severe as they mingle between consciousness and delirium. Through it all Nina thinks of her daughter. "How can Allechka be without a mother?" she thinks, "How can I die and do that to her?" Nina conjectures as she blurrily looks at the small, thin child who lies close to her. "Allechka, take care of Papa if Mummy can't," she struggles to say. "If there is such a thing as God, please help me," she pleads, praying for Allechka's sake.

It's impossible for Nick to continue to stand by watching his wife slip away in front of his own eyes. Doctors are useless in these cases, if they're to be found at all. In desperation he looks through the medicine cabinet and finds some crystallized mercurochrome. He knows its use as a topical antibiotic, and its potential deadliness if ingested. Surmising, however, that Nina's organs are swollen from infection, he mixes a solution of a trace amount of the mercurochrome in some water.

"Nina," he says, sitting next to her bloated body on the sofa. "We know you are dying. We don't need to pretend. I've mixed a very small amount of mercurochrome in this water to fight the infection. You decide if you want to drink it or not." He brushes her fine hair off of her face and looks beyond the gray pallor into her sunken eyes. No one can be sure of the outcome. Nina, beyond everything she's been through, is truly frightened as she nods and allows Nick to lift her head to the glass he places at her lips. She sips the lukewarm water. It tastes bitter. She swallows and lets her head fall back.

20

THE ESCAPE
1942

Josephine walks determinedly past the restaurant, filled with high-ranking Nazi officers, on the first floor of the apartment building she owns. Looking straight ahead, slightly down, and not making eye contact is the best way to avoid any form of communication whatsoever. It's been a very difficult two years since the death of her 86-year-old mother. For Josephine's mother (also named Josephine) had continued to be the woman who made the world's complexity and savagery comprehensible. It wasn't until her death that Josephine realized just how much she had counted on her for stability. With both her parents dead, her husband executed in Siberia, and her youngest son back in Leningrad, there has been little pleasure in life for Josephine.

She hastens her step, walking by the entrance to the

restaurant, ignoring the loud patrons at the bar listening to the radio, with its continual droning of Germany's victories in Russia. Although the restaurant manager pays his rent to her, there is no need for Josephine to stop by for any reason today. Instead, she has other business to address at her office: to inform some of her tenants of another dictate imposed upon her and them concerning the harboring of "undesirables."

She turns the corner and starts up the broad, marble staircase of the large lobby of this particularly old and ornate building. Nothing pleases her more than to not hear any of the continual propaganda of the Nazi army's surrounding of Leningrad, the city where three of her four children live. It was her old home and where her nieces and in-laws still live. Still, she's heard of civilians supposedly running to the front line to join the Nazis in order to save themselves from starvation caused by the oppressions of Stalin. The Nazis, she knows, cause the starvation.

Knowledge of nearly two million starving Leningrader's causes her horrific nightmares and tremors at night. Who comes visiting from another world, she does not know. But what is true is that at times Nina has been there with her, and Vova, and her husband Leonid. All have come in dreams or visions as a way to say good-bye.

Josephine hears the sound of her heavy heels on the otherwise silent corridors leading to her and her secretary's offices. The heavy black shoes are barbarically unattractive to her, as is the suit jacket and skirt she wears, which have replaced her fine silk dresses of the

1930's. She's worn nothing but black since May, 1941, eight months ago.

In her distress, she thinks of Vera. It wasn't enough that the doctors removed her daughter's uterus against her will. Late in the evening, after Josephine had left visiting her youngest daughter in the hospital, a nurse came by and delivered a "sweet soup." The soup was poison. The coroner's report simply stated, "heart attack." A heart attack for her 29-year-old daughter, the daughter who played Moonlight Sonata and Chopin so well on the piano, who donated her free time before she became too ill to help less fortunate villagers, who was always so meekly mannered. Indeed, Josephine knew better, later finding out the truth directly from the hospital administration.

Yet, what is she to do with her ensuing rage? She is forced to only contemplate her emotions rather than act upon them. The controlling eavesdropping performed by her own government continues to condemn each and every citizen's communications, work, and life. The where, when, if, and how of daily existence is constantly interpreted with suspicion and condemnation by the insanely conservative, pseudo-religious doctrine imposed by the leader whom the masses ignorantly elevate.

Bread rations increased to 300 grams February 11th. On the

15th, Nina felt well enough to get out of bed and dress for the first time, before once again lying down for the rest of the day. Nick notes this in his journal as its second-to-last entry. The neighbor woman had been using coupons to get bread for everyone. But, on February 23rd, Nina insists on going back to the breadlines herself. As she makes her way downstairs, she notices the apartment manager's son. The little boy says hello and then brags to her, "My father has died, but my mother and I are leaving the city."

Nina unable to humor his fantasy, simply says, "No, you can't get out of here."

He looks up at her, surprised, and says, "Oh, but yes. People with children can, and we already have tickets."

Nina can't believe what she hears, but must find out for sure. Weak and exhausted, she walks, nonetheless, in the bitter frozen Leningrad February. Beyond boarded-up windows, lifeless restaurants, the ruins of buildings that had been hit by mortars and then scavenged for firewood, and to the Central Committee Office. As she walks, she notices, as if for the last time, how the faces on the sidewalks are all utterly despondent and hopeless. The joy that is inherently Russian, even through the hardest of times, isn't there. It is as if the city is possessed and can't shake off these terrible demons.

Reaching Committee Headquarters she goes up to the administrator, who has a relatively plump face compared to the hollow cheekbones and swollen stomachs of most Leningraders. Nina looks at her and asks, "Is there a way for families to leave the city, Comrade?"

The woman answers, "Yes, it's true." She explains how families with small children have been allowed to get train tickets, which transfer them to the frozen Lake Ladoga. The lake has become a natural break in the continuous frontline of the surrounding Nazi troops. Convoys across the lake are becoming more regular. It is these convoys that are able to bring food into the city and take small numbers of people out. Families are the chosen few.

Nina, humbled by gratitude and energized by hope, rushes home to tell Nick.

❧

Morning comes and light filters into their tattered, barren apartment that no longer bears any resemblance to what once was a home. But today there is hope. Layering their clothing, they pack only the barest of necessities in a small bag. Nick wears six pairs of pants on his shrunken form. Nina packs her remaining jewelry into the pockets of a summer jacket she wears beneath her winter coats.

Nina is the last to leave, as Nick carries Allechka's sled down the stairs and coaxes his daughter alongside. One last time she glances across what's left in the apartment's cold emptiness. The furniture, purchased, bartered for, made, and inherited, lies in scraps. Nearly all of the books, wooden objects, and toys have been burned. The remainder is left in disarray. Nick has already informed their closest friends of their departure. He's also left a note at the manager's office instructing friends, family, old coworkers–whoever may come in search of them after the siege–they had managed to leave Leningrad. He leaves the forwarding address of his father as well.

Nina shuts the door on the rubble of a once-contented life. As she does so, she sees the hand-painted porcelain plates given to her by her father, still on the uppermost shelf of the kitchen wall. Each shows the roses that he loved so much. But the plates are too heavy to be carried. The sight of them, soon to be lost forever, makes her ill with grief. Turning, she shuts the door and slowly they begin the long and arduous walk down the stairs and away from the sure death that is Leningrad.

Breathlessly, they push open the front door that seems as if it carries the weight of a tomb. They stop and catch their breath before the frozen wind hits. Numb and exhausted, they go no farther than the snow-covered sidewalk. Nina wonders, "How can we get to the train station when we can't even walk?" Both know they won't have the strength to walk the distance to the train station.

Then, as can only happen in a fantasy, one lone truck stalls on the street directly in front of them. The woman driver tries the ignition and works the pedal as Nick walks over to the window. "We cannot walk," he shouts through the glass. "We're starving and we must try to make it to the station where we can get tickets to leave the city. I will give you two packets of cigarettes if you take us there."

The woman nods her head, opens the window, and agrees. "I will only take you to the bridge," she tells him as she takes the cigarettes. "Climb in the back," she instructs. Nick follows her orders helping his daughter and wife onto the back of the truck. Together they ride in bitter cold through the desolate, Leningrad streets and through the city of their birth, the home they had loved through so many difficulties. Nostalgia is no longer in their hearts, only a wish for survival.

Directly ahead is the deceptively picturesque, elegant bridge that straddles the now-frigid Neva River. Beyond is their station. The truck stops with a jerk and the driver hails them to get off. With weak legs they dismount, standing at the beginning of the frozen icy bridge. The wind blows with a howling echo as a fierce, icy blast picks up the snow from the frozen waters below and wraps it around the bridge's steel frames. Slowly they push the sled with Allechka and their bags, looking forward, one cautious foot in front of the other, using every ounce of energy left in their frail bodies. As they arrive halfway across, the sled tips over on an icy drift. Nick and Nina do not know if they have the energy to right it. But slowly and painfully they do, and continue their march to the station, never once looking behind them.

The station is full of bodies, some dead, many more barely alive lying quietly on the floor in huddled groups, and waiting for the arrival of the trains. But, amazingly, there is food: three fingers of a murky soup for the entire family made up of indistinguishable ingredients in a makeshift tin bowl. Nina has a hard time holding it down. Nick immediately goes to the ticket window and stands in line. He shows the birth certificates and papers for his wife and daughter, which show they are still alive. The clerk hands him three tickets. They have three magical tickets for the train out of Leningrad and for one of the few trains that have access to the frozen Lake Ladoga. More valuable than gold, these three tickets to freedom and food mean they have a chance at life once again.

Nick returns and the three stay close together amidst the masses of hungry civilians. They will be on the fifth train out today. The first has not yet arrived at the departure gate. Nick worries that they may not be able to withstand waiting for the fifth. Then as the first train arrives, those passengers begin making their weary yet determined way to the doors. Nick ushers Nina and Allechka forward. Nina does not argue. Directly, he walks to the rifle-bearing soldier guarding access to the train. "We are starving here. My wife is sick and dying and my little girl is, too. We are scheduled for the fifth train, but we don't know if we will make it that long, and need to get out as fast as possible." He shows the guard two packets of cigarettes. The guard obliges, and Nick, Nina, and Allechka are allowed access.

The train moves its short distance across the forlorn city and stops at the station nearest the lake, which borders the very edge of its territory. Everyone is ordered out and into the deep snow and raging winter weather. Nina panics, yelling at Nick, "Why did we come here, if only to die in the snow? It would be better to die in our beds!"

But then, in the minutes that count as hours to frightened people, several trucks arrive. These trucks are to take them over Lake

Ladoga through the only break in the line of enemy troops that has circled the city for eight months. Amongst the first to climb aboard, they huddle in the back. All around, they hear the shots of gunfire and then the sound of cannon. Allechka shakes with cold and fear as Nick rocks her in his arms. "It will be all right, Allulia," he repeats over and over again, reassuring her and himself at the same time.

The trucks successfully cross the lake and then stop at the train station nearest its shore. Their abandoned city is beyond sight in the swirling white freeze of snow. This time a train is waiting. It's an empty cattle train, old and rusted, as if it were left over from the age of the Tsars. Nick, Nina, and Allechka clumsily struggle through the wide-open wooden doors, and onto the damp, hay-filled floors. They wait while others climb in, eventually crowding the rectangular boxcar with their scrawny rag-covered bodies.

The train journeys through the white-forested, Russian countryside. Then it stops. A military train at a station up ahead is given precedence over the fleeing Leningraders. The passengers get out and relieve themselves in the forest. Nina gets out and walks a small distance away from the others so that she cannot be seen. Suddenly, the train starts moving again. Those nearby jump in as it begins to pick up speed. Nina runs through the high drifts as quickly as she can. The train continues to forge forward yet faster, oblivious to Nina's screams for help. "To the door, just make it to the door...," she thinks, as she pushes herself to slog through the deep snow. Nick yells, unable to help, "Come, Nina, come, come."

Every fiber in Nina's body pushes forward to survive.

Projections of freezing to death, stranded alone in the forest watching the train speed away, shoot through her mind. Yet somehow she's able to get close to the open door. She stretches out her arms and gloved hands to the opening; three relatively sturdy men grab a hand each and the fur of her collar, and she feels herself lifted up and forward. Nina falls onto the floor of the cattle car, her lungs burning. Even here the city wants to keep her in its own dying arms.

❧

Village women who come near the tracks and offer some food accompany the next stop. Nick gets the watery soup and a piece of bread. Allechka says, "What a big piece of bread," never having seen such a large portion and too young to recall life before the food rations decreased.

Regardless of the food, they are suffering from eight months of starvation. Others on the train are in equally bad or worse physical and mental condition as the endless hours merge into days. Nina cannot help but learn to recognize the look that comes on one's face as a precursor of death.

The train continues, at times stopping for hours, then starting again. A once-pretty, now-emaciated, Russian girl about the same age as Allechka sits nearby constantly on the lap of her aunt, against the side of the car. Her nickname is Olenka for "little deer" because she has large beautiful eyes. The aunt and uncle had rescued her from the city taking her from the aunt's sister, who along with the girl's father, were starved beyond the physical effort needed to make the trip themselves. They hoped their daughter, pretending to be the aunt and uncle's daughter, would make it to a better life.

Nick allows Allechka to offer her possible friend the very last morsel of remaining cat meat they've brought. But she doesn't eat. After awhile, Allechka's efforts have exhausted her to the point of sleep. She rests her head near the side of the boxcar. While Allechka sleeps, Olenka becomes restless like the dying do. Nick and Nina watch as the little girl's body convulses on her aunt's lap until she lies still in death. Men open the door, take her lifeless corpse, and fling it out onto the frozen, Russian earth. The aunt cries and tells Nick and Nina that before she left, her sister told her that she had a nightmare in which she was searching for her daughter in the snow and couldn't find her. The nightmare has come true.

Allechka wakes from her nap with her hair frozen to the wall of the boxcar. "Where is Olenka," she asks, as her father gently releases her hair from the boards. He looks her in the eyes with a knowing sadness and holds her close. "It will all be well soon," is all he can say. Allechka is now frightened as she looks around the train worried that to look listless or pale would mean she may disappear, too.

With no means of cleaning oneself and very little warmth, everyone on the train continues to wear their same layers of clothing unceasingly as they sit for endless hours, and then days, crammed like cattle next to one another. Rumors spread about a thief onboard, which Nina uses as an excuse to remain on the train as Nick continues to get allotments of soup and bread from infrequent, remote stops along the way.

The train makes its journey south as the grasping hand of death continues to reach Leningrad's fleeing victims. An obviously once-elegant blond woman sits close to the wall at the same side of the boxcar, restlessly and continually combing her pretty, long hair. One morning she wakes and frantically combs her hair as usual before laying back down, apparently asleep. She never wakes. Her organs dried up beyond the salvation of food's aid. Her heart nourished itself at the expense of her body, leaving her nothing to digest. She, too, is thrown into the abyss of deep snow as the train relentlessly continues.

Nina does not remember the specifics of this long, grueling ride on this train smelling of dirt and death as it heads on blindly. She does notice the weather has changed from bitter cold to mild as the weeks roll into April. Days have been lost waiting while military trains use the tracks. Nina remains delusional with exhaustion as she removes layers of clothing only to expose more of her thin frame, and her body, still unable to absorb nutrition, doesn't respond to their diet of soup and bread.

Though he's retained his intellectual stamina, Nick functions on a fraction of his prior body weight. His flesh hangs on his bones beneath more than one layer of pants. But he continues to work on solutions in the hay-filled boxcar, now contaminated with the feces and smell of death from the original load of too-starved-to-recover passengers. At a train station in mid-central Russia, Nick is able to negotiate the family onto a standard passenger train that will take them close to Armavir, in the Caucasus region of Russia. Nick's father and sister live not too far from Armavir, which is as far south as Bucharest or Venice is in relation to Northern Europe.

Allechka sits on one side of the seat with her father, Nina sits across from them. Even though the child has eaten soup and bread, her little stomach still yearns for more nourishing food. Nick is able to revive the story of the rich uncle that will be providing macaroni shortly. Allechka has some hope that it may come true. To break the monotony of her pleas for more food, Nina takes a handkerchief from Nick and ties a knot at its end for Allechka to use as a toy. Allechka begins to tell the knotted hanky the story of the rich uncle, adding that he will bring potatoes and bread, too.

Finally, after several weeks of ceaseless travel, the train stops at the Armavir station. Armavir is a relatively large city and not unfamiliar to Nick, who had visited his father's house here in the past. Once a central hub linking the coastal resort cities, Armavir has now been transformed into a strategic, Communist-managed depot where oil and grains are shipped from this always-fertile region.

There has been no means by which to notify Nick's father, Mikhail, or sister, Shura, that they were coming; therefore there is no one to pick them up at the station. Public transportation is no more readily available here than it was in Leningrad. Only horses and buggies cart women, children, and old men.

Nick quickly assesses the surroundings and walks to a farmer on a cart. "Comrade, can you tell me which way to Vasvechenskaya," he asks, knowing the answer. The man points the right way, which assures Nick of his honesty. Nina straightens her own and her daughter's hair and pushes it up under their hats in an effort to look as normal and appealing as a woman and her daughter can who have just survived starving or freezing to death. The two wait nearby. Nick walks over to his wife. He knows she has two gold watches; one in her possession to keep safe for Vova and the other, a gift from her father for her eighteenth birthday. He tells her that the man won't accept paper money but wants gold. One of the watches will have to be sacrificed.

Nina is too malnourished to argue. Instinct already tells her that Vova will not need his watch, and having lost everything else from her father, she gives over her brother's. "What can the watch do other than tell time," she reassures herself as she hands it over to her husband. Nick presents the watch. The old farmer smiles and announces how pleased his wife will be as he allows the three to struggle onto the back of the cart. Then, still hungry, pale, exhausted, and dirty, they arrive suddenly, like snow in the night, on the doorstep of Nick's father, Michael, and sister, Shura. Their spirits are alive though their bodies are nearly dead. Greeted with surprise and embraces, the three collapse into the comfort of their temporary new home, feeling as if their time on this earth had nearly been robbed from them as clearly as Vova's watch was.

Nina begins another decline; the adrenaline that allowed her to make it this far has left her body, leaving her emaciated and drained. Recovery again is only a glimmer in her fading, exhausted eyes. Nick is unable to rest for long. Every nerve in his body motivates him to get up and seek the markets where he will buy as much food as he and his sister can possibly carry.

Artillery and tanks, war planes and the Nazi armed forces destroy homes and decimate villages on the not-too-distant horizon. Animals flee the Blitzkrieg that tramples over homes and fields and the lives of their inhabitants. And at a field office, Nazi officers finish writing the draft of their invasion plan; they will most certainly invade the entire region within the next four months.

21

THE CAUCASUS
APRIL 1942 TO JANUARY 1943

Although mischievous in his youth, Nick has always been thought of as the wisest in the family. He had plenty of friends growing up and got into a fair amount of trouble with his male companions. Using a very clever mind, Nick led them in adventures and misadventures. He also kept very busy inventing devices to make life easier around the house. Both his father and mother felt everything he did was right and smart.

Most of the family were and are simple people even though, starting with his grandfather, all since have had formal educations. His grandfather was freed from serfdom by his botanical innovations and sent away to school in St. Petersburg. His father Mikhael followed in his footsteps by getting a formal education there, as well. He later married a schoolteacher (Nicholas's and Shura's mother) and returned to a simple country life. After Nick moved to live and work in St. Petersburg, his family felt the loss and missed his humor and charismatic presence.

Shura, his sister, had also been a teacher before the war. Her first pregnancy with her son Tusia came at a time when her husband had been recruited to work in Siberia. Mikhael suggested she remain home, as Siberia was not a good place to raise a child in his estimation. She took his advice, divorced, remarried, and birthed a second son, Tallic. Both are now teenagers.

Even though Shura had sometimes felt frustrated by the affections showered on her brother when they were children, she is thrilled to see him and his family. She affirms that even though the house is small, they can arrange it so all will be comfortable. And indeed it is. Upon entering there are benches and chairs surrounding a table with a dimly-lit lamp. The cement oven on the other side of the house not only serves as the stove to prepare food but also to keep the house warm. The main room contains a comfortable couch where Mikhael naps, and comfortable chairs. The bedrooms are in the back of the house, and there are lofts where the children sleep. Allechka, for now, will sleep with her parents in one of the empty bedrooms.

The reunion is celebrated with heartfelt joy. Nick is treated like a soldier home from the front, and Nina and Allechka are welcomed with open arms. Food is prepared in their honor and placed before the three. Vodka is served, cigarettes smoked, and laughter and chatting carried out until well into the morning hours on many nights. Father asks about news in Leningrad, wanting to know what is happening there—how did they survive; what did they do to keep warm and find food—while continuing to shower Nick with praise for using his cleverness and intelligence to save his family.

For days all Allechka wants is food and bed. But as she becomes more alert, she, too, is comforted as Papoon, the name she gives her grandfather Mikhael, fawns over her. "Allechka, come sit on my lap…what a darling child…so smart. Look she looks just like her father and smart just like him. She will become a real brain! She will be a professor for sure!! Forget bed."

As days pass, rest, food, and family help Nick resume his old habits. His father instructs him to fix the stove, saying, "It never worked well and now it is causing smoke." Then relenting by saying, "Everything is fine. Do it tomorrow. We need not worry today."

Nick also begins looking for administrative and engineering work in the village. But there is none as the region is mostly supported by agriculture and mining. The fact that he is not in the military becomes annoying to him, based upon the reaction of the village people. To create a diversion from the subject he walks with a cane, just as he occasionally did in Leningrad. This does not help his psychological state. He constantly reminds himself this cannot be a permanent solution. Yet the war rages. Nothing is normal for him.

While Nick and Allechka now amazingly grow healthier, Nina does not. She continues to lie on the couch, unable to move. Her thoughts are of her brothers, Vova and Leonya. Leonya, she knows, is with the army fighting against the Germans somewhere—but where, and is he still alive? And dear, beautiful, idealistic baby Vova, who had risked everything to come back to Leningrad, who was starving, has he survived? An internal struggle is taking place within her. "Everything gone…the apartment abandoned…they starved us…" Her random thoughts are extreme, confused, paralyzing, and they fluctuate between dreams asleep and semi-conscious imagination.

It takes several weeks for Nina to show slow signs of recovery from exhaustion, starvation and shock, but she begins to show color in her cheeks as she eats, sleeps, and talks more and more with family members. A letter arrives from Leonya, who is in Leningrad and obtained the forwarding address from Nick and Nina's apartment manager. Nick keeps the letter to himself at first, but then shares it with his wife when he feels she's well enough to accept it. Nina eventually reads that Leonya, upon returning from his post and seeking answers to Vova's demise, had received nothing but a torn piece of brown paper from a Leningrad hospital. On it, written in Vova's fine handwriting, were the words: *How can you all leave me here to die? There is no food. I can't stand or walk, and this is my third visit to the hospital – I've almost died twice already, yet no one has come for me.*

The letter goes on to scold Nina for not providing Vova food. It states that he can't believe she left without helping him. Apparently Irinka, Leonya's wife, had also gone to the hospital, but by then even Vova's coat had been stolen. And when he, Leonya, returned to Vova's apartment, he found that Aunt Natasha and cousin Irina had taken everything, except for one packed suitcase, which was lying in the middle of the room.

Nina is horrorstruck when she reads the letter. Her brother is dead!! Furthermore, she wonders, how was her sister-in-law, Irinka, capable of visiting the hospital to get Vova's camel-hair coat, but could not bring him any food while he was still alive? "Not even a crumb of bread…," she thinks in anger that is turning to rage. "And what of his hospital rations? The nurses must have eaten those." She needs to blame someone, forgetting the complete lack of any available food in Leningrad. Completely dumbfounded by the inhumane selfishness of her aunt and cousin, it is difficult for Nina to comprehend how they also stole her brother's mahogany furniture and all of his fine German suits, knowingly leaving him to die alone. She sits in anguish, blindly holding the letter, tears forming in her eyes.

Spring has turned to summer and the clear skies reflect light off of the corn stalks growing in the garden. As little, four-year-old Allechka runs through them, her blond hair makes her invisible. Often she sits next to her grandfather on the wide porch encircling the small, rectangular cottage and listens as he rocks in his chair and tells her stories of animals. Allechka innately adores these stories as animals' lives seem so simple and natural, unclouded compared with the lives of people.

It's been over two months since Nina lay near death on the sofa and a month since she's been able to spend long periods of time awake and alert. But tomatoes are ripe, and the Party office has recruited Shura and herself to pick them. Working in the fields in the Caucasus summer is grueling, dirty work. But Nina is familiar with this. After all, she's picked vegetables in gardens since the time of the Revolution. It doesn't bother her much that her hands have become callused and she's often tired when she arrives home in the evening. For she is stronger now, and as she picks the vine-ripened tomatoes, she keeps a good perspective thinking of how good it is to even have tomatoes to pick—and of how she doesn't have to starve any longer.

A warplane flies overhead. As Nina looks up into the hot blue sky, she thinks to herself how wonderful it would be to have a plane like that. How wonderful it would have been to fly that plane straight to her starving brother when he was still alive in Leningrad, pick him up, and bring him to all the food they have here. But he is dead. And she will never reconcile how their country could have possibly allowed a man such as he, and all the men like him, to die.

Summer drives into August and rumors start to circulate that the Germans are advancing against surrounding villages. Again, the haunting hint of fear can be heard in people's voices, heralding the onslaught of an enemy. Leningrad is still entombed, and the advancing front is only thirty miles away from Moscow. The oil-rich Caucasus region is obviously a target the Germans can't resist. No one is sure when, but everyone knows they are coming.

Neither Nina nor Nick knows why they are still alive, other than by a miracle. And if you've experienced one miracle, you believe another can happen again. Nick and Nina, however, do not choose to test this belief alone. As has been their habit since the inception of the war, they sit face to face across the kitchen table and talk late into the evening. What are the possibilities? What should they do? What are their options?

Information in the village is gathered mostly by word of mouth. The anxiety level is mounting as villagers exchange information that, "…the Germans are coming, the Germans are coming," as they rush to collect durable goods, dried goods, firewood, and whatever else they can in preparation against the inevitable devastation. The Nazis are simply moving too fast, there are little or no fortifications, and almost all of the Russian troops are away fighting in Stalingrad.

Nina remembers the fears and rumors that circulated around Leningrad before the siege. And even farther back, twenty-five years ago, the knock on the door of her parents' apartment in Tsarskoe Selo to announce, "The Bolsheviks are coming, the Bolsheviks are coming." This sudden and rancorous mass hysteria is not new to her ears. Experience has taught her that, even as a defenseless child, she has survived all this chaos and awakened to new days in new places. The Germans do not frighten her this time because she understands the situation now.

It may seem like an odd idea, but Nick, always a proponent of invention, has been using his time to dig a deep trench in the front yard, has surrounded it with logs, and stocked it with food, water, medicine and blankets in case the house is destroyed.

In the meantime, Allechka has enjoyed playing in the sandy garden and watching her papa dig the hole. The sounds of increasing gunfire and distant bombs don't bother her so long as food hasn't been taken away, and that hasn't happened with both Mummy and Auntie Shura cooking all the time.

❧

Morning turns to afternoon this hot, August day. It finds the entire family at home. The advance of the Nazis has precluded any further work in the fields for Nina and Shura. The sun burns wickedly in the sky, targeting its light on the trees and corn stalks in the yard. Tension can be felt in the small cottage, cutting the normally languid roll of the summertime heat. The sounds of war grow closer. The air seems to grow heavy and still, as the languid sounds of nature are drowned out by the unrelenting sounds of advancing troops. The Nazis are now just outside the village, in surrounding forest and fields, destroying what remains of the summer crop.

Nick has taken it upon himself to signal the alarm. The enemy is too close now. He knows it's time to tell everyone to gather what he or she can and hide in the ditch. A momentary panic ensues as the family does as he suggests, and all take shelter in the warm earth of the side-garden shelter.

Enclosing the large yard is a tall wooden fence; the walls

345

of a fortress in a childhood game, yet this is no game. Any activity outside the yard can only be heard. Airplanes fly above, filling the sky with the turbulent noise of engines. Armies march, fight, or retreat. Artillery shells stream by with a sickening whizzing sound, then explode. The extent of the decimation is anyone's guess. The family simply waits…quietly, patiently, resignedly waits.

Suddenly, the front gate bursts open. To their amazement, it's a village girl who runs into the yard and shouts, "The Germans have taken the village. They're here!" Everyone continues to lie still in the dirt, surrounded by supplies, knowing that their village is being consumed by a wave of German troops descending upon it. The sound of fighting in the distance begins to subside. Eventually it is quiet. "What is happening," Nick's nephew whispers.

"I don't know, just wait," Nick responds patiently.

Several more hours pass, when Mikhael stands up and announces that he's had enough. "It's dinnertime," he says matter-of-factly. "I eat my dinner promptly at 5:00 PM. Today will be no exception!" he concludes as he begins to move towards the house. Nick tries to reason with him, telling him he may die if he goes back into the house. Mikhael insists, continuing to badger his son, "I'm seventy-five, I've lived this way all of my life. I won't stop now," and with that he proceeds to the house. Shura complains that she also must go in now to prepare the dinner.

Nick realizes he won't be able to control his obstinate father. He also realizes that the Germans have taken the village by now. It won't be long before they come to the house. When they do, it is best they have a plan. Nina reassures her husband, reminding him that, to the Germans, they are not soldiers but only a family living in the countryside. And Nina's nationality is German.

In this regard, Nick and Nina work better together as a team than in the usual individual roles of husband and wife. Where he is emotional, she is strictly rational. As in the past, she presents the issues sometimes as a complaint. Nick then calculates the solution, and bounces it off of her. Nina, after eliminating Russian emotion, generally agrees. Together they take action.

They've agreed they need a plan. Nick proposed that they set up a table, place a bottle of vodka in the middle of it, and sit down, as usual, to dinner. Nick reminds his wife that she should speak German when the Nazis come, to offer them the vodka. Nina thinks over the setup, but suggests she wait on the porch instead. "Perhaps they won't need to come in at all," she says. Nick strongly disagrees. But Nina insists, claiming she is not any more afraid of them than the Communists. Besides, she isn't hungry. "If they do insist on coming in," she says, "We'll support our plan with the vodka."

Shura, Tusia, Tallic, Nick, and Allechka go into the house, prepare their evening meal, and sit at the table. In the center, they place the vodka. Nina remains on the porch, in Papoon's rocking chair. The pattern of its creaking reminds her of the sound of a tennis ball hitting the court. She keeps her competitive strength, as her mind remains alert, still, patient, and confident.

Suddenly, the wooden gate bursts open with a crash that sounds as if the door is splintering off of its hinges. Nina refrains from showing any reaction. A young German man Vova's age, wearing a handkerchief over his mouth to protect himself from the dust, strides up the path and quickly approaches the house. He appears to Nina as tired and frayed, but on guard. It's obvious to her that he's alone, and she can see his motorcycle outside the gate.

Nina greets him, "Guten Tag." The German statement is not highly unusual to him in these southern Russian regions. Germans had emigrated here since the time of Catherine the Great, and entire German villages, though pillaged and mostly de-Germanized by Stalin's purges, have been encountered in the Crimea west of here.

His eyes remain on the door. "Was wünschen Sie hier, heute? Was wünschen Sie?" Nina asks what he wants here, and then adds that he should stop. He ignores her, approaches the front door, and grabs his pistol.

Nina fearlessly reaches for his arm as every part of her being demands her own authority and every bit of her protective, strong nature is pushed to the surface through sheer adrenalin and willpower. "Nein! Halt, bitte!" she shouts. He pushes her aside and kicks the door open. There he sees a family sitting around the table eating dinner. Nick calmly says, "Come in," in German he learned from his wife earlier that day. He gestures to the young man to come closer to the table.

The officer pauses, and then holsters the gun. Nina follows him from behind, encouraging him to enter as well. He sits down and accepts a shot glass of vodka with a slight smile. Nina also smiles and asks, "Would you like something to eat?"

"Yah," he answers, as he swallows the vodka.

Nina does most of the talking speaking naturally in German. The conversation continues due to the officer's growing inebriation, and he begins to share details. He has been in the area for several days and met other Germans from Russia. Nazi officials are aware that the Caucasus region had an established population of German farmers and are under strict orders to no longer alienate them. The Nazis have learned that their harsh treatment of captives in the Ukraine only set the native population, who might have been more accommodating, against them with a vengeance. They are to change their take-over tactics and are told to be less confrontational as each situation presents itself. His other comrades are in the villages and surrounding cities. There aren't enough of them to travel in pairs house to house.

They are now being "liberated," he explains. "Isn't it true that every single German-Russian family has been spared the oppressions imposed upon them by the Communist regime," he asks rhetorically. "Are we not saving you from the persecutions and executions of Stalin; from communal living, from confiscation of your lands, or from being imprisoned in Stalin's labor camps?" He continues, "We can be looked on as a window to the world for the oppressed German peoples in Russia."

They continue to talk, and Nick, through Nina, asks the question, "Where will you be going next?" The officer pulls out a map and shows them exactly where the troops are heading. Nina dares not look up, thinking this man a fool for actually exposing the army's advance. "But we have his trust now," she thinks.

When the time comes to share personal information with the officer, Nina makes the quick decision to identify herself with her German maiden name. It's a sly decision, but necessary. It's clear to her that her German name will come in far more handily with these people, just as her marriage to a pure Russian and his protective non-bourgeoisie family name had provided her protection during Stalin's purges, assassinations and mass murders. If St. Petersburg had changed its name to Petrograd during the first war and then to Leningrad to reflect the times then she could change her name as well. Katschalin was far too Russian for a city that is now occupied by the Nazi German army. Siewert will be a much more comforting name in their new situation amongst Germans.

The supper finishes when the officer leaves, staggering a bit on his way out. Both Nick and Nina know the inevitable report to the new, occupying military office of information should be good.

Nina stands at the sink washing dishes from the morning meal. She awoke early as usual today and put on her cream-colored dress with the small pink flowers that she had sewn before the invasion. She lifts the stained coffee cups and plates with bits of egg and rinses them under the warm, soapy water. She looks out the kitchen window at the garden beyond where Allechka now plays.

A loud knock is heard at the door. Nina, startled, drops the plate back in the sink. It splashes down, drowning in the water. She hears German spoken in a harsh and loud voice over her husband's Russian. She quickly picks up the towel by the sink, dries her hands, and walks to the entrance hall where the brazen Nazi officer is trying to talk to Nick.

"Guten Morgen, was wünschen Sie heute," she asks in a friendly yet incredulous manner. The soldier disregards her and proceeds to unscrew a light bulb from the front hall. Nina chastises him. Grandfather Mikhael shouts from his bathroom to "shut the door," as he is getting cold in his bathtub. "You won't take our light bulbs," Nina commands in an authoritative manner. "How dare you come in here and treat us this way, we will have none of this!" she continues, as she follows him to the next room.

He turns to her piercing through her with his annoyed and tired eyes. She has seen these eyes before, and they do nothing to intimidate her. Nina repeats her remarks, and shows him to the door. The Nazi understands this language, this attitude, these directions, and leaves the house.

❧

Vasvechenskaya is no longer a Communist-controlled village. That it is Russian is not to be denied, but the Communist Party is no longer present. The Communist Party officials no longer hold power.

They have been replaced. The new party is the Nazi Party. Though lesser administrators in the smaller, surrounding cities still hold their positions, the Communist Party leaders no longer do. Instead, a new power is now in control—and is an oppressive force all the same. It is an oppressor who is equally as willing to murder innocent civilians for their differing beliefs or for their birth heritage or race or creed or class.

A black limousine, extremely unusual for the territory, pulls up outside the house. Inside the car are a driver and an officer. The two exit the car and knock on the door of the household. Nina answers. They identify themselves, and the officer asks, "Sind Sie Nina Siewert?"

"Ja, Ich bin Nina Siewert," Nina answers and directly asks their purpose, completely comfortable with the use of her maiden name.

The officer grips her arm, in both a manner trying to feign camaraderie and, at the same time, force and coercion saying, "Wir haben Arbeit fur Sie, meine Volksdeutscherin."

"What kind of work," Nina asks, knowing she will have to go with them.

As they travel in the back seat of the automobile thoughts race through her mind, "How like the Communists these Nazis are. Am I to be sent away from my family? Will I be interrogated, executed?" She will not let them make her afraid. Living under Stalin for so many years has taught her what to do. She hasn't done anything wrong and has managed to escape years of terror when those around her had been sent to Siberia or worse.

The officers take her to a large mansion that has been transformed into the commandant's office. Pictures of their Führer, their own virulent madman, adorn the walls. A high-ranking Nazi officer enters the room and sits behind his desk. "You are a Volksdeutscher and, as such, will be able to serve the Fatherland as an interpreter," he says. "Today we have some villagers coming in to tell us of their inventories of livestock and crops. We must assess this in order to feed your German brothers-in-arms."

Nina receives this statement with a mocking laugh to herself. The gleam in her eye appearing to be approval to the officer, but thoughts are of her brother abandoning the Nazi Army; it is not *her* brothers who are in arms.

"Verstehen Sie? Do you understand?" His question brings her out of her thoughts.

Unflinching, sitting straight and erect in the chair, she looks the officer square in the eye and says nothing. Years of experience to not only appear to be unaffected but to feel unaffected come into play at this moment.

She is taught how to salute correctly with her arm raised in the air and slightly to the side. She complies, thinking how utterly foolish this man's game is. Inwardly she mocks the movement. The reason for the salute is not important to her. It has to be done and that is the end of it.

The German army controls all the land to the west through France. Russia has now been opened to the rest of central and western Europe. Some of the townspeople are actually relieved, seeing the invaders as a way out of Stalin's Russian nightmare.

Nina's job continues day after day. Farmers come and go throughout the day and week. They talk of the harvest and tell of their numbers of cows, sheep, chickens, and pigs. Nina takes notes, translating the information into German. On one particular occurrence a simple farmwoman comes into the office with her cow. The woman explains that she lives alone and this, her only cow, is just nine months old.

Reminded of the difficulty of farm life from her own teen-age experience, Nina feels pity for the woman. Nina knows that cows younger than six months are not yet confiscated. "You must tell us that the cow is six months old and we won't take her," she tells the woman, realizing that if she were heard, she could be arrested or shot. The woman does as instructed and corrects herself to Nina, saying the cow is five-and-one- half months. Nina marks the number down in German, and the two are allowed to leave.

Nina is reasonably paid for her work, but each day she has to enter the office of the enemy. Every evening she comes home and acts as if nothing is out of the ordinary, all the while realizing that nothing has been ordinary for as long as she can remember, since the long-past Revolution of her late childhood.

As she works, she wonders when this will all end. Thinking of the monkeys that are characterized as seeing, hearing, and speaking no evil, she is sworn to secrecy. Yet she is no monkey and cannot nor will not be controlled. She has already lived her entire adult life in a crippled, oppressive society, and has, through it all, retained her belief in freedom of thought and her ability to rationally detect right from wrong. Primarily she has never abandoned the formality and manners of the now-devastated Tsarist bourgeoisie from the old era in which she was born.

While translating some documents in a large, common room of the mansion, she is interrupted by a co-worker. The man identifies himself as Oscar von Kursell, the brother of Claus, Nina's cousin's husband. "Are you Nina Siewert, cousin to Tatiana Siewert?" Oscar asks.

Nina remembers Tatiana, the daughter of her Uncle Roman, the cousin who escaped the Revolution because her mother, Claudia, took them to the Baltic States, during the first war. Yet she responds with an immediate and emphatic, "No, no, no. You must be mistaken." Alarmed at being recognized, Nina has never met this man before and doesn't want to identify herself. Her maiden name is a guise to be used only with the Nazi armies, only to help her and her family stay safe. She doesn't want to be known. This is only a stepping stone—a job that will last as long as necessary before she can get out and away, no longer recognized by the Communists as ever having been here. In her mind, she believes she must not ever be classified as a propagandist.

Oscar is taken aback. "But surely there is only one Nina Siewert," he thinks. He knows of her. His brother, an amateur genealogist, has always been fond of the whole family and had mentioned her. Nonetheless, Oscar goes about his business. He won't ask her any more questions. Obviously she doesn't want to be bothered, and it is not his place to disturb pretty, female co-workers. Perhaps he will write his brother tonight.

❧

Nina is amongst the first to hear of developments in the German war machine. She understands how this army and these people operate. What they must be thinking is beyond comprehension. The most obvious information is passed amongst the translators, officials, and other office assistants. The war in Stalingrad is going very badly for the Nazis. There is no way to hide this.

She also learns of the difficulties encountered while maneuvering through, and then defending, the steep Caucasus Mountains. The Germans brought in moose, which are comfortable in mountainous terrain and are unpredictable, dangerous animals; yet the Nazi advances were still deterred. The terrain was too steep in some areas, and the Russian army snipers held the Nazi advance. It seems apparent the Germans will not be able to continue, and, in fact, their advance is being repelled.

Soon, the office is abuzz. Decisions are made rapidly. The

command has come to withdraw, even though the Nazis do not believe in withdrawal. They believe that their cause is only to advance or to hold their line. Withdrawal means defeat, and defeat is not tolerated. The office falls into disarray, leadership is changed, and the course of business so quickly and efficiently set up is now just as efficiently altered.

Russians of German descent that live in the village, and others who are being held as political prisoners, or who are under Communist scrutiny, come to ask for help, to ask to be withdrawn as well. Orders are placed to allow some German nationals to leave, to be evacuated with the Nazis.

Nicholas has constantly reminded Nina of how temporary this occupation is. It has been beyond clear to him that any further Nazi advance into Russia is hopeless. He believes there is no way, no matter how long it takes, the Russian people will allow the country to be ruled by Hitler; no way Stalin will allow a foreign invader to take over Russian soil. Both Nicholas and Mikhail know that since the Mongolian invasions the whole of Russia has never been taken over. "Simply impossible," he reminds his wife as news of the Stalingrad battle is discussed. "We've seen this coming for months now. How long has it been? It was August when they took over and now it's January," says Nick during a heated debate over the family dinner table.

Nina writes to her mother that evening, as letters can still be sent to Berlin. Although the lines of family communication have been opened, Nina does not give too many specifics. She knows the

Nazis are far too busy to be reading letters from a German national to her mother. In fact, there are far too few men left in the capital to do so. Besides, she isn't even certain that her mother is still in Berlin. After all, wars force people to move, and there isn't the time or the means to notify family of their destination. But she continues to write only the news, after years of living with spies, one imagines is innocuous enough for any form of spy to allow through. The letter reads as follows:

Dear Mother,

I am afraid that the Communists are advancing toward our village. As you know, our family has been persecuted for the last 25 years. If we stay here, we will surely be sent to Siberia. Nick believes we must withdraw. We would like to come to Berlin.

Affectionately, your daughter,
Nina

Rapidly enough, given the expediency of the now-retreating Nazi troops, Nina receives word back from her mother. She learns that, given Berlin's function, situations are not the way they used to be. Josephine accepts Nina's decision but lets her know that life won't be much better in Berlin than what Nina has already experienced elsewhere. Furthermore, Josephine will use what influence she can to prepare the necessary papers to bring her daughter out of Russia.

No decision is an ideal one. Yet what can Nina and Nick do? Go to the capital of the Russian enemy in the middle of the war, or stay in Russia and most likely be executed? For them the choices are few; they can't go back, they can't stay. Nick, Nina, and Allechka will pack their few belongings, say goodbye to their relatives, and leave. The initial paperwork required for them to emigrate has been approved, making them part of the displaced masses fleeing the constant chaos of war and repression.

22

FLEEING RUSSIA
JANUARY TO APRIL 1943

Nick, Nina and Allechka climb onto the horse cart this chilly January morning, once again with few possessions, as they begin the journey to Berlin. Once again they take their newly-repaired, thick, Leningrad coats along with new clothes. Once again they leave much of what they've been able to accumulate, including most of Allechka's new toys. It will be cold in Berlin. The timing of the Nazi retreat and the resulting movement of many civilians has come in an inconvenient season. With this departure they will leave behind their birthplaces, the country of their childhoods, educations, customs, and their lost relatives. Hopes and dreams have turned to nightmares.

The ride to Armavir is quite different from their arrival nearly one year ago. Armavir is also different. The last time they were here it was a Russian city, one that saved them from the Nazis and the starvation of Leningrad. Now it is a Nazi-controlled city, and one that will serve as their escape from retribution by the Communists. The city that bore the brunt of an invasion is now being evacuated, not only by its invaders, but also by its oppressed citizenry. Those who have approval flood the train station. These include Nazis, German nationalists, and Russians with advanced skills. Amongst them also are the long-suffering bourgeoisie. Most of these families have been devastated, but there are still a few, like Nina's, who have survived the terror of Stalin and the fumblings of the Nazi regime.

Nina is now considered a *Volksdeutscher*–someone from a German family who settled in Russia and made it their home. Thousands of them helped create European cities here. Centuries later they are forced to flee to a country that is no longer anything like the country their ancestors left. In this surreal moment they are all Germans from Russia going back to Germany through a Russian city occupied by the German Nazi army.

Silently the family sits amidst their former countrymen on the train. The route will be northward and then slightly westward through the Ukraine and then Poland. But no one knows exactly how long it will take them to get to Berlin. Beyond this, they aren't even sure if they will reach Berlin, how they will find Josephine, or if the train will be attacked by the Russian army and everyone killed as traitors.

As the train starts through the countryside, all they see is devastation. The Nazis in their retreat continue their assault on land, people, and crops. Nick is enraged by what he sees. All around are retreating troops, destruction, displaced people, entire villages in disarray. Nina keeps Allechka away from the windows.

As the train moves into the forest, Nina remembers. The only other time she had left Russia was to go to Finland, to the dachas. Now she is leaving her homeland for what she knows will be the rest of her life. She can never return nor has any desire to return. Yet a part of her mourns its passing. It was the country that her brother Vova had come back to–her brother now dead of starvation. It was the country she loved with all the passion that Russians know; passion born of struggle and hardship; passion with no translation. She is Russian-born, and throughout all the terror and revolt and horror, something spoke to her…once.

The people have changed; the intellectuals, the artists, the gifted, and well-educated have been killed. The country is run by political opportunists and dictated to by a paranoid killer. Family, associates, and friends have been exiled, sent to Siberia, and killed. Tens of thousands are starving to death in Leningrad. Millions are now being displaced.

Nina rarely saw an intelligent expression as she went out in public in recent years. Everyone learned how to feign vacuous disinterest. When well-practiced, this expression indicated one appeared to have nothing on one's mind. It was painted on her own face a thousand times as she left the house, not knowing for sure who was a spy, who would report her, or who would be offended by the slightest glimmer of thought or creativity.

Nina looks out the window and sees the birch trees. Yet even they, in their majesty, in their delicate paper-like, thin, white bark, seem saddened. Their leaves don't sparkle, and their bark appears ashen, as if their soft skin has turned a shade paler in their distress as they witnessed the years of savagery around them. That they still stand is a testament to Mother Nature. But even these trees appear silent, sullen, and mournfully rigid, incapable of bending with the wind.

The White Guards she once imagined the birches to be as a child–protecting the princesses on a voyage–are no longer. They have all been murdered. These Communists are not her people. These strangers in the countryside who berate their people, suffocate their creativity, and murder their independence, are not her people. She wants nothing more of them and convinces herself that she hates this place and these strange people who had allowed brother, uncle, aunt and cousins to starve, who exiled her father, assassinated her uncle, and divided and devastated her family. She hates them. She pretends she *wants* to leave.

Yet, deep in Nina's heart, she feels the loss of her homeland. She feels the sorrow of leaving a relationship turned bad. She does not want these memories, these feelings. She is leaving her country for something better. It is time to look ahead. For her family's sake many decisions will now be up to her. She does not relish negotiating through a country she's never seen and finding a mother she's never truly known. But as is her nature, she won't regret the past. They will face events as they come. For today, they must each do what needs to done; and for Nina that is to sit on a train, be silent, and be a mother.

Nina turns her gaze from the window and looks at Allechka, who is still at the age where everything is like a game. Perhaps, Nina hopes, her daughter won't remember Russia at all. Perhaps this will be for the best.

Nick sits nearest the aisle next to his daughter. A tear falls down his cheek, but he does not lift a hand to wipe it. It is a tear better left to create a path where more will follow. He can no longer imagine what he will find at end of this journey. The disruption and displacement have drained his body and mind, and he never foresaw these horrific events.

He's used his creativity time and again, setting the stage with cigarettes or vodka, creating scenarios to protect his family. He's utilized tricks he learned as a child in the country from Russian gypsies (all now exterminated) to outmaneuver, outrun, outsmart an enemy. If there were a way, he would beg for help from the spiritual world.

In that mystical realm he's witnessed miracles in the face of tragedy which could not be rationally explained. For surely his education and life experiences alone have not helped him live through the punishments of starvation and loss of all he had built for himself. And what fate brought him to find solace in once-lost family, only to be overrun by the monstrous presence of the Nazi army? He, too, is leaving all he knows behind, to go to a foreign country, to be surrounded by people whose customs and belief systems have threatened his Russia; he will have to live in the midst of warring strangers. What might fate hold for him, a Slavic Russian, considered by the Nazis to be low on the scale of evolution? They are now refugees, he and his little family.

Their train continues into hours and then days. Less important than troops, military equipment and supplies, it is more often delayed than allowed to move forward. When the trains do move, they pass through devastated countryside that is the same in its ruin. All around are disrupted lives, false allegiances, incomprehensible fear, legalized murder, powerful insanity, orphaned children, homelessness, poverty, anger, confusion, brutality, starvation, and repression. Nick's observation of troops and the dispossessed along the way and in stations make it clear to him that the Nazis are indeed capable of the atrocious behavior they had been rumored to have conducted in Russia. And though he maintains a strong countenance, he cannot help but become more and more outraged by the obvious cruelty around him. The daily barrage of angry, foreign tongues creates a constant fear that at any moment his family will be surrendered to the whims of war.

The train stops on this particular occasion at a Polish village. The motley assortment of fellow political exiles and refugees are walked through the bombarded, formerly picturesque town to what once was a schoolhouse. The children here have obviously not had normal lives since the outbreak of the war. There is no school, and no laughter from students resonating in the stony corridors; only a shelter for displaced persons. Makeshift bedding materials lie upon the cold floors where people wait for not just hours but days. But there is a cafeteria, and, although the rooms are poorly heated, they provide shelter from the dampness of the freezing rain.

Weeks come and go, and the school becomes more of a prison. But tonight, this April 15th, Allechka plays with friends as Nina walks to the cafeteria. It's Allechka's fifth birthday today, and Nina has an idea to get a piece of bread with butter and sugar to make something sweet to celebrate. She uses her most courteous German to ask the cook for sugar. Her general tone, she realizes, has become more harsh and authoritative. Her daughter's birthday reminds Nina of her own age, and makes her imagine how it will be to see her mother for the first time in fourteen years. "What will she think of me," Nina wonders, as she successfully brings the sweet treat back to the rooms where her daughter plays.

It isn't long after this special day that the Nazi guards come to retrieve the trainload of weary travelers. The family and several others are escorted from the school, through the village, and back to the station.

Nick holds onto Allechka, feeling helpless as they walk to and board the train. Their travels continue as they move out of this village whose name will not be remembered. It is better left behind in Poland. They pass through forest and villages with similar, war-torn, hopeless appearances, until the train stops again. They are in a Polish border town not much different from the last. They've all become the same, as dark in spirit as the now-gray winter sky, as desolate as the wet, chilly weather, and as helpless as the severe uniforms and cold faces of soldiers remind them they are.

Again, everyone is ordered off, through the station, out to the muddy street. There are no buses or automobiles to take these fleeing foreign refugees, only horse-driven buggies. Once again Nina rides on a shaky wooden cart, herded like an animal and ushered into a displaced-persons camp that once housed old horse stables and grooms' quarters. There are only stalls and hay to spend the night or nights, depending on each family's situation. Fear permeates the air as some families are escorted away. One by one, Nina, Nick and Allechka are searched and checked for disease by a German doctor.

❧

Josephine walks briskly across the busy Berlin avenue. It's been a trying two months since she's been aware of her daughter's evacuation from the Caucasus. Berlin has restrictions and documentation requirements beyond those of other German cities, and getting her daughter into Berlin hasn't proven easy. She's already seen four lower- ranking Nazi officers, has earlier been refused the last necessary documents, and now must be prompt to meet with a higher-ranking official this afternoon.

It's been against her better judgment to have Nina come to Berlin. After all, Britain has been targeting the city with bombing raids since November. And this atrocious extremism that is the political power of the moment continues to commit arrests and

367

persecutions without mercy. It isn't that Josephine hasn't seen this repression before, for she has survived the Russian Revolution and witnessed the rise of Bolshevism and its destruction with the even more repressive rise of Stalinist Communism. The insanity that has been Hitler over the last seven years has also brought about the abandonment of her son, Vova, and the murder of her youngest daughter, Vera, by the Nazis.

Although she's survived these catastrophes, she's also hardened. At first she felt shame at having the audacity to bring four children into the world. Then, after hope of a new-found life in Berlin had decayed, she grew tired of blaming herself. There seemed nothing left after the ceaseless atrocities brought on by political, power-driven men in this tired and brutal life. Now, with the potential arrival of her eldest daughter Nina and Nina's family, she fears it may already be too late for all of them. The war will doom everything. What is the use in hoping for anything different?

Nonetheless, indignantly she walks up the strict stone stairs of the Reichstag building. As a German citizen and landowner she will not be stopped. She *will* bring her daughter and her daughter's family to Berlin.

Nick and Nina, once again feeling less than human in an animal stall that is shelter for the desperate, are alarmed by the shout of a Nazi guard, "Siewert family…report immediately…Siewert family…report immediately." Nina's use of her maiden name is still in force. Nick, Nina, and Allechka quickly gather their few, now dirty possessions. Given exit papers, they walk alone through the streets of another anonymous town to the train station. Once there, they stand in a madhouse of refugees. Nina walks with a tight grip on Allechka's hand. Nick clutches the documents. Together the three move quickly to the platform indicating "Berlin."

As they push forward, Nina sees row upon row of prisoners with the Star of David on their garments being pushed by guards in the opposite direction. Suddenly, a woman holds out her baby, her lips miming something foreign to Nina. "Take her, take her," Nina interprets all too slowly. Nina hesitates. It's all going too quickly. Nina only registers the thought to grab the baby when the nameless woman is pushed forward, pulling her doomed child close to her again. Nina continues forward with the flow of people moving her toward the train.

The image repeats in her mind a thousand times, haunting her. She thinks to herself, "I could have helped her and taken her baby… I wanted to help her… She moved so fast…. I couldn't think fast enough. Oh, to have another child, to save the life of that child, but how did it happen? She considers this abrupt experience again as she makes her way through the rushing, pushing, clinging, bumping crowd. And once on the train the haunting memory is repeated… then again and again….

As the train crosses the German-occupied Polish border into

Germany, Nick remains unhappy and angry. He's glad to be leaving the displaced-persons camp, but, from what he's seen, must not imagine what they might find. They head deep into the cauldron of the Nazi state to ironically find the security of family. The contradictions are becoming too absurd for Nick's comprehension. He begins to lose his ability to maintain his mental calm. The sound of squadrons of airplanes and the sight of herded civilians and clanking soldiers with their cold steel weapons become more pronounced and jarring to his tired mind.

The orderly train begins its forward motion, and then stops. Guards enter and shout to the evacuees, "Return all jewelry," as if it were taken from them; as if it had belonged to the Nazis. Wrapped tightly next to Nina's body, sewn into her coat, is her gold watch and ring. Nick carries his Leica camera sewn inside his coat.

Nina will have nothing to do with this, her anger becoming her protector. Adamantly, she thinks, "Why should I give up all my possessions? I've brought them all the way from Leningrad and they are mine." Pondering the risk, she believes they cannot search everyone; she'll remain still with no response to the commands. "He who gives up loses," she thinks to herself.

The guard makes his way down the aisle and stops above the seated family. "Do you have anything to declare," he says in a strong, authoritative voice. Nina, immediately answers with a strong, unflinching, "Nein."

Nick, however, is less self-assured. He's completely unfamiliar with these people, and what he's seen so far fills him with anxiety about what they are capable of doing. He hesitates briefly and then says, "Nein." Immediately, he is asked to stand up. The guard feels his coat and his beloved camera. Instantly, he tears at the lining, takes the camera, and moves on. Nick sits down, this time more angry than frightened. After all, he has his paperwork, he is not a criminal, and they took nothing of Nina's. It is *his* camera and they have no right in taking it. Nina, showing no sympathy, only quips, "You should have hidden it better." The train moves on. Nick sits feeling betrayed by his wife while he has been robbed; his anger turns slowly into resentment.

23

B E R L I N
1943

As the train gets closer to the capital of the Third Reich, suburban towns have replaced forests. It continues to be obvious that something is wrong. The streets and schools appear to be neat and orderly, but in-between the neatness and superficial placidity looms a quiet desperation that is evident in the occasional bombed-out buildings. Nina senses that this is not Germany at a normal time. But what does Nina know of normal times? And what she knows of Germany or Berlin has only been gleaned from letters, and her knowledge of its people and language has come from her family.

Arriving in the grandiose Hauptbahnhof (Central Station), they witness the axis where the war machine hums. People move briskly on the active train platforms, their subtle dissonance not obviously apparent, yet intuitively felt. It is Berlin in the spring of

1943, weary from four years of war and becoming edgy about the war not yet won. Yet the city and its people are trapped by their leader's will to persist, all the while maintaining a deadly façade of inevitable victory with a sense of tainted, false glory.

Nick reaches for their bags, anxious not only about the inner conflict he feels here, but also how it will be living with his mother-in-law. From what he understands of her temperament, he is doubtful. And although he's not a communist sympathizer in the least, Josephine's bourgeois upbringing and privileged existence already disturbs him.

Nick, Nina and Allechka exit the train and touch the concrete platform of German ground. They walk crowded close together amidst the other passengers toward the center of the station. Nina is not sure her mother will have the slightest idea which train she is on. She does have the address of her mother's flat, and in the worst case she and Nick have money to get them there. She considers what she will say after these fourteen years. What will her mother look like? Information was always so diluted by the time it reached her in a self-edited and then censored letter. And any photographs were rare.

Then from the corner of her eye she sees a thin yet solid, refined yet simply-dressed woman with an upright, almost severe posture walking toward her. In front of her is a miniature baby carriage. "I think that's Mother; it must be," Nina says, turning to Nick. Stopping him and Allechka, she walks toward her mother and smiles. Josephine takes her gloved hand, raises it, and gives her daughter a firm handshake.

"And this is our little Allechka. This is for you," Josephine acknowledges her only grandchild, and then pushes the doll's carriage nearer the child. "We will call you Annichen or Anni now," she announces, changing Allechka's name to the more–acceptable Germanic translation in an instant.

Allechka silently observes the strange formal appearance and approach of this unusual lady. She has never received such a gift before and looks at it quizzically, wondering where the doll is.

Nina is flustered and surprised by her mother's presence and the efficiency with which she must have been informed of the exact train on which Nina, Nick and "Anni" had arrived. It makes her feel as if she is a little girl again, and not the mature adult she has become. She is not yet confident in how to respond to Josephine. Her mother remains aloof as always, and therefore Nina will remain aloof as well. There is no room for overwhelming and useless sentimentality, especially in public.

Josephine's thoughts are quick and clear. Nina appears to her to be more severe than she would have imagined. Pretty all the same, but obviously not polished as she had hoped. She knew the conditions were poor, but her daughter's letters had suggested otherwise. She's always trusted Nina to be strong and extremely capable; more capable, in fact, than Josephine had sometimes proven to be under the same circumstances. She wasn't aware of the toll this trait would take on her daughter's appearance. Nina's choice of wardrobe leaves much to be desired, and, to continue her judgment, so does her daughter's choice of husband.

The newly-reunited family makes its way through the shuffling crowd of Berliners to the subway for their ride to Josephine's apartment on the outlying west side of the city. Nick is not happy about the renaming of his daughter. He also begins to see the nature of his wife, via her mother, for the first time. But this is neither the time nor place to say anything. For now he will surrender himself to the new authority of his mother-in-law, as he walks helplessly outside his own country.

Nina walks first, behind her mother, into the nicely appointed, moderately sized apartment. A large china cabinet with crystal bowls, vases, and porcelain figurines sits to one side of the room. Two chairs are upholstered in silk, and the windows are treated with white lace curtains. The two silk needlepoint portraits Josephine brought with her from Russia adorn one wall in the living room, which also contains a peach-and-cream-colored silk sofa and two more chairs with small pillows on them. Josephine walks the trio through the apartment where they see two finely decorated bedrooms and a small adjoining sewing room. The kitchen and dinette are on the opposite side of the apartment, bathed in light that shows off their cleanliness. Nina has not seen such refined, simple luxury for many years. The products in the kitchen and bathroom have not been available in Russia even before the war. Everything appears to be clean, new, and functioning, not sloppy, used, or badly made.

They are shown to the bedroom which they will share and then allowed to wash and prepare for their evening meal. It is strange to be here. How different it would be if it were merely for a visit, but here they have come to live, with no jobs, no sense of understanding of the place, in a city turned in upon itself in its vengeful war, and Nick and Anni do not speak the language. They have come as displaced persons—as immigrants—to Nina's mother's very private home.

The family eats dinner together in the dining room. There has been no need to wait in a long line for their share of rations. The meal has been prepared for them. Josephine has never learned to cook. Anni is unaccustomed to so much well-prepared food, but eats politely what she can with urgings from Nina.

Josephine, at first, tries to make sure to include Nick in conversation by speaking Russian to him. Otherwise, she speaks German to her daughter. This makes Nick feel even more excluded. The strange old-world airs and restrictive, controlled social graces of his mother-in-law offend him in a cerebral way. He was taught to despise these bourgeois standards, and is himself more down-to-earth, more open.

Josephine is conservative, proper, and, at first, silent about the feelings or the tragedies and opportunities that have beset her. But Nina is curious. After the meal is concluded and the adults retired to Josephine's sitting room, Nina and Josephine speak freely. Nina asks, at the first opportunity, "Tell me about the family, Mother. Tell me about Vera. What has happened?" Josephine's face is sober as she begins. She pauses for a moment; a hesitation pre-cursing some considered thought before speaking. Nina's mind is open yet patiently waits for a response.

"Vera became very sick," her mother explains. "She began to tell me that people were whispering at her when no one was around. She told me how these people hated me. Her expression was incredible. I thought she could get better, and she seemed to at times, but instead the episodes became more frequent and kept getting worse."

Nina sees her mother's loss of composure for only the second time in her life. When her father was sent to Siberia for the first time, Josephine had simply shut herself up in her room. Now she sees the pain and emotion on her mother's face that normally remained reserved and indifferent.

Josephine continues, incited to explain in further detail, "I couldn't take her out in public any longer. Once she kicked me while we were in the middle of the sidewalk, and at other times committed acts unbecoming a woman. I didn't know what to do. One day she jumped from our second story balcony, and that was my limit. I no longer could protect her from hurting herself."

Josephine doesn't wait for a response and uncharacteristically explains further, "The doctor couldn't treat her and sedatives didn't work for long. And although I didn't want to, I finally took her to the hospital. I had no choice."

Josephine pauses momentarily as Nina listens, not interrupting. She then regains a stiff outer countenance as she says, "What was beyond my imagined fear came true. The authorities, Nazi administrators, gave her what is known as a "*sweet soup*," after she had been in the hospital for a month. The "*soup*" put an end to her life." Nina becomes obviously angered, but Josephine continues, "They claim that any German who remains ill for longer than a month and all those declared mentally incompetent–Vera had been diagnosed as being schizophrenic–are considered a threat and an imposition to the German race. This is what happened to your sister," Josephine concludes.

Nina's anger is unleashed as memories of her little sister surface; there she is in the back of a small carriage being pulled by her brother at the cottages in Finland, and later, walking in the gardens of the palaces at Tsarskoe Selo. Always so sensitive, maybe too sensitive, Nina surmises, knowing that any expression to her mother would not only be insensitive but out of order. But as she digests this information, she wonders, with all that the German people had invented and created and developed in music, philosophy, art, and science, how could they have resorted to this atrocious behavior? *They* are not her people. *This* will not be her true home.

As weeks go by, Nina is reunited with many of her extended family; her grandmother (her father's mother) Olga, now in her late eighties; and her old German tutor; her father's sisters, Aunt Stella and Aunt Anita, who live together; there are her mother's brothers, single and elderly, whom she remembers from summer times at the

Finnish dachas; her father's brother, Uncle Roman, visits, as does her Aunt Claudia and her cousins Swetlana, Tatiana, and Kiril. They meet even more extended distant relatives on both sides. Anni has played with her cousin, Boris, grandson of Josephine's sister Emma, in their elaborate apartment that takes up several floors of an entire building. Boris's playroom on the top floor contains a functioning miniature train scaled to the size of the children.

On this particular night, a Claus von Kursell arrives alone to dinner. His wife, Cousin Tatiana, Uncle Roman's daughter, is absent due to having fallen ill with the flu. Formally dressed for dinner according to his aristocratic upbringing, he speaks perfect French and Russian. A hobby of his is genealogy, so he takes particular interest in asking many questions. And though Nina has never met him before, she is impressed with him. As the maid serves dessert, Claus directs his glance across the table at Nina. "Why did you tell my brother Oscar that you didn't know my wife or any of your family," he asks abruptly, yet with polished diplomatic politeness.

Nina remembers the occasion at the mansion in the Caucasus where she ran into Oscar as a fellow translator, and quickly responds, "Because I was afraid I would be called a propagandist." Josephine is startled, having heard nothing of this before.

"But why? You weren't being threatened by the Bolsheviks," Claus persists, using the old-school term for the Communists.

Nina, now somewhat flustered, but like her mother not one to be intimidated, replies, "I could not afford to be questioned." Continuing, she says, "I simply needed to be as unobtrusive as possible. I learned that after the Revolution and it has kept me alive so far." Claus understands it is the end of this subject. He has also felt the treachery of the Bolsheviks. Curious and observant in his youth, he recognized the unacceptable acts of the new, Russian leadership. He understands Nina's transference of fear and subterfuge to the Nazi regime.

ɞ

It is a beautiful, late spring day in this orderly city, and Anni enjoys the sunshine by posing on the front steps of her grandmother's apartment building as her father snaps photographs. She's dressed quite finely with the ever-customary, large bow in her braided shoulder-length blonde hair. She likes flirting with her papa and the camera, and feels important and all grown up.

Nick has borrowed his mother-in-law's camera. It does little to alleviate the resentment he still feels over the loss of his cherished Leica. In fact it makes him all the more aware of how little he took from his lost life in Leningrad. He'd truly like to purchase another, but finding employment as a Russian-speaking engineer is impossible. And he refuses to be reduced to sweeping the streets of Berlin. Focusing on his daughter today, however, allows him some escape. He wants to use the façade of the ornate stone entranceway. To him it is much like the city—now an illusion of false grandeur.

Josephine takes Nina via the subway to the family properties.

Most stops contain civilians and many uniformed officer and soldiers. And, although they are underground, Nina can sense the commotion above. For above is the hub of the German war machine, the headquarters of the Reich, the environs of the dictator and the crux of the madness. They pass through the station that yields to Unter den Linden, the neoclassic Brandenburg Gate, and then the station for the old opera house. It is only one more stop before they arrive at Friedenstrasse. They leave the subway and walk a short distance until they reach the corner where two large avenues meet, forming a triangle.

Here, throughout these large, central-city blocks are apartments, garages, shops, and offices; all properties developed by Nina's grandfather Carl. Josephine controls them all. Her brothers Carl and Wilhelm inherited the automobile empire her father had built at the turn of the century when he traveled between St. Petersburg and Berlin. This left a vast estate of buildings, properties and land for the daughters. Her sister, Tante Lulya, now deceased, could not at the time inherit anything while still in Russia. And her sister Emma was uninterested in managing them, already too rich to be concerned. So Josephine was allowed the inheritance as well as the responsibility to both maintain the multiple mortgages and reap the financial rewards of so much property.

Nina's response is to herself and to herself only. She is dumbfounded that all of this belongs to her mother. How could this be? How could she have been laboring in the fields for all these years? How could she have been fleeing from starvation, near death, with threadbare clothes and six-day work weeks, when her family owned all of this?

Josephine makes no inquiries into her daughter's feelings or state of mind. She takes her directly to her office and introduces her to her secretary. Josephine simply states, "It's your turn to help manage this now, Nina. My secretary will show you how."

Over the next few, increasingly warm days Nina learns how to collect rent and write letters when rent is past due. She documents mortgage payments and utility bills and begins to work with the tenants when small repair issues become necessary. But there are few men in the city, and the female tenants have been fairly cooperative, fixing their own leaky faucets and clogged toilets. Of course, there are nightly air raids taking place. Bombs had already begun to fall on the city since the previous November. Soon repairs may be a greater problem.

∾

Anni looks at her papa inquisitively as he ties three suitcases together and makes a bed in the adjoining sewing room. "Why are you going to sleep on this, Papa?" she asks. He avoids her question and continues his work. "Stop, Daddy," she says louder. But he doesn't listen.

Anni is disturbed by the arguments, instinctively sensing Papa has been nervous and upset although she is too young to hypothesize why. She simply overhears arguments, especially those between Papa and Omi (German for "grandmother") Josephine. Once she heard Papa tell Omi, "Get on your knees and beg forgiveness." She doesn't know what this means but heard her omi apologize.

Nick's outrage has grown to the point where he refuses to learn German. Still unable to work as summer has entered its hot, weary August days, he despises being here near the center of this "Reich." Hadn't they suffered enough from these Germans? Needless to say, not least in his mind is his own intolerable situation, as he uses his cane to cower from accusing stares from passersby of "Why are you, a relatively young man, still here?"

In addition to this, he finds it utterly preposterous, watching the Nazis march about and self-righteously proclaim their insecure dominance over the other peoples of the world. He despises them and yet is subjected to what he convinces himself is their hideous language, their strange unaffectionate formalities, their atrocious Nazi saluting, day and night. And the bombing is increasing; incendiary bombs (which produce firestorms) and nightly British air raids are making their nights a special kind of hell..........again.

Anni lies in her bed next to her mummy. Papa no longer sits by the window with the light of his cigarette glowing. She wonders why he sleeps alone, feeling less than confident and abandoned as the airplanes fly above. Whose airplanes fly above she also does not know. She comforts herself now. There is no other choice. She holds tight to her new "Bärchen." "He's just next door," she says to the toy bear as she drifts off to sleep.

24

THE NEW ONSLAUGHT
1943

The sting of an early fall chill is noticeably biting; yet, to Nick, Nina, and Anni, it is mild compared to the frigidity of the Russian fall. Nina wears her best coat from Leningrad. Nick and Anni have new ones purchased by Josephine. Where Josephine has been restrictive in her spending for her daughter, her attitude toward Anni has been a different story. Anni now has new clothes, but better yet, a roomful of new toys. Against one wall of the guest room she shares with Nina, are pretty glass shelves. Among an assortment of toys are delicate glass figurines representing small animals, which line the shelves, and a big, brown Steiff teddy bear lies on her pillow.

Although providing for minimal needs for her daughter and son-in-law, Josephine has been, as usual, conservative. Income from the property rentals has become stagnant and sometimes nonexistent with so many men in the military or now dead, and the inappropriateness of evicting widows who pay rent late or not at all during the war speaks for itself. In addition to this, two of the twelve buildings have been nearly destroyed by bombing along with the loss of many civilian lives.

The Allied Forces have continued bombing raids on Berlin. Thousands of airplanes fly like so many locusts over Germany on a daily basis. They blanket the skies like huge formations of geese flying south for the winter. But these are not geese. These are weapons sent to destroy and decimate the populations below. In their bellies they hold deadly cargo which lays waste to this ancient capitol. They come with the shrieks of sirens and are followed by inevitable, random destruction.

Nina's work for her mother has ended almost as soon as it had begun. Josephine no longer finds it safe or reasonable for Nina to go across town to the office, leaving it to the competence of her secretary. Other social activities have also been suspended, leaving them mostly silent prisoners in Josephine's apartment.

Bombings are regular; sirens howl twice a day with punctuality, and the orderly Berliners are confused by so much disarray. How often can a broom clean up broken walls and shattered concrete? What happens when the house the broom is contained in no longer has any walls? This obtrusive destruction not only frightens but also perplexes the people attempting to go about their business. They now must walk around the piles of debris to continue their normal regimen of daily chores. There is a degree of madness to the lack of order in an already irrational city, and a strange order to the madness.

From the window of her mother's apartment, Nina looks out on the devastation the bombings have caused as she wonders at the state of this war. Whole buildings are empty where fires raged the night before. Others are intact. All the elements exist, the straight lines of the Boulevard below, perfectly proportioned, well-manicured buildings, well-dressed Berliners active on the street, and then empty space, rubble and a charred building where the symmetry is broken. Cardboard replaces window glass. And after each attack when the cardboard is jettisoned out on the boulevard neighbors then quarrel over whose cardboard is whose. Nina often considers how old men who have created this atrocity sleep on fine beds in well-appointed homes while young men are off dying in the fields.

As evening approaches the family sits to a dinner prepared as usual by Nina. It consists of sausage and potatoes and some not-very-fresh vegetables. The cook has been dismissed since traversing across the city has become too hazardous and being away from her family too dangerous. Sirens howl and an air raid begins, unusual for this time in the early evening. Dinner is only half finished.

Nina and Josephine routinely grab a few medicines, canned and prepared foods, and water left by the door for these occurrences. Together with Nick and Nina they walk out the door and join neighboring women, elderly men, and children. All walk down the hall to the staircase, down one flight of stairs to the first floor, and through a hallway to the narrow set of stairs leading to the cellar.

Anni dislikes the cellar, but at least it is different from the one in Leningrad where she grew ill. She has friends here and a big sandbox in the center to play in. and is happy that Omi is with them. It isn't that she is so much bothered by the sirens and bomb bursts; she has become used to them and they have always been a part of her life. It is more the dampness of the air, the utter absence of light and the anxiety of the adults around her; all these things make her afraid as well.

The raining incendiary bombs have stopped their storm. Sirens howl again, signifying the all-clear for inhabitants to leave their cellars and return to their homes. Anni, her mummy, papa, and omi walk up the stairs and back to the apartment. It's all become so routine that no one makes a big fuss over it anymore. Nick, Nina, and Josephine resume their places at the dining table where the dinner still stands, cold and uneaten. Anni has lost her appetite and is allowed to excuse herself to play in her room.

Before she enters, she is stopped at the door. There, to her surprise, is a hole in the wall and an unexploded incendiary bomb propped at an angle directly in her toy corner. All of her delicate glass animals are shattered and strewn haphazardly as are the glass shelves. Anni rushes back to the table. Breathlessly she says, "Papa, a bomb is sticking in the building right into my toys!"

Nick hesitates, looking at Anni as if she were momentarily insane. Then he tells her, "Anni, go back and play in your room." Anni listens as calmly as she is capable as he continues, "There aren't any more bombs, the siren went off, and we need to be calm. Your toys are okay. Now go back to your room and I will come in awhile to put you to bed."

Anni is confused. She wonders why grown-ups won't believe her. "Perhaps I am imagining it," she thinks, and returns to the room. Sure enough, "Bärchen" is in shreds on the floor, and a bomb is partially stuck in the wall. She edges very near the bomb and picks up the pieces of her teddy bear; there is an arm, nearer is part of the head with one eye hanging on a thread; here are some more threads. She collects the pieces and starts to sob as she walks back out to the kitchen where the adults are still gathered.

Nina and Nick stop talking and look at their daughter holding her pieces of blackened teddy bear. They are horrified. Nick runs into the bedroom as Nina and Josephine follow, where they stand staring at an unexploded bomb. Josephine calls the building's manager and begins to collect her precious jewelry and some bags where she has her most valuable possessions ready to take to the cellar. Nick and Nina grab Anni and hurry out of the building.

The manager immediately knocks frantically door to door as everyone runs out of the building expecting the bomb to explode at any moment. Soon a corps of detonation experts and volunteer soldiers arrive. Little Anni has lost her beloved teddy bear and cannot contain the stream of tears that flows from her eyes. Hours later everyone is allowed to return from the street and sidewalks to their apartments. Boards are placed over the hole in the wall. The war is getting worse.

$\boldsymbol{\mathcal{CS}}$

The trips to the cellar become more frequent and the sirens become less predictable. Anni is growing more tired of these trips, sometimes awakened just as she drifts to sleep. She doesn't care to play at this hour. She asks why they can't stop the sirens. But the howling continues and it's time to go to the basement again.

As Anni shuffles along she passes the ground-floor apartment where two elderly ladies live. Peeking in the door as she holds Mummy's hand, she sees a large, white teddy bear sitting on the foyer bureau. "Please make sure to take your teddy bear," Anni says to one of the ladies as she stops in their doorway. "Mine got hit by a bomb," she explains.

One of the women pauses, goes to the bureau, takes the bear, and hands it to Anni. "You may take him to the basement with you and take care of him," she says.

Anni holds the temporary replacement close to her heart, and walks with her parents the remaining distance down the hall and stairwell into the cellar. Anni names him "Bärchen the Second," and strokes him as the bombs explode outside. "Everything will be okay, soon you will be able to go back home to your little place on the bureau," she repeats over and over, soothed by the soft faux fur.

The raid eventually ends, and all return home. Anni stops to knock on the door of the old ladies' apartment. (The two women decided to remain in their apartment at the last minute.) As one sister answers she announces, "Your little bear is well but he is very frightened."

"Since you were such a good little caregiver, you can keep him," responds the eldest sister.

Anni's pale face lights up, accepting the gift with delight. She can now express joy with a new friend after losing her friends so often, imaginary or otherwise. She tells them she will be sure to always take care of her little Bärchen.

⅌

The intensified endless assault continues to beat on the small family. This gnawing city war continues to ebb and flow, intensified with the days. Entire buildings are left burning after the persistent air assaults, leaving brigades of civilians to line up handing buckets to one another until the smoldering fires are put out. Rows of chimneys stand silhouetted against the sky where entire buildings once stood.

It becomes increasingly impossible to keep a true perspective of one's individual life when there is an enforced sense of normalcy that is imposed upon Berlin by an iron-fisted dictator. People still dine in cafes and the zoo remains open even though the giraffes and some of the other animals have been killed. Daily activities during the shorter periods of time outside the cellar continue. Food is purchased at the markets that are not bombed out, toiletries are maintained as best as possible, clothes are washed, conversation is made between the family members, and like Leningrad during the beginning of the Siege, the symphony orchestra still performs for those still able to listen. Nonetheless, everyone is extremely aware of the possibility of it all ceasing on any given day. They try to live as they had, yet nothing in common is remembered as the days merge together in the lives of these increasingly shell-shocked, traumatized subjects of the aggression that is war.

Nick, however, finds it increasingly difficult to pretend. The sights of the collapsed neighboring apartment building and streets filled with rubble have likewise eroded his patience in others' persistence to make everything *seem* normal. His nerves have never fully recovered after leaving Russia. To him Berlin has been but a façade waiting to be dismantled. The pains in his chest are only a manifestation of the conflict in his mind over what to do next and where to go in this mad world.

Yet the Nazi war machine continues as the capital's bureaucracy dictates its unmanageable atrocities. The night air stinks of burning rubble as the inevitable rears its familiar face. After only nine months since their arrival in Berlin, they must yet again run for their lives. For there is another fierce threat to their survival that does not come in the shape of a bomb or bullet but in the guise of a political belief system that sees them as the worst of the enemy. The Communists are coming.

This is another familiar, yet surreal, moment to Nina. It had been years before with her mother, at the apartment in "the Tsars City" of Tsarskoe Selo that the family watched and waited in horror, as the Bolsheviks-turned-communists turned their country and lives upside-down. The Russians come from the East as the American and British come from the West to free Berlin from the atrocities of the Nazis. Now the Nazis–who had been the outer enemy in Leningrad–are what protect them from the advancing Communists, from whom they are defectors. Whose side is whose doesn't really matter, as neither side has offered any peace, freedom, protection, or civil rights. And now, in the course of one year, the sides have changed. The enemy is from within, outside and all around.

The cold, damp, basement air and earthen-and-concrete floor send chills through Anni's tired body as she sits one more time, Bärchen in hand, in the cellar with her parents and Omi. A good portion of the day and evening is spent here. Living is now done mostly underground. "Mummy, look at the bird," Anni points to the old women who gave her Bärchen and now sit together in a corner with a parrot in a cage.

Nina observes the vignette of elderly women with a brilliantly-colored bird. Its colorful feathers and sturdy grasp on its wooden perch give Nina a comforting sense of calm and a childlike, reflective memory of events and symbols that have subconscious meaning to her stemming from the summers of her youth.

"Go ahead Anni, it's a parrot, you can visit it," she urges her daughter toward the bird.

Anni makes her way across the congested basement of familiar faces. "Hello. Why have you brought your parrot?"

One sister explains, "Three days ago the bombs shook the building so much that when we returned to our apartment we found the cage on the ground, the door open, and our parrot gone."

"But you have your parrot now," replies Anni, with a little frown.

"This afternoon while we were eating, my sister noticed the china cabinet door mysteriously opening. She looked inside and found our little parrot, apparently hiding like we are. Now we're making sure he's all right, just like you protect your Bärchen."

For this short conversation, Anni is happy. She imagines that from now on, and as long as they all have to hide in the basement, Bärchen will also have a friend to play with. She asks her mummy if she, too, can one day have a parrot. Nina agrees with a smile.

❧

Anni had fallen asleep a couple of hours ago but is awakened to the wrenching sound of what sounds like thousands of high-pitched sirens. It's time to put her shoes on, always right next to the bed, and bring Bärchen to safety. Her papa quickly runs into the room and grabs her hand. The bombings are more suddenly upon them tonight. Explosions reverberate below, shaking the earth and illuminating the sky.

The basement is eerily silent as everyone stares at each other, the floor, and the walls. Exhaustion hangs in the air. The children are too sleepy and weary of the attacks to play. They cling to their favorite toys and just wait. Silence is followed by the whizzing sounds of the burning incendiary bombs. The ground trembles. The walls shudder like cracking branches. Then suddenly the entire building is shaken with a thunderous crash. Dust falls from the ceiling. People gasp in horror at what possibly could be happening above.

Red embers and black smoke seep from below the door before it bursts open to reveal nothing but rubble blocking it. There is no exit. Anni squeezes Bärchen with all of her strength, as she looks at her father's face–then her mother's. Both are tense, unflinching. Smoke intensifies as Nina places a handkerchief in a pail of water prepared for this purpose. She covers Anni's mouth and nose with the soaked fabric, and then puts another against her own face. Anni holds the handkerchief tight against her little mouth and nose, her eyes burning and welling up with tears.

Nick and the other men hack on the wall with picks and shovels, thinking they might be able to break through to the adjoining basement. They are still attacking the wall as the cellar becomes darker with the acrid stench of their burning building. Fortunately men from the adjoining basement hear the frantic sounds of desperate pounding, screaming, and wailing from the basement next door. They, too, grab their pick axes and begin to bore a hole from their side. Everyone hears the sound of the rescuers coming from the other side of the wall.

Piece by piece, the wall is compromised until a small hole appears. All are relieved that escape from this tomb is assured. Indeed, the hole breaks larger as the men on both sides feverishly claw at it. When the hole is large enough for an adult to get through, the men drop their shovels and begin to help the women and children. Nick grabs for Nina, Anni and Josephine. Anni clutches at her Bärchen as she escapes the smoke-filled room. Men on the other side pull the coughing, gagging inhabitants into their cellar and up the stairs. Anni scampers through the hole, holding tightly onto her Bärchen. Nina follows with Josephine. Nick is not far behind.

From outside their building Josephine, Nick, Nina, and Anni look up through flames and smoke. The apartment above theirs is on fire but their second-floor apartment is not—at least not yet. The windows have shattered and some walls are sheared off. Neighbors rush to quench the fire with buckets of water. The family decides they have a chance to salvage some of their belongings if they act quickly.

Josephine and Nina find their way up a rubble-infested stairwell to Josephine's apartment with pieces of torn cloth tied over their mouths and noses. Once in, they fill bags and pillowcases with jewelry, silverware, clothes, and photo albums and toss them to Anni and Nick through a gaping hole where the wall once was.

Although the wall between the kitchen and the living room is missing, the doorframe still stands. Nina and Josephine continue to walk through the standing doorway out of habit, rushing between the rooms. Nina takes the silver, wedding-anniversary tray of her grandparents and adds it to the salvaged possessions. The marble tabletop and front-hall mirror are smashed from the direct it of a incendiary bomb which now sits cooling in the ground-floor apartment below. Much of the silk furniture and lace window curtains is disintegrated and smoke-stained and is left strewn all over the remaining rooms. The crystal and china cabinet–amazingly still intact but emptied of its most vital antique ornaments–is too heavy to move, and so is left abandoned as a symbol of what had been elegant in the apartment.

Nick, watching from the sidewalk below, thinks the women have gone insane. He holds his daughter's hand and looks at her then up into a dark sky filled with floating red embers from a cityscape lit only by fire. In resignation, he asks Anni, "Why do you think that the sky is so red?"

Anni responds, "I think that God is showing us how much blood we have shed this very night."

"From the mouth of an innocent child…," Nick thinks.

25

EVACUATION FROM THE CAPITAL OF THE THIRD REICH
1943

As morning arrives, the train makes it way out of the of the buzzing train station, city, and suburbs crowded with a load of anxious-to-hysterical Berliners. It was as difficult for Josephine to accept leaving Berlin as it had been for her to leave St. Petersburg. Then the harshness of the situation of the First World War was simply a hindrance. Now her home is destroyed and she is forced to listen to Nick, who convinced her to accept the opportunity offered them and others, now called "those who flee bombs," to relocate in Langweilig, a small village outside of Berlin, where they are promised housing.

It's been an uncomfortable ride—Josephine, stern and stifled; Nina, concerned about the loss of her mother's wealth; Anni, not capable of accepting the loss of her new friends and home; and Nick, ever aware of the train's direction not away from, but closer to the

East and the mouth of the advancing Communists. Out the windows of the moving train, all have seen the advanced destruction the war has brought. Where before, on Nina's and Nick's trip to Berlin, order was maintained around bombed-out buildings, now rubble is only heaped next to more rubble on the streets, and smoldering ruins still smolder.

Beyond Josephine's muted, formal appearance is a woman in reluctant acceptance. She was in her late thirties, as Nina is now, the last time conditions required she leave her home. Then she fled to the countryside when the Bolsheviks relocated her family from the renamed and demoted Leningrad, no longer the capital of Russia. Then, too, she left all of her worldly goods: fine furniture, velvet draperies, Persian rugs, china, chandeliers, and family heirlooms. Now for a second time in her life she flees to the countryside, this time from the capital city of Berlin, where her personal wealth has been greater than that of her and her husband's in Tsarist Russia. This second occurrence, finding her now in her early sixties, is even more devastating—if levels of misery could possibly be assigned traumatic events.

Nina sits, silent in her seat, stunned, while acknowledging her mother's earlier warnings that things would not be much better in Berlin. Both the motion of the train and the uncanny repetition of fleeing war and political regimes take her back, first, to leaving St. Petersburg as a child, when servants transported cartloads of furnishing, art work, clothing and toys. Second, it reminds her of her move to the countryside with everything lost to the Bolsheviks;

and third, their move out of Leningrad, leaving behind the relatively well-equipped life she had managed for herself.

It is still incomprehensible to her that her mother has owned so much property, and it is beyond what her rational mind can accept that all of it is being bombed as the Communists yet again advance. But there in the past were Father, Vera and Vova, all…dead…now. She can't allow herself to remember. The loss of these material things pales in comparison to loss of her family members. Still, hauntingly the vision of her apartment door closing on her poor father's hand-painted porcelain plates reemerges as she compares it to walking out of her mother's abandoned apartment.

Nick has been desperate to remove himself and his family from Berlin. All of his sensibilities, rationality, and intuition have been screaming at him to get out for the months since they arrived. He has been, all at the same time, aware, unnerved and tired of the restless activity of droning Berlin in its fight to maintain control over its citizens. The public harangues, dictates, falsified victories, and propaganda by the abominable Nazi Party have only affirmed his contrary opinions. Their paraded flags and emblems advertise a just cause for its people, which is all camouflage for Hitler's warped opportunism. Nick has longed to get out, and now they have a chance to do just that.

After a short train ride from the German capital, they've arrived in Langweilig. The village's military central command has expedited the availability of rooms for some of these migrating Berliners. Apartments, guest bedrooms and garages and stalls are left empty in many cases due to decimated populations from arrests, evictions, and men slain as soldiers. Josephine's imperturbable sense of entitlement manifests itself in two apartments directly across the hall from one another in an old German chateau-style, residential building located in the village center.

Days merge into one week, then ten. Josephine spends hours on the phone with her secretary. The shelling and bombing have hit another building, the rental market is no longer functioning yet the bank continues to demand payment on its mortgages.

As Christmas approaches there isn't much to celebrate, but they are grateful to have each other, the warmth of a place to live, and food. This is as much as can be asked for. It is unfortunate that Nick and Josephine do not see eye to eye on most things. In fact, this continued conflict has also taken its toll on Nick and Nina's relationship as partners in this desperate struggle for survival.

Nick quickly grows disenchanted with the village, obedience to his mother-in-law's pocket book and commands, and the repeated interrogations by officials. At least in Russia he could read the eyes of the Communists and understand their body language and movements. Here in this village, the Nazis make him feel unprotected and off-guard with their brazen arrogance and cruelty. And most obvious of all to him is the repressed fear of the war. He knows which way it is going. It has been clear to him since before he left Russia. After all, hadn't they evacuated Russia because Germany was retreating in the first place?

After Anni is tucked in Nick approaches his wife to discuss

their current living situation. He wants to move. Nina responds with disbelief, in customary fashion, "Are you crazy?" Nick persists. He knows there are far too many soldiers, and though they are safe for the moment, they are clearly still within allied bombing range. Nina eventually relents, and together they approach Josephine.

It is immediately clear that she has no interest in going any further into to the countryside. She disliked the countryside in Russia and the thought of it here reminds her of the poverty and isolation she had experienced there. The city is life to her, the country is emotional death. This village is as much of the countryside as is palatable. Josephine will remain. Nick has grown weary of constant dissension between, his wife, his mother-in-law and himself. He has made a valiant effort in trying to convince Josephine to leave.

The next question on his mind is money. To his extreme displeasure they have been dependent upon her financially since the 1,000 DM they brought with them from Russia has long been used up. He humbles himself to ask her. Josephine allows them 700 DM. She also gives him something of eventual importance–key addresses of contacts and family throughout the country–should they be separated, perhaps indefinitely.

In other ways, the weeks here have not been idly spent. Nick has been able to communicate in Russian and broken German with village men, fleeing émigrés, and farmers, and has determined the safest place to move. A small village, about three hours' walk, through country roads now covered in snow, remains untouched and is heavily forested. Nick has been able to confirm a family there will take them in. He purchases another sled and supplies, and Nick, Anni, and Nina walk the three miles to the small hamlet of Zullighoven.

Nina trudges in stoic silence through the wintry landscape of this 1943 December frost. She misses the bond that had been developing between her and her mother even more than when she was first separated from her in Leningrad. The sound of the snow crunching over the dirt road is all that can be heard in an almost eerie silence. With their warm sweaters and winter coats and packages resting on Anni, who sits on the sled, they make their way through the forest-lined, sparsely-traveled distance to their fate in an out-of-the-way German village in the middle of World War II. Unfortunately, even this seemingly quaint and more isolated retreat does not dismiss the fact that the war is coming closer. They've grown sensitive to their intuitions as they prepare to save themselves however they can.

26

In the German Countryside
1944–1945

Autumn colors are speckled throughout the woodsy landscape. The air is cool and brisk. Fighter convoys of planes can be heard flying overhead. The Russians are advancing from the east and they've made definitive headway. The Americans are advancing from the west, forging across Germany's great rivers. Nina notices birds flying south for the winter. Airplanes haven't completely disrupted their migration patterns.

There is no money to be made by Nina as she picks first tomatoes earlier in the summer and now potatoes in the late fall. All able-bodied women are to do any work necessary to feed troops of the Fatherland. The farmwomen here are not too different from those in the Caucasus. In reality they are all related. It is the German farmers from these areas that 170 years ago migrated to the Russian foothills. In the 1870's they began leaving Russia for places as far away as Kansas and South Dakota in the United States in order to avoid religious persecution and obligatory military conscription in the Tsar's army. Those remaining were sent to Siberia by the hundreds of thousands during Stalin's recent purges.

Working in the fields prevents Nina from making any more of her three-hour trips to Langweilig to get supplies and visit with her mother. Josephine had moved back to Berlin early in 1944, then back to Langweilig, only to return finally to Berlin again when her secretary died in a bombing attack. Nina was hurt by the decision as it reminded her of Josephine leaving Russia for Berlin. But, she justified, it is she and Nick who had moved away from Berlin this time.

It's Anni's first day of school today. In April she turned six, and as fall has begun, she is allowed late entrance into this farming community's kindergarten. Nick picks her up from the small schoolhouse. Anni shows him her gift. "See Papa, it's my first-day-of-school present," she says as she shows him the cone-shaped paper filled with fruit, nuts, and miniature candles. "I sat in the front seat and made friends with Liesel who sat next to me," she enthusiastically continues. Nick smiles as he takes her hand and walks past the neighboring houses.

Later he'll make notes of her clever statements in very small, penciled, Cyrillic letters in his little black journal. He's already recorded her earlier questions such as: "Is God wealthy; Why; Does he have many toys;" "Papa, why did Jesus Christ wear long hair?"

He noted his reply, "Anni, formerly everyone wore long hair."

"And you also, Papa?" she asked.

Christmas arrives, a holiday outlawed in Russia, but not completely unfamiliar to Nick or Nina, who celebrated it as children before the Revolution. Nick cuts down a small fir tree, carefully places cotton on its branches, and folds origami swan ornaments out of paper. Adding candles and pinecones gilded with some yellow paint, he creates a Christmas tree—a *Tanenbaum*.

Anni is amazed. It's the most magnificent thing she's ever seen. After she tells some friends, the word is passed, and soon children and parents alike come to the house to look. It's the first Christmas she's ever experienced and the most popular she's ever been. Then on Christmas Eve, a oddly-dressed man arrives who hands out presents of fruits and nuts. Not fooled for long, little Anni asks her mother, "Why does Papa dress like a funny man?"

New Year's Eve passes into 1945. The threat of confrontation is undeniably increasing. There are few places on earth that do not hear the news declaring the progress of the Allied troops into the heart of Germany and the expected surrender. Zulighoven is aware of this fact as well.

By mid-February Dresden, center of the Baroque Humanism that once symbolized what was best in Germany, has been obliterated by incendiary bombing—wiping out thousands of fleeing refugees. The Russians, the feared communist Russians, have advanced well into Poland and are moving quickly on to Berlin. Buggies and carts, heading to the west and filled with those escaping eventual Communist takeover, pass through their village.

Nina and the neighbor woman make coffee for the cold and frantic Russian and German-Russian émigré families who tell them of the brutality of the Russians, the rape of women and the unrestrained anger of the Russian army now unleashed. She hears of the murder of entire villages of young German boys, and further realizes the extent of the suffering is beyond comprehension on both sides.

Nick has heard these stories, too. Were it not for Anni's schooling and happiness he would have insisted on leaving long ago. Both he and Nina agree that capture by Russians will mean execution, imprisonment, or Siberia—and an orphanage for Anni—in the best of cases. It's agreed the time has come to leave at once. They'll take the sled and walk back to Langweilig, where they can hopefully take a train to the west. Nick rationalizes that if they continue to head west, it will be more likely to be taken over by the Americans.

⅋

Nina packs the remaining suitcases in frustration. She sets aside some non-essential items in a box that will have to be left behind. Their worldly goods, though of little material value, have grown in these months in this remote village. And Nina has grown exhausted from having to leave things behind.

They do not leave until late afternoon and this journey is not met with anticipation of anything good. Nick places the now nearly-seven-year-old–and much larger–Anni on the sled, along with two suitcases and a sack, they leave the room they've made a home of, say good bye to the family who befriended them, and walk into the snowy, white landscape on their three-hour journey back to Langweilig.

The pine trees bow toward the earth as they creak and moan with the wind pushing their heavy, snow-laden limbs. Their sounds evoke the unspoken anticipation between Nick, Nina and Anni as they walk into the inevitable climax of war. Nearing the larger village, it is obvious they are not the only ones to have made the decision to leave. The village is in chaos. Sleds, carts, pedestrians, a few horses, and weary, cold travelers crowd the streets in an effort to avoid the approaching Russians.

The train station is the hub of this surrounding chaos. People climb through windows of the waiting trains. Meanwhile shouted rumors fly of the Russian invasion of nearby towns, "The women were raped," goes one; "The men were all killed," is another. Nick has procured tickets, but only to another, not-too-distant village. Passengers are only allowed to travel a limited distance, he tells Nina.

Together they lift Anni onto the tall steps leading up onto the train and immediately follow her on board as the train departs the gate and heads south toward Czechoslovakia. As required, they get off where obliged. Here, too, mounting hysteria has begun to overrun the station. Those fleeing the larger cities are overrunning towns. The inhabitants of larger villages are occupying smaller villages. Everyone–displaced persons, refugees, political exiles from previously-conquered Russian territories, Germans, even some deserting Nazis–are trying to get away from the advancing Russian army. But the war is not quite over. The military has not conceded defeat. Hitler still shouts orders to his henchmen, and Nazis continue to control, execute, and threaten.

Nick makes his way immediately to the ticket counter and returns, again successful. "If anyone should ask," he tells his wife after they are seated on board, "we're going to your mother's. Tell them she's in the next village. Look on the map and remember the name." They roll forward awhile and then exit the train. They repeat the same strategy. The next train arrives, they enter, and they travel more kilometers down the track. They continue, moving south and slightly west. And through it all they pass surreal visions of groups of people struggling to go westward away from Russians, leaving behind the homeless, the despondent, or those already entrapped. The horrors of these last days of Nazi-controlled Germany are beyond comprehension.

Finally, they pass into the former Czechoslovakia, once an ancient German colony again under German control, arriving at a very small village called Branda. Numb to the incessant turmoil, they make their final stop. They have traveled as far as their exhausted minds and bodies will allow. However, Nick is determined to go still farther outside the village. He asks some of the locals and obtains the information he needs. Exhausted beyond argument and mentally numbed, they begin to walk again. Outside the village, past the schoolhouse, beyond a field, is an even smaller enclave of five large homes owned by forest rangers and their families. Hopefully they can find a room there.

Cobblestone streets have turned to slushy, snow-covered dirt road, the trees become denser, casting shadows with the fading light. All is silent. Winter and war have stifled the sounds of nature. A slight breeze carries with it a damp chill as they pass a small field and see an outline of brick houses in the distance beyond the trees.

They turn the corner of narrow dirt cross-road and are abruptly stopped. The road is barricaded with felled logs. Even here, the war is made evident. Nick holds Anni's hand and guides her around the barricade. Nina follows. A threesome of strangers in this unfamiliar land, they stand together as Nick knocks on the door of the first house. A woman answers. Nina asks for her father or husband. She's with her young son, and another family already occupies the spare bedroom. Down the road, she suggests, is another house. Perhaps they can try there.

Into the farthest reaches of the countryside they've come to be as far away from the eventual onslaught as possible. Terrified, they know it is only a matter of time. A million troops have been massed by the Communists for the final invasion of Berlin. The Americans have passed the Rhine and the Ruhr. The clock keeps ticking nearer doom or salvation.

They knock on the door of this second, larger house. Greeted and invited in, they are shown up the stairs by the owner, a forest ranger, to a room in the back corner of the second floor. Two other couples and one elderly woman already occupy the other rooms here. The ranger and his wife use a room on the ground floor.

Anni is comfortable with these strangers. Nina and Nick's fear of capture by the Russians has not been relieved. But they realize that they've run far enough with no place left to hide and have no capacity to go anywhere else. They must wait and hope that the Americans capture them. This ceaseless pattern of flight and hide that started so many years ago has to come to an end. And though reasonably comfortable here, weary and dispossessed, they are without a nation to call home.

As the days pass, Nick finds it increasingly hard to entertain himself by recording poetic verse, philosophical queries, or the clever inquiries of his daughter; his nerves begin to prey on his mind. One happy moment is Anni's birthday; on April 15 she turns seven. But she receives no gifts, just the comfort of food, and the façade of safety in a dense forest enclave, in the late spring of 1945.

27

ATTACK
MAY 1945

It is twilight and the sound of the late spring's crickets and birds are droned out by the clashing thuds of artillery and bombing somewhere in the distance. Nick and Nina rehash their decisions thus far, deliberating their fate. Neither can conjecture with any assurance what might happen for the war continues unabated. Although it seems as if this dreadful conflict should have reached its apex by now, it hasn't. Still they believe the time must, by all accounts, be near. They can feel it in their souls.

They know that the deep forest also contains soldiers. Every square meter of land can be potentially dangerous. Yet Anni still plays with the forester family's dachshund in the sandbox in the yard. After all, the war has been going on for more than half her life, and Nina and Nick haven't the heart to keep her confined in the house all day.

Anni tilts her head back as she watches a large metal object fall from the sky and bounce onto the field nearby. "Mama, Papa," she shouts, and runs upstairs where her parents sit at their small table. "A bomb dropped but didn't explode. I saw it bounce on the field," she yells. Although they've known her to be correct before, it seems far-fetched to them that a bomb could bounce. Nick again consoles her, ushering her away as he so often has in the past.

Anni returns to the sandbox dejected, wondering when they will ever take her seriously. Looking to the field, she sees the foresters and farmers all surrounding the spot where the round object landed. She ignores the real world, and again enters the land of make-believe by building a house made out of sand. Shortly thereafter some of the villagers inform her parents and the other residents that a gas tank was ejected from a passing plane. Everyone ran to it to see if they could extract the excess fuel.

It is not long after this that a very large explosion wakes Anni from her sleep. She wonders if it might be an exploding building in the village. But she's heard an explosion this loud before and knows it is not good. She also knows that Papa will come to take care of her and her mother if it were a real emergency, so she goes back to sleep.

She doesn't know how long after, but again she awakens. This time it's to the sound of the owner telling Papa it's time to go to the basement. Anni cries as Nick holds her hand down the flight of stairs, through the kitchen and to the cellar. Anni is sleepy and doesn't want to go. She remembers the time in Berlin when the building collapsed and began to burn and running to the basement presaged the worst of the worst.

Nick feels her fear in her sweaty little palm and resistant tug. It pains him to lead , the most precious person in his life to the cold cellar, but he has no choice. The shelling is very loud and very close.

Together they huddle on the dirt floor amidst canning tins and fruit jars. Explosions coalesce nearby, as the field Anni had observed earlier in the week is targeted by what sounds like hundreds of bombs. Earlier that evening the villagers lit candles in the field to act as a decoy to the bombers. All the houses have since had blackout cloth on the windows. The decoy worked. The forester goes up the creaking stairway and opens the door. Shortly thereafter, he returns and tells the group they can feel safe in going back upstairs. There is no sign of damage and no sounds of attack–momentarily.

Nina reheats the soup on the small burner in their room. No one is hungry. Nick's anxiety cannot be camouflaged as he uncharacteristically tells his wife that he thinks they are going to die. Neither knows their fate. Communist propaganda about American capitalists does not dampen their spirits as much as the possibility of death by bombs, tanks, fire, machine guns, capture, torture, or murder by the Communists does.

That evening, as usual, blackout cloth is placed over the windows, and the doors are bolted shut. Anni watches the glowing embers of her father's cigarette in the darkened room. Then tanks vibrate the earth below, as snipers are heard in the nearby forest.

Again, the forest ranger knocks on the door. Nina recalls the last advance of the other invaders–the Bolsheviks–when she was Anni's age, and is not daunted. She helps Anni put on her shoes and then puts on her own, as Nick takes their daughter's hand. Quickly and quietly they rush beyond the kitchen and down to the cellar. The others crowd around as the owner bolts the doorway.

The fighting outside the house is excruciating. Bombs explode as if on the doorstep. Bullets ricochet off trees and walls. Surrounding trees crash from the burden of oncoming tanks. Machine guns spatter and heavy artillery whizzes by, decimating what once was a dark and beautiful forest. Nick, Nina, and Anni squeeze each other tightly. The entire house shakes with a tremendous, tortuous thud as mason jars crash to the floor and dust falls on their hair and faces.

One of the men shouts hysterically as he rushes up the stairs, "We have to get out. They'll throw a grenade in here. We'll all die!" Panicked, the others begin to move to the stairwell as well. "Wait," the man shouts as the sound of bullets splinter off the outside door directly above them.

The sense of being surrounded wraps around each person's consciousness as an odd, momentary silence ensues. One of the men takes a stick, ties a white handkerchief to it, pushes open the storm door leading directly outside, and waves it through the opening. Suddenly, the door is flung open. An American marine holding a shotgun yells and ushers everyone out.

Nick, Nina, and Anni follow up the stairs. Anni cries, Nick's heart twists in pain, and Nina succumbs to the terror in fearful rigidity. Outside in the light of day, everyone is motioned to line up against the outside, bullet-riddled garage door. There they stand, women crying and men petrified. One thing is confirmed, however—the uniforms and emblems *are* American. Shortly after the troops finish their search of the house, all are simply told they can return. Dazed by the episode, and finding they are still alive, it is all they can do to start walking back into the house.

Nick surveys the damage. Directly through the main room of the house and out the back wall is a huge hole, obviously created by a tank. Nina notices the Americans lying about in the woods and asks if they are dead. A soldier responds that they are not.

Nina and Nick retreat to their room, which is mostly undamaged. Some men can be heard communicating with the soldiers left behind. The entire mood quickly lightens. Off in the distance sounds of ammunition can be heard, but that, too, fades like a thunderstorm advanced by the wind behind it.

Nina sits across from Nick at their table. What do they do now? They have survived and the Americans don't seem to want to harm them. An entirely different problem has arisen: who are they to trust?

Anni is contented. The soldiers are nice to her and she's met a chocolate-colored man. She plays in the sandbox. To her it matters little that the Americans are here. As long as the adults seem happy and the gunfire has subsided, the soldiers and outside devastation brought by war is normal for her. Besides, she knows her mama and papa can see her from the second-floor window.

Nick answers a knock on the bedroom door. An American soldier enters, looks briefly around, and glances at Nick's cane. Nina and Nick speak no English and this American speaks little German or Russian, but they try to make sense of each other. The mood is cautiously friendly as the three continue. The soldier then leaves, shutting the door behind him. Nina and Nick become startled when they hear the door lock.

Nina immediately walks to the window where she spots Anni playing below. Anni looks up and sees her mother, wondering what she wants. "Allechka come to the door and unlock it, dear" Nina says. Anni immediately knows that something is up given her mother's artificially calm and earnest demeanor. Wondering whether she's in trouble or not, she walks into the house, up he stairs, and to the locked door. The key is still in it. She turns the key and pushes open the door. Nina and Nick walk quickly into the hallway and then stop. The soldier is also standing there. In his hands is a bottle of wine.

They all re-enter the room. Nick and the American drink and try to speak to each other. The wine bonds them. There are no words to describe their sense of relief. Nina walks over to the burner near the small table where the two men are sitting, points to a pan and says, "Eier?" He understands her offer to cook him eggs and nods. "Wie viel," she asks, and the soldier responds by lifting three fingers. There *are* only three eggs she realizes.

The American asks Nick "You go back to Russia? You want to go?" Nick understands as a shudder runs through his body. "Nyet,

Nein," he quickly and vehemently states, with symbolic gestures of his hand and arms pushing the question down and away. Nina understands as well, walks over to him and uses German, Russian, and even the French term for "no."

The American tries to clarify, "You Russian; Russian our friends; we take you back to Russia." Nina desperately adds a more lengthy, emphatic answer, "No, we don't want to go to Russia, we under no circumstances want to be turned over to the Russians." The soldier seems to understand, although it is clear to all he does not realize the threat his communist allies represent to their freedom.

The conversation continues for a little longer, and then sleepily, the soldier motions to the bed. Nina gestures for him to use it by laying her head sideways upon her folded hands, then pointing to him and to the bed. Nick and Nina sit and speak quietly at the table, glancing curiously at their guest until he wakes up. He wishes them well and leaves.

The Nazi Party is soon thereafter banished, Hitler is dead; there is no more fighting and Germany has been conquered. The Allied Forces pushing from the west and the Russians moving from the east have succeeded in ending the war in Europe, but Germany is now an occupied territory yet to be re-defined. There is, however, still a need to hide from the Russian threat; in the Russian occupied territories, as well as in some American and British sectors, Russian evacuees are being turned back to the Communists where they face retaliation and banishment for their supposed cowardice. Many are sent to Siberia or murdered.

For Nick and Nina this is still a foreign land with a new government and new rules. Nick concerns himself immediately with answering his questions of what exactly are the new rules, can this government be trusted; will it be permanent; how will they personally be affected. Most important now is the continued business of living. Nick and Nina are not foresters. They have no family in this rural area, no work that is suitable for them, and they are running out of money.

Within days, Nick and Nina discuss the options that Nick has been researching for another move. Berlin is destroyed and Russian occupied; it is no longer an option. Nina has suggested another city, Marburg-an-der-Lahn, where her cousin Milka, daughter of wealthy Aunt Emma, has lived since before the war. Nick has kept the names and addresses Josephine gave them upon their leaving her. Marburg is in the southwest region and in the American sector. Together Nick and Nina have weighed the pros and cons before agreeing they'll leave for Marburg tomorrow.

Nina with Kotya

1939 postcard sent from Leonya in Leningrad to Berlin

Nina and her father-in-law Mikhael in the Caucuses just after escape from the seige, 1942

Vova

Nina's passport photograph

Nick and Anni, approximately 1949

Nina, Anni and Nick in Marburg apartment. Anni sits at a little desk that was a gift received on her last birthday before moving from Marburg. It was purchased by her father, Nicholas, who was able to buy the desk when stores finally began selling more consumer goods after the war. It was left behind.

Book 4

28

MARBURG-AN-DER-LAHN
LIFE AMONGST THE GHOSTS OF WWII
1945–1946

A medieval fortress stands alone, overlooking a village it has protected for centuries inside cold, stone walls. Perched on a hill above Marburg-an-der-Lahn, it has stood witness to wars and famines, plagues and power struggles. Below, on the hillside, is the old part of town, where beautiful old homes stand in a picturesque landscape. Their gardens grow vegetables desperately needed by the disheveled and hungry population below. This city, not decimated by target bombing, is left physically intact. The devastation is emotional and psychological, nonetheless. The architecture remains, but the lives of the people will never again be the same.

This train ride is the last extension of a five-day journey through June's heat and humidity. It has been far superior to the horse and cart that took Nick, Nina and Anni on part of their journey across the barren, still-smoldering German countryside. Finally this train has arrived in the placid Marburg-an-der-Lahn station. The family departs to the normal sounds of civilians and American post-war troops. No longer are there desperate commanding officers shouting orders to their soldiers or shrieking loudspeakers directing fleeing victims of war or tortured souls en route to their demise.

Reappearing from their sojourn in the wilderness and forests, the three once more emerge from the country and into a large town. This is a newly-occupied, military-controlled and punished Germany—a country shaking trauma and disorientation from its collective consciousness, and looking with clearer eyes at the utter obliteration of its old structures, politics, beliefs, lies, and actions. Only now gaining awareness that comes before healing its citizens scavenge for food and shelter and for what is left of their divided, bleeding souls.

Nick and Anni wait at the train station as Nina goes to the address given by her mother. The address is for her cousin Milka and Milka's son Boris. Milka is the daughter of Josephine's wealthiest sibling Emma. She moved here after her husband, a high-ranking Bulgarian aristocrat and official, had been murdered and her apartment building had been destroyed. She and her son escaped the explosion that killed her husband. It happened two years earlier at the funeral procession of a deceased Nazi official. Her husband had been a pallbearer. She and her son had arrived late. Fortunate for them, they had been unable to enter the church when a bomb exploded, killing her husband and many others inside the church, and propelling Milka and Boris onto the street from the doorway where they had been standing.

Nina wonders if she will find her cousin still here as she walks through the wrought iron gate and between two tall maple trees. Arriving at the front entrance of the neatly-maintained building she looks on the roster next to the mailbox. And yes, the name is here. She knocks on the door. Milka, not completely sure who the thin and exhausted stranger is, answers, questioning, "Nina?" Together they walk into the small apartment's parlor and sit on the sofa.

After introductory formalities have been made Nina goes on to explain, "Nick and Anni are at the train station as I wasn't sure to even find you here." She then continues, "I'm sorry to ask you this, but, as I've mentioned, we have just arrived here and have no place to stay."

Milka expresses relief that Nick and Anni are still alive. "I thought, seeing you here alone, that…Nina, we have only two bedrooms and my mother, your aunt Emma and my son Boris are here also. I don't know how we can manage with two families in so few rooms in this apartment…. I know of a building where people, refugees mostly from other cities and those from the east, can stay. We can help you look for an apartment. I'm so sorry."

Nina, disappointed, understands. It's clear that Milka was challenged to find this apartment in this southern city during the war in the first place. And it is obviously not large enough to provide for another family. But Nina hasn't much time to reminisce today; without a home, in a foreign city, and with her husband and daughter at the train station still waiting for her, she excuses herself.

Nina returns to the station, finds Nick and Anni, and tells Nick the news. Nick is glad that at least there is a shelter where they will be able to sleep and eat. The refugee shelter, bleak and overcrowded, will have to serve for the time being. In the meantime, they'll have food rations. But food is impossibly scarce. This has been the problem for Nina since before the Revolution, and here it is happening once more. In fact, everything is impossibly scarce. A good part of the economy is based on the black market, from what can be traded amongst people of the heirlooms and consumer goods they've been able to save from before the war. In addition to this, CARE packages from the United States sometimes fill the gap.

There are also no apartments to be found. The city is swollen with refugees from surrounding cities that were bombed beyond recognition, and others like Nick and Nina, who left to flee the Russian-occupied or threatened zones. All scavenge for jobs, food, and shelter. It appears as if they will have to practice their patience in the absence of so many necessities. But how long can this patience hold out? How long can they live with so little before they grow weary of not only the lack of food and shelter but also the disillusionment brought on by this strange and foreign country?

Nina's solution as always is to keep busy and try to make whatever extra money she can. She's done so for the past week by filling in for a sick acquaintance at the American Canteen. During this week, Nick, Anni and she eat well, as the leftovers are free for the taking. Anni even received a donut, which she wondered about, having never seen anything quite like before.

On another occasion, Anni receives a large orange from an American soldier. Before she gets a chance to bring it home and show her mother, another little German girl that Anni thought was her friend, steals it and runs home. Anni tells Nina, who becomes furious and immediately speaks with the girl's mother. The girl's mother apologizes and tells Nina that the next orange the little girl gets, she will give to Anni. The promise is kept when Anni later brings home an orange, but it's much smaller than the one she originally had. Yet another lesson learnt for Anni in this strange, new, competitive climate.

However, Anni is contented to play with her second cousin Boris, who is almost the same age as she, in the sandbox behind the apartment building. She's played with him before when they both were in Berlin two years ago. She remembers that he had a huge bedroom suite with separate playroom that contained a choo-choo train and tracks all around its perimeter. Boris would ride the front, child-sized car, pretending to be going off to work, and Anni would wave to him like a good wife.

As the dust begins to settle on the immediate aftermath of the war, much more information is obtained. Nina receives a response from her mother as well as telephone communication when she visits Milka. Josephine survived the Russian takeover of Berlin. Her damaged, but not completely ruined, west-side apartment is in the section taken over by the Americans. In order to save herself from being raped by Russian soldiers like so many other women, she dressed and acted like a very old woman. When one soldier was about to rape her, his comrade dissuaded him, by saying, "what do you want with an old woman like that?" A younger woman very nearby her in the basement shortly after the final invasion was not so lucky. The Communist soldiers proceeded to brutally rape her until the girl's mother threw herself upon her daughter's still struggling body and begged the Russian soldiers to take her instead.

❧

Nina, with the help of her cousin and aunt, finally finds an apartment. The first they've had since Leningrad, it is also much smaller—one room in the attic of a strangely configured building. Originally intended for college students, there are four other one-room apartments also in this attic. over one wall sits a little, round window that looks over many other rooftops and six stories to the ground below. On another wall sits a large metal furnace that is also usable for cooking. The upstairs units all share the toilet. And the communal kitchen is on the fifth floor below, where Nina will get water for cooking and cleaning. Nina's able to get two beds, a sofa, and some dishes from charity. Later she'll try to purchase some material to make curtains and a tablecloth.

Nick has spent a good portion of his time looking for work. Dressed in the dress shirt and suit his mother-in-law purchased for him while they lived in Berlin, he often feels more humbled than proud. This, along with his lack of competency in German, prohibits him from obtaining the type of position that his education and engineering management experience in Russia should otherwise merit. The only jobs that are competitively available for him are basic labor positions, which are unacceptable to him. This new freedom is somewhat disappointing. Opportunity to make a decent, quality life for himself and his family is what he's wanted, and opportunities are hard to come by in this impoverished, defeated land. For now it is apparent that he must be content with what he has.

In order to thwart his anger and growing depression, he begins to study religions. The Communists squelched all study or practice of formal religion or informal spirituality, believing religion to be a bourgeois tool for exploitation. Throughout these recent years past he has seen miracles that were well beyond explanation and has been amazed at the fact that they've survived by some unimaginable odds. Might it mean that he's not supposed to be dead? And what do others believe that he can learn from? Is there more to know? Might there be some answers? Nina also believes that only by some miracle was she saved from dying of starvation in Leningrad. And who can explain the truck stalling in front of the apartment as they began their journey to the train station? They never would have otherwise made it. On the other hand, what can account for this terrible war?

Nina also cannot find work in her field of expertise–drafting. So she falls into the habit of finding work where she can get it. At times she is a cleaning woman, and at others she is a seamstress. The relationship between her and her husband has become strained from the war and now that they live in such a small place matrimonial expectations are difficult to fulfill. They argue over their lack of money and the rationale of finding meaningful work. One area of compromise, if only for the sake of propriety, has been Nina's use of her married name again.

❧

As the months pass it is clear that all of Josephine's rental property is completely in the Russian-controlled zone. Josephine has been given permission to maintain the rents of one building if she agrees to live in it. She's refused, so there will be no further rents forthcoming. Nina's request for financial aid also has been heard. But Josephine will only be able to send a small amount of money. Hardly enough, both Nick and Nina agree, to provide for extra food or cloth needed to sew new clothes.

Nina is distraught over her mother's lack of motivation to send any further monies to her or her family. Josephine maintains her determined self-control and her reserved demeanor even in this shocking loss of so much. Seemingly overnight she has lost control of an enormous amount of wealth which took her father's lifetime to create. Yet, she must take it in stride, for what other choice has she. This is life; she consoles herself with numerous Russian proverbs of the land of her birth, where its inhabitants throughout the centuries have experienced repeated loss, suffering, and upheaval. And yet many still survived, and so will she.

Spiritual seeking alone has not alleviated Nick's financial difficulties. Through the weeks he's kept an ear to discussions among other uprooted people, he has continued to look for work. Fate finally offers him a new opportunity to use his mechanical talents.

One day an acquaintance asks him if he knows anyone who can fix a watch. Nick responds that he can. Immediately he sets up his tool area in the corner of his narrow apartment and takes apart the entire watch, making paper cutouts of where each of the gears and assemblies go. Finding the suspect spring, he repairs it with a soldering iron, puts the parts together, and replaces the watch face and glass. After this successful repair he communicates with the Russian and German old men who spend hours in the park playing games, marketing his capabilities. One refers a client, who then refers two more. He feels the first hint of satisfaction and purpose creeping back into his life.

Through his ever-expanding network of acquaintances in his religious studies, he develops a friendship with a fellow Russian émigré-turned-Methodist-minister; they philosophize, complain and rehash their experiences. He also begins to narrow down his religious explorations. Christianity, being the most familiar to him and his pre-communist Russian culture is the one he chooses. Within Christianity, he is convinced, Methodism offers the freest range of practice. With his friend's assistance, he converts to Methodism. Nick introduces his wife and daughter to the church and places Anni in Sunday church school.

As fall approaches, Anni also begins grade school with the other children. She doesn't make friends very easily and is still very small and frail, having suffered so many years of hunger and limited foods. Since the war's midpoint, she's never been able to recover her good sleeping habits. Sometimes she has terrible nightmares that border on hallucinations in which she can't differentiate reality from fantasy. The better-dressed and fed little girls taunt her in the classroom. Once they encircled her outside of the house until Boris chased them all away. She doesn't know what's wrong. It hurts her deeply that the other little girls taunt her by repeating, "Little Russian…little Russian."

As winter approaches and Nina watches Anni and a little friend play, she becomes preoccupied with her daughter's thin physique. Neither Nick nor Nina can tolerate the belligerent behavior their daughter is subjected to. The betterment of her life is something they both can agree upon—a common cord that holds them together now that the war's demise has torn at the very fabric of their relationship. Through various church groups, Swiss families have been hosting war-torn German children for three-month periods to help them recuperate physically, and hopefully mentally, from the devastation of the war. Families pick children from photographs and bring each in turn to their homes. Nick and Nina agree that sending Anni away, for the first time in their lives together, can only be for the best. Anni takes the information with well-placed reservation. She only becomes measurably enthusiastic when she learns that Boris, her cousin, will also be going come spring.

29

ANNI
1946–1948

Eight-year-old Anni cheerfully climbs onto the train car with her brown cardboard suitcase filled with her best clothes. Carloads of young eight to eleven-year-old boys and girls, like so many of the Pied Piper's flock, are ready to leave the village. It is the first time in Anni's entire life she's ever been separated from her parents. In the recent past, she's seen families torn apart, children without parents, parents searching for lost children, and all ages of the dying or dead. In Berlin, she acted coquettishly in order to endear herself to others in case the worst happened to her family. Thoughts of losing her parents concern her to a degree, as the train full of cheering children leaves the station. Nonetheless, she waves bravely to her mother and father on the platform. One thing she's glad about is that her cousin Boris is with her.

The train stops in Switzerland and Anni and all of the children are taken to a hospital to be inspected for afflictions. The hospital is made up of one long, tall, brick building with a pointed roof and large, surrounding, wooden porch and one separate, smaller building used for terminal-care patients. The larger building that Anni is taken to has the feeling of a displaced-persons camp, and, even though it is well lit, feels dark and unwelcoming. Anni's good mood turns quickly sour and subdued as one by one the children are inspected. Boris is allowed to go on with the other children, separating her from her only security. Anni is told she will have to be held back.

Feeling desperately alone, she cries and waits. Within time, a nurse comes to tell her why she is waiting. The nurse, quite directly says that she is a carrier of scarlet fever. Anni protests, "But I don't feel sick." The incident on the cattle train leaving Leningrad comes to the surface of her memory. She recalls the feeling of terror when she awoke from her nap to find men throwing the body of her sick friend out into the snow.

The nurse interrupts her and tries to calm her down by explaining, "You aren't sick but you can make other children sick unless you're cured." Anni is still terribly upset as the brusk but friendly nurse tries to sooth her by pointing out the pretty mountains outside , and telling her that they can call her "Annichen" here. The icy mountains do little to comfort her, as she contemplates yet another name change. She doesn't like it much, but she accepts it as what grownups do each time her family relocates. A nun takes her by her hand and escorts her to the hospital room she will be living in; as they walk the corridor, Anni figures it's something she can live with.

The hallways seem grim, sterile, lonely, and cold. There are no other children here. Next door to her room she notices a man presumably dead, his entire body and face is covered with a blanket. She holds back her sobs, wondering how her parent's could have sent her here, where they are, and what happened to the life that was supposed to become better by coming here.

"Which bed would you like," asks the nun pointing to the two beds in the room. One normal-size bed has metal devices hanging from the ceiling. The other is only slightly bigger than a crib. Annichen considers them for a moment. The metal-device bed seems odd and frightening, and even though the crib bed is very small, it's nearer the window and sunlight. The nun tells her in a calculating, instructive tone, that whatever she chooses will be hers for the duration, so she had better choose well.

"This little bed will be just fine," Annichen says, choosing the small bed, and holding back her tears to be on good behavior. The nun leaves. Anni, alone and un-consoled, curls up in a fetal position on her new little bed, far away from her family, and cries herself to sleep.

After a couple of days Anni realizes that the bed she chose is too short, and the larger bed may not be so bad. She asks the nun if she can change and is told very harshly, "You were told you could only make the decision once and now that the decision is made there will be no changing it." This same nun also belittles her. When the doctor enters her room, the nun introduces her condescendingly as "Our little Russian." "But I'm half German," Anni protests, hoping that she might be treated better, if she's thought of as German. But this achieves nothing in her favor.

As days pass, Anni remains isolated in her room. There's a little courtyard outside her window, but when she asks if she can go outside to play there, she is told "No." Meals are brought to her as if she were in a prison cell. Once per week she is given a chocolate bar, which she hides in the dresser next to her bed, and eats slowly over the course of the week. She is also not given any toys, but only paper and pencils so she can send letters home to her parents. Cleverly, Nina and she devised a plan before she left, in which, if things were going well, she would put O's on the page, and if things were going poorly she would put X's. Anni puts big X's on the bottom of the page knowing that someone will read the letter. Sure enough the nun asks her what the X's are for. "Only kisses," Annichen replies ever so politely.

One day, Anni's nun reports in sick and a different, younger nun comes to see her. This nun, decidedly more kindly, gives her a chocolate bar two days in a row. "Why am I getting chocolate bars every day," Anni asks, wondering if she has deserved a special treat. The new nun tells her that she was supposed to get a chocolate bar every day. After Anni says she hadn't, the new nun confirms she will, from now on, get one everyday.

Shortly thereafter, Anni also gets a little plastic doll to play with. This is consoling, but only to a degree. The hours alone seem endless and it's hard to spend so much time crying. Even though the weather has become warmer, and Anni can leave her window open, bars protect the window just outside the screen. But she is able to befriend the gardener who has recently worked outside her room. One day, as a surprise, he brings a kitten for Anni to play with. She loves kitties and it's the first she's been able to play with since losing her own cat in that horrible winter in Leningrad.

After four long weeks and a hard-learned ability to adapt to this difficult situation, Annichen is told that she is cured of being a carrier of scarlet fever. The time has finally come for her to leave the hospital and go to her foster parents in the countryside. She packs the cardboard suitcase, relieved to be leaving, but wary of what awaits her. Again heading off to more strangers, she isn't sure they will be any nicer than the people she has already met.

Nina sits at the small table nearest the heater/stove to read the letters from her daughter and mother. The X's in Anni's letter outrage her, yet her hands are tied. She doesn't mention this to Nick, knowing that he would be adamant in his response and knowing how protective he is of his daughter. The rift between her and her husband has never healed. Something drastic and damaging happened during the years of continual shelling, relocating, and loss of livelihoods that has never been resolved between them. Nina can't resolve this alone, and neither of them seems able to make restitution for any wrong-doing on either side. So she resolves instead that it is better to say nothing at all, sometimes remaining silent with her husband for days or weeks.

Nick has managed to rent one of the other closet-like rooms down the hall from their sixth-floor attic apartment. This has become an office and his personal retreat. Proudly he displays a sign on the front door stating *Uhrmacher* (clock and watch repairman) for visiting clients. Solving the riddles of more and more clocks and watches, he's happy to not be arguing with his wife, whom he now calls by her Russian maiden name Nina Leonidovna. Often he eats alone in his office surrounded only by the sounds of ticking clocks. His favorite is an old French clock, obviously of superior quality, for which he's built a simple wooden housing. When he isn't repairing these clocks and watches, he invents designs, analyzes technical problems, studies languages and religion, builds miniature models, and tries to draw conclusions from the insanity that he has lived through. His business grows to a reasonable level, as a good number of timepieces were damaged or broken during the hostilities. Perhaps, he surmises, that the atrocities of the war were so great that even time had no business moving forward.

When Anni's train arrives at the Pratteln Station, two sisters, Marichen and Lily, and their brother Hans meet her. The siblings are friendly and gentle toward her. They take her suitcase and transport her in a horse and buggy to their large, stone home built in the midst of a meadow with a view of snow-covered, majestic mountains in the background. Here she has a fluffy goose-down bed in a room all to herself. Indeed, things are much, much better here.

Her eighth birthday comes and she is given a new, warm, wool sweater, a doll, and other new toys. Every Sunday they have a big dinner which includes beef, potatoes cooked in creamy butter, and thick slices of brown bread. Easter arrives with an Easter egg-hunt for Annichen and her new friends in the garden, to her surprise and delight there are hidden chocolate eggs and small presents. As spring commences, early planting season arrives. Anni helps by sitting on a little seat on the back of a horse-pulled plow. Her reward is lunches of thick bread with butter on it and big chunks of cheese.

One day, however, Anni has a big fright. The sisters and brother have all gone to the village at the same time. Anni is left to play alone in the garden with new friend. Accidentally, they leave the gate open and Daisy, the family cow, escapes. Anni and her friend are upset and worried. They decide to walk out the gate and down the road toward the village. There, they find the cow by the village well. Together they coax her back to the farmhouse, telling no one of their misadventure. They know Daisy can't tell either.

Unfortunately the months here end quickly, especially since she had to spend one of her three allotted months in that horrible hospital. But she now has so many gifts that her one cardboard suitcase no longer holds them all. The siblings offer her a new suitcase so that she has two to hold all her clothes and gifts. On the way to the train station, sadness wells up while saying goodbye to her new family. She'll miss them and the mountains of Switzerland, both of which have created loving memories for her.

ɛᴈ

Home in the attic apartment in Marburg-an-der-Lahn, Anni tells her papa of her adventures. She purposely doesn't reveal too many details of her experience in the hospital. Why burden him with any more information than he needs to know about being sick? Besides, no one has asked her how she feels about her trip.

It's odd to her, but all of a sudden everyone wants to be her friend. The other little girls in the neighborhood no longer make such a fuss about her being a Russian girl, and, true, her blond hair is brighter from so much sunshine and her body is more filled out.

One day Anni notices that her mummy has received a package from Omi Josephine. One of the items is a paper lantern. Before the war, people would string up strands of these for parties and picnics. Nina gives Anni the lantern and a candle. Anni finds it interesting and shows it to her girlfriend, Liesel. Liesel remembers her mother having one that is now stored in the attic. She fetches it. Shortly thereafter, Eva, a wealthy neighbor girl, comes outside to see what Anni and Liesel are playing with. Of course she has a nicer one, which she runs to get. When she comes back and lights it, it catches on fire and burns, to both Anni and Liesel's great delight. Eva's grandmother runs out on the street, scolding her granddaughter to come right in.

Liesel and Anni keep theirs lit and walk up and down the street. Together they sing a traditional song that they recently learned in school. It goes, "Laterne, Laterne, Sonne, Mond, und Sternen," meaning "Lantern, lantern, sun, moon and stars." They enjoy themselves until bedtime, promising they will go back out again the next day.

The following evening Eva joins them with yet another lantern and her best friend. Now there are four children walking the streets with lanterns and singing. The third night other children join them, and soon even smaller children come accompanied by their parents. The groups become an impressive procession of children and adults walking the streets of Marburg-an-der-Lahn, singing this pleasant and peaceful song which rises to the upper stories of buildings, inviting families to join in.

This lasts for several weeks, and like many things, begins to get boring for Anni for whom the event has lost its charm now that it isn't any longer her and Liesel's own, unique event. The girls are amongst the first to drop out. Soon some of the other initiators drop out, leaving the newcomers. Shortly thereafter the local newspaper publishes an article about the event. It states, "...the procession composed of children looking like so many fireflies coming out of the ashes of war...finding joy and happiness with these old and forgotten items..." Anni is pleased that even though she isn't mentioned personally, it is rather amazing that she and her girlfriend started such an event.

Anni continues to grow quickly enough that her always-oversized clothes eventually do occasionally fit. But this is short-lived before a new set of oversized clothes are obtained by Nina. Now that the last days of summer have coalesced into much cooler fall weather, and Anni has outgrown last fall's wardrobe, she again wears a sweater and pants that are two sizes too big. Also unfortunate are today's overcast clouds and chilly downpour, requiring Anni's presence indoors for yet another day. Being indoors with Mummy all day isn't exactly a lot of fun for this ten-year-old girl, especially since Mummy spends the entire weekend day cleaning the whole apartment until it is spotless.

Perhaps she can visit papa across the hall in his office to relieve her boredom. Her toy bird is broken and maybe he can repair it. Actually, she visits him quite often. He's even made a swing that he normally uses as a tool to repair watches but extra sturdy so that Anni can play on it. Besides, he's fun to be with, talks with her, and includes her in some of his adult thinking about a whole range of subjects. He also shows her some of the interesting inventions and paper toys he makes.

Anni prances out the door, across the strange round hallway, and into Nick's small office. Once there, she sets her broken toy down and begins talking. His conversational subject, sometimes as diverse as gypsies or tarot card readings, has turned to religion today. This raises a question for Anni.

"Papa," Anni asks, "Will God repair my bird if I ask him to?"

"He will if he wants to," replies Nick.

"Why doesn't He try," she thinks. She'll ask God to repair the bird, leave for now, and come back later. Nick doesn't convince her otherwise.

Sure enough she leaves for a while, thinking the whole time of the miracle that may happen to her wooden bird when she returns. Later, Anni excitedly knocks on her papa's door. Nick opens it and there, just inside, on the table, is the wooden bird. It's exactly as she left it…broken.

The look on her face tells all. Nick says nothing. Perhaps it was too soon, she conjectures. And then decides to come back again tomorrow. Nick does not dissuade her.

Papa is in his office early, and after Anni has eaten her breakfast and dressed she'll joyfully visit him. She raps on the door and there on the large, wooden, work bench on the far side wall, within clear view, is the bird. It's in pieces, exactly as she had left it, untouched. Disappointed but not dissuaded, she doesn't ask any questions. Papa had said that if God wanted to, He would fix the bird. Perhaps she'll be on extra-good behavior today. Leaving again, she'll return daily for the rest of the week.

Patiently, she returns one last time. The bird still remains unmoved. Finally in desperation, she pleads, "Why hasn't God fixed my bird? I've come every day and it's still laying here broken."

"God did not think it was necessary to fix your bird," Nick

responds.

Anni pauses for a moment and then asks, "Papa, will you fix it?"

"Yes, my dear Allulia, I will," Nick says using his most endearing nickname.

She knows better than to be a little pest, so doesn't return for two days. When the day has come, she knocks on his door. He opens with a smile. And there on the wooden bench is the bird, sitting upright again with its floppy wooden wings prepared to fly.

"How silly of me to ask God to do such a small task when he has the whole world to look after," she thinks. "God has given me Papa, and now Papa has fixed my bird," she concludes.

30

PASSAGE BEYOND
1949

The entire eastern European stage has fallen more deeply into the controlling hands of Communist Russia. The Atomic Age and aggressions of the Cold War in its infancy has awoken the United States and its western allies from their naiveté to Stalin's true intentions. Nick and Nina have felt the heat of their old Communist oppressor breathing down their necks during the years they've been trying to make a living in Germany. Yet, they miss their people in Russia, and Germany has neither become a comfortable home nor has it been very successful in its own struggle out of post-war guilt and economic gloom.

Nick received the letter from the Argentinean Council, dated December 12, 1948, just before Christmas. They were sorry, but he and his family did not qualify for immigration into their country. This frustrates and unnerves him, for Argentina was a choice made only because he felt it a good possibility for someone of his economic and social status to gain acceptance. The reality is that the family's quality of life has not improved much in Germany. Even though Nick has his watch and clock business, it is irregular work, and once the clock or watch is repaired the customer is gone. New customers are always required, and the work necessary to obtain them has nothing to do with the technical qualifications that make Nick a self-educated expert.

To make matters worse, Nick has never felt as though he fits in here, from the day he entered the train and left Russia behind to the present. And he's angered at how poorly his daughter has been allowed to assimilate as well. The language barrier has posed a challenge for her. Because of this she was retained for an extra year in kindergarten. The few friends her age she did make are now advanced to a higher grade. This poses even more social distance and has been yet another excuse for continued teasing.

Nina, too, has found neither Marburg-an-der-Lahn, nor Germany for that matter, to be fortuitous for what she's expected from her life. She, 42, her husband, 45, feel regret for what little they have to show in their middle-aged years. She still carts water up flights of stairs, cooks entire paltry meals on one burner, and re sews donated clothing to try to keep some semblance of pride. This is a far, far cry from what she was initially raised to expect out of a dignified life. And if it weren't for her husband, she would have moved closer to her mother in Berlin. After all, she loves her mother and her mother loves her, even though neither is capable of showing it—their relationship ever a distant one. Nina struggles with her resentment of her mother's refusal to help her financially.

Leningrad and Russia are additional points of anger for her. She'll never forgive the political regime for killing her father or assisting in the starvation of her brother Vova, Uncle Eric, and cousin Elena. She'll never understand how the Russian Communists weren't capable of getting food to the millions who starved to death in that most horrendous siege. Writing to Leonya, her eldest brother and only living sibling, who is still in Leningrad, or her other relatives and cousins, would only endanger them. It would leave them exposed to the continuing, seemingly endless, tyrannical recriminations of Stalin against his people. The last time she remembered walking down the boulevards of Leningrad before the war, the intelligent, sensitive, and sophisticated faces were already gone. No, Russia is dead for her forever.

But Nick *has* continued strategizing and planning during the four-plus years they've lived in Germany. Besides writing to embassies in South America, he's quizzed friends on word of better opportunities elsewhere and maintained a long-distance correspondence with his fellow émigré, the Methodist minister who immigrated to America and has lived in Port Huron, Michigan, for the past several years.

Through much legwork he's processed the paperwork necessary to be considered for immigration to the United States. It's been a requirement of the authorities there for candidates to have a sponsor family in the United States. Via his friend, Serge, and Serge's Port Huron-based Methodist church, a sponsoring farming family located in Ubly, Michigan, has been recruited to "foster" Nick, Nina and Anni in return for one year of labor on their farm. The first hurdle is an intensive physical examination.

⁔

Once again it is the bitter cold of winter when the family must move. It is January of 1949, and Germany is still in the throws of the economic and social disaster it has created, much like Russia has been since after its Civil War. But there is hope this day for a new and better life. Nick and Nina talked late into the night about the prospects for life in the United States. After their farm labor in Ubly is finished, Nick hopes they may possibly move to Detroit. Detroit is the auto capital of the world and Nick knows both of them have the capabilities to work there; Nick with his engineering background and Nina with her drafting expertise. Nina has been open to this idea. After all, it was her grandfather Carl who traveled between Berlin and St. Petersburg before World War One developing an automobile empire in two countries; the grandfather who had saved her from drowning twice. Recent communication with her mother in Berlin has made it clear that not only was her grandfather's property confiscated in Russia all those years back, but the properties he developed in Berlin, which Josephine later inherited, are now

450

completely in the control of the Russians as well. It has become treacherous to even attempt to visit them in the Eastern Sector of the city. Those in Russian control are, indeed, lost.

Packing takes its toll as always and Nina is forced to make choices between what to take in their one suitcase and what to leave behind. How often, she wonders, has she had to leave almost everything behind? It seems to be an endless cycle. Of some consolation is that the furniture, including the boxy and worn sofa and side chair, had been rented with the apartment and are not great losses. The dishes were obtained from charity. And they've had little opportunity to accumulate possessions of any real value. Nonetheless, leaving those things which have made them meagerly comfortable is upsetting.

Since they aren't sure they will be able to immigrate until after they pass physicals in Bremen, they will need to keep the apartment available in the event they return. Nick is most concerned with his high blood pressure and chest pains which have been occurring for years. They'll give Milka and Emma the key on their way out. Should they be approved to leave, they'll contact the apartment manager, who has agreed to contact a charity to pick up their remaining boxes.

Nina works furiously and extremely conscientiously cleaning every corner, wall, ceiling, and fixture of the apartment. While she washes the hard wood floors on her hands and knees, she considers what her new home will be like. What will it be like working for nothing for wealthy American farmers in the town of Ubly until their debt is paid?" She scrubs some more. Doubt sets off negative thoughts: the immediate prospects there don't seem very appealing; hasn't mother Josephine been right before when she told me not to go; has moving been the right decision; why are we really moving after all? Nina stops scrubbing and puts her hands on either side of her forehead, rocking her body forward and back to ease the rush of anxiety.

Anni plays with Boris on the stairway. "Look Anni, a wreath," Boris says as he takes it from against the wall where a neighbor had left it to be thrown away. He throws it down one flight of stairs and then the next. Anni watches gleefully as tiny dry pine needles spray fragments all around the hallway like a rain of forest green.

It isn't long before Nina, to her extreme and exhausted displeasure, becomes aware of the disaster in the stairwell. She scolds Anni and then Boris, who runs home. Anni feels both deceived by her cousin and guilty about the fun of spraying the shedding wreath, and she promises to never make a mess like this again. Nina commences sweeping every stairwell of the six-story apartment building.

Nick removes his metal "Uhrmacher" sign from the door of his office with a screwdriver from his tool box he made in Leningrad. He has managed to carry it through all of their travails so far. He feels sadness as he locks the door on his box of scrap gears, metal carvings, and the swing Anni played on. But the cleaning, the packing, offloading of books and knickknacks, return of the last repaired, endlessly-ticking clock and watch and dismantling of the living space called home is complete.

Nina's dressed Anni in the nice wool dress she made and

a little, cream sweater with a monogram of a poodle in the upper corner. She's placed a big, cream-colored bow, as usual, on top of Anni's french-braided, long, blonde hair. Anni is happy with her appearance except for the floppy bow, and happier to be wearing an outfit that isn't too big. Nick wears his customary, round, thick, black-framed glasses, and neatly-tailored and ironed, dark suit. His receding hair is slicked back which shows off his broad forehead. Nina dresses herself in a fashionable, oversized, ruffled-collar blouse, a plain skirt, and matching, brown jacket. They'll take a picture when they make it to Bremen and memorialize this moment in time with Nick's camera.

❧

The train will be leaving for Bremen shortly. It's frigid outside and the lack of clouds leaves no ceiling to harbor the warmth of the earth. February will come in a few days, and they will hopefully be on their way to Hamburg to catch the ship to America. There will be few goodbyes today except for fond wishes from Milka and Emma when they drop off the keys on their way to the train station.

Nina turns the key in the door giving her last review to the disturbed, but not vacant, apartment. She shivers with the recollection of the times she has locked the door on apartments normally still brimming with her or her mother's personal possessions, never to return. But the thought doesn't last long for they have a train to catch.

Like so many train rides before, the noise of metal wheels against the rails of the track usher in the movement of change in their lives. There is a major difference from so many times before: the villages they pass through are at peace. There isn't much to talk about. They've all been here before, feeling hope mixed with anxiety, moving into the unknown, the only continuity in their lives has been the ever-present desire to survive if not progress. Each chapter has presented this family with new surroundings, new threats, and new opportunities. They have managed to remake themselves every time.

The train arrives at the unfamiliar Bremen station. Bremen is much larger than Marburg and more morose in atmosphere. It had suffered major damage during the war. The rubble has been cleared but there are holes in the pattern of the city where buildings once stood. There are vacuums of emptiness where life once took place, and an entire generation of what should have been working men is missing.

They are given the address of a small studio apartment with beds and a desk where they will have to stay while their paperwork is being finalized. Physical examinations will begin, one at a time, as soon as possible. Nick is scheduled last.

His day comes. It is bitter cold in a bitter, strange city. Anni knows of these physicals and remembers all too clearly the torture she experienced in Switzerland when she was found to be a "carrier." She is petrified and does not want to be left behind. She would not be able to live, she feels, if she were to be too sick to go and abandoned as an orphan.

Nina does not worry. Being the most at home with German professionals, to her this is just a routine that she will practice patience with. Before too long both she and Anni exit the doctor's examining room. By all expectations they have passed. For now, they'll go back to the apartment and wait for Nick.

Waiting in the lobby for so long has given Nick too much time to think. He knows that if any of the three of them fail to pass the examination, all will be refused entry to American ground. Failing the examination has all the implications of a life of quiet desperation in a country he has never become a part of, and defeat in a defeated land. Finally, the office assistant ushers him into the examining room. His doctor arrives and is typical of a middle-aged, highly-educated, German professional who appears to have the rigid character, lack of humor, and authoritative mannerisms that make Nick uncomfortable.

Even though he had met some well educated, elderly Germans before the war, and managed a few in his factory, the war seems to have cemented those aspects of German personality he cares for the least. The atrocities of the burning villages near his father's home as the train headed for Berlin, the masses of homeless and disenfranchised peoples, the poverty of soul he felt in the wake of Jews being corralled and "directed" through border-town stations, and the anxiety he felt as his coat was ripped open and his camera confiscated, come back to him in a snapshot of adrenalin-pumping fear. It is this personality, this cold, holier-than-thou personality that Nick is reminded of as his German doctor, now employed by the American military, examines him with final authority in determining his and his family's ability to gain access to a better life elsewhere.

Nick returns very tired to the warm, little room where Nina has held off the dinner she prepared on the single burner. Very upset, as if personally wounded, he tells Nina about failing the blood-pressure test. "But I have rescheduled a second test tomorrow and have passed everything else," he says downheartedly. Nina understands his anxiety, and knows there is little she can do to fix either his blood pressure or the personal demons that still haunt him. Recalling Leningrad's cold clasp on her until the very end, it appears that this time it is he that is being held back by Germany.

The cold temperatures keep Nina and Anni apartment-bound the second day of their stay. There is little to do except wait for Papa to return with the news. Anni plays with her one teddy bear she's been able to bring along and a doll Nina has made by tying a knot in a kitchen towel. Nina considers writing her mother, yet there is no final determination to write about.

Nick sits on a hard, wooden chair in a large, poorly-heated room arranged with many empty tables and chairs before he is shown into a small, private room. Medical testing instruments hang from the walls, and the smell of sterilizer burns his nostrils. Jars of medicines and shiny, silvery equipment in jars of blue solution stare at him. He feels as if he's going to be invaded, knowing his future hangs in the balance of today's events. Tired of his future always being affected by others' decisions, he thinks of calming thoughts of his childhood in the Russian countryside to still his nerves.

The second day's doctor is Russian.

Anni looks out the window at fluttering large snowflakes that coalesce on the window ledge, trees, and ground far below while she watches for her papa's return. Nina moves between watching with her and reading the newspaper at the little desk. She's used to waiting with little information, attempting to maintain confidence with a day's possibilities, but today is particularly trying. This decision has never felt completely right to her, but going back to Marburg now would not be easy either.

Though they speak the same language, and though they find themselves both in a foreign country together, this Russian professional and Nick are many worlds apart. The doctor is, either by choice or by necessity, a Communist. Nick's role as an emigrating ex-Russian, now given an opportunity to leave for America, makes him despised. Nick is terrorized. This comrade has the authority in their homeland to report and condemn other Russians to Siberia, as in fact, does every comrade. This same doctor is one more amongst the living, persecuted masses, which Nick and Nina ran from.

The stethoscope is cold against Nick's chest. He tries to think of the icy Russian winters that he loves so much, but can only smell the breath of the tired Communist victor. He is reminded of being a young fourteen-year-old boy, watching the revolution unfold on the streets of his village; and then, as a factory manager, watching his co-workers disappear into Siberian work camps for no explicable reason. Fear over his own comrade makes him angry, but he knows he passed the line of irreconcilable differences when his family lived in the Caucasus under the auspices of the Nazi regime.

Anni sees her papa walking toward their building and notices his heaviness as he uses his cane for balance in the freezing slush. She calls Nina to come to the window. "Papa's coming," she says excitedly as Nina looks out the window, the pupils of her dark brown eyes contract in recognition of the dejected stride she sees. She hopes the familiarity of his body language is deceiving her now.

Anni listens as her papa passionately describes his experience with the Russian doctor. That her papa can fear anybody or anything is incomprehensible to her, but it appears that this doctor did make Papa feel uncomfortable.

Yet a well-worn and well-utilized part of Nick, the survivor, had taken over. Having found a way out of so many life-threatening tragedies in the past, he was not about to be turned back now. Using his mental bag of Russian ruses, tricks, and manipulations, in the end, he negotiated for one more chance to see another doctor and take the failed blood-pressure test over again.

All have another sleepless night. Another extremely cold day in Bremen follows. It's is February 1st, 1949, and so cold that even the sky takes on an even, crystal-like deepness to it's blue hue, like the deceptive color of the ocean which looks it's most invitingly deepest and darkest blue when at its coldest.

Nick is in the doctor's office, when after a slight, courteous rap on the door, an American doctor enters. The doctor tries to speak

German but can't very well. He sets down his large stack of papers which threaten to fall, almost knocking over the big glass jar filled with the icy blue liquid. Nick laughs. Preoccupied with procedures, the doctor looks at his paperwork and mumbles something under his breath that Nick has difficulty understanding. He looks at Nick, smiles and comments, "…simple test…blood pressure…in America…nurses do…bothered with…no nurses…Germany…"

Nick listens and observes this man's odd and somehow comforting behavior as he places the blood pressure strap around Nick's arm. The American seems strangely out of place here, but in a good way. He is a man who hasn't suffered the drudgeries and deficiencies and absolute poverty of living under oppressive regimes that Nick has experienced. All the same there appears to be a relaxed sophistication in his bearing.

The doctor tries to say something again in German, but can't. Finding his language attempt humorous, he laughs, and then both of them laugh about not understanding. The doctor shrugs his shoulders and arms in the universal sign of "What am I supposed to do?"

Nina waits in anxious isolation, glancing at the city sprinkled by a light flurry of snow. She thinks about her past and remembers seeing her mother wait for her father's return from his old office in St. Petersburg. That was another life and another world. And then there was the waiting, the incessant waiting, for her attackers. There were the Bolsheviks, the Nazi's, the Communists, and the Americans. Always an impending doom she always survived. Now she sits uprooted even from her small apartment in Marburg, waiting to find out if she can leave for the promises of a country where she knows no one.

"Momma, here comes Papa ," Anni's voice is heard a pitch higher than normal as she first notices her father walking down the street toward the apartment. Nina takes her focus away from her thoughts and the mesmerizing barrier the snowflakes have created. Here is her husband walking briskly, confidently, even buoyantly toward them. Mother and daughter rush to the door and hold it open as they hear his footsteps. Smiling, he says, "We're going to America!"

The ship will sail from Hamburg in three days' time. Only one last European train ride through the frozen forests between Bremen and Hamburg before they embark on longest journey to the greatest hope they have for a peaceful life in America. Nick cleverly sets up his camera to take a picture of the three of them wearing their nice outfits they wore when leaving Marburg. Nick smirks, Nina holds her back straight and her head up regally, as she has seen her mother do, and Anni innocently, yet without a smile, looks into the bright flash that marks this momentous victory.

31

NEW YORK
1949

The ship assigned, the *Jumping Marine*, is a moderately sized military boat-turned-passenger-ship with its guns removed. Anni is excited. She's never seen such a big ship before, let alone been offered a ride in one. She lets herself fantasize about what her mother and father have told her; that she will finally "meet the rich uncle" and will have a good life. Papa will be happy working as an engineer after their stay on the farm in Ubly, and mummy can work as a draftsman. And she will meet nice Americans, the type that gave her the chocolate bars and the orange and the extra food at the canteen. Nice Americans like the ones who made the Nazi soldiers go away.

But what about American children, she can't help but wonder. Will they be like the little German girls who teased her about her accent, or like the ones who called her "little Russian girl"? Will she not quite fit in? Will she be held back? Will the teachers be mean to her? She doesn't know the language and has never fully identified or been accepted as a little German, even though she can hardly recall being a little Russian. In America, she convinces herself, she'll try hard to be just like them, to fit in, to be likeable.

Nina fears the water. Her childhood memories of nearly drowning have never been forgotten. And now from the docks of the partially repaired harbor she can only see an endless supply of it. The harbor looks out on the Atlantic Ocean which separates this old continent from a newer one; a continent remote and isolated from any remaining family. But then again, so few of the family remain. This old continent holds only memories. For now, she won't dwell too much on the past or try to read too much into the meanings of so much loss and change. The business of daily living concerns her most, and right now that involves crossing the Atlantic Ocean.

Inside the women's dormitory cabin, Anni jumps onto the top bunk nearest the window with the doll and wooden toys she's been given by the friendly American steward. Nina puts the suitcase and a bag she's been given with its toothbrush and comb on the lower bunk. Nick places his things in the hull bunks with the rest of the men, then joins Anni and Nina on deck to watch Germany recede from view.

The boat pulls away from the harbor. The city, now becoming the horizon, the last German city Nick or Nina will ever see, is still rebuilding from its firebombed core. There is no family to wish them a safe trip. As ever, it's only the three of them headed to an altogether-new destination in the crisp, clear shadows of a short, cold winter's day.

Anni feels sad as the boat begins its fourteen-day trip across the Atlantic Ocean. But that's okay. She'll do what she has always done to entertain herself; she'll play with her new friends and toys, and talk with Papa. And tonight, after dinner, after trying new foods like grapefruit and bananas, she'll love watching "Bugs Bunny," just like the American children do. She'll watch and listen to the American English words. Maybe she'll ask to be called "Ann." After all, like a chameleon, she's changed her name often enough. It seems "Ann" is her name in America, and Papa and Mummy will surely agree. It's important to fit in.

The swelling ocean waves keep Nina seasick in her bunk, unable to eat much for most of the trip. When not completely out of sorts, she has time to think. A lifetime's worth of memories have already formed in her 43 years, it will take almost as long to make restitution for what she's suffered. The old world is vanishing into the coffers of her imagination, her past merely resonating in her subconscious. She will have to build a new life for herself. She will have to remake herself…just once more.

The heaving, winter waves have subsided for two days. It's long enough for Nina to regain her bearings and take a rare trip to the deck where she meets up with Nick and Ann. Together they stand on the gray, windswept steel deck, bundled up in their long, thick, brown coats and hats. Nick takes a photo of Nina and Ann with another fellow traveler. Nina, not fond of the weather, holds the collar of her coat tightly until the flash of the camera freezes this moment of time. Somehow the years of stress haven't been too harsh on her pretty features, even though they have hardened her.

Days pass slowly on this ship in an endless, harsh sea. And then Nina hears them. She can't be mistaken, as she's always had a good sense for them. They've called to her since childhood. She's saved them, befriended them, kept them in a cage, and watched them fly away. Nick has explained that any sign of birds will mean there's land nearby. Nina and Ann leave their cabin and immediately head to the deck. There isn't just one, but flocks. Flocks of gulls in the distance are heading for the boat, shrilling with promise of approaching land. Then through the endless continuous gray, they see the Statue of Liberty. Hundreds of pigeons freely soar above and around them, the same birds that live in all big cities. Like Nina, Nick, Ann and Josephine back in Berlin, these birds are survivors, dissuaded neither by climate nor circumstance.

Nick has quickly joined them. Other passengers come on deck. Innately enamored with the statue's significance, Nick, Nina, and Ann, as so many before them, are the new recipients of Liberty's continuing story. Berlin and St. Petersburg are behind them. In the distance beyond the statue rise tall buildings–the skyscrapers.

And below them, "All those cars…," says Nick, amazed at the technology and abundance of so many people, each in his own vehicle. He's not seen anything like this before. But it's another metropolis; another giant city that they must traverse to get to the farm where they are expected. He knows he will only see it briefly and then never again. It will not be their final destination. But, for a moment, on the deck of this aging, transformed warship, it symbolizes a new life…and perhaps a permanent home.

Anni holds tightly to her mother's hand. No matter what lies ahead, her parents are the most important things in the world. Without them everything would be meaningless. Having been too disappointed by her experiences in the past, she cannot become overwhelmingly excited now. However, she cannot help but feel the energy of those around her.

Nick then suddenly takes his cane, lifts it high in the air, and throws it overboard. It floats briefly on the choppy, gray surf, and then it sinks, swallowed by a wave. Ann looks at him, incredulous. "Papa, what are you doing?" She has never seen him without his cane.

"I've never needed it dear," he responds.

"But why?"

"Because children talk," he says to his vaguely-understanding daughter.

Nina and Nick exchange an intense look. Nina understands how difficult it was for him to pretend for so long. It was in agony that he made the decision to avoid the draft into Stalin's army so long ago. He knew his family would not have survived without him. The shame he felt as one of so few younger men not in the army followed him until they left Germany. He used the cane around the apartments in Russia and Germany because he knew that under

Stalin and Hitler even a child's naive comment would mean certain death for her parents. Avoidance of Hitler's army was an added pleasure. Finally, he kept the cane even four years into the peace that followed, because he could not let go of the anticipation that "it" could all happen again…at any time.

The boat slowly makes it way to Ellis Island, as all three stand exposed to the hope that the past will not haunt their present.

Epilogue

NINA

The ninety-eight-year-old Nina sits on her plush, yellow, rocking chair in the living room of her northern Michigan condominium. To the right is a dark wooden, old-fashioned, china cabinet with beautiful German, antique, crystal vases, engraved with the letters JS (for Josephine Siewert) a set of silver spoons, and miniature, silver salt cellars with individual serving spoons. A box, strewn with yellowing black and white photos, and an old photo album from the beginning of the last century lie open on the short, rectangular table in front of her.

Nina, speaking in broken English says, "I almost drrrowned. I zplashed in zee vater vis all my might. I could not get out and knew I vas drrrowning. My granfazer reached into ze vater vis his gold-handled valking stick. My zandals slipped on ze muddy duurt next to ze river by ze cottages. He alvays saved my life. I don't know, maybe zat's vy I vas alvays his favorite."

I, Robert, her grandson, listen intently. I've heard most of these stories throughout my (then) thirty-eight years. Fascinated with hearing first-hand accounts of life during the time of the last Tsar, I remain quiet and let her weave her tales, as she often jumps from one decade to the next, but always returns to her early childhood in Finland and in the bold and tumultuous city of St. Petersburg.

How fortunate that she is still alive after all these years to tell me the stories of life during the Tsars, of the Revolution and the World Wars, of the dictators, and even of the beautiful Russian countryside. And yet it is strange and maddening that so many violent things are still happening today, as if we, humankind, have failed to learn our lessons.

Nina sips her hot tea and offers another sugar cookie, moving quickly between stories and time periods of the most horrific tyrants and events in history with the finesse and clarity of mind normally not found in someone her age. Amazed, I sit taking in every word. How I love this wonderful, strong, and courageous woman—my grandmother, my omi. And how I miss not having been able to meet my grandfather; the wonderfully complex, passionate, self-sacrificing, obstinate, and humorous Nick, who died in 1963 while Ann, my mother, was still pregnant with me. He had worked as a draftsman in Detroit, never regaining his prior professional stature. And Josephine, such an elegant and timelessly strong woman, who lived in West Berlin to the ripe old age of 86. She died in 1967 before I was able to see her. I will never get to know Vova, idealistic, handsome, charming, and tragic; nor entrepreneurial automobile enthusiast, Grandfather Carl, who died at 90 in Berlin; nor Leonya, whose daughter Tatiana found my grandmother through a *Glasnost*-era letter. I will never truly know the heart of Grandfather Leonid, Omi's father, whom the Soviet Union later exonerated as having committed no crimes. All of them enliven and intrigue me. It's almost as if they are still around giving advice and whispering encouragement.

It's getting late and I notice that even though old Omi is still enjoying the conversation, it probably would be best to let her conserve her energy for today. We can talk again later. I shut the photo album opened to the page with the picture of the beautiful young woman, taken at a rocky beach, who wears a large-brimmed hat with a feather. I collect Grandfather Nick's little black book written in tiny, penciled Cyrillic Russian words, and the seven pages which are the beginning of a book Nick had begun, called *From the Life of Ann K.*

What they must have experienced and with what fortitude and strength they overcame such incredible obstacles. They endured tragedies our society will be doomed to repeat if we don't learn from them. An idea forms as I say goodbye to Omi. Perhaps I'll start where Nick left off. Perhaps I'll write a book.

The End

Author's Note

The previous chapters are based upon actual incidents. While I was writing this story, I re-interviewed my grandmother, Nina, taping and videoing what I could. I also interviewed my mother, obtained and reviewed a tape made by Claus von Kursell and Swetlana Siewert (sent to me from Swetlana's niece, Kira), and used a little black book that my grandfather kept, chronicling events which occurred during and after the siege of Leningrad. The Prologue was copied verbatim from his documents.

As we all know, memory is both fallible and conditional. Events are remembered based upon the perception of the storyteller's experiences, and the societal, intellectual and emotional factors that influence the way he or she looks at the world. Considering this, I've included historical background where possible to add further depth and broader societal episodes. While I've made every attempt to maintain the accuracy of the stories told to me, the feelings, mental cognition, processing of information, some dialogue, and descriptions of actual locations have been interpreted to facilitate the telling of this story as a novel.

Scenes have been reconstructed to be as true to the nature, character, look and feel of the period as researched and provided by her in years shortly after their occurrence.

Carmichael, Joel, *An illustrated History of Russia*. New York, Reynal & C

Dunmore, Elena, *The Siege*. New York, Grove Press, 2001.

Dyck, Peter J., *Troubles and Triumphs 1914-1924*. Springstein, Manitoba, Canada, 1981.

Elliott, David, *New Worlds, Russian Art and Society 1900-1937*. New York, Rizzoli, 1986.

Froncek, Thomas, *The Horizon Book of the Arts of Russia*. New York, American Heritage, 1970.

Kaiser, Daniel H., *The Workers' Revolution in Russia, 1917; the View From Below*. New York, Cambridge University Press, 1987.

Karpovich, Michael, *Imperial Russia 1801-1917*. New York, Holt, Rinehart and Winston, 1961.

Kochan, Miriam, *The Last Days of Imperial Russia, 1910-17.* New York, Macmillian Publishing Co., Inc., 1976.

Mann, Golo, *The History of Germany Since 1789.* New York, Praeger,1968.

Massie, Suzanne, *Land of the Firebird; the Beauty of Old Russia.* New York, Simon & Schuster, 1980.

Mrazkova, Daniel, *The Russian War: 1941-1945.* New York, Dutton, 1977.

Murrell, Kathleen Berton, *Russia.* New York, Dorling Kindersley, 1990.

Nabakov, Vladimir, *Speak, Memory, An Autobiography Revisited.* New York, Vintage International, 1989.

Nishen, Verlag Dirk, *A Portrait of Tsarist Russia; Unknown Photographs From The Soviet Archives.* New York, Pantheon, 1989.

Riasanovsky, Nicholas V., *A History of Russia, Second Edition.* New York, Oxford University Press, 1969.

Riske, Edith Edelgard, *Flight for Survival, A Step Ahead of The Russians in 1945.* Ontario, CA, Riske, 1993.

Ross, Stewart, *The USSR Under Stalin.* East Sussex, England, Wayland, 1991.

Seton-Watson, Hugh, *The Decline of Imperial Russia 1855-1914.* New York, Praeger, 1967.

Speier, Hans, *From the Ashes of Disgrace: A Journal from Germany 1945-1955.* Amherst, University of Massachusetts Press, 1981.

Tolstoy, Valdimir, Bibikova, Irina, Cooke, Catherine, *Street Art of the*

Revolution; Festivals and Celebrations in Russia 1918-1933. New York, Vendome, 1990.

Tompkins, Stuart Ramsay, *Russia Through the Ages; From the Scythians to the Soviets*. New York, Prentice-Hall, 1940.

Treadgold, Donald W., *Twentieth Century Russia, Sixth Edition*. Boulder, Westview Press, 1987.

Viltchkovsky, *Tsarskoe Selo*, 1910, forward by Bob Atchison. Internet, Alexanderpalace.org.

Walkin, Jacob, *The Rise of Democracy In Pre-Revolutionary Russia*. London, Thames and Hudson, 1963.

Wechsberg, Joseph, *In Leningrad*. New York, Doubleday, 1977.

Werth, Alexander, *Russia at War 1941-1945*. New York, Dutton & Co., 1964.

Videos

"The Architect of Doom," First Run Features, New York, Peter Cohen Producer, 1991.

"Cities At War: The Doomed City – Berlin," Simon & Schuster Video, Simon & Schuster, Inc. 1986,, Berlin : The Bettmann Archive 62159-9

"Russian Ark," A Film By Alexander Sokurov. A Wellspring Presentation of a Hermitage Bridge Studio and Egolitossell Film AG Production World Sales Celluloid Dreams (www. Wellspring.com/russianark). 2002 Egolli Tossell Film AktienGesellschft & Hermitage Bridge Studio. New York.

"The Wonderful Horrible Life of Leni Reifenstahl," Kino Video, Kino International Corp., 1993, New York.